LIGHTNING AND LACE

BY

DiAnn Mills

BARBOUR
PUBLISHING

DEDICATION

To Larry and Martha Dyke.
Good friends are a gift from God.

I THEREFORE, THE PRISONER OF THE LORD,
BESEECH YOU THAT YE WALK WORTHY
OF THE VOCATION WHEREWITH YE ARE CALLED.
EPHESIANS 4:1

CHAPTER 1

In the predawn hours when earth stood ready to relinquish its cloak of darkness, Bonnie Kahler reached to touch the opposite side of the bed. Empty. Just as it had been for the past two years, nine months, and nineteen days. Every morning she woke with the hope that Ben hadn't been taken from her and his body didn't lie in a cold grave while she struggled to keep a feeble hold onto sanity.

Some days Bonnie believed she could cast aside her sorrow and raise her children alone. She could be strong and decisive and not let her widowhood affect her every step. On those days, she believed God still cared about her and He would show her how to fight the blackness engulfing her soul.

This was not one of those days.

Bonnie drew back her hand and took a deep breath. Her head pounded. Zack and Michael Paul needed breakfast and a smiling mother before they left for school. Lydia Anne needed a mother who played dolls and dressed her sun-kissed hair with ribbons and bows. All three of her children deserved a mother who understood she carried the roles of both parents. The boys loved to fish, but she hated the thought of handling dirty worms and slimy fish. Far too long she'd expected her brothers and stepfather to fill Ben's shoes.

Help me, Lord. I want to climb out of this selfish hole and live for You.

I want only truth in everything I do.

Refusing to wallow in self-pity one minute longer, Bonnie swung her legs over the side of the bed and walked to the open window. She pushed aside the curtains and listened to the rooster give his call to morning and the cattle low in response. This had been Ben's favorite time of the day.

"Bonnie, come watch the sunrise. It's prettier than most," he'd say. And she'd crawl out of bed to join him. Not because she shared his enthusiasm for the day's beginnings, but because she loved him.

Today the sun barely lit the horizon in colors matching the fall leaves carpeting the ground outside her home. Odd how they glittered like jewels in the pale moonlight when only a half-moon illuminated them before the sun pushed it from sight. Autumn ushered in painful memories of Ben's last days—the persistent cough that decimated his body and took his spirit to a place where she could not go.

She slowly turned to the nightstand where Ben's Bible rested. Most days she shrank back from looking at it and exploring the words that promised to sustain her. But she always thought about reading the familiar passages. Beside the Bible sat an empty wine bottle. She startled. Had she drunk that much last night? A friend had suggested she drink a small glass of wine when she couldn't sleep. Last night, the wine had tasted as sweet as her life had been with Ben, but today guilt consumed more than an empty flask. Her family would be appalled. Seeking their guidance crossed her mind, but she was too ashamed of her inability to cope after all these months.

"I will not give in to this," she whispered. "Dear Jesus, help me."

The day's activities scrolled across her mind. She needed to meet with Thomas in the next few minutes. He was a good foreman who knew her failings, yet he always took the time to review the past week's work and show her where every penny was being spent or earned for the Morning Star Ranch. Soon, maybe today, she'd take more interest in the ranch.

Michael Paul wanted to take piano lessons, and today she'd make the arrangements with her sister-in-law to teach him. Lydia Anne needed more attention from her mother, the kind of attention that didn't result in frustration and tears from both of them.

A twinge of fear took root in Bonnie's heart. She'd been summoned by Zack's teacher. His behavior at school had been deteriorating steadily since his father died.

"Don't make excuses for him," her mother had said. "Force him to face up to the consequences of his mistakes. If you don't, he'll continue to torment Michael Paul and Lydia Anne. The older he gets, the more his tendency will be to bully you. Now is the time for Zack to understand rules and authority."

How could Bonnie instill those values in her son when she couldn't bring herself to discipline him? He grieved for his father. All of them did. How could she help her precious children when she shared their misery?

Bonnie lifted her shoulders and swept her fingertips across the Bible, a milestone, for she hadn't been able to complete that small gesture of respect for months. Her other hand grasped the wine bottle, and she set it by the chamber pot.

I'll drink tea to help me sleep. I'll listen in church this week, and I'll try very hard to take Mama's advice. She nodded to punctuate her thoughts. The reverend planned to retire soon; perhaps she'd garner the strength to ask him for advice before he did so.

With more determination than she'd felt in months, Bonnie dressed and descended the stairs to begin her duties for the day. She heard Juanita humming a Spanish tune in the kitchen and smelled the nutty aroma of coffee.

"*Buenos dias*, Miss Bonnie." Juanita clasped her small hands together and smiled broadly. "Another beautiful day, I think. *Si?*" She poured Bonnie coffee and added a brilliant smile.

"Thank you." Bonnie wrapped her fingers around the cup. She envied Juanita's iridescence—always happy, beautiful, passionate about her faith. "I think the day is as beautiful as you and I choose."

"Then we choose the best."

Forcing a smile, Bonnie told herself that soon she'd not force joy. It would return. Life was about to change. It had to. A rap on the door indicated that Thomas had arrived to discuss ranch business, and today Bonnie planned to listen.

Travis Whitworth didn't believe in luck or coincidence, but he did believe in a nudging of the Spirit. And right this very minute, he felt a wagonload of apprehension. Standing at the Kahlerville train station with bag in hand, he glanced around for someone to direct him to the parsonage. There he'd meet the retiring Reverend John Rainer and begin to learn his duties as the new preacher. Excitement should have taken over his senses, but instead, he questioned his calling. Had he misunderstood God's direction? Or did the quivering in his bones come from what had happened at his last church?

Nonsense. No one here knew his past, and he doubted if anyone would. Even his own mother wouldn't recognize him. Maybe the wild hair, baggy clothes, and spectacles weren't necessary. But looking pleasing to women had disrupted his ministry before, and he intended for it never to happen again. The train slowly chugged away while smoke curled up and disappeared, reminding him of how God had forgiven him. The matter had been settled; here he'd make a difference in God's kingdom.

Travis made his way down the street, noting the warm weather that felt more like summer back home in Tennessee. He'd miss the hills and the change of seasons. Right now the leaves painted the hills in scarlet, gold, and orange. Geese migrated south, and a touch of cool air paved the way for winter. More than home, he'd miss his family, but they were glad he'd left. Sadness settled on him, and he shook his head. God had given him a second chance.

An older couple made their way toward him. "Excuse me. Can you direct me to the parsonage?"

The man nodded while the woman patted his arm.

"Turn around and head down the street. Go past the train station and around the bend. It'll be on your left beside the church. The schoolhouse is across the road."

"Are you the new preacher?" the woman asked. She bent over slightly, but her voice sounded strong.

"Yes, ma'am. My name is Travis Whitworth."

The matchstick thin man reached out to shake his hand. "Eli and Nellie Parker."

"It's a pleasure. You have a pretty town."

"Hmm." The woman studied him, then frowned. "No man alive can take Reverend Rainer's place."

Travis expected this, especially since the man had been at Piney Woods Church for forty years. "I don't intend to take his place, ma'am. I only want to shepherd the church with God's help. I pray you'll have patience with me until I learn more about the congregation."

"Where's your wife?" the woman asked, the wrinkles in her face intensifying.

"I don't have one."

"Who'll lead the women and make sure the poor and needy folks are taken care of? I don't understand how you can do your job without a wife to help you."

Travis hadn't anticipated the firing of questions so soon. "I believe this gives the women an opportunity to serve the church and community. But I promise I'll do my best." He tipped his hat to the couple. "Good day, Mr. and Mrs. Parker. Thank you for the directions."

He turned toward the road and saw where it curved and disappeared in a canopy of pine trees. Sort of like his life. A horse and rider trotted by, nearly running him over. What a reception.

Once Travis rounded the bend, he breathed in the picturesque countryside. Birds serenaded him, and for a moment he relaxed. Up ahead and to the right of him he heard voices. He stopped in the road, and the distinct sound of boys arguing seized his attention. He focused on the trees and made his way closer to them.

"Your pa died 'cause he couldn't stand being around you."

"Liar. He was sick."

"Yeah. He had you for a son."

The sharp smack of a punch broke the otherwise peaceful afternoon. One of the boys cursed, and the struggle continued. Travis left his bag at the side of the road and headed for them. He stepped into the middle of them and grabbed each boy by the shoulder.

"Whoa, boys. Shouldn't you be in school?"

One of the boys, a dark-haired youth of about twelve, wiped a trickle of blood from his mouth. He scowled at Travis. "That's none of your business."

Travis shook his head and glanced at a red-haired boy whose shirt had been ripped nearly in two. A purplish bruise encircled his eye, providing no doubt as to who was winning this fistfight. "So do you think it's none of my business?"

"We don't need you, mister," the red-haired boy said, nearly out of breath.

The dark-haired one laughed and jerked from Travis's hold. "I'll teach you a lesson, Clay—one you'll never forget." He lunged forward, but Travis grabbed him.

"We're heading to the school." Travis shoved both of the boys ahead of him. "Fighting doesn't solve a thing."

The boys tried to shrug his hold, but years of hard work in the Tennessee hills had made Travis strong. The dark-haired boy cursed again. His pa needed to take a switch to his backside—or was this the boy whose pa had died?

The schoolhouse loomed ahead, but the children were obviously inside tending to their lessons. By forcing the boys into the building, he'd humiliate them. For a moment, he wished he had a rope to tie them up before he fetched the teacher. He paused before mounting the schoolhouse steps and debated the best way to handle the mess he'd gotten himself into. The door opened, and a woman stood before him.

Shock etched her face. "Zack, what is going on?"

The dark-haired boy shook off Travis's hold. "Clay started it, Mama. I didn't want to get beat up, so I hit back."

Travis had sincere doubts about the truth in Zack's words.

"That's a lie," Clay said. "He started it by saying my ma was bigger than a cow and ugly."

Zack swallowed hard. "That's not true, Mama. Please believe me. He said Papa died 'cause I was a bad son."

The woman's face softened, and she reached out for him to take her hand. "I believe you." She tilted her head and eyed Travis.

For the first time, Travis studied the woman, a little lady with sky blue eyes. He saw the resemblance between her and Zack, except she had hair the color of wheat. Apparently she was the schoolteacher, too.

"And who are you?" she asked.

"Travis Whitworth, ma'am. I was walking past the woods and heard the boys scuffling."

"He threatened to beat me," Zack said. "I begged him to bring us to school."

Travis wished he'd never interrupted the boys. Zack obviously had more than a little experience in manipulating his mother. He stole a look at Clay from the corner of his eye. Fear had captured the boy. No doubt Zack had practice in bullying others.

The woman stiffened. "How dare you speak to these boys this way?"

"Ma'am, I said nothing of the sort. I simply broke up the fight and brought the boys here. If you'll excuse me, I'll be on my way."

She shook her fist at him. "I have a good mind to report you to the sheriff. A grown man has no right threatening young boys."

Shock settled on Travis. Had he come to the wrong town? "I assure you I had the best intentions in breaking up the fight, but if you feel you must contact the sheriff, I'd be happy to talk with him. I can be contacted through Reverend Rainer."

Frustrated and angry, Travis took long strides to the road to retrieve his bag. No wonder the reverend of this town was retiring. The citizens of Kahlerville offered as much welcome as an aggravated rattler.

CHAPTER 2

Travis reached to pick up his bag and too late discovered a wasp flitting above the handle. The nuisance sank its stinger deep into his palm. Travis yelped and dropped the bag. A second wasp attacked the top of the same hand. What had he done to deserve this? Immediately his hand swelled and burned. If he believed in bad omens, he'd purchase a ticket for the next train out of here. Made him wonder if Satan himself had taken up residence in this seemingly quiet town.

Once free of the wasps, he examined his hand to pull out the stingers. Both were embedded, and unless he was ready to dig out flesh with his pocket knife, he'd have to wait until he met up with Reverend Rainer's wife. He shook his hand vigorously in an effort to shake off the throb from his wrist to his fingertips. Snatching up his bag, Travis once again walked toward the parsonage. The church was visible from the schoolyard. In fact, he'd seen the house and church while escorting the boys to school, but he hadn't had the opportunity to study the buildings then. Now he took in every board, every shrub, every neatly planted flower surrounding the church. He shielded his eyes against the afternoon sun and peered up at the steeple. *My church to watch over for God as long as He sees fit.* When the wasp stings caused him to drop his bag and rub the area around his palm and on top of his hand, Travis recalled the moments in his life that had seemed perfect just before a stab of evil spoiled the beauty. With cautious wisdom, he grabbed the wooden handle and ventured farther.

He walked around the well-maintained whitewashed building, the sparkling clean windows, and...there in the middle was a stained-glass window. A picture of Jesus portrayed as the Good Shepherd glistened in vivid colors of green, red, and blue, reminding Travis of the enormity of his calling and the need for the Good Shepherd to carry him. Travis smiled, one of the few times so far that day.

Rose bushes climbed up the side of the church as if by next spring they would strive to cover all of the building in a mixture of blossoms and thorns. Ah, another reminder of life's goodness and adversities. He made his way behind the church, where a tree-lined, narrow wagon path led to a fenced cemetery. *Life and death, all a part of this earthly journey.*

He moved on to the opposite side of the church, where another stained-glass window depicted Jesus in the garden of Gethsemane. Pausing for a moment, Travis smelled the faint sweetness of wildflowers then made his way back to the front of the building. Flowers bloomed at his feet. Someone cared about these neatly kept grounds. He paused and glanced up at the double doors, then mounted the steps. His home-for-wayward-wasps bag landed with a plop on the wooden landing. With his heart thumping like a scared rabbit, he removed his tattered hat and opened the door.

A slight mustiness met his nostrils—a blend of old hymnals and wood. For a moment, he savored every delicious scent and envisioned every pew filled with worshippers. Light oak enriched the room, from the benches, to the window casings, to the pulpit, and on to a life-sized cross mounted in the back. The two stained-glass windows were more striking from the inside. Momentarily, he forgot about the mishaps since arriving in town. *Thank You, Lord, for allowing me to serve You in this beautiful church. May I never disappoint You again.*

With purposeful steps, Travis focused his body and heart on the pulpit. His boots thundered against the wooden floor much like the echo of the words from a powerful sermon. Scaring folks to death with a threat of hell had never been his way of preaching. Nevertheless, after his encounter with the wasps, he could sense a good sermon coming on. A Bible lay open on the pulpit, and when he curiously glanced to see the passage, his gaze fixed on Isaiah 6:8: "I heard the voice of the Lord, saying, Whom shall I send, and who will go for us? Then said I, Here am I; send me."

Travis chuckled. The irony of this broken preacher being used by God for a divine purpose brought more of a hearty laugh. And when he considered the problems he'd encountered since his feet hit the train station here in Kahlerville, he laughed again.

"Good afternoon." A man's voice echoed from the back of the church.

Travis glanced up from the pulpit to a tall, elderly man whom he believed to be Reverend John Rainer, the man whose shoes he must attempt to fill. The reverend's thick, snow-white hair reminded him of an old prophet, possibly Isaiah himself.

"Afternoon. You must be this church's reverend."

"I am. At least for a while longer."

Travis wasted no time in moving toward him. "That's why I'm here. I'm Travis Whitworth."

A broad smile spread over the older gentleman's face. "I think it's a mighty fine day when a man of God comes to town."

"Looks like Kahlerville now has two of us." Travis's hand throbbed from the wasp stings, but he still reached out to shake the older man's hand. "The church is beautiful."

"Thank you. We have good people here."

And I hope to meet them soon.

"Come on over to the parsonage and meet my wife. We've been waiting for you. Got a room ready."

"I hope I won't be a bother to y'all." *Hope she doesn't mind lending me a needle to dig out these stingers.*

"Of course not. Repairs are being made on the house that will serve as the new parsonage, since my wife and I will remain in the old parsonage here. It will be about another week before they're completed."

"I'm a fair hand at carpentry work. I'd be glad to help."

He chuckled. "We have more than God's work in common. We'll both lend a hand on the project."

Although Travis understood he was being carefully scrutinized and would be for the weeks and months to come, he did see an air of respect in the older man's eyes. Travis breathed an inward sigh of relief. He'd hopefully found a friend.

A young boy about eight or nine years old exploded through the doorway with a little girl right behind him—screaming. The boy, with yellow-white hair that tickled his collar, stopped and whirled around, then picked up the little girl. He kissed her on the cheek. She had her own cascade of sun-colored curls. The scene touched Travis—the impulsive boy retracing his steps to soothe an unhappy child. He saw a sermon coming on and promised himself not to forget it.

"Sorry, Grandpa," the boy said. "I raced up to see you and didn't know Lydia Anne was right behind."

"Perhaps you should speak to my guest." Reverend Rainer took the distressed little girl from his arms. She snuggled up against his coat, and he, too, kissed her cheek.

The boy took note of Travis and stepped forward with an outstretched hand. "Excuse the interruption, sir. My name is Michael Paul Kahler."

"Travis Whitworth. And I'm pleased to make your acquaintance. Is the town named after your father?"

"No, sir. It was named after my great-grandfather." The boy pointed up at the little girl. "This is my sister. I reckon you heard her coming. She's Lydia Anne."

"Sorry, sir, for carryin' on," the little girl said.

Travis smiled. Pretty little thing. "Apology accepted, Miss Lydia Anne."

Reverend Rainer righted the little girl to her feet. "My grand-children, Mr. Whitworth."

"Call me Travis. Congratulations on such fine grandchildren."

"We are a little partial to them."

Michael Paul turned to his grandfather. "Shall we wait outside until you're finished with Mr. Whitworth?"

"Not because of me." Travis focused on the older man. "Unless we have something to discuss that can't wait."

"I'd rather get you settled into the house. Michael Paul, this gentleman will be the new reverend."

The boy's eyes widened. "My grandpa needs a rest, and we're going to do more fishing."

The reverend's gaze swept back to the open door. "Is your mother with you?"

"No, sir. She's at the school talking to Zack's teacher." Michael Paul frowned. "He did it again, fighting at school, and Miss Scott was real mad."

Travis sensed the blood drain from his face. Surely the same fatherless Zack who had been knee-deep in a fight less than an hour ago was not the reverend's grandson. Or his mother the reverend's daughter. Confusion—and a little anxiety—swept over him.

"Did your mother send you to fetch me?" the reverend asked.

"No, sir. She just said she'd come by the parsonage once she finished."

"And Zack is there, too?"

"Yes, sir. He was scrubbing blackboards when I left."

When Michael Paul spoke this time, Travis saw the resemblance between him and the woman he'd met earlier. Did he dare confess his role at the schoolhouse?

"Why don't you take your sister to see your grandma?" the reverend said. "We'll be right along."

In the next instant, the children disappeared, leaving Travis be-wildered as to what to say.

"I wasn't prepared for you to hear family business the moment we met." The reverend shook his head.

"I understand. But I'm used to dealing with uncomfortable situations. In fact, I believe I've already met your grandson and daughter." He hadn't formed his words exactly right, and he, the new preacher, should be precise—and tactful.

The older man lifted a brow curiously. "How could that be since you just arrived?"

Travis cleared his throat. "On the road here. Uh, your grandson and another boy were fighting."

"Then you've seen his difficult temperament."

"Yes, sir. I have."

"I'd like to hear what happened from you before I hear it from Zack."

Travis braved forward, wondering if Zack was as good at convincing his grandfather as he was at convincing his mother. ". . .So after I got stung, I snatched up my bag and walked here." He omitted how upset the reverend's daughter had been with him.

"I'm really sorry. I've been meeting the train for the past several days looking for you, and the one day I miss becomes quite unfortunate. Did you get those stingers out?"

"Not yet. I thought I'd trouble your wife for a needle."

"Then let's get you taken care of right now."

"No harm done at all. Perhaps I'll have an opportunity to meet with your grandson. I'd like to think boys will be boys, and—"

Travis's response died in midstream as the church's door opened and the same woman he'd angered earlier stood before them.

If he'd not already tasted her anger, he'd have thought an ethereal being had floated in to make certain his first day in Kahlerville was filled with splendor. She wore a pale blue dress—something he hadn't noticed before. And her blond hair gave him all the more reason why she could be mistaken for a messenger from God.

"Good afternoon, Reverend. Mama said you were here. Do you

have a few minutes?" She moved closer, but in doing so, she must have seen Travis. "Excuse me. I didn't know you had a visitor." Her eyes widened, and recognition flickered bright, then hot.

"We met earlier." Travis nodded. "Travis Whitworth."

"Indeed we have. I'm Mrs. Kahler."

He focused on the reverend. "I believe I'll gather up my bag on the steps and introduce myself to your wife."

"I'd rather you didn't," Mrs. Kahler said. "From what Zack has said about your threatening him, I fear you might harm my other children or my mother."

Travis took a deep breath. Her absurd statement didn't warrant his wasting breath to respond, so he didn't. But, oh, he wanted to.

"Bonnie, this gentleman is the new reverend. He's been called to take my place. I don't believe he's a threat to the children or Jocelyn."

<hr />

All of Bonnie's early morning resolve to conduct her life with wisdom and grace collapsed like a corncrib toppled by a windstorm. This. . . this beggar-looking fellow with unkempt hair and beard was the new reverend? A nasty taste rose in her mouth. Why, he didn't have the decency to wear a properly fitted suit. But just as quickly, her motherly instincts squeezed her heart.

"Sir, my son does not lie," she said as calmly as possible.

"Perhaps he mistook my eagerness to break up the fight with Clay as another matter. Both boys were upset."

"Zack was nearly in tears. First the other boy insults him, and then he is threatened by a stranger." Bonnie trembled with a nagging thought that her son may have lied.

"Ma'am, I stated this before, and I will again. My role involved breaking up the fight and escorting the boys to school. I give you my word. I did not mean to disrupt your school or cause you grief over my interference."

"I'm not the schoolteacher." Did this unkempt man think she'd take his word over that of her son? Why were so many people against Zack unless—

"Bonnie," the reverend began, "Mr. Whitworth is a guest."

She startled and immediately regretted her behavior in the presence of her stepfather, the reverend. "I apologize, Reverend. Mr. Whitworth and I will discuss this matter at another time."

Mr. Whitworth cleared his throat. His face appeared to ripen to a tomato red. "I'm finished with the discussion, Mrs. Kahler."

"How dare you?" she asked. "Kindly admit your error and be done with it."

Travis turned his attention to the reverend. "Sir, I think it best that I secure lodging at the boardinghouse. I appreciate your hospitality and your warm welcome, but I'm afraid my presence here might be a problem."

The reverend raised his hand, moistened his lips, and gave Mrs. Kahler a smile. "Bonnie, you wanted to talk to me earlier. If you could wait here, I will escort Mr. Whitworth to the parsonage and return."

Anger and a sensation that she might be wrong swept over her. "Yes, of course." She blinked back the tears and seated herself on a pew. Surely, Zack had not lied to her. Surely not. Surely not.

CHAPTER 3

The longer Bonnie waited, the more she pondered all the times Zack had insisted he told the truth while others insisted otherwise. Miss Scott had declared that if he pulled one more prank, he'd not be welcome to return to school.

Today marked the first time Zack had ever accused an adult of lying. As she contemplated the many times she had believed him over his brother, sister, and other children, incidents plodded across her mind. Michael Paul seemed to be clumsy—or was Zack hitting him? And Lydia Anne just last week had gotten an ugly bruise on her arm. She had said Zack did it, but he declared she'd fallen from the rope swing. Why would her precious son, the only one of her dear children who looked like their father, lie and hurt others?

Bonnie thought she'd be ill. Deep in her spirit, she now knew the times that Zack had been in trouble were his fault. She'd made excuses for him in the belief he was innocent and good. And now this horrible realization of how wrong she'd been made her furious— mostly at herself.

At the ranch, Thomas had made it clear that Zack could not ride with the ranch hands, and she had thought it was because he might get hurt. Now she wondered differently. Her son didn't have friends, and Mama refused to keep him with the other children for any length of time. She said he caused trouble.

This morning when Bonnie had resolved to live as a godly woman, she knew it also meant listening to the truth no matter how it hurt. And it did hurt—badly.

Today at school, Zack's teacher said he rarely completed his homework and constantly disrupted the class. When the woman cried, Bonnie was determined to have her replaced. Obviously the teacher had not been trained in controlling her students' behavior. Now Bonnie felt so foolish—and angry. Tomorrow morning she'd apologize and insist Zack do the same.

What about Mr. Whitworth? She cringed at what she'd said to him. The man must have spoken the truth; he had no reason to accuse Zack of wrongdoing. To think she'd been ready to ask the reverend's assistance to discredit the man.

Ben, this is your fault. You left me to raise these children, and I don't know how. I can't even take care of myself.

Running and hiding from everyone in town had made a lot of sense in the past, but the days of allowing someone else to manage her life were gone. Blinking back the tears, she resolved to handle the matter without another drop of embarrassment to the reverend and Mama. Once she and the children were home, she and Zack would have a long talk. Her son knew the difference between right and wrong. No matter how much he hurt from losing his father, she wouldn't permit his behavior to continue.

Standing from the pew, she whisked the dampness from beneath her eyes. Mr. Whitworth and the reverend deserved an apology. She swallowed hard and stood on trembling legs. Heaven forbid, but she wanted a drink to settle her nerves. Shaking her head, she made her way from the church and down the steps.

Her gaze rested on Mr. Whitworth, who walked her way at a fast clip. Such a peculiar-looking fellow, as though he'd forgotten a trip to the barber. His suit flapped much too wide in the fall breeze, as though he might take wing and fly. Perhaps he'd gone through hard times or an illness and hadn't been able to purchase properly fitting clothes.

The closer Mr. Whitworth came, the more timid she grew. With all of that hair covering his face like an unplowed field, how could she discern his temperament? Could Zack have caused more problems, or was this all her own doing? Perhaps he'd thought through her earlier remarks and returned to discuss the matter, or could Zack have insulted him again?

"Mr. Whitworth." Her voice lacked the bravery she envisioned. "May I have a word with you?"

"And I with you," he said. "I must apologize for my rudeness."

A twist of guilt assaulted her. He did have a kind voice. "No, sir, I am the one who accused you unfairly. At least I believe so."

He took a rather ragged breath. Obviously she had upset him earlier, and the ordeal would plague her for many days.

"I believe," she said before losing her courage, "that my son has deceived me on too many occasions. To say I am humiliated does not convey how very sorry I am."

"Do not concern yourself a moment longer, Mrs. Kahler. I could have handled the situation with the boys and you much better than I did."

"Thank you. As a widow, I sometimes overlook things about my children that others do see." She noticed the reverend leave the parsonage and walk toward them. She waved and waited. Both apologies could be done at the same time.

With a shiver, she glanced back at Mr. Whitworth. His right hand was covered with what looked like baking soda.

"Wasp stings," he said, as if reading her mind.

"I'm sorry. Usually the reverend keeps their nests knocked down. I hope it feels better soon."

"And it does." He smiled. "It happened before I got here."

The reverend made his way to them. "I'm ready to speak with you now," he said.

"It's not important." Bonnie's heart beat faster than a train at full speed. "What is more important is that I apologize to you as I have to Mr. Whitworth. I am now convinced that Zack has deceived me many times. I intend to take care of it promptly."

"Good," the reverend said barely above a whisper. "I'm here if you need me. And I know your brothers are, too."

"I may need to call on all of you." She forced a smile, however; contacting Morgan or Grant to help her with Zack would never happen. They had perfect children.

"How are things at the ranch?" the reverend asked.

Relaxing slightly, she welcomed the change of conversation. "I do need roof repairs completed to the house. Can you recommend someone? The ranch hands are very busy."

"I'd be glad to do the repairs," Mr. Whitworth said. "I'm handy with wood and carpentry."

She startled. "But sir, don't you have a lot of work at the church to do?"

"Yes, indeed, but I can spare a few hours."

She took a deep breath. "I appreciate this very much. The job can wait until next week." She laughed. "Unless it rains." *Good. Giving the poor man a few extra dollars will ease my conscience and possibly pay his way to the barber and a good tailor.* "Excuse me, I'm going to say hello to Mama and find my children."

Her heart was a little lighter with apologies out of the way and a means to repair the roof. Then she remembered Zack. This couldn't be as difficult as she feared. The children sat on the porch steps with Mama, eating cookies the size of the moon. A platter piled high with more teetered precariously on the porch swing, while the aroma of ginger swirled through the air.

"We need to head home," she said with a smile. How she loved her beautiful children. "I see Mama is feeding you molasses ginger cookies."

"And they're still warm. Would you like one?" Mama asked. When she turned her head, the afternoon sun picked up the white in her hair. It hadn't grayed but had slowly transformed from pale yellow to a shimmering white.

"I could never resist your cookies."

"It wouldn't hurt if you'd eat a dozen. Put a little meat on your bones."

Mama's teasing held a good bit of truth, but Bonnie intended for everything about her life to change.

"I'll get you one." Lydia Anne popped up to fetch one from the platter and handed it to her mother.

"I want to go fishing when I get home." Zack picked up a stone and threw it.

His request nearly soured Bonnie's stomach. "I don't think so."

"Why not?"

"Excuse me, but I believe you need to mind your manners, young man."

"I need to get away by myself after this horrible day."

Why was her heart pounding so hard? "I said no. You and I have a few things to discuss."

"Like what?"

"Zachary Hayden Kahler, the conversation is finished. Now you may go sit in the wagon while I talk to Mama."

His eyes flashed rebellion unlike she'd seen since he was a toddler, but she wasn't in the habit of refusing his requests, either. Zack stomped off to the wagon, and she started to call him back for his insolence, but she already trembled from the confrontation.

Mama's eyes met hers, and the smile there calmed her a little.

"Please let Zack go fishing," Michael Paul whispered. "He'll be mad if you don't."

Bonnie took Zack's place on the step beside her middle son. "He will not go fishing." She tilted her head. "Why do you care if he's angry with me?"

" 'Cause he hits." Lydia Anne brushed the cookie crumbs from her dress.

Bonnie clasped her hands in her lap. She'd cry, but tears were useless with no answers to the problems. "I'm sorry," she said. "I'm going to be a better mother. I promise. Zack will not bully you or Michael Paul from this day on."

All the way back to the ranch, Zack's surly mood pushed her to the brink of exhaustion. He drove the wagon while complaining about his miserable day. By the time they arrived home, she decided her dealings with him could wait until tomorrow.

"Why did Grandpa have that beggar inside the parsonage?" Zack asked. "I started to tell him how the man had threatened me, but I thought you would."

"Mr. Whitworth is the new reverend," she said. "But no matter if he is a poor man in need, he deserves your respect. And I don't believe he threatened you today."

"You'd take a stranger's word over your son's?"

Determination gave Bonnie fresh courage. She nodded at Michael Paul and Lydia Anne. "Run along and let one of the ranch hands know we've returned so they can unhitch the wagon. Your brother and I are going to have a talk."

"About what?" Zack asked.

She peered into the face of her son, and her heart plummeted. So much like Ben on the outside but so angry on the inside. "Walk with me to the back porch." A few moments later, she seized the opportunity before losing nerve. "We are going to settle a few matters right now. The fight at school today and your behavior of late. . .it has to stop. Miss Scott will not tolerate any more interruptions in her class."

"I told you what happened."

His voice rose, and she inwardly admitted the husky sound frightened her. When had his voice begun to change?

"I believed you in the past when it was your word against that of another child, but today proved to me that you have been lying."

He started to protest, but she raised her hand to stop him.

"No more fighting, no matter what the reason. You will mind your manners in the presence of adults and obey your teacher. And if I find one more bruise or mark on Lydia Anne or Michael Paul, I swear I will take a switch to you."

"Why should you care what I do?" he said with a toss of his head that sent his dark hair spilling across his forehead. "You don't care about any of us anyway. When Papa died, you crawled into his grave with him."

"Inside the house. To your room." Emotion burned her throat.

"No, I won't." He planted both feet firmly in front of her. His gaze met hers squarely. "I'm going fishing."

Quivering uncontrollably, she clenched her fists. "You will be punished."

"You never whipped me before, and Mama, if you haven't looked lately, I'm the same size as you are."

He whirled around and raced toward the barn. And she was powerless to stop him.

⁓⊙⊙⊙⁓

Travis heard the grandfather clock from downstairs chime, and he prepared himself for dinner at six thirty, his first night in Kahlerville, Texas. He'd offered to help Mrs. Rainer, but she had refused. The older woman staunchly stated the only male she permitted in her kitchen was her husband.

Travis removed his spectacles and set them atop his well-worn, black leather Bible resting on the dresser. He didn't need the eyeglasses to see but rather to give the impression that he couldn't. While waiting to board the Northern Pacific in Fort Smith, Arkansas, he'd found them in a general store. They were perfect for what he needed to complete his new look.

He hesitated before descending the stairs. An image of Bonnie Kahler flashed across his mind. What a beautiful woman, but the pain in her eyes told of her unhappiness. He'd do his best to help her, but her son Zack already had the upper hand. Travis could see the rebellion with his eyes closed. She'd have to get strong before the boy took over the household. Not a good situation for any of them.

He sighed. Maybe he was sensing things in the Kahler family that weren't there, but he'd watched a lot of widows get overrun by strong-willed sons. The situation reminded him of wildflowers in a briar patch.

A man wanted a pretty wife with good children. Made him feel fulfilled and happy. And children needed a father. But unless Mrs. Kahler found a way to settle down her oldest son, she'd have nothing to look forward to but heartache.

He'd pray for Mrs. Kahler and her little family. He'd also shepherd Piney Woods Church and do a little carpentry work. Nothing else. Praise God, he had enough sense not to step into her life with two left feet.

CHAPTER  4

That evening after dinner, Bonnie sat in the parlor with Michael Paul and Lydia Anne. She tried to concentrate on her middle son as he read his little sister a story, but Zack hadn't returned, and her mind and body churned with every ticking of the clock. Michael Paul said nothing about his brother's absence. Why should he? She'd already broken her promise. If she couldn't stop Zack from going fishing, how could she stop him from bullying his brother and sister?

Outside, she heard a wagon stop in front of the house. Her worst fears assailed her. What if something had happened to Zack and she'd been unable to hinder his plans? He could have slipped on the riverbank or been bitten by a cottonmouth. Why hadn't she gone looking for him? Had she grown so afraid of confrontation that she didn't care what happened to her son? Bonnie attempted to collect her composure.

"Would you like for me to answer the door?" Michael Paul asked.

She glanced his way and saw the compassion in his eyes. Dear Michael Paul, at eight years old, wanted to shelter his mother. "I'll see who has come to visit," she said. "But thank you. Your reading is very good." Yet she hadn't really heard him.

She made her way to the door. Footsteps sounded on the porch, and then the knock startled her. Bonnie took a deep breath and opened the door.

Oh, no, not the Hillmans. "Good evening, Sylvia, Lester. How kind of you to stop by." She opened the door wide and smiled as they walked into her home.

"Oh, we won't be long," Sylvia said with a voice so soft and sweet that it must rival the heavenly host. "We simply wanted to see how you and the children are doing."

"We are managing very well. Come on into the parlor. Michael Paul has been reading to us."

Lester glanced around, his contemptuous attitude dominating the room. "Where is that other strapping son of yours?"

"Zack went fishing and hasn't returned."

"I always catch the best fish at night." Lester seated himself beside his wife on the sofa.

Bonnie held her breath and hoped her daughter didn't say anything that Lester and Sylvia Hillman didn't need to hear. "Lydia Anne, would you like to help me with coffee and apple pie for our guests?"

Juanita stood in the doorway. "No need, Miss Bonnie. I'll bring it for you."

"Thank you." Bonnie continued to smile after Juanita disappeared. "I don't know what I'd do without her."

"I'm glad Mr. Kahler was able to provide for you long after his demise," Sylvia said.

"Yes, ma'am." *Oh, why couldn't she have visited without Lester like she's done in the past?*

Lester cleared his throat. "How is the ranch?"

"My foreman, Thomas Reynolds, does an excellent job of running things—and keeping me informed."

"I'd be glad to go through the books for you," Lester said. "You could bring them to me at the bank, or I'd be glad to ride out here."

"I appreciate your offer, Lester, but I'm really fine. My time of grieving needs to come to an end, and that means becoming more involved with the ranch. Actually, I'm excited about it."

Bonnie did not need the town banker meddling in her affairs.

She had enough problems without adding more.

"Your children are beautiful," Sylvia said. "And they always look so nice."

"Grandma made me a new dress," Lydia Anne said.

"I'd love to see it." Sylvia smiled into Bonnie's face. "May I?"

Bonnie understood the woman's need to be around children. She and Lester had none of their own, and the town's children became a substitute. "Of course. Lydia Anne, would you like to show her?"

The little girl's blue eyes danced. She slipped her hand into Sylvia's and started up the stairs. A moment later, the back door slammed, and Bonnie realized Zack must have come home.

"I'll see how many fish Zack caught," Michael Paul said.

In the next moment, Bonnie was alone with Lester.

"I have a fine bottle of wine for you," Lester said. "It's in the back of the carriage."

"Please, I don't need any more. I'm sleeping quite well on my own without it."

"Nonsense. It will calm you down after dealing with the children. I'll get it and be back before Sylvia returns."

He slipped out the door before she had an opportunity to protest further. Lester was used to people doing what he said, and Bonnie worried that he might tell others about supplying her with wine. She'd simply store it somewhere. She shuddered at the thought of her family discovering she'd been drinking. It was bad enough she'd begun accepting the gifts of wine from Lester with the "just between us" agreement, but the drinking had gotten out of hand as the empty bottle proved this morning.

Lester returned with the wine, and Bonnie set it in the sideboard. Whatever would she do if Juanita found it? As soon as the Hillmans left and everyone was in bed, Bonnie would move the bottle upstairs.

"Please, no more," she whispered. "I have no use for it."

He chuckled. "Show me the full bottles, and I'll stop bringing them."

"This is the last time that I ask you politely to stop."

"And how would the good reverend and his wife feel about your indulgence in spirits?"

A shiver raced up and down her arms. If Ben were alive, Lester would never speak to her in such a way. Voices from the kitchen seized her attention, and her thoughts flew to Zack.

"Six big fish," Michael Paul said. "Where did you go?"

"Upstream a little," Zack said. "Next time I'll take you with me."

Bonnie swallowed hard. How long before Michael Paul no longer sought her permission to do things? Suddenly life seemed to spin in all directions, as though she were a child's toy. Her resolve from this morning flashed across her mind. She must reach out and grab hold of her life and those she loved. But how? *Jesus, help me.*

"Let's see those fish," Lester said. "I'm glad you permit Zack to do a few things on his own. He's growing up, and a young man needs time to think about life and what he wants to do. I'd be glad to take him fishing or hunting."

She clenched her fists. "Morgan and Grant can do those things."

"But your brothers are busy men. Morgan's law practice and Grant's medical responsibilities don't offer much time outside of their own families."

"The reverend is looking forward to spending his days with the children, too."

Lester smiled. She used to think he was a pleasing man to look at with dark eyes and hair like Ben. He and Sylvia had been through a rough time when he had fathered two boys by a woman who once owned the town's brothel. The woman had left town with the children, and Lester had become more involved with church. He and Sylvia appeared happy, but Bonnie wondered. What would she do if he turned his affections to her? The possibility had not crept into her thoughts until tonight. His persistence with the wine alarmed her.

"I gave the reverend a sizable check this afternoon," Lester said.

"He said it would help with the orphans and widows—not you, of course."

She despised the implication. This ended tonight.

I'm an Andrews. My daddy started the biggest ranch in the area before he died, and my mama built it on her own while raising three children. If Mama did it, so can I.

⌘

Travis had been in Kahlerville for two days. He'd been introduced to more people than he could remember. Most of them were skeptical about his new position, if not downright rude, and he understood taking the reverend's place might ruffle a few feathers. Looked like he'd have to prove himself. The reverend had apologized more than once for the way he'd been treated, but each time Travis had reassured him that the transition would take time.

In a few short minutes, the reverend and Mrs. Rainer's family were expected for dinner. He'd met Mrs. Kahler but not Morgan and Grant Andrews and their families. They were influential in the community, and he hoped to make them friends. The tantalizing aroma of roast beef and potatoes swirled up the stairs and moved him not to delay a moment longer. His stomach had rumbled for hours, and he'd spent a good bit of the afternoon in prayer for tonight. The sound of voices told him the time had come.

Travis made his way down the stairs and into the dining room. The reverend stood with his back to him amid a swarm of people. He saw Mrs. Kahler, but she was talking to another woman. *Lord, help me here.* He touched the reverend on his back. The introductions were about to begin.

"The food smells wonderful," Travis said.

The reverend turned and grasped his hand. "Good. You're here. Let me introduce you to everyone."

"Do you think the new preacher is ready for us?" a man asked. "After all, you're asking him to put up with seven stubborn, independent adults and eight lively children." He stuck out his hand. "Morgan Andrews. I'm the oldest of the clan. This beautiful, auburn-haired woman is my wife, Casey, and these are our children: Chad, Lark, and Daniel."

"Pleased to meet you." Travis listened to Grant Andrews introduce his dark-haired petite wife, Jenny, and their two little girls, Rebecca and Rachel. At least he'd already met Mrs. Kahler and her children.

Near the end of dinner, Travis placed his fork beside his plate and focused his attention on the reverend at the head of the table. "The folks here refer to you as Reverend Rainer or just Reverend. I'm not used to using that title and hoped you might suggest something."

"What did they call you back home?" The reverend picked up a jar of apple butter.

"Mostly Brother Whitworth by the congregation and Brother Travis by close friends. Although some did call me Preacher."

"What do you prefer?"

"Brother Whitworth to start with and then Brother Travis as soon as folks feel comfortable. I also think the name difference will help make it look like I'm not taking your place. What do the rest of you think?"

Heads nodded, and Travis relaxed slightly.

"I think that will work fine," the reverend said.

"Do you plan on getting a haircut before Sunday?" Zack asked, then snickered.

"Zack Kahler." Mrs. Kahler stood from the table. "Leave the room this instant."

"Can I take my plate?" he asked.

"No. You are finished with dinner." Her face matched the white tablecloth.

Zack scooted his chair back, still snickering. He grabbed a biscuit and left the room, banging the outside door in his wake.

"I'm so sorry," Mrs. Kahler said. "I need to take the children and go home."

"Sit down, Bonnie. Leaving is exactly what Zack wants," Morgan said. "I'll go talk to him in a little bit."

She slowly sat. Her shoulders lifted and fell.

"Perhaps I'm the one who needs to talk to him," Travis said. "He and I started out badly."

"Zack doesn't get along with anyone," Morgan said. "Don't waste your time."

Tension sparked the air.

"He's grieving over Ben," Mrs. Kahler said. "I know that is no excuse for his behavior, but—"

"You're right." Grant tossed his napkin on the table. "Every family dinner we have is spoiled by Zack's impudent behavior."

"And he's getting worse. I hear what happens at school," Morgan said.

"Maybe we should simply stay away." Mrs. Kahler's voice rose, and her lips quivered.

Travis wanted to hush the rising voices. He didn't think this was the first time the siblings' words had flown at each other over Zack's behavior.

"What good would that do?" Mrs. Rainer said. "I'd rather we not discuss this any further tonight. Brother Travis is our guest, and the children don't need to hear any of this."

Travis stood. "I could take the children for a walk if you need to talk."

"Are you saying that we *should* talk about Zack? I am quite capable of taking care of my own son's behavior." Mrs. Kahler's cheeks flamed red.

Travis sensed his own face growing warm beneath his beard. "Mrs. Kahler, I'm attempting to be accommodating. I'll do whatever I can to help."

"The problem is that none of you have any sympathy for what the poor child or my other children have gone through in losing their father." Mrs. Kahler stiffened.

35

Morgan shook his finger in his sister's face. "He is no longer a child, Bonnie. And you may not have noticed, but Michael Paul and Lydia Anne are well behaved. Zack is fighting and causing trouble wherever he goes." He stopped abruptly and glanced at Travis, then his mother. "I apologize for this outburst. You're right. Our discussion is not appropriate for our guest or our children."

"And I apologize, too," Grant said. "We're not helping the situation at all."

"Well, you can continue your dinner in peace, because the Kahlers are leaving." Bonnie nodded at Michael Paul and Lydia Anne. In the next instant, the three were gone from the table and out the front door.

The reverend rubbed his face. No one said a word.

"I lost my temper," Morgan said. "I just heard an earful from Chad and Lark before we got here. Guess I was already angry." He gave each of his children a stern look. "All of you are old enough to understand that you don't repeat family business."

"Yes, sir," the three echoed.

Grant's daughters said nothing. Travis believed they were afraid to speak.

"Brother Travis, I hope the rest of your congregation is easier to deal with than we are," Morgan said. "I was fixin' to offer my help with whatever you need, but I have a feeling we need you more than you need us."

CHAPTER  5

Bonnie tossed and turned while the rest of the house slept. She heard every sound outside her window, from the dogs scrapping to insects serenading the night. She despised what had happened that evening—from the incident with Zack to the angry words shared with her brothers. What made matters worse was that Morgan and Grant were right. Horribly, honestly right.

All of her life, she'd let others take care of her: her parents, Morgan, and Ben. Grant had refused to coddle her, and later Mama had as well. If she thought about it for very long, she realized Mama and Grant had shown the most love. Now she must guide and parent her children, and she lacked the knowledge or the strength. But she could find what she needed.

Zack's disrespectful comment proved to her that he had to be reined in or the words of her brothers would haunt her forever. She hated her inability to control her oldest. She stared out the window into the inky blackness, lit only by a half-moon. The morning might look better, but first she needed sleep. A little wine always pushed aside whatever bothered her. She could almost taste it. . .feel the warmth trickling down her throat. . .and the moment her mind dulled to the pain. It rested mere feet from her bed.

No! I will not. Those days are over.

The longer she fretted about the future of her children and how she wanted desperately to rise victorious as a strong woman and mother, the more she craved a glass of wine. Guilt scraped its fingers through her heart, but it didn't stop the desire to simply sleep and forget.

Bonnie's head pounded. She could win this war of weakness. She must. Her children's lives lay in the balance. Throwing back the coverlet, she rose from the bed and dressed. Stealing across the floor, she reached into the wardrobe and pulled out the bottle of wine from the corner. She wrapped a shawl around it and crept downstairs, holding the beloved enemy to her heart. The stairs creaked with every step she took.

Once in the kitchen, she reached for the kerosene lantern from the table and lit it. With its light, she made her way outside to the shed and found a shovel. The three dogs, a mixture of whatever stray mutt spent a few days in Buttercup's company, pushed each other aside for her attention, which, oddly enough, gave her some sense of ease.

She resolved to bury the bottle behind the barn where no one would find it. A small hole would do. If Lester produced another bottle, she'd refuse it, even to the point of letting Sylvia know about her husband's gifts. Bonnie knew she'd been wrong in accepting the wine and even more wrong in drinking to forget her grief, and she wouldn't continue the ruse any longer.

She slammed the shovel into the ground and turned over one clod then two. The smell of fresh earth met her nostrils, bringing back a flood of memories of when she used to watch Ben dig worms for his and the boys' fishing days.

"Miss Bonnie, are you all right?"

She nearly fell over the shovel. "Land sakes, Thomas, you frightened me."

He reached out and steadied her. "Ma'am, you did the same to me."

Bonnie massaged her right temple. "I'm not sure what to say." *The truth?* "Can you keep another secret for me?"

"Yes ma'am. I've done so in the past, and I will again."

In the shadows, his deep voice, mellowed with age and simple wisdom, gave her more determination to complete the task and admit her wrongdoing. "Remember when you found some months ago. . .after. . .I—"

"I remember."

She sighed and braved on. "I'm burying this bottle as a way of burying that habit."

"I see. Would you like me to do it for you?"

"No, thank you. This is something I must do. My children need me. This ranch needs me, and I have to be strong." Emotion crawled up her throat, and she forced it back down. "I depend on you way too much, and that's not fair."

"But you've had it hard since Ben passed on."

Just the mention of his name caused her to gasp. Oh, how she missed him. "I appreciate your sympathy. Yet I know it's no excuse to take on detestable vices or not make Ben proud of me. I want him to look down from heaven and not worry about poor Bonnie and his children." She stopped herself before uttering another word. "My, I've said far too much."

"I understand, and I'll keep your secrets."

"It's easier to talk in the dark."

"You can always talk to me. No one ever hears about it but the Lord."

"This ranch never would have made it without you. You're worth your weight in gold. Tomorrow I want to start learning more about everything you do."

"Are you sure? It'll take a lot of time."

"I'm positive. I want folks to say that I'm just like the rest of my family. I'll pay you extra for your effort."

He laughed lightly. "No thanks. Seeing you take an interest in things is payment enough for me. Me and the Lord been talkin' about you. Hope you don't mind."

"Not at all. I need all the prayers I can get. And Zack. . ." She took a breath. "He needs prayers, too."

"Yes, ma'am. He's had a hard time of it. You want me to leave you alone or wait till you're finished?"

"Best wait. Your presence keeps me accountable."

When the hole was large enough, she slammed the shovel onto the bottle's neck and broke it. Glass tumbled into the hole with the wine. She piled dirt on top with a fierce vengeance.

"I'll put the shovel away," he said.

"No, I need to do this whole thing. All my life, somebody's been doing things for me that I could do myself."

Once the task was completed and she had made her way back inside the house, she took a moment to remember the many nights she and Ben had crept outside to watch the stars. Yawning, she mounted the stairs, feeling very satisfied and amazingly lighthearted. She slipped inside the door of each child's room and planted a kiss on a sweet cheek. Only Zack awoke.

"What's wrong, Mama?" he asked through a sleep-laden voice.

"Nothing." She touched his head and wove her fingers through his hair. "I love you, Zack, and I know you aren't happy. I won't let you get by with any more bad behavior. Loving you means making you mind."

"I don't think you can do it."

She smiled in the darkness. Odd how burying a bottle of wine could give her such confidence. "I'm not sure how, but I will find a way."

Zack turned over and pulled the sheet over his face.

"Hiding from the truth doesn't make it any less the truth," she said. "You may be too old to whip, but there are other ways."

"How?"

"Military school."

The sheet whipped back. "I'd run away."

"And do what? Lie? Steal? The law would find you and punish you worse than I ever could. You're hurting, Zack. Why not talk to Grandpa or one of your uncles?"

"They don't care about me. No one does."

"Like I said before, I love you. All of our family cares about you." Bonnie didn't attempt to continue the conversation. She'd taken a giant step this night, and tomorrow she'd take another.

"I'll hurt Michael Paul and Lydia Anne if you try to stop me from doing what I want."

"You'd hurt the ones who love you?" A tear slipped from her eye. To think this was only the beginning of making up for all of her mistakes.

❧◈❧

Early Saturday morning, Travis and the reverend walked down the road away from town. Dew-kissed leaves glistened in the early sunlight, and birds called to one another in bright song.

"I want to learn all there is to know about Piney Woods Church before tomorrow." Travis laughed. "I sound like a kid."

"Just eager. We do church simple here in Kahlerville. Sunday morning, evening, and Wednesday night prayer meetin'. Sunday school is at nine with church at ten, and we usually have revival services in early spring. Deacons meet once a month, and the ladies have a Bible study with Jocelyn every Thursday morning."

Travis smiled. "Good. What about a choir?"

"Not regularly. Grant's wife, Jenny, plays piano and has organized folks to sing on special occasions."

"I'm hoping we could start one. Do you think many would be interested?"

"I think you'd have a good turnout. When would you practice?"

Travis considered the church week. "Most likely Wednesday evenings before prayer meetin'. I'll put the matter to prayer."

"And I will, too. Heard you singing last night. Right pleasing voice. I suspect we could have a fine choir." He paused. "I just remembered something. An old friend of mine said he heard you preach a revival. Said it greatly moved him, much like the preaching he remembered as a young man."

Travis startled. Did the reverend's old friend reveal any other information about him? "What was his name?"

"Adam Edwards. Said he was passing through a small community near Knoxville at the time."

"I don't recall the man." Travis forced a chuckle. "Anything else I should know? My singing could have stopped a few from showing back up at the next service."

"That was all he said. Are you ready to start preaching? I was thinking about Sunday morning."

"Sure. Might as well get started. I'd like to visit a few folks today and see what kind of reception I get without you beside me." Travis grinned. "Can you suggest a few? I'd like to meet those who won't be running me out of town with buckshot in my behind."

The reverend laughed. "Once we get back to the house, I'll see what I can do about a list of agreeable folk and where to find them."

After breakfast and prayer, with his shoulders erect, Travis walked into town, his frayed Bible tucked under his arm. His hat, worn thin around the brim, fit his bushy hair comfortably, but the slightly large pants would have fallen to his ankles if not for his suspenders. With a quick brush of his hand, he wiped off his dirt-covered boots and wondered at the picture he must be presenting.

Call me Jeremiah, he inwardly chuckled, *or John the Baptist. I've come from the wilderness with a word from the Lord.*

He visited various businesses and stopped by homes to introduce himself. Wherever he went, Travis carried a small notepad. When he met a new face, he jotted down the name and something that would help him remember that person. Most of the townspeople were polite, but a few acted apprehensive—wanting to know where he'd come from, if he had a family, did he believe in the Bible, and countless other questions.

He called upon the banker, Lester Hillman, a dandy-looking man who dressed more like he owned a bank in New York or Boston instead of in a small town in Texas. The two men stood in the lobby of the bank. "Come back at another time. One day next week," he said. "I enjoy giving to those in need, and I'm asking you to keep me informed about situations in which I can help. Did the reverend tell you I'm the largest contributor?"

No, he didn't, but do you know Jesus? "The reverend and I haven't had an opportunity to discuss all the members."

Travis stopped by the telegraph office and made conversation with a spindly, toothless old man, Jake Weathers, who openly stated no preacher would ever be as good as John Rainer.

"Probably not," Travis said. "I just hope ya'll have patience with me while I learn from him."

"Won't take nary a bit of patience," the old man grumbled. "Either you have it or ya don't."

"Well, with God's help, I'll do my best." Travis tipped his hat. "Thank you for your time. I look forward to seeing you on Sunday morning."

The man who owned the livery ran him off. He told Travis he didn't need God; religion never gave him a thing but trouble. Picking up a pitchfork, the owner indicated he wasn't a bit afraid of the devil, either. Travis still invited him to church.

The barber, also the undertaker, proved to be friendly and offered a free haircut and shave. Travis politely declined but inwardly found the offer amusing. He knew exactly how badly he needed to be groomed.

Midmorning he stopped by the lumberyard. The reverend had suggested he visit the owner, Frank Kahler, who was in charge of fixing up Travis's soon-to-be home. The man was also Bonnie Kahler's brother-in-law.

The front door stood open, inviting in the light breezes of the

September day. Travis inhaled the sweet smell of sawdust, and the hearty sound of "Mornin' " instantly put him at ease.

"I'm looking for Frank Kahler," Travis explained to a huge, square-looking fellow wearing overalls and hosting a wide grin. "Is he around?"

"That would be me. What can I do for you?"

"I'm Brother Travis Whitworth. Reverend Rainer suggested I stop by and introduce myself." He stuck out his hand and received a vigorous shake.

"I'm pleased to meet you. Follow me on out here." Frank walked outside to where logs were being loaded onto a wagon, and Travis followed. "Has the reverend told you about the new parsonage?"

"He said you were in charge of fixin' it up."

"Yes, sir, I am." He laid the last log on the wagon bed. "That'll do it," Frank said to the mule driver. He turned his attention back to Travis. "Do you want to take a look at the house? My wife is there sanding woodwork, and I know she'd really like to meet you."

Travis agreed, and Frank drove a wagon through Kahlerville and past the town's businesses. They soon discovered a common love of carpentry, and their conversation turned to types of wood and methods of construction.

"This house once belonged to my brother," Frank said. "He lived here until he got married; then a young couple stayed in it about two years before they bought a farm of their own. My brother passed on, and his widow deeded it over to the church."

"I've met Mrs. Kahler. A fine woman."

"My brother sure loved her." They stopped in front of a small, freshly whitewashed house sitting back off the road. Travis admired the new roof and paned windows. It suited him just fine.

Stepping up onto the front porch, he welcomed the woodsy scent, the feel of sawdust scattering beneath his boots, and the whisking sound of someone sanding wood. He'd always enjoyed the feel of wood in his hands.

"Looks to me like you've done more than fix this house up. Why, it looks and smells brand-new."

"The reverend was real concerned that you had a good place to live."

"Frank, I'd have been happy sleeping under the stars."

"Ellen," Frank called through the open doorway, "I've got someone here for you to meet."

"Just come on back," a soft voice said. "But tread lightly. The baby's asleep."

The big man cringed. "Guess I'd better not talk so loud."

Travis nodded knowingly. "I have a lot of nieces and nephews. Mamas always have work to do while their babies sleep."

They entered the parlor, where Ellen Kahler stood wiping the sawdust from her hands. Travis simply grinned; the house sparkled with fine workmanship. Frank showed him the kitchen and two bedrooms, then returned to the parlor.

Frank gave an admiring glance at the baby resting peacefully on a quilt in the corner. He wrapped a muscled arm around a tiny, fair woman.

"This is my wife, Ellen, and our baby, Frank Jr.," Frank said. "And this is Brother Whitworth, the new preacher."

Ellen extended her hand shyly, and Travis looked into the face of a strawberry blond with peach-colored freckles dotted across her nose. Frank towered over the tiny woman, wordlessly expressing his devotion to her.

"Welcome to Kahlerville," she said. "I'm sure the Rainers are glad you're here. They do need to slow down a bit. I hear you're from Tennessee."

"Yes, ma'am. Not far from Erwin."

"I lived near there until I was fifteen, but you don't look familiar."

Travis coughed. "My home and church was pretty far up in the hills." He pointed to the sleeping baby. "Good-looking boy."

"Thank you. He's been teethin' and a mite fussy with it. I wanted to have more done on the sanding—"

"Ma'am, let me help," Travis said and took another appreciative glance around him. "My, this looks fine. You folks are going to a lot of trouble."

"Brother Whitworth is a carpenter, too," Frank explained.

"Like Jesus," she said. At that moment the baby began to cry. She scooped him up, and he immediately quieted.

Travis glanced at the two doting over Frank Jr. "There's nothing I like better, other than preachin', than to be working with wood. I'd be honored if you'd let me lend a hand. You folks have plenty to do on your own."

"Well," Frank began, "we could use another man. Would you be willing to help a few of us next Wednesday? We could probably have it ready by Friday."

"I'll be here," Travis said. "And thanks."

"I need to write my mother a letter," Ellen said. "I'll ask her about your family and church."

Travis fought to keep his composure. The last thing he needed was folks learning about what had happened in Tennessee—the problems in his church because he'd made a few bad choices.

CHAPTER  6

Travis took a deep breath, willed his knees to stop shaking, and quickly breathed another prayer before stepping up to the pulpit of the Piney Woods Church. A hush swept over the crowd, and Travis knew without a doubt that his words would set the mood for how the congregation accepted their new preacher. Hostile looks from a few folks didn't give him much confidence.

Oh, Lord, it's been a long time since we've done this together. I'm not so sure I still can preach. Help me.

"Folks, I stand before you this morning feeling very humble that our Lord has seen fit to bring me here to your town, your church. Over the past few days, I've met a number of you, and I appreciate the fine welcome and all the help Reverend Rainer has given me. Every preacher dreams of shepherding a church that loves Jesus and is eager to do His work. I know this is a Jesus-loving church.

"Some of you have expressed concern about me taking the reverend's place. Just let me say that I have no desire to ever replace your fine reverend and—"

"Amen," a man said.

"I'm glad you agree with me, sir." Travis's heart knocked against his chest. "It would be impossible to put all of that wisdom into another man. But with all of us working together, we can continue what God has begun through Reverend Rainer's fine ministry.

"I imagine y'all have questions. So after the service, Mrs. Rainer and some of the other ladies have arranged a reception at the parsonage. Everyone's welcome."

"Right now, let's worship together in song by turning in our hymnals to page 118, 'Blessed Assurance.' You folks certainly have a fine pianist. I could listen to Mrs. Andrews play from sunup to sundown."

Once the hymn began, Travis felt his nervousness fade slightly as he focused on the words. "This is my story. This is my song. Praising my Savior all the day long."

What would these good people think if they knew why he'd left his church in the Tennessee hills? Why hadn't he thought to change his name? Anyone could find out what a miserable job he'd done there—and the resulting disaster.

"Today's message is taken from Genesis. God has placed a series of sermons on my heart about the spiritual journey of Jacob. Would you follow along in your Bibles in Genesis 25:21 as Isaac prays for God to give him and Rebekah a child."

Preaching about Jacob the deceiver hit an ironic chord. Maybe the sermon was more for him than it was for the good people sizing him up like a new crop of potatoes. At the end of his message, he invited those who wanted to make Jesus the Lord of their lives to step forward. None came.

No surprise. He wanted to step down from the pulpit, walk out the door, and catch the next train out of town. He forced a smile and glanced out at the people. The reverend and Mrs. Rainer's family were all there. A couple of the folks who had expressed regret at the reverend's retirement weren't seated among the congregation. One elderly couple—Mr. and Mrs. Parker—frowned.

Maybe they knew the truth after all.

At the parsonage, folks helped themselves to a picnic lunch and ate on the grass. Some were polite. The barber offered his services again, and Lester Hillman told him how much money he'd put into the collection plate again. His wife blushed. Travis wondered if the woman ever questioned her husband on his mannerisms. Everyone needed accountability.

Travis realized he wouldn't last long if the good Lord didn't provide a miracle.

Early Monday morning, as the sun peered over the horizon, Travis rode to the Kahler ranch. He stopped at the front gate of the elegant white home belonging to Mrs. Bonnie Kahler. His gaze trailed up the structure with its stylish angles and chimneys that emerged from the many roofs. The trim work looked like it was done by an expert—the horizontal clapboards and fish scale shingles all painted in a deep green that reminded him of the Tennessee hills.

Travis glanced upward to a towerlike structure on the second floor and saw Mrs. Kahler looking down upon him through one of the windows. When she saw him staring back, she quickly pulled the drapes together. He almost waved.

The rich earth beneath his feet looked moist as though someone had just watered the flowering plants, and not a single weed threatened to choke any of them. His gaze moved to the veranda, where a pair of rocking chairs looked as inviting as a fresh-baked apple pie. Huge baskets of ferns dripped water ever so lightly unto the wooden porch. Travis clearly heard the hustle and bustle of ranch hands in the distance. He couldn't make out their whoops and hollers, but nevertheless they were there. A cow bawled. A dog barked.

Travis planted his foot on the first step leading up to the carved oak door, then hesitated. He'd already offended Mrs. Kahler more than once. Perhaps he should take care of his errand at the back door like other hired folks. After all, he did come with a job to do.

Travis retraced his steps to the front of the house, then followed a path to the back door. A young Mexican woman answered his call and in broken English asked what he wanted.

He removed his hat. "I'm Brother Travis Whitworth, here to repair the roof."

She disappeared, leaving him standing outside. He suspected his workmanship may not be to Mrs. Kahler's standards. Before he had an opportunity to further question his abilities, however, she stood at the door, dressed in a pale gray and ivory dress. He attempted to ignore what her beauty did to him. A man of God had no right to think of such things; the past had already proved that.

"I didn't know if you would truly come this morning," she said with her hands neatly folded in front of her. "But I'm glad you did. Are you settling in?"

Travis couldn't stop the smile. Mrs. Kahler had a way of looking at him that made him want to look at her all day. "I'm doing fine, thank you. The reverend and his wife are gracious people." He pulled his gaze away from her lovely face and glanced up at the roof. "I've allowed two days to do the repairs. I hope it's long enough."

"I'm sure it will be fine." She nodded, and for a moment he doubted his ability to climb onto the roof. "I'll have my foreman show you about. Have a good day, Brother Whitworth."

Bonnie called for Zack to escort Travis to one of the stables. The boy appeared annoyed at the request, but he didn't argue with his mother. Travis started to bid her a good morning, but the door shut soundly before he could speak.

"All right, son, lead the way," Travis said.

"I'm not your son," the boy said.

Travis rubbed beneath his nose. *Must I always be offending some member of this family?* "I'm sorry, Zack."

"You don't have to put on airs with me, Preacher, 'cause I don't care about anything you have to say. You're hired help, that's all."

"You must have gotten up on the wrong side of the bed," Travis said.

"That's none of your business."

"Disrespect is my business." Travis swung his stride ahead of the boy and eyed him squarely. "And you have been taught how to respect others."

"I don't have to do anything I don't want to."

The rebellion in Zack's stance told Travis this boy would have to fall hard before he walked straight.

"If you would give me a chance, I'd like to be your friend, but friendship means each of us has to treat the other fairly."

"I don't need any preacher friends." Zack pointed to the stable door. "The foreman's in there. His name's Thomas. I'm headin' to school."

A short time later, Travis nailed pieces of shingle onto the roof of the house. My, how he loved the touch and smell of wood. Somehow knowing the Lord worked as a carpenter made him feel just a little closer to Him. The sun crept across the sky, warming his back and removing any traces of early morning chill.

Travis whistled his favorite hymn of the day—"Abide with Me"—until the words and melody took form. One hymn after another filled the air around him while he worked and considered the sermon for Wednesday night. He'd nearly drowned with Sunday morning's pitiful message, but at least he had a second chance. He prayed his words would be filled with the Holy Spirit—and not Travis Whitworth. He pondered over scripture passages, rolling the meanings around in his mind. Nothing came to mind, so he kept singing on through the afternoon.

Zack. The boy's spiteful words repeated through his mind again. Not only did Zack need to learn respect for himself and others, but more important, he needed to find a relationship with Jesus.

Such a job You have given me, Lord.

"Brother Whitworth," a young voice called.

Travis peered around one of the chimneys to see Michael Paul staring up and shielding his eyes against the afternoon sun.

"Yes, Michael Paul. Did you have a fine day at school?"

"Yes, sir. Juanita has fried chicken, green beans, corn bread, and cold buttermilk for you." Michael Paul held up a basket and pitcher for Travis to see.

"Wonderful. I'm powerful hungry." He made his way across the steep roof onto a ladder bringing him down beside the boy. "Would you like to share this with me?"

"No, sir. I had lunch at school, and we'll have dinner later on. Thank you just the same."

"How about visiting with me for a spell?"

"I'd be glad to." Michael Paul followed him to the back steps.

While Travis ate, he chatted with the boy. His lively conversation revealed that he was a whole lot different than his older brother.

"Brother Whitworth," Michael Paul began slowly. "I—I sure enjoy your singing."

"Thanks," Travis said. "Do you like music?"

"Yes, sir. My aunt Jenny is going to give me piano lessons. When I'm by myself, I sing, too."

Travis ruffled the boy's hair. "Perhaps we need to sing together. What do you say to working on some hymns with me?"

Michael Paul reddened slightly, but he did manage a smile. "I don't think I'm nearly as good as you."

"All the good Lord wants is a joyful noise."

"I can do that."

Travis placed the fork and empty plate back into the basket. "Do you have any chores right now?"

The young boy shook his head.

"Well, why don't you stay and visit a while longer? Talking would sure make the time go by faster, especially with a young lad who likes my singing."

"I have to ask my mother, but I 'spect it will be just fine."

"Would you tell her and Miss Juanita that I appreciated this fine food?"

Michael Paul nodded and disappeared with the empty basket and pitcher, and Travis resumed his position on the roof. *Now he's a good boy. Real pleasant and talkative. I hope Mrs. Kahler allows him to spend some time with me. He may be the first one of the Kahler family that I can call a friend.*

"Brother Whitworth." Michael Paul cupped his hand around his mouth. "Mama says I can talk to you until Lydia Anne wakes up from her nap. Then I have to play with her."

"Good. Why don't you tell me the things you like to do best?" Travis asked.

In between hammerings, Travis listened to Michael Paul talk about the ranch, school, his uncles, grandparents, and favorite songs, but he said nothing about his mother or older brother.

Once Travis completed all the repair work and the foreman gave his approval, Michael Paul helped Travis gather up the tools and pieces of wood. Together they placed them in a storage shed. Lydia Anne had not yet woken from her nap, so Travis seized the opportunity not only to thank the boy, but also to praise him for his assistance.

"I couldn't have gotten this work done so fast if you hadn't been here," Travis said. "I thought it would take me two days."

"I didn't do anything."

"Yes, you did. You talked to me and kept me interested, and the roof nearly repaired itself. Before I go, I need to tell your mother the roof is fixed and the foreman approved it. Shall we tell her together?"

Michael Paul nodded. The sound of arguing from inside the house caused the boy to stiffen. Travis heard the voices and recognized Zack and Mrs. Kahler.

"I should hurry on back to town. I reckon having Thomas look at the roof is enough. If your mother has any questions or needs more work done, she can contact me at the parsonage," Travis said. "Would you give her my best?"

"Yes, sir." Michael Paul's gaze swung toward the house.

The voices rose louder. This family was not headed for disaster; it was already there.

CHAPTER 7

Bonnie handed Thomas a steaming mug of coffee before he gave her the morning report. The foals born last spring were doing well. Cattle prices were up. A nearby rancher had offered her a good price to sire a couple of his mares.

Thomas's gaze kept drifting toward the kitchen. She nearly giggled.

"Those biscuits sure smell extra good," he said. "Cookie burned ours this morning."

She figured it was Juanita and not her cooking that attracted Thomas. "Juanita, please get this man a plateful of breakfast. Can't send a man to work without a full stomach. If there's any custard pie left from last night, he might like a piece to go with it."

"Thanks." He took a gulp of coffee. "The cattle are looking good. We'll get a fair price at the stockyards this year."

She'd thought it might be good to send Zack to Fort Worth with the drive, providing he started listening to her. But now wasn't the time to mention it to Thomas. "I want to take a look at the ranch today—see what I've been ignoring. Do you have time to ride with me?" she asked. "And sometime soon, I want to know how many head of cattle and horses we have."

"Yes, ma'am. I'll have Wildflower saddled after the young'uns are gone to school." He rubbed his jaw. "Somebody shot the thievin' coyote that kept takin' your chickens. Found it this morning with a bullet between the eyes."

"Splendid. Now Juanita won't be complaining. I'll let you tell her about it."

He grinned. "I don't know who got it, but I heard the shot in the middle of the night. Odd none of the men owned up to it, 'cause that was some fancy shootin'."

She laughed, and it felt good. "Doesn't matter. It's dead, and the chickens are safe." She walked out onto the back porch with him, both sipping coffee. Juanita brought him a generous plateful. The smile between them told Bonnie her suspicions were correct. Age didn't matter when it came to love, and Juanita was a good twenty years younger than Thomas. "You'd better eat your breakfast before the other hands find out."

"Will do," he said and snatched up a slice of ham.

"I've lost track of our horses. I remember we had five foals last spring."

"Miss Bonnie, are you wanting to learn all about ranchin' in one week?"

"You forget where I come from."

"That's right. You just need remindin'." He chuckled, then stared up at the sky. "Might rain. You don't want to get wet."

"I'll wear a slicker." Talking about the ranch—the home she and Ben had shared—made her feel alive again. If only she'd found interest before, perhaps her life would not have been so consumed with self-pity. And she'd have been a better mother.

"If it doesn't rain, I'd like to take Lydia Anne. I want her to start riding." She paused. "Do we still have the saddle that Zack and Michael Paul learned in?"

"It's in the tack barn." Thomas grinned from one scraggly bearded jaw to the other.

"I don't want my daughter to be afraid of anything." *Not pampered and spoiled like me.* "Michael Paul needs to learn how to shoot a bow and arrow. I remember Zack used to have one."

"I got it, too."

"And I'll be settling my oldest son before I ask you to help him with anything."

"Thanks, Miss Bonnie. He'll be all right."

She knew he was merely being polite, but the affirmation helped.

Within the half hour, she called the boys for breakfast. A ranch hand always drove them to town for school, and it was nearly time to leave. Michael Paul bounded down the steps.

"Where's your brother?" Bonnie asked.

"Haven't seen him since last night." He avoided her eyes.

Gathering up her skirts, she hurried up the steps. They'd argued again before he went to bed. But fussin' between them occurred on a regular basis. He'd been in another fight and had a black eye to prove it.

"One more fight, Zack, and I'm talking to my brothers about finding a good military school back East," she had said to him.

"Told you before I'll run away."

His final words echoed in her mind. First she knocked and called his name. Nothing. Then she opened the door.

Bonnie gasped. Zack's bed was empty. It hadn't been slept in, and his window was open over the back porch.

Since Travis had repaired Bonnie's roof in just one day, on Tuesday morning he and the reverend joined Frank Kahler to help finish his house a day earlier than planned. They were supposed to sand the floors and cut the inside doors. Maybe on Wednesday they could stain them all before the evening service. Some folks had donated furniture, including a fine desk from Morgan Andrews. Those things would be delivered on Thursday. Then he could move in on Friday or

Saturday and hang the doors himself.

"As much as I enjoy Mrs. Rainer's cooking, I'm looking forward to living here," Travis said.

"We're expecting you to show up anytime you're hungry, but I expect you'll have plenty of invitations." He chuckled. "Watch out someone doesn't try to marry you off to one of their daughters."

Travis touched his bushy hair and beard. "I believe only a lady who needs glasses would give me a second look."

"Or one who looks at the heart," Frank said. "I have the most beautiful wife in these parts, and look at me. I more resemble a bear than a man."

Travis shook his head. "I imagine I'll be married to the church instead of a woman."

"You never know what God has in mind. A good woman is a blessing, and children make a man feel complete." The reverend nodded to punctuate his words.

Travis knew the truth. The past haunted him like a worried demon.

Before he could form a reply, someone knocked on the open front door and called out for the reverend. "I'm sorry to bother you, but this is important."

"Come on back, Bonnie. Do you need to talk to me in private?"

One quick glimpse at her reddened eyes and face caused Travis to feel more than a little uncomfortable. What had Zack done now?

"Yes, please," she said.

"Should Brother Travis join me?"

"I suppose."

Travis heard the hesitancy, but he accompanied the reverend to the front porch anyway. One little woman should not have to bear such anguish alone.

"It's Zack." She swallowed hard. "We had an argument last night about another of his fistfights and his disrespect for others. I thought he went to bed, but instead he left home. His bed wasn't slept in. I—I didn't discover he was missing until this morning."

"Do you have any idea where he might have gone?" the reverend asked.

She shook her head. "I brought the carriage into town, took Michael Paul to school, and left Lydia Anne with Mama. I came here before going to see Morgan or the sheriff."

The reverend wrapped his arms around her trembling shoulders. "I'll go with you to see Morgan. What about Grant?"

"He wouldn't go there. Grant's made it clear that Zack isn't welcome with the little girls." She moistened her lips. "Can't say I blame him."

"Anything I can do?" Travis caught her gaze, and for a moment he believed he'd do about anything to help her find Zack.

"No, thank you. We'll find him." She dabbed beneath her eyes and turned from him.

"Is he on horseback?" the reverend asked.

"No. I'm sure he realized one of the ranch hands would've caught him taking a horse."

"Then he couldn't have gone far. Any friends that he might have gone to?"

"Reverend, Zack has gotten so ornery that I don't think he has any friends left."

The older man pressed his lips together. "All right. I imagine Morgan will have some ideas. Maybe Chad's seen him."

"I really would like to help, but I understand," Travis said. Despite their differences, she was a lovely woman. But a pretty face had once gotten him into a heap of trouble. "I'll be right here with Frank and praying for you." His attention focused on Eustes Arthur, the town sheriff, making his way toward them at a fast pace.

"Mrs. Kahler." Sheriff Arthur frowned.

She whirled around and greeted him with a pleasant smile.

"This isn't a social call," he said. "I've got your boy in jail."

Mrs. Kahler's face blanched, and her shock yanked at Travis's heart. Zack needed a firm hand, a man's hand.

"He's just a boy." Her voice rose. "And you're treating him like a criminal."

"Your boy was caught red-handed, stealing a saddle at the livery. Where was he going to put it? And you know what's done to horse thieves in this part of the country."

Her hand flew to her mouth, then she took a deep breath. "I'm sure there's been a mistake." She turned to the reverend. "If you would kindly get Morgan, I'll walk over to the jail with Sheriff Arthur." Her skirts swished by as she stepped down from the porch. In the next instant, the sheriff followed.

The reverend threw Travis a wary glance, and he understood exactly what was expected of him. Hurrying back into the house, he found Frank. "I've got an errand to run. I'll be back as soon as I can."

When he caught up with Mrs. Kahler and the sheriff, she tossed Travis a look that would have stopped a cornered polecat.

"I don't need your help, Brother Whitworth. This is family business."

He ignored her dismissal and kept step beside her.

"You are one stubborn man," she said barely above a whisper.

"I'm a man of God. We go where we're led, even when we aren't wanted."

"Obviously."

Inside the jail, Mrs. Kahler nearly crumpled at the sight of Zack sitting in a cell.

"What have you done?" she asked evenly.

Good. Don't let him get off with this easily.

"It's all a mistake." Zack stood and peered at his mother with the same woeful eyes that Travis had seen that first day in town. "I walked most of the night and fell asleep in the livery. I was using the saddle for a pillow."

"I don't know if you're telling the truth or not." She turned to the sheriff. "Please unlock the cell. My brother will straighten this out."

Sheriff Arthur blew out an exasperated sigh. "Mrs. Kahler, you've got to get your son under control. If he's like this at twelve, what's he going to be like at thirteen, fifteen, or seventeen? Mark my words, if you don't get ahold of Zack, he'll end up in prison—or hung."

She stiffened. "Right now, I demand you release him. I will handle his discipline if the situation calls for it."

The sheriff had long since turned a vivid shade of red. "Not until you tell me that something's going to be done about all the trouble he's getting into."

"How dare you talk about my son this way? Why, if his father were alive, you wouldn't be talking to me like this."

"If Ben were here, none of this would be taking place. Zack's mean streak would have been taken care of behind the woodshed."

"Zack knows what's going to happen because of his behavior."

"No!" Zack backed up until he was against the cell wall. "I'd rather stay here."

Anger grew between mother and son, much like corn bread and milk on a sour stomach. Zack attempted to look brave, but Travis saw more than an angry boy. He saw a cry for help. A nudging in Travis's spirit made him want to head back to sanding floors with Frank, but he'd stay and do whatever was needed.

Within the hour, the reverend and Morgan joined them. Neither man looked a bit happy over the circumstances.

"My job is to keep the law," Sheriff Arthur said. "If this boy were grown, he'd be facing a whole lot more than an angry family."

"Excuse me," Travis said. "Would you consider releasing him to me? I can continue his schooling and keep him busy."

"If Zack is going to stay with anyone, it will be with my mother and the reverend," Bonnie said.

"I think not," Morgan said quietly. "I'm not putting an undue burden on Mama or the reverend. It's time they took life a little easier."

"You're talking about Zack living with a complete stranger.

Besides, it wouldn't be long. I've. . .I've decided to send him to a military school back East."

Morgan remained unmoved. "That's a good decision, but he doesn't need to live with Mama and the reverend until we can make arrangements."

"Then let me have him for a while," Travis said with no display of emotion. "I'd like to try to help. If Zack could change, then he wouldn't need to leave his family."

The room grew silent as everyone waited for Mrs. Kahler to speak. Tears streamed down her face.

"What about me?" Zack asked. "I don't want to live with no preacher."

"You can take him," she said, regaining her composure. "He can be very difficult, and I am no good at disciplining him. I'm willing to try anything, but I won't have him mistreated."

"I'd not hurt him, Mrs. Kahler." He reached into his pocket and pulled out a clean handkerchief for her. She took it and offered a faint smile, giving him the courage to continue. "I can't move into my new home until the end of the week—"

"Both of them can stay at the parsonage until then," the reverend said. "And Travis can start Zack's schooling right away."

Travis wondered exactly what he'd gotten himself into. Granted, he had nephews, and he knew what the Bible said about raising children, but he didn't know where to begin with a rebellious, half-grown man. At least he could turn to the reverend and the boy's uncles for insight into what his relationship had been with his father. Zack didn't have respect for others, least of all himself. Oh, but the Lord had gotten him into a fine mess.

A leaded silence filled the small office while the sheriff unlocked the cell. Travis met the reverend's gaze. He saw frustration and worry etched on the older man's face. No point in letting the reverend see his own misgivings about handling Zack. Of course, most folks thought Travis was older because of his bushy hair and beard.

"I'll stop by the school and inform his teacher," Mrs. Kahler said.

"Thank you, ma'am. I promise to do a good job with his schooling."

"I won't stay with that ugly, do-gooder preacher." Zack shoved his hands inside his suspenders. "Let me come home, and I'll be better."

Travis listened to Zack attempt to manipulate his mother. He had to admit the boy knew what to say and how to say it.

"You don't care for me at all, do you?" Zack said. "You're kicking me out."

"I believe you ran away," she said.

"Ever since Papa died, all you care about is yourself. Now that I'm in a little trouble, you don't want me anymore." Zack clenched his fists and took a step toward his mother, but Travis stood between them.

"Zack, calm down. Beginning this moment, you won't be talking to your mother this way."

"Amen," Morgan said. "Good luck, Brother Travis. I'm tired of dealing with him."

The boy's eyes blazed with anger—anger that must have been brewing for more than two years. "Good. Mama's a bad mother, and the rest of you just want to get rid of me."

Mrs. Kahler touched his shoulder, but he shrugged her off. "There's no need to cite my faults. I know what they are. But above all things, I am still your mother. Say and think about me as you will, but the real truth is I love you. It would be easy to take you home and hire a tutor and go on about our business as though nothing has happened, but that wouldn't do you a bit of good. I've allowed you to become wild and a bully. But it's all out of my hands at this point. Brother Travis has offered to help, and I'm consenting to it. In the meantime, I'm asking Morgan and Grant to find a military school. The future is up to you. You can learn how to behave, or you can continue as you are and face the consequences of an undisciplined life."

A deafening silence permeated the room. She turned to Travis, her chin lifted high. "I will not attempt to see my son until he wants to see me or you tell me the time is right. I'll have one of the hands bring his clothes. I—I appreciate what you're trying to do." She gathered up her skirts and left the office.

CHAPTER 8

The house seemed strangely quiet that night at dinner. Michael Paul and Lydia Anne said little even though Juanita had prepared their favorite chicken and dumplings. It was Zack's favorite, too. Bonnie's bite of dumpling hung in her throat until she sensed she'd be ill. The forlorn looks on the children's faces told her they weren't faring much better. She needed to reassure them about their brother but not tell them what might happen if Zack didn't learn to respect others and himself.

"Will Zack get food while he's at Brother Whitworth's?" Lydia Anne asked.

"Of course he will," Michael Paul said a bit gruffly.

Bonnie had to address their worries. "Don't you want your brother to be nice again like he used to be?"

Lydia Anne nodded, but her gaze stayed fixed on her plate. "I don't remember when Zack was nice all the time. But I miss him."

"I miss him, too, but unless he learns to have respect for us and mind those who are older and wiser, all of us will be miserable."

"You mean Zack's not happy, either?" Michael Paul asked.

"What do you think?"

He seemed to ponder her question for a moment. "No, he's not. What can the new preacher do that's different?"

"I'm hoping a man of God can help him see where he's wrong, and in turn, Zack will want to change."

"Then he'll come home?" Lydia Anne asked.

"Of course. Our family needs to be together."

"What if Zack likes being miserable?" Michael Paul asked. "Will he go to jail?"

A knot tightened in her stomach. She understood that unless Zack found purpose in his life, his future held no hope. "We will simply pray that God is able to reach him."

"I'm going to pray every night," Michael Paul said. "Zack hits me and says bad things, but I don't want him in jail."

"Me, either," Lydia Anne said with a dainty shrug. "Sometimes he's a little nice. Just most times he's not."

"When can we visit him?" Michael Paul asked.

"Brother Whitworth will let us know."

Her younger son frowned. "He's not our father. I don't think Zack will listen to him. At least I'll see him at school."

"Brother Travis is planning to teach Zack."

Michael Paul stared at her curiously. "Is he already in jail? Zack is going to be real mad. Maybe run away again."

Bonnie's heart plummeted. Again her threat of military school bannered across her mind, and now she must follow through. If she backed down from this, Zack would never respect her. This was all so very difficult. Even her other children doubted Brother Travis could make a difference.

❦

Travis shared dinner with the reverend and Mrs. Rainer without Zack. The boy had cursed in the presence of his grandparents, and Travis had ordered him to his room without the benefit of a meal. The boy had simply grown angrier.

"You did the right thing," the reverend said at dinner. "I wanted to take him out behind the woodshed."

"Not as badly as I did," Mrs. Rainer said. "Where on earth did he learn those words?"

"Maybe the ranch hands," the reverend said. "Hard to say. May have picked them up at school."

"You took on a big job with our grandson." Mrs. Rainer leaned in closer to the table. "Morgan and Grant had their rebellious moments, as most boys do. But neither of them compared to the ugliness I see in Zack."

Travis wondered if he'd lost some of his God-given good sense to try to help Zack. But the boy despised him, and his actions could cause a preacher to lose his faith.

"I'm sure God will give me direction," Travis said.

"More like a coat of armor." The reverend half chuckled. "Seriously, he didn't used to be this way."

Travis nodded. "Pretty close to his father?"

"They did everything together," the reverend said. "Zack didn't cry at the funeral and has been like this ever since."

Mrs. Rainer dabbed at her eyes. "Bonnie lost her papa at his age, too. I feel sorry for him, but he's shutting us all out from his life. I pray military school won't be necessary. Then I'm afraid we'll lose him for good."

"I'm not familiar with any to recommend, and," Travis paused to carefully form his words, "I'm not family. My intentions are not to interfere but to help." He hesitated again. "Since Zack lost his father, I really don't want to see him lose the rest of his family, too."

"I agree," the reverend said. "The problem is if he doesn't learn to control his temper, Michael Paul, Lydia Anne, and Bonnie will not be safe. Sure glad Morgan settled the problem with the saddle. For once, Zack might have told the truth."

Travis silently agreed. He started to apologize for continuing an unpleasant topic during dinner, but someone knocked at the door.

Mrs. Rainer excused herself to answer it. Most likely she was pleased not to discuss her grandson's wild ways.

"Evenin', Grant. Are you alone?"

"Yes, just me, Mama."

"How about some coffee and pie?"

"Sounds good. I need to talk to the reverend and Brother Travis."

"You can do both."

While greetings were made and pie and coffee served, Travis noted that Grant resembled his mother with light coloring, although his hair was darker than hers and Mrs. Kahler's. Worry lines furrowed Grant's forehead.

"We had another problem at Heaven's Gate last night." Grant nodded at Travis. "That's a home where women can find shelter from ways of life that don't honor God."

"The reverend mentioned it to me. I believe your wife, Morgan's wife, and Mrs. Hillman oversee the home."

"Yes. We've had a few instances of late that alarm us." He glanced at his mother.

"Go ahead, Grant. I know what's been happening there," she said.

"The same girl who was beaten about six weeks ago was beaten again." He laid his fork beside the plate. "I treated Rosie. Tried to get her to tell me who'd hurt her, but she refused to give me a name. She has to be covering up for someone, but who? And why?"

"You want me to talk to her?" the reverend asked.

"I'd appreciate it. I'm afraid she might not survive another beating. If we could find out who's responsible, then we could have him arrested."

"Do you mind if I ask a question?" Travis asked. Once Grant and the reverend affirmed him, he braved forward. "So this young woman worked in a house of ill repute?"

"Yes, but she's been living for the Lord almost a year," the reverend said. "She's barely twenty years old and has been attending church. Bonnie and Jenny have been teaching her how to read and write, and she's been doing housework for Sylvia Hillman. Now that is a good woman. She volunteers more than Bonnie and Jenny. She wanted to take Rosie home with her, but the girl refused."

"Do you have a suspect?"

"I don't," Grant said. "No one has seen any men around Heaven's Gate, unless she's slipping out at night." He leaned back on the legs of his chair. "There's no reason to keep the man's name secret unless he's threatened to kill her."

"I remember the last time," Mrs. Rainer said. "How badly is she hurt?"

Grant set his jaw. "Ugly. Makes me want to tear someone apart."

"I can tell by the look on your face that I need to leave the room." She stood from the table and picked up a few of the empty dishes. "I'll be in the kitchen."

"Thanks, Mama." Grant waited until the door between the dining room and kitchen closed. "I'll be real honest here. Whoever is beating Rosie is careful not to damage her face. She's black and blue from the neck down, and her left arm is broken."

"She must be frightened to death." The reverend shook his head. "Is she back at the home or with you and Jenny?"

"Heaven's Gate. I don't think she'd have sought help if one of the other girls hadn't found her. I talked to Eustes, and he plans to have one of his deputies keep an eye on her."

Travis wondered what kind of man purposely hit a woman. A weak one, at best. "I'd be glad to talk to Rosie," he said. "Maybe a new face might help the situation. Then again, the reverend here has wisdom and the look of a father figure."

"The last time Jocelyn went with me, and Rosie wouldn't breathe a word of what happened." He paused. "Brother Travis, I'd like to see about her in the morning. Mind going along?"

"Be glad to." A hammering in Travis's head nearly blinded him. The past always seemed to attack him when he least expected. *Trying to help a woman who once lived in a brothel?* The thought made him shake to his shoes.

"Thanks." Grant took a sip of coffee. "Where's Zack?"

"I'm getting Jocelyn," the reverend said. "Brother Travis can give you that story."

A few moments later, Grant stared into Travis's face. "Sure glad I stopped over here tonight. Military school, huh? I'll visit with Morgan tomorrow. I imagine he knows more about those things than I do. Like you, Brother Travis, I want to see Zack like he used to be."

"I think that expecting him to be the happy boy y'all knew when his father was alive is unlikely. It's impossible to lose someone and then behave as though it never happened. He can find happiness, but he has to trust God again and understand he has a good life ahead of him. The change would be a blessing for all of you."

"And we'd owe you a tremendous debt," Grant said.

"If we are blessed to see a change in Zack, it is God who is owed the thanks."

Later on, as Travis finished reading in his room at a small desk, he pulled out paper and pen to figure out how he was going to school Zack. He already knew the main textbook would be the Bible. Within the covers of those pages, he hoped to build lessons that would help Zack in reading, writing, spelling, ancient history, geography, and hopefully, spirituality. Tomorrow, Travis planned to visit the schoolteacher for help in math. He'd learned she didn't want the boy back in her class. He shrugged. The idea of teaching Zack a little Greek and Latin had crossed his mind. For a moment, Travis wondered if the education he'd received in seminary had been intended for more than preaching the gospel.

Travis believed God knew all along about how he'd fail at his church in Tennessee and all the horrible gossip and lies that followed. And God knew about the problems here in Kahlerville and his taking on Zack Kahler. Travis blew out an exasperated sigh. The idea of teaching and parenting a twelve-year-old scared him to death. He'd rather take on a town full of heathens. At least he'd have an idea where to begin. *God, if You had this all figured out, then*

You must have a plan in this, too.

His thoughts trailed to Zack's mother, but no sooner did the image of her face rise in his mind then he pushed it away. His work in Kahlerville did not involve anything to do with a woman, other than tending to the needs of her soul. He stood from the chair and stretched. Before he went to bed, he needed to make sure Zack understood his commitment—whether Zack wanted to hear it or not.

In the darkness, he made his way down the hallway to the boy's room. Travis knocked once, twice. No response. He twisted the knob and stepped inside a dark room, half expecting him to be gone.

"I have nothing to say to you, Preacher."

"Good. I came to tell you something."

"I don't want to hear it."

"Then cover your ears, because I intend to say my piece. I'm your last hope—me and God—if you want to stay in Kahlerville and not be sent to a military school. I'm giving you my word that I will do all I can to help you."

"I don't want your help."

"I thought you weren't listening. Anyway, tomorrow morning you'll be up at five o'clock. We'll have early devotions together, then take a walk before breakfast to discuss what God said to us during our Bible reading. After breakfast begins school. While I'm your teacher, we'll work on the same things your teacher taught. You're mine until I give you a break. I also plan to teach a few different subjects."

"Like what?"

"Learning carpentry, hunting, and fishing for starters."

Silence. But then Travis didn't expect an answer, and maybe he'd planned all this because deep down he wanted to be that father figure for Zack. Why, he had no idea.

CHAPTER  9

"How did you fare your first morning with Zack?" Reverend Rainer asked as he and Travis walked past the general store and on to Heaven's Gate.

Travis laughed. Might as well find humor in the mess he'd gotten himself into, or he'd give up on the boy the first day. And he certainly didn't want to think about stepping into Heaven's Gate and living through his demons. "I roused him at five just as I warned him the night before. When he failed to acknowledge me the second time, I pulled back his quilt and shook him."

"Whoa. I don't know if I'd have been that brave."

"Well, I'm questioning my sanity. Anyway, after he let me know about his displeasure, I lit the lantern and told him to get dressed or he wouldn't get breakfast. Figured after going without dinner, he'd be right-smart hungry. That worked. We read the same Bible passage and took a walk before breakfast to discuss it."

"What scripture?"

Travis grinned. " 'Follow me, and I will make you fishers of men.' We talked about what that meant." He shrugged. "I talked, and he looked bored."

"I probably would have chosen the prodigal son."

"It crossed my mind. But I'm saving that whole chapter of Luke

15 for when I think he's ready. So I asked Zack if he liked to fish and told him if he could behave himself for three days, we'd go fishing."

"What did he say?"

"Said he preferred to go fishing by himself."

The reverend chuckled. "I shouldn't be laughing here, but I see the worms in what Zack is doing." He laughed aloud. "Pardon my choice of words. But your plan does make good sense."

"I was awake most of the night praying about it. I won't give him any slack, but I will let him know I care."

"What's he doing now?"

"Writing a paper about one thing he likes about his mother. This will be the first of many, and I figure when we're done, we'll give them to the right folks. If he refuses, then he can go to bed without dinner again. I also see a lot of merit in having him write a paper about what he likes about himself."

"You're a good man, Travis. I hope Zack sees and understands what you're doing real soon. And I hope this town treats you right."

You wouldn't be so certain about my character if you knew what happened.

"Are his other grandparents living?"

"Yes. Pete and MayBelle own the general store and the feed store."

"I remember meeting them. Does Zack see them often?"

"He did until he was caught stealing candy from the store."

Would the reports about Zack never end?

A few minutes later, they stood outside a fairly new two-story house. If not for the sign on the gate that read "Heaven's Gate," Travis would have thought a family lived there. Any mirth he might have felt earlier vanished in light of what had happened to one of the girls housed in this charitable home.

"A brothel once stood here," the reverend said as though reading Travis's mind. "It burned, leaving the occupants homeless. Jenny had this house built for the girls who were ready to start over again. She,

Sylvia, Bonnie, and sometimes Casey, Morgan's wife, teach the girls all kinds of things, from sewing and cooking to Bible study."

Mrs. Hillman stepped out onto the front porch, hands perched on her hips. She was a tall woman, not comely, but her heart shone through her smile. He didn't doubt for one minute that heaven had taken notice of Sylvia Hillman. Everywhere he turned, she was ministering to folks. Strange couple, Lester and Sylvia.

"I saw you two coming. Are you here to see my Rosie?"

"We sure are," the reverend said. "I wanted her to have an opportunity to talk to Brother Travis personally."

Mrs. Hillman stuck out her hand. "It's a pleasure to see you again. Rosie told me how she liked your preaching."

"That was right nice of her." Travis figured the poor girl must be deaf. His sermon last Sunday had been barely tolerable, and tonight's prayer meeting had best be a sight better, or he'd lose his congregation before he even began.

"Is she feelin' up to visitors?" the reverend asked.

"I'm sure of it. Lester is with her now, reading scripture to her and the other girls." She blinked. "He's such a caring man. Why, he's offered Laura a job at the bank and said he'd train her himself."

"That is a fine man," the reverend said.

The two men followed Sylvia inside and up the stairs. Travis plastered on a smile while his insides fought with his heart. Whoever had done this to a poor girl who was trying hard to live a right life ought to be horsewhipped. An image of Felicia flashed across his mind, and he shuddered. He'd done his best to keep her away from a brothel, but all it had accomplished was his losing his church—and any respect from those who mattered. Maybe he could do better this time. He prayed so.

At this moment, Travis needed to put aside his personal feelings about Lester and praise God for a man who went out of his way to help society's unwanted.

Lester closed the Bible and stood when the reverend and Travis entered the bedroom. He shook hands with both of them. Two other young women stood and greeted them politely and then bent over Rosie to kiss her cheek. A moment later, the other young women left the room.

"Good for you two to come." Lester smiled down at Rosie. "We just finished reading from the Psalms. I'll leave you, since I need to get to the bank." He smiled at Rosie. "You're doing fine. Remember all we talked about, and I'll check on you soon."

Lester left them alone. A tear trickled down Rosie's cheek, and she whisked it away with her right hand. Her left arm lay bandaged against the side of her body. The injured young woman with jet black hair and olive skin looked to be from Mexico.

"Hello, Rosie, I brought Brother Whitworth with me."

"Thank you for coming," she said.

"Do you feel up to us visiting?" the reverend asked.

She hesitated and nodded. Why had she refused to name the man who had attacked her? The reverend pulled a chair close to her bed, and Travis did the same.

The reverend took her hand. "Won't you tell someone who did this to you?" His voice was barely above a whisper.

"I can't." Another tear slipped from her eye, and the reverend wiped it away.

Jesus, help her.

"Are you afraid?"

She nodded. "It's not just me but others who might get hurt."

"Not if the sheriff arrests him."

"I can't take that chance."

"And what if it happens again?"

"Please, Reverend. It's impossible. All I can do is mend and forgive. . .and forget."

"I understand, but you're letting a cruel man go unpunished."

"Look at what I once was. It's fittin'."

Travis wanted to come out of his chair, but he swallowed the indignation threatening to boil over. "Miss Rosie, no one deserves this."

She offered a faint smile. "Tonight's prayer meetin', and I'll miss your sermon."

"We'll pray for you," Travis said.

"Thank you." Rosie's eyelids fluttered. "Don't know why I'm so tired. Must be the medicine Doc Grant gave me."

Travis glanced at the reverend, who nodded toward the door.

"Brother Whitworth and I'd like to come back and see you again. Is that all right?"

"Of course," she whispered through closed eyes. "You are my Jesus. You and Mrs. Rainer, Mrs. Hillman, Jenny, Bonnie, Casey. . ."

The two men left the room. Nothing settled. No name to bring to Sheriff Arthur.

<hr />

Bonnie basked in the cool wind blowing against her face. How long had it been since she had felt this content? Lydia Anne sat in front of her, laughing and giggling, not the least bit afraid of racing over the pastureland with the spotted mare heaving beneath them. They'd ridden over most of the ranch with Thomas this morning, seeing parts of her land that Bonnie had long neglected. A spirit of newness and anticipation had taken hold, and she treasured it.

Finally, she pulled the mare to a walk. "We're going to wear out Indian Sun," she said.

"Can I ride by myself?" Lydia Anne asked.

"Very soon. In fact, we might start this afternoon when you wake from your nap."

Thomas laughed. "I think the Kahler womenfolk might be entering the horse races next Fourth of July."

"We might," Bonnie said. "And we might win."

"Would Zack be able to watch us?" Lydia Anne asked.

For a little while, Bonnie had pushed aside her concern for her oldest son. "I should hope so. We'd need him to cheer us on."

She glanced at Thomas, and he gave her a reassuring smile. Bonnie appreciated this fine man, weathered with the knowledge only experience could give. Juanita was one lucky woman.

As they rode back to the house, two riders approached them. She recognized the men as her brothers. Fear tightened her throat. Had something happened to one of her sons?

"Everything is fine with Zack and Michael Paul," Morgan said as soon as they were within talking distance. "I saw that look on your face."

She sighed and praised God at the same time. "What brings both of you out here?"

"First of all, you look wonderful," Grant said.

"Thank you, Doctor. Lydia Anne and I were checking on the cattle and horses."

"We had fun," the little girl said. "More fun than baking cookies or planting flowers."

"More fun than the new kittens we found this morning?"

Lydia Anne tilted her head. "I can't decide."

The men laughed, but obviously the little girl didn't understand. Bonnie kissed her wind-flushed cheeks.

"Good to see you, Thomas," Morgan said. "Glad you're here with Bonnie. We wanted to talk to both of you."

Bonnie looked down at her daughter. Lydia Anne didn't need to hear anything that could frighten her.

"Hey, little lady," Grant said. "How about riding back with your Uncle Grant and showing me those new kittens?"

Lydia Anne glanced up at Bonnie. "Can I, Mama?"

"I don't see why not." She rode closer to Grant so he could lift the little girl onto his horse.

"Can we run like Mama and me?"

Grant's gaze flew to Bonnie's. "You were racing with her?"

She laughed. "We're tough, aren't we, Lydia Anne?"

"Yes, ma'am. This afternoon Mama is going to teach me how to ride real fast."

"Walk first." Bonnie smiled into the sky blue eyes of her precious daughter. "Have a good time."

Grant rode away, leaving her alone with Morgan and Thomas.

"Is there something I should know?"

"Rosie was beaten again," Morgan said.

Bonnie gripped the saddle horn. "How is she?"

"Grant patched her up, and she's at Heaven's Gate. She won't tell anyone who did it—just like the last time."

"That makes no sense."

"I agree." He turned to Thomas. "Sure glad Bonnie has you to watch over things."

"I promised Ben before he left that I'd keep an eye on his family."

"Good. Guess you figured that's why Grant and I rode out here. We're worried about our little sister."

"No need. I always have someone guarding the house."

Bonnie's eyes widened. "Thanks, Thomas. I had no idea."

He grinned. "Ben told me to be sly as a fox."

She could almost hear Ben giving those instructions. In the past, she'd have shed a few tears, but today the thought warmed her.

"My thanks to you." Morgan's shoulders lifted and fell. "We'll sure sleep a lot better."

"You're welcome. We've all sort of adopted Miss Bonnie and the young'uns."

"See, I'll be fine," she said.

"Grant's right. You're looking much better. We both want to apologize for the way we've handled things. I haven't been very understanding."

"You two were simply being the big brothers you've always been. I'm trying real hard to get on with my life. Not that I won't be making mistakes."

"Let us help in any way we can."

She swallowed a lump in her throat. "Would you continue to look into a military school for Zack? I have to be prepared in case Brother Travis isn't able to work a miracle." She attempted to sound objective, but her voice broke.

"Sure. All of us are praying for him. Chad feels real bad about what's happened."

"They used to be close. Maybe they will be again."

"I hope so," he said. "A long time ago, I vowed to stop hovering over you and let you make your own decisions."

"I was eighteen when you made that statement. And you were courtin' Casey at the time."

"I'm still working on it."

Bonnie laughed, then sobered. "Papa spoiled me. So did you. Then Ben. Mama and Grant attempted to make me strong, but it never happened. Now I have three children to raise, and I intend to make my family and Ben proud. After all, I have Andrews blood flowing through my veins."

"Do Ben's folks know about Zack?"

She nodded. "I stopped there after I left the sheriff's office. I think they would have liked for me to bring him there, but they're getting up in years, too. I regret my assumption that Mama and the reverend would take Zack." She glanced away. "I regret so much, but God is talking to me."

"A lot has happened in a few short days."

"I guess so. Morgan, I appreciate all you and Grant have done for me. I love you."

"Haven't heard that in a long time."

"I haven't loved myself in a long time. And I have miles to go. I'm sure we'll share a few more disagreements."

"You'll make it, Bonnie. I'm sure of it."

But her words had sounded braver than what she felt. Her mind said she needed a drink, deserved one after the past few days. Her heart told her otherwise, and she clung to God like a newborn. *Think about others. Be gracious and compassionate.*

She'd planned to stay home from prayer meeting tonight to avoid Zack, but now she wondered if she should sit with Rosie. Seemed like there was always something to be doing. She wanted to talk to Brother Whitworth to see how Zack was doing. She didn't want to put too much hope in what the man was attempting, but to have her son happy and at peace seemed like a dream. Would life ever get easier?

CHAPTER 10

"If you would like to have the peace that passeth all understanding in your life, now is the time to come forward and ask Jesus to live in your heart."

How many times had Travis given that invitation over the years? But this time it was Wednesday night prayer meetin' at the Piney Woods Church. When he held revivals in other churches, folks used to come forward. But never in his own church. Ten years of preaching, and not one soul was saved in the Tennessee hills church. No wonder his brothers had asked him to leave—among other reasons.

Travis listened to Jenny Andrews play piano. She had the gift. He looked out at the congregation. Mrs. Kahler wasn't there, but he hadn't expected her. Zack sat in the front row at Travis's request. He looked like he'd rather be cleaning out horse stalls.

Suddenly his heart nearly stopped. In the middle pew on the left side, a young man rose and made his way down front. Could it be? Had God honored Travis's prayers to bless this church and call lost souls to Him? He nearly cried. A soul for the Lord. Heaven must be singing.

Thank You, Lord, for allowing Your Spirit to move through this church.

"What can I do for you, son?" Travis asked the young man.

80

"I'd like to live for Jesus. I thought I was Christian, but I think I was only foolin' myself."

"What's your name?"

"Timothy Detterman."

Travis laid his hand on Timothy's shoulder. "Let's pray."

For the second night in a row, Travis lay awake praying—this time in gratitude for God blessing his ministry and for a new soul entered into the Book of Life. On Friday, instead of Saturday, he'd move into his new home with Zack. His original plans had been thwarted when problems arose first with Zack, then with Rosie. But being a preacher meant his hours were not his own. Interruptions came like baby rabbits in spring.

He started to sing—not too loud. Didn't want to wake up the household. *"Blest be the tie that binds. . ."*

Sure would be nice if Zack started acting more civil. Truth be known, any change might take weeks.

"Our hearts in Christian love. . ."

The boy hadn't gotten dinner again. The idea of writing something nice about his mother was more than he could handle. A growing boy needed his dinner, but it was Zack's choice.

"The fellowship of kindred minds. . ."

Pete and MayBelle Kahler thanked him tonight for what he was doing for their grandson. Travis hoped he wouldn't disappoint them.

"Is like to that above."

Maybe he could talk to Mrs. Kahler about having Michael Paul join him for a song.

On Thursday Bonnie fretted about Brother Travis and Zack moving into their new home without her there to help. She'd send canned fruits and vegetables along with a smoked ham, bacon, eggs, and beef for the pounding on Saturday morning. All the folks from church would be donating food and housekeeping items for Brother Whitworth's new home. Mercy, Zack could eat a whole dozen eggs by himself. She nearly had to tie herself to a chair to keep from riding into town. One of the hands delivered a bed for Zack so he wouldn't have to sleep on the floor, and her mother offered a small dresser for his clothes.

Come Sunday morning, she'd be in church, perhaps sitting in the back where her son couldn't see her. She'd love to know if he missed her. Then again, she'd rather not know. Most likely his mean streak still ran strong. Her thoughts rolled to Brother Travis. Took a good man to take on a troublesome child.

"Miss Bonnie, Mr. Hillman is riding in," Juanita said.

"Is Sylvia with him?"

"No. He's by himself."

Bonnie frowned. The thought of hiding toyed with her mind. That man must have memorized the moment and hour when Lydia Anne took her nap. Once he left today, she'd mention the problem to Thomas.

When a rap at the door announced his arrival, Juanita answered it. Bonnie glanced about the kitchen. The apples were ready for canning, and Juanita had beans and sausage simmering. She'd wanted to read the *Cattleman's Report* and go over the latest figures of beef prices. Wasting time with the obnoxious Lester Hillman would put her in a surly mood. *I'll get rid of him and feel good about it.*

With a deep breath, she untied her apron, hung it on a hook, and headed down the hallway.

"Good afternoon, Bonnie." Lester removed his fancy hat. "I thought little Lydia Anne might be resting so we could talk."

She forced a smile as Juanita set Lester's hat on a small table in the hallway, then walked by. If only her sweet cook would stay by her side instead of bringing coffee for the two of them. "Yes, she's resting. Is something wrong? Has Rosie grown worse? When I visited her yesterday, she appeared to be doing better." She gestured toward the parlor, remembering his previous visit and the unwanted bottle of wine.

"Everything is fine, and Rosie is on the mend. However, she still refuses to name her assailant. My word, what is she afraid of?"

"I wish I knew."

He waited for her to seat herself on an overstuffed chair, then sat on the sofa. Lester Hillman was no more a gentleman than the pigs wallowing in foot-deep mud. He might have the people of Kahlerville fooled, but not Bonnie.

"What brings you to the Morning Star?"

He smiled. "To see how the Widow Kahler is doing. With what happened to Rosie, Sylvia and I are concerned about your safety."

"Thank you, but no need. My brothers have alerted Thomas."

"Wonderful."

"So you have ridden out here for nothing. I hope the bank doesn't suffer in your absence."

"It's never for nothing when it comes to seeing your lovely face."

Anger simmered near the top of her head. "Lester, your remark is not appropriate for a married man."

He smiled, revealing all of his perfectly white teeth. "I have a gift for you."

"I don't want it."

"You mean you haven't finished the other bottle?"

"Truthfully, I destroyed it. I told you the last time not to bring me any more wine."

A saddened look swept over his face. "What has changed your mind?"

"I sleep fine without it. Needless to say, it is another mark of impropriety."

"I could say the same about you accepting it."

"Perhaps I should confess my indiscretion to Sylvia. In fact, I shall do so at the earliest convenience."

Lester's face reddened. Ah, she'd challenged him.

"I've already told her," he said.

She recognized a lie when she heard one. "Then I have you to thank, but the apology will come from me."

A hammer could not have softened the stone-hard look on his face. "I advise you to think twice about that. Sylvia is a genteel woman who believes the best in everyone. I'm sure you wouldn't want your image marred."

"So you lied and haven't told her."

"Does it matter? Gossip about you will damage the fine reputation of your entire family."

Lester was right; hurting Sylvia only served to make Bonnie look like a less than proper lady. Juanita brought in a silver tray of coffee and set it on the table between them.

"Thank you, Juanita."

Lester repeated Bonnie's gratitude. Usually he complimented Juanita about something, but his thoughts were obviously elsewhere. Once she left the parlor, he added sugar and cream to his coffee. Not Bonnie—she drank hers black and strong like the rest of her family.

"I do have a reason to speak with you," he said. "However, your unappreciative mannerisms cast a shadow on my good intentions."

"Lester, get on with it. Simply tell me why you're here."

"My, Sylvia would be appalled at your rudeness."

"Some people bring out the worst in me." *Just leave, Lester.*

"Tsk. Tsk. I heard you were looking for a military school for Zack."

Irritation settled on her more than before. "And where did you hear that?"

"I overheard Pete and MayBelle discussing it before church started on Wednesday evening."

"I doubt if those measures will be necessary."

He chuckled. "Brother Whitworth isn't even married. How do

you expect him to handle an unruly boy like Zack?"

"God can do the impossible."

"Sounds like you've been listening to the reverend. I have a friend who is affiliated with Fishburne Military School in Virginia. It's a fine establishment. May be exactly what the boy needs. Sylvia and I talked last night, and I could write a letter of recommendation."

"Why?"

He smiled. "My Christian duty." He glanced around the room as though toying with his next words. "I'd like to help, Bonnie. That's all."

She doubted if the offer sprang from his relationship with God. "And what would you want from me in return?"

"Why do you question something Sylvia and I want to do for you?"

"Because I know you better than most people. You always have a reason for doing things, and it always benefits you."

He opened his mouth to speak, but a knock at the door silenced him.

"My, what a busy afternoon this is," she said. Whoever stood on the opposite side of the door was welcome.

She stood. "I'll see to the door," she called to Juanita.

Her heart pounded. *Let it be Thomas. He'll be able to tell that I'm uncomfortable.* She swung open the door and silently thanked God.

"Brother Travis, how good to see you. Won't you come in?" Her relief in seeing him caused her to relax. "I've been wanting to speak with you about Zack."

He stepped into the hallway and turned toward the parlor. The autumn wind had whipped his unruly hair and bushy beard every which way. "I'm sorry, Mrs. Kahler. I see you have a visitor. Afternoon, Lester."

"Afternoon, Brother Whitworth. How's your charge?"

"Doing fine. I left him working on arithmetic."

Bonnie wanted to throw her arms around the wild-looking preacher's neck.

"I can come back at another time," Brother Travis said.

She shook her head. "Nonsense. Mr. Hillman was just leaving." Swinging her attention to Lester, she offered her most pleasant smile. "Thank you so much for your generous offer, and please thank Sylvia for me. I am grateful, but it won't be necessary. Morgan and Grant are handling the situation."

"I understand. Once I'm back in town, I plan to see Morgan. We might be able to do some business together for the bank. I'll mention our conversation to him, too."

Bonnie wanted to throw him out on his ear. She refused to be obligated to Lester, even if Fishburne was the finest school in the country. She picked up his hat and walked into the parlor. He tossed her a superior look and followed her to the door.

"Please tell dear Sylvia that I missed her today, and I'll chat with her on Sunday about Rosie."

Once Lester left, she realized that she never wanted him in her home again without Sylvia accompanying him. His words today had reinforced her sentiments about him. She neither trusted nor respected him.

"Kindly sit in the parlor, Brother Travis, and I'll pour you a cup of coffee."

"It's not necessary. I won't be long."

"Nonsense. I would like to have a fresh cup. How do you like yours?"

"Black." He hastily removed his hat, and she placed it on the small hallway table in the exact location where Lester's had lain. "I wanted to talk to you about Zack," he said.

"I see. Oh dear, I hope this doesn't mean you are giving up." She ushered him into the parlor. "Please excuse me for a moment while I fetch you a cup." She could have asked Juanita, but Lester's visit had shaken her, and she needed to regain her composure for Brother Whitworth.

Once she had the silver pot in hand and had poured each of

them a hot cup of coffee, she seated herself in the same overstuffed chair where she'd conversed with the despicable Lester. "How can I help you?"

Travis rubbed his palms on his pant legs, then reached for his cup. "I understand this may be painful, but can you tell me about Zack's relationship with his father? I took the liberty of asking the reverend and your mother, and they said the two were very close."

"Inseparable." Emotion welled up inside her, and she fought hard to dismiss it. "Ben believed in spending time with his children. He loved teaching them—everything from the value of education to fishing."

"Does Michael Paul exhibit any of the same problems as Zack?"

"Not at all. He's a peaceful boy, always wanting to please." She hesitated. "Michael Paul cried at his father's funeral. Zack has never shed a tear."

Brother Travis appeared to ponder her words. "Have you two talked about how he feels about losing his father?"

His question probed deeper than she wanted to think. "I have had such a grievous period since Ben's death that I have. . ." A tear slipped down her cheek, then another. "I have neglected my children. I'm ashamed to admit this, but if Zack had wanted to talk to me, I probably wouldn't have been able to listen."

Brother Travis pulled a handkerchief from his pocket and handed it to her. Their fingers brushed, and she realized that she had not touched another man aside from the reverend and her brothers since Ben's death.

"Thank you. Seems you always have a supply of handkerchiefs. I have your other one done up."

"Glad to be of service." He shifted. "Perhaps I should go since this is upsetting you."

"Please stay. This is for Zack, and I need to help my son." She dabbed the handkerchief to her nose. "How is he?"

"Oh, about the same. I have his time scheduled so he won't be idle. He has a sharp mind, and I think with time we'll make progress. What are some of his favorite pastimes?"

"Fishing is his favorite. He liked riding with his father, and Ben had been teaching him to use a rifle and hunt. I gave him his father's Springfield, one from the War Between the States. But it has a nasty recoil."

He nodded. "Good. I want to reward him with those things."

"Has he asked about us?"

"No. Right now he's getting used to me. I think once we're moved tomorrow, we'll make more progress."

"He is so angry with me."

Brother Travis shook his head. "I don't think he's angry with you. I believe his bad feelings are aimed toward himself." He paused. "Is there any reason why Zack would blame himself for his father's passing?"

How horrible. "Absolutely not. Ben had a lung ailment. There was nothing anyone could have done. Have you had experience with a situation like ours before?"

"No. I'm simply counting on God to lead me. I want to help your son, and I won't give up. I've said this before, but I believe a boy needs to be with his family."

His compassion caressed her heart. What a dear man. "I sincerely appreciate what you're doing—and for the handkerchief. I'll have it done up for you, too."

He stood, rather awkwardly. "Thank you, Mrs. Kahler. Again, I didn't mean to upset you. I hope you don't expect a change in your son too soon. My guess is that it will take awhile."

"I understand." The heartache over losing Ben had taken longer to conquer than she'd ever anticipated. "I'd like to apologize again for the way I treated you when we first met."

"Well, I look more like a tramp than a man of God." He smiled. "I'll be leaving now." At the door he hesitated, then slowly turned around. "Michael Paul is quite fond of music. I suggested to him that we might sing together for a service, but we need your permission."

"He loves music, and I think it's a fine idea. I'll let him know."

"He's a fine boy, too. All of your children are good."

Bonnie needed to hear those words. The town's new preacher was a true blessing. If he looked half as good as the soothing sound of his voice, then he'd be one fine-looking man. She silently questioned why he kept all of that hair. Maybe he felt kin to John the Baptist or one of the ancient prophets. Instantly, she warmed at her thoughts.

"You are welcome anytime you choose to visit. Thomas said the roof never looked better."

He laughed, a cheery sound. Reminded her of peace and wisdom and children, all in one. "I'll make sure the reverend or your mother accompanies me the next time I come. I wouldn't want folks talking."

Oh, please, Lord, don't let anyone gossip about any man and me. "A very good idea. I think Zack is a very lucky boy."

"Let's wait until I have any success before thanking me."

Once he left, she leaned back against the door and slowly slid to the floor. Her precious babies—all of them had suffered because of her selfishness. Tears flowed swiftly, the ones she swore would not surface again. Brother Travis had saved her from the ill-mannered Lester Hillman, and she realized he'd seen her disgust with the town's banker. Bonnie had grown afraid of the man, who professed to be a caring Christian. His threats were serious, but if she went to Morgan or Grant, Sylvia would be hurt one more time, and the woman treasured her husband. Lester had nearly destroyed her with his illicit relationship with the owner of a brothel more than two years ago. This might push her into an early grave. Many times she wondered why Sylvia had stayed with him after his adulterous affair.

I'm being so judgmental. Lester did have some fine qualities, especially when it came to helping Sylvia at Heaven's Gate or giving to the poor.

"Miss Bonnie, are you all right?" Juanita's hand touched her shoulder.

Bonnie swiped at her cheeks and below her eyes. "I didn't mean to do this again."

"You loved Mr. Ben. God doesn't expect you to forget." She sighed. "I thought Mr. Hillman or Brother Whitworth might have done this."

She glanced up at Juanita. "Oh, no, not Brother Whitworth. I don't think he knows how to be unkind."

"Mr. Hillman is not like his wife. Excuse me, but I think he's evil."

"You've heard the things he's said, haven't you?"

"So sorry, Miss Bonnie. I will not tell anyone."

So Juanita knew what Bonnie was afraid to say. Today she'd talk to Thomas about watching the house for Lester. A glass of wine tugged at her senses. It would settle her down, relax the trembling. But she neither had any nor wanted to give in to the temptation.

CHAPTER  11

On Sunday morning, Travis had much to be thankful for. He had a fine new home. His congregation had surprised him yesterday with food and other household items for a pounding, and for the first time since he'd been placed in Travis's care, Zack had dinner. Of course he complained about Travis's cooking—comparing it to what he'd cleaned out of horse stalls.

"You have a choice here, Zack," Travis had said.

He frowned. "What's that?"

"You could do what you've done for dinner since we started keeping company." Travis stabbed the shoe-leather pork chop. "Although, I'm having second thoughts about it, too."

Zack frowned. "How much bread do we have?"

"Enough for us to split it." Travis picked up the loaf of bread given by one of the church folks. He tore it in half and gave Zack his portion. "We can split the gravy."

"Is this the best you can cook?"

"You're welcome to try anytime you like."

Now Travis glanced at the front pew and nearly laughed at Zack. Heavy eyelids slid almost shut. He must think that sitting on the first pew gave him the right to sleep. Not in God's church where Travis preached. He'd already warned Zack that they'd discuss the service during lunch. His gaze took in the rest of the worshippers. Mrs. Kahler, with Michael Paul and Lydia Anne, slipped into the back pew.

He remembered the first time he had seen the children's mother—a little angel with a crown of pale gold. From all he'd seen in this short amount of time, she was trying to live her life for the Lord. Instantly, he chastised himself for concentrating on Bonnie Kahler instead of God. Hadn't those kinds of thoughts gotten him into enough trouble? Except Bonnie Kahler had nothing in common with Felicia except that both women needed help putting their lives in order. He smiled at the reverend and Mrs. Rainer. How wonderful to some day have a woman sitting beside him, supporting him. . . loving him when he'd made mistakes.

"Good morning." Travis raised his hands to signal the beginning of the service. " 'This is the day which the Lord hath made; we will rejoice and be glad in it.' This morning I'm rejoicing because of a new home that's filled with food, furniture, and all I need to be more than comfortable, supplied by God and all of you wonderful people."

"Amen," said Jake Weathers.

Travis nearly laughed. That old man had to be older than the town and had a voice that reminded him of rumbling thunder.

At the close of the service, Zack disappeared. Maybe he'd seen his mother and wanted to avoid her. One of the families had invited Travis for lunch, and normally he'd have accepted. But this family didn't know about Zack, and Travis wasn't so sure the boy had found his manners well enough to attend a social event. Today the two of them would eat Brother Travis's cooking. Not real appetizing, but they wouldn't starve.

At their new home, he found Zack sitting on the front porch. He had changed from his Sunday clothes into overalls—dirty ones. Tomorrow Travis needed to wash clothes, and Zack could help.

"You left in a big hurry."

Zack frowned. "I saw Mama there."

"She's a member of our church, too."

"I thought she'd stay home." He shrugged. "Mama doesn't like unpleasant things. Tends to stay away. But I think she's changing."

Travis sat on the step beside him. "How?"

"Like she's gotten religion or something."

Travis laughed. "Does that bother you?"

Zack picked up a stone and tossed it toward the street. His silence was all the response Travis needed.

"Your mama wants to get stronger. Be a good mother. She wants good things for you, too."

The boy threw another stone.

"She drinks."

Travis had to think about his answer to this one. *Mrs. Kahler drank spirits?*

"You don't believe me, do you?"

"I never accused you of lying."

"Well, she does. Every night in her room. I've seen the bottle on her nightstand, mostly near empty and empty. Papa used to say only a weak person drank."

"And you think your mama is weak? Is that why you don't have any respect for her?"

"She doesn't care about us. Just herself. I bet she's been sitting with Miss Rosie at Heaven's Gate and not even thinking about us."

"You mean you, Michael Paul, and Lydia Anne?"

" 'Course. Who else would I be talking about?"

"Well, Zack," he said. "I have it on good report that she took Lydia Anne with her to Heaven's Gate, and Michael Paul was at school. I saw her yesterday, and she asked about you and asked when she could see you."

He stiffened. "She probably wanted to know how soon I'd be ready to leave for military school."

"Not at all. What she wants is her family back together."

"I can't believe that. I know my mama, and she's living in the past when my papa was alive."

"I see there's nothing I can say to change your mind. God will have to show you the truth. Nobody on this earth is perfect, and we all have to forgive each other. Why don't you think on it while I fix us something to eat? I believe you love your mama as much as she loves you."

All the while Travis busied himself with frying pork and potatoes, he pondered Zack's accusation about his mother drinking. He refused to ask her about such a thing, but that wouldn't stop him from praying about it. Sighing, he glanced out the front door for a glimpse of Zack's head. Secrets always caused the most hurt. He should know. And getting folks to talk about what plagued them was real hard. Most folks thought their problems were no one's business and talking about them was kin to sin.

Suddenly an idea took form. Journals for Zack and his mother. Even if they kept their troubles to themselves and God, it might help them deal with the deep hurt. He'd check at the general store. In the meantime, he'd ask Mrs. Rainer or the reverend to accompany him one day this week to call on Mrs. Kahler. Maybe he'd borrow a couple of fishing poles. He'd lean them up against the back porch just in case Zack decided to behave for three days. After all, if the Lord could resurrect in that amount of time, Zack Kahler could find a reason to go fishing.

Why couldn't Bonnie Kahler be old and ugly with a voice like a raspy old man and a wart on the end of her nose? He chuckled. She'd not be too happy with his thoughts.

In a way, God had given him a second chance on more than shepherding a church. He'd given him a chance to live again. He wanted to believe that by helping Zack, he'd make up for the mistakes he'd made in the past. Trying to convince Felicia to leave the brothel hadn't been wrong; it was how he'd gone about it.

On Monday morning, after he and Zack went through their new

morning schedule, washed clothes, and hung them on the line, Travis set Zack to work on some arithmetic that Miss Scott had recommended. Travis set out to visit Miss Rosie at Heaven's Gate and to the general store for the journals.

At Heaven's Gate, Jenny Andrews answered the door with her youngest daughter, Rachel, clinging to her skirts. She ushered him into the parlor where Miss Rosie sat propped on a sofa in the parlor and talking with the young women whom he recognized from his former visit. Mrs. Andrews had been playing a familiar hymn on the piano for them.

"Listening to Mrs. Andrews is better than church." He took a seat on a chair that wasn't made for men. "I don't have to give a sermon."

The women laughed, and he noted the color in Miss Rosie's cheeks was a little pinker.

"How are all of you this fine day?" he asked. "And our Miss Rosie?"

They all echoed how well they were doing, even Miss Rosie.

He turned his attention to the beaten girl. "Is there anything I can do for you?"

"No, sir. I'm healing fine. Soon I'll be back working for Mrs. Hillman again."

"Don't rush yourself. Looks to me like there are lots of folks willing to take care of you."

"That's what we keep telling her," Laura, a red-haired young woman, said. "The weather is beautiful, and she can read all day long."

"But I need to do my part," Rosie said. "I feel guilty with all of you doing the work."

"I do miss your cooking," Laura said. "I think about it all the time I'm working for Mr. Hillman at the bank."

"And now I have to make my own breakfast," Daisy, a tall young woman, said.

Travis gazed into Rosie's olive-skinned face and smiled. "You have wonderful friends here. Take time to heal, and I'll stop by again."

As he made his way to the general store, he talked to God about Rosie. *Lord, I pray whoever did this to her leaves her alone.* With the loving people around her, surely she'd be safe. *And then there's Zack. . .and his mother.*

⚜

"What am I supposed to do with this?" Zack turned the journal over in his hands. His eyes widened. "It doesn't have any words."

"It's not supposed to have any words." Travis wanted to laugh, but Zack was serious. "It's a journal for you to write in."

"You want me to write a book?"

This time Travis swallowed his mirth. "Not at all. A journal is for personal thoughts. Things you want to say but don't necessarily want other folks to read."

Zack stared down at the book; his dark hair fell over his forehead. "Secret things?"

"Yes. Just yours. You could write down all the things you remember about your father."

"Why?"

Lord, does this boy trust anyone? "Because things have happened in your life that are painful and hard, and the days ahead may not be easy. The treasured times you had with your father may one day be forgotten."

"I don't want it." He slapped the book on the table.

"I'm not surprised, so I'll put it in your room."

Zack crossed his arms over his chest. "You can't make me write a word."

"You're right. I can't." With those words, Travis wrapped his fingers around the journal, walked to Zack's room, and laid it on his bed. With a deep breath, he made his way outside into the cool air before he said things a good preacher never said. God must have as much for him to learn as Zack.

CHAPTER  12

Bonnie listened to Sylvia explain the Bible lesson to Rosie, Laura, and Daisy. She focused on the woman's serene face and how her passion for the Lord came through every word. What a wonderful woman to lead these ladies in biblical ways. How could such a godly woman have such a horrible husband? She'd do anything for Sylvia; the woman deserved a special mansion in heaven for what Lester had put her through and what she'd done for others.

Bonnie thought back over Lester's visit. For the first time, she questioned if Sylvia was aware when he came calling at the Morning Star without her. Suddenly Bonnie felt dirty. She should have mentioned those times to Sylvia in case Lester had omitted telling her. Bonnie's past dealings with him hadn't been morally or spiritually right. All she could do now was step forward as a proper woman. Back in the beginning when Ben had first died and her life had been consumed in grief, she had thought Lester wanted only to help.

"Paul told Timothy to take a little wine for the sake of his health," Lester had said. "It's a biblical statement; something you can bank on." He chuckled. "Seriously, I heard you tell Sylvia that you were unable to sleep. A glass of wine in the evening would help you rest. Your children need a mother who is able to perform the responsibilities of both parents."

And so it began.

I've been very foolish. She'd been a willing party to not letting Sylvia know about his gifts of wine.

"Sylvia disapproves of drinking except for medicinal purposes," he'd said. "I didn't tell her about the wine, and I suggest you keep the information to yourself."

Naturally, the woman would have objected, and deceiving her was wrong. Why hadn't Bonnie used a little common sense? The thought of the implications not only churned her stomach but also needled at her conscience.

Lester's previous visit had come close to frightening her. Why had he become so insistent after her refusal of wine, why so eager to find a military school for Zack? Why should he care? If he truly was living for the Lord, he wouldn't have visited her without Sylvia or given her that first bottle of wine. A gnawing suspicion caused her to feel slightly queasy. Did Lester want her dependent upon him? Why?

She nearly gasped. He'd been involved with the woman who'd owned the brothel. They'd had two sons together. Surely Lester wasn't looking for another adulterous relationship. If she had gotten to the point of needing the wine on a daily basis, then she'd be beholden to Lester. He could demand whatever he wanted from her, and she'd be forced to comply. She'd come dangerously close to being in that position. How utterly disgusting. Poor Sylvia. Lester didn't deserve his wife's kindness. She was devoted to him, the love clearly written in her eyes.

"Mrs. Kahler," Sylvia said. "Would you like to answer Rosie's question?"

She hadn't heard a word. How humiliating. Bonnie moistened her lips. "I'm a little uncomfortable in responding."

"Please, don't be." Rosie brushed back her silky black hair. "I know the type of life I lived before Jesus entered my life. I simply want to know if the woman at the well will be in heaven."

Bonnie's heart thumped against her chest. "I believe only Jesus knows the answer to that question. But if the woman was sincere in repenting of her sins and her desire was to live in obedience to His ways, then she will be with us in heaven."

The sadness on Rosie's face brightened. She'd gone through so much pain from the beating. How sweet to see a glimpse of happiness. Whoever had hurt her needed a taste of a horsewhip, and Bonnie would gladly oblige.

"Thank you," Rosie said. "One day, that woman and I will have much to talk about and much to thank Jesus for."

Bonnie slipped from her chair and bent to Rosie's side. She took the young woman's hand. "I pray your life grows in the joy that only comes from our Savior. You deserve so much, Rosie. The future will be brighter for you because of your faith."

"Do you really think so? I feel forgiven, and I talk to our Lord. . . ." Emotions appeared to consume her. "I talk to Jesus all the time."

"He lives inside you. I can see it in your face. Soon you will be healed, and your life will grow brighter. I'm sure of it."

Just as Travis set aside his Bible and notes for that evening's prayer meeting and turned his attention to Sunday's sermon—when he would officially become the pastor of Piney Woods Church—he heard a knock at the door. With his mind whirling with what he thought God wanted him to say on Sunday, he stumbled to answer the door. *Do I use Hebrews 11, the chapter about faith? Or do I use Romans 8 and talk about what it means to be a true believer?*

"Afternoon, Brother Whitworth. Can I have a moment of your time?" Lester Hillman smiled as though a rancher had just deposited a huge sum of money into his bank.

Travis swung open the door. "Sure, come on in."

"Is Zack here?"

"He's doing schoolwork on the back porch."

"Looks like you're doing a fine job with him. He needs a firm hand."

"He's doing well. Sometimes understanding accomplishes more than discipline."

"Can we take a little walk? This is private, and I wouldn't want the boy to hear our conversation."

Travis made his way to the back porch and let Zack know he'd be gone for a little while with Lester. Zack glanced up, his dark eyes stormy, but he said nothing. Later Travis planned to ask why. Their relationship had eased into more silence than communication, which was better than listening to Zack's rebellious comments and Travis having to decide how to handle the situation. However, he was no closer to finding out why the boy insisted on taking a wayward stand against authority.

Outside, the two men walked in silence several feet from the house. Curiosity had nearly gotten the best of Travis.

"What can I do for you, Lester?"

"It's a delicate matter, and I need your word that no one finds out that I revealed this grim information to you."

"I'm a man of God. Only He would cause me to repeat your words."

"Thank you. I'm real concerned about Bonnie Kahler. She's. . . she's takin' to drinking."

"Are you certain?" Travis recalled Zack's accusation about the same thing. He hated the thought of her indulging in spirits.

"Oh, yes. Sylvia and I visit the Morning Star on occasion to check on Mrs. Kahler and the children. We've seen her in such a sad situation that she slurred her words and could barely stand. I think her Mexican housekeeper is raising the children, and goodness knows what they are learning from the ranch hands. My guess is Zack picked up his bad ways from those men."

"That is very unfortunate. Are you asking me to talk to her?"

"I believe she'd be angry. At least when my dear Sylvia tried, she lost her temper and denied drinking at all. My dear Sylvia doesn't know I've come to you for assistance, and I don't want her to know, either. She works so very hard at Heaven's Gate that this would upset her greatly." He paused and stuffed his hands into his trouser pockets. "I hate to think what this would do to Bonnie's parents and brothers. They are such fine families and contribute greatly to our community."

"Other than prayer and a possible confrontation, what do you think I should do?"

"Sylvia believes Bonnie is unfit to continue working at Heaven's Gate. She's afraid liquor will be brought into the home, and it would be very easy for the young ladies there to slip back into old ways. We certainly don't want the home to become another brothel. Excuse me, Brother Whitworth, but I don't think my conclusions are wrong."

"I see, and yes, a situation such as you speak of would be a problem."

"That is where we feel you could be of assistance." Lester's tone sounded as if every word pained him. "We'd like for you to dissuade her from volunteering at the home."

"Why me? Shouldn't a decision of this serious nature come from Mrs. Jenny Andrews, who owns the home? Besides, I've never seen any indication of Mrs. Kahler's drinking or of her behaving in a manner that isn't appropriate. Her family has not mentioned this to me, either."

"Heaven's Gate utilizes volunteers from Piney Woods Church. You are now the overseer of that much-needed ministry. Mrs. Andrews delegated the responsibility of running the home to the reverend right after it was built."

"I can't dismiss Mrs. Kahler unless I see for myself that she is unable to fulfill her duties. In my opinion, you should take your concerns to Jenny Andrews and to the reverend and Mrs. Rainer."

"Why, Mrs. Andrews is very busy with her family and assisting her husband in his medical practice, and the reverend and Mrs. Rainer are too old to deal with any more problems in their lives. They are very distraught about Zack and appear to be consumed with worry about him."

Why did Travis not believe a single word of Lester's declaration?

"I understand all you've told me, and I appreciate your concern about Mrs. Kahler in light of your wife's devotion to Heaven's Gate. But I will not tell her that her goodwill to those living at the home is no longer needed."

Lester stiffened. "Then you give me no choice. My wife's peace of mind means more to me than life itself. If you refuse to help in this matter, I will be forced to withdraw all of my financial support from the church."

Anger buzzed in Travis's ears. "I'll not be threatened. The Lord will provide for our church with or without your money."

"Perhaps Piney Woods needs a pastor who can better lead its members."

"That's not your decision to make."

"But my money speaks for me."

"I believe the good people of Piney Woods can tell the difference between being led by money and following the Lord. Good day, Lester. I have a sermon to prepare."

Travis turned on his heel and headed back to the house. Bonnie Kahler drinking? A bad influence on those living at Heaven's Gate? Miss Juanita raising the children? What was the real reason why Lester had come by? What did he have against Bonnie? She'd been quite upset with Lester the day Travis visited the Morning Star. She'd been trembling when Travis first arrived, and her face had been drained of color.

If she truly had a problem with strong drink, then a drive out to her ranch with the reverend and Mrs. Rainer was in order.

Up ahead, Zack leaned over the porch railing. His lanky frame was but a hint of the man to come, a handsome lad with dark hair and eyes that must have been his father's. A twist of something Travis had never felt before left him sad and longing. The idea of marriage and one day a family had gone by the wayside. But he hoped that someday God would bless him with a wife and children despite his many faults. He waved at Zack. No point letting the boy know Lester had made him angry.

"What did he want?" Zack asked.

"Church business. Did you get your reading done?"

"Yes, sir."

Travis's eyes widened, and he grinned. "Sure do appreciate the kind words."

"I'm hungry."

Travis laughed. This was the first time the boy had been civil—even if his stomach was the reason. "So am I. Let me see what I can cook for us. Your grandpa sent some of his famous biscuits."

"I could make a whole meal on them."

Travis swung an arm around Zack's shoulders, and the boy didn't flinch. "I'll slice some ham and fry it up and bring out the apple butter."

"I'll get the plates and pour some buttermilk. Brother Whitworth?"

"Yes, but Brother Travis sounds better between us men."

"Thanks. I—I don't like Lester Hillman. He's not what folks think he is." He shrugged. "I know he helps out with the poor folks, but he's not like the men in my family."

Travis didn't know how to reply. Especially when he had sensed a few flaws in the man's character himself.

"Do you have a good reason?"

Zack shrugged. "He shouldn't look at Mama the way he does."

Suddenly Lester's demands about Mrs. Kahler's supposed drinking problem made sense. An accusation spread over Travis's mind like a creeping vine that choked everything it touched.

CHAPTER 13

Travis fretted over leaving Zack alone while he visited Mrs. Kahler, but if the woman was in fact drinking, the boy didn't need to view it. Instead he gave him chores and schoolwork to do over the afternoon hours, and he asked Mrs. Rainer to accompany him to the Morning Star Ranch.

"I'd like to talk to Mrs. Kahler, but I don't want to call on her alone," Travis had said. "It doesn't look fittin'."

"I agree. Some folks just look for something to gossip about. I always enjoy a ride to Bonnie's ranch, and the afternoon is a good time. The reverend takes a nap then, so I won't be missed." The woman nodded to punctuate each word.

Travis imagined Mrs. Kahler would someday look like her mother— the same sky blue eyes and wheat-colored hair that had merely whitened and not grayed. He hoped if Mrs. Kahler did have a problem with spirits, her mother would mention it to him before they arrived.

The two took the reverend's buggy and horse. If not for a cold rain, the ride would have been pleasant. Mrs. Rainer chatted about her family and church life, which eased Travis's mind. He always feared folks would inquire about his last church.

"Morgan and Casey live on the ranch that my first husband and I homesteaded," she said.

"The Double H, right?"

"Yes, it stands for Hayden's Heaven." Mrs. Rainer smiled, and he figured she was remembering days gone by.

"So Zack was named after his grandfather—Zachary Hayden. He and I will have to discuss his namesake."

"Are you making any headway with my grandson?"

He shrugged. "I like to think we are, but he's keeping something from me. I can feel it in my bones." *And I hope it's not anything to do with his mother drinking.*

"With a young boy, it's difficult to tell. All boys seem to go through a time when life doesn't make sense to them, and when a tragedy occurs. . .well, only God can restore them."

"Sounds like you know from experience."

She laughed. "Oh, I do. Both my boys had rough periods for a while. Grant was sixteen when he gave me trouble. He simply missed his father and got to mixin' with the wrong boys. Refused to listen to me. Forced me to be mama and papa to him. But Morgan had the real tragedy."

"You don't need to tell me this unless you want."

"Hmm. I will because the story is a part of our family, and you're giving of yourself to pull us back together. The story is not a secret. Most folks in town remember it all." She hesitated and glanced away for a moment. "Morgan's first wife was brutally murdered by an outlaw."

Travis startled. "I forget this part of the country had been pretty wild."

"Still is, Brother Travis. My Morgan blamed himself because he wasn't at home when it happened. He took off after the killer, and that's when he met Casey." She eyed him critically. "What I'm about to tell you is not to be repeated. None of the children know this but Chad, and we prefer to keep it that way until the others are a little more grown."

"I understand."

"Casey was a part of the outlaw band that killed Morgan's wife.

She'd been a part of the group since she was fourteen and finally fled in hopes of finding a new life. Her reputation had been built on the gang's reputation, not on anything she'd ever done. Casey and Morgan fell in love but had a hard go of it. They both had pasts that haunted them and kept them apart. God healed their pain and made a way for them to marry." She took a deep breath. "I know that families pass things on to each other, and I fear young Zack may have inherited his uncle's tendencies to handle grief through anger."

"I see. Your secret is safe with me, and I pray Zack soon finds peace."

She patted his arm. "I believe my daughter is finally on the right path. Bonnie came to see me a few days ago and asked for forgiveness. She admitted to grieving so that she'd neglected her children, the ranch, and her relationship with the Lord."

"Praise God," Travis whispered.

"Jenny happened to be there at the time, and she did the same with her. We all had a good cry." Mrs. Rainer laughed. "Brother Travis, the reverend and I decided that the Lord has sent you to help this crippled family be whole again."

I doubt your confidence, Mrs. Rainer. You don't know what happened in Tennessee.

"Bonnie is taking a new interest in the ranch and even having Lydia Anne learn how to ride." Her eyes sparkled with Bonnie's renewed enthusiasm for her family. Mrs. Rainer was a hearty woman, the type this country needed to stay strong.

"I don't think I have a thing to do with how the Lord is working in your family. He's answering prayers from a godly family."

"Shush, now. We all know different."

She talked on about church matters, helping him bide the time to the Morning Star. Soon the rain stopped, and rolling pastures filled with cattle and horses came into view. He wanted this afternoon to answer the question about Mrs. Kahler's presumed drinking. Travis had never been patient in waiting to learn the truth about a matter.

Bonnie met them on the front porch with a sweet smile and a hug for her mother. Travis inhaled for a scent of alcohol but smelled nothing but the freshness of the woman who had captured his mind in more ways than one.

"Are you making apple butter?" Mrs. Rainer asked once they were inside the house. "Smells heavenly."

"Juanita and I finished by noon. I'll send a jar back with each of you. I'm so pleased you came to see me." She smiled at Travis. "I have your other handkerchief ready for you. And how is my Zack?"

"Oh, I have him busy this afternoon. He's memorizing his first Latin words, cutting wood, and preparing vegetables for stew."

Her eyes widened. "He knows nothing about cooking."

Travis laughed. "We men have to learn a few things to survive. I put on some beef before leaving, and he's to add the rest."

"I hope it's palatable."

"So do I. It wouldn't look good for the new reverend and his charge to starve, although we've survived on a few meals of the reverend's biscuits."

"I'd gladly give up a meal for them." Bonnie laughed, a pleasing sound he'd never grow tired of hearing.

He allowed himself to stare into her eyes and thought he'd drown in their depths. Ben Kahler had left behind a beautiful woman. She gestured toward the parlor where he'd enjoyed her company before, but Mrs. Rainer stopped her.

"I want to sip coffee in the kitchen and visit. You know how I frown on all those lady peculiarities."

Bonnie laughed. "I just brewed a fresh pot and haven't tasted a drop." She peered at Travis. "Is that fine with you?"

"I'm from the Tennessee hills, Mrs. Kahler. Most of us don't have fancy parlors or elegant coffee cups."

"Then come along. Juanita, we have two very important people for coffee."

"Sí, Miss Bonnie," came a response from the kitchen.

Travis instantly relaxed. He sensed warmth here despite the turmoil, and certainly Mrs. Kahler had not been drinking. Still it bothered him that both Zack and Lester had accused her of such. He pushed the puzzlement from his mind. Good coffee and the company of three fine women held his attention—for the moment.

After Mrs. Kahler poured coffee for them all, she sat at the kitchen table with them. "Are you here to see me on business?" she asked.

Mrs. Rainer nodded at Travis. "Brother Travis asked me to accompany him. Sir, I guess you are to answer my daughter's question."

He nearly laughed at Mrs. Rainer's bluntness, but he did appreciate her ways. "I wanted to see how you are doing in Zack's absence." His words were partially true.

"I worry about him, but I'm keeping busy with Michael Paul and Lydia Anne." Bonnie glanced at her mother. "Mama, don't you dare leave until she wakes up from her nap. Anyway, Thomas is reacquainting me with the ranch. Lydia Anne is learning to ride, and Michael Paul has taken a new interest in the cattle business as well as the piano. I'm looking forward to watching him grow up." Her shoulders lifted and fell daintily. "We are doing well, but we miss Zack. Or rather, we have missed the old Zack for a long time."

"I'm praying he'll return to you soon."

"But he must abandon his anger," she said. "I cannot threaten military school and not be prepared to follow through." She stared into her cup. "Has he opened up his heart to you?"

Travis hesitated. "I'd rather not say until we spend more time together."

"You're thinking he might stretch the truth about things?"

The thought of hurting her with what Zack and Lester had said clawed at his heart. "I want him to trust me with everything. Then he and I can sort out the truth and work through his troubles."

Sadness shadowed her delicate features. "A boy should be able to come to his mother with the things that burden him. I pray that day comes soon."

"It will, Mrs. Kahler. God is faithful."

Dear Lord, don't let this kind lady suffer too long.

Within the half hour, Lydia Anne woke and was delighted to see her grandma.

"Can I show you the horses?" the little girl asked Mrs. Rainer. "Mama lets me ride by myself."

"Oh yes, show me." Mrs. Rainer stood from the table and reached for her granddaughter's hand. "We'll leave your mama and Brother Travis to talk and drink coffee."

Once the two left and Juanita excused herself to tend to something outside, Travis realized the utter helplessness of being alone with Bonnie Kahler.

"Now that we are without other ears, is there anything you need to tell me about Zack?" The earnest look in her face nearly made him speechless—and he was a preacher.

"I think any preconceived ideas or notions I might have need more time."

She tilted her head and glanced into her cup. "I've made many mistakes as a mother. I deeply regret them."

She'd said this before, but her past must really be bothering her. "God forgives our misdeeds, and I have plenty of my own."

"You're an answer to prayer, and I'll forever be indebted." Her soft voice reached down into his soul and gave him confidence that perhaps he could help her son.

Without another spoken word, she reached out and touched his arm. If not for his shirt and jacket covering it, he'd surely have been burned.

~~⌐◎⌐~~

"What do you think about taking a walk this morning to the parsonage?" Travis asked Zack a week after he'd visited Mrs. Kahler. "The reverend and your grandma asked us for breakfast. He and I have a few things to discuss afterwards."

Zack's face brightened.

"From the look on your face, you don't mind giving up a couple of hours of schoolwork."

"No, sir. Or your cooking." He yawned.

"Very funny. Do you miss your school friends?"

A strange look swept over the boy's face, one Travis couldn't quite read. "Miss Scott hates me."

"I hardly think she *hates* you. More like she had her fill of your behavior."

"Same thing. Both of you say exactly what you think." Bitterness tipped his words.

"That's right. She doesn't like the trouble you caused in her class-room. Has nothing to do with the young man inside of Zack Kahler."

"You're talkin' in riddles."

"One day you'll understand what I mean."

The anger and rebellion surfaced in Zack's eyes. Travis regretted the miserable state of the boy, but he'd been there—and not so long ago.

"All right, let's go," Travis said. "Along the way, we can talk about this morning's reading—King David putting Uriah in the front lines to get him killed."

"Are you thinking I'll say it was all right 'cause he was the king?"

Travis picked up his Bible and opened the door, motioning for Zack to step through. "I have no idea what you think. That's why I asked."

"I don't understand why God didn't hit him with a bolt of lightning for what he did. He knew better. Looks like murder to me."

"If you were God, how would you have handled it?"

Zack shrugged—his familiar response. "I'm not God."

"If God gave all of us what we deserve, none of us would be alive."

Travis couldn't get another word out of Zack. He'd like to think his charge was reflecting on the morning's Bible reading, but Travis had a hunch other more pressing matters raced through the boy's mind. The boy's heavy eyelids showed he hadn't gotten much sleep during the night.

The closer they drew to the parsonage, the faster Zack walked.

"You must be powerful hungry," Travis said.

"Sure am."

"Do you want to walk back to the schoolhouse? This early no one should be about, and it's been a long time since you were there."

"Not today."

Travis lifted his head and peered off in the direction of the school. He startled. What was flapping in the breeze? He stopped dead center in the middle of the road.

"Well, if that don't beat all." He chuckled. "Zack, take a look at that tree in the schoolyard."

Zack stood beside him. "What is it?"

"Looks like somebody strung up a woman's clothes in the branches." Travis planted his hands on his hips. A woman's unmentionables flapped in the breeze. Three pairs of them. "We ought to see what we can do about getting them out of there. Miss Scott will be real upset."

"I wonder who did that."

The way Zack asked the question drove an arrow of suspicion straight into Travis's mind. "Whoever hung those clothes up there had to be pretty spry."

"I imagine so."

"Clever, too. But there was a sky full of stars last night."

"Yes, sir."

"I doubt if the culprit had any help. Probably did it by himself."

"Most likely."

They walked closer and spotted the reverend in the schoolyard. He stared up into the tree, obviously wondering how to retrieve the clothes.

"Morning," Travis called. "Somebody's been up to mischief."

"If I wasn't a preacher, I'd laugh," the reverend said. "Best we set those clothes free before Miss Scott gets here."

"Aw, leave 'em alone, Grandpa."

"Now, Zack, I know you don't care for the teacher, but she deserves your respect." The reverend reached for the nearest branch.

"We'll do that, Reverend. I don't think Mrs. Rainer would approve of you climbing trees." Travis fought an urge to laugh. He glanced at Zack, whose face was the color of a ripe apple. "Should we summon the sheriff?"

"Oh, we don't need to bother him," Zack said.

Travis swallowed another laugh, but he couldn't let him get by with this. "So, Zack, how long did it take you to string up Miss Scott's clothes? Now I understand why you're tired this morning."

Zack didn't say a word.

"Did you do this?" the reverend asked.

"Ah. . .yes, sir."

Travis cleared his throat and focused his attention on Zack. "I wonder if that lightning bolt is anywhere close."

Zack took a deep breath. "How did you know?"

"I didn't for sure. Just guessed. But you're going to bring down every piece of those clothes. Are they Miss Scott's?"

"Yes, sir."

"Did you steal them from her clothesline?"

"Yes, sir."

"Not one bite of breakfast until you've finished and apologized to Miss Scott."

Zack winced. "Do I have to apologize?"

Travis narrowed his gaze. "Do you really think I'd let you get by easily?"

"No, sir." He sighed. "Can I wait until the other kids get here?"

Travis raised a brow.

Zack blew out an exasperated sigh and headed to the tree. Later Travis would have a good laugh. From the mirth on the reverend's face, they'd both remember this prank for a long time.

CHAPTER  14

Bonnie slowed her mare as she neared the entrance to the Double H, Morgan and Casey's ranch. She owed her sister-in-law a bushel basket of apologies for the years of leaning on her and the rest of the family far too much. Guilt had kept Bonnie awake the preceding night, and it was time she did something about it. She'd apologized to Mama and Jenny, and she should have done the same with Casey that day, too.

"Mama, I like riding to Aunt Casey's ranch," Lydia Anne said. "Can we do this everywhere we go?"

Bonnie laughed. "Sometimes we must conduct ourselves like proper ladies and use a buggy or carriage, but we'll ride together as much as we can. As soon as you can ride by yourself, we'll come visiting Aunt Casey, and you can show her how well you can handle a horse."

"Goody." She tilted her head and looked into her mother's face. "I'm glad you're happy now."

Bonnie kissed her forehead. "Me, too."

Casey met them on the front porch with a bushel basket in hand. A second basket sat on a wagon bed. A gust of wind toyed with her auburn hair, and she brushed it back. "Good morning. Are you two enjoying this cool weather?"

"No, ma'am," Lydia Anne said. "We're enjoying this ride together."

Casey shielded her eyes from the sun. "I've been meaning to stop by. How are you?"

"That is why I'm here." Bonnie swung down from Wildflower. "Can we talk a bit?" She peered at the wagon. "Looks like you're going apple pickin'. Need some help?"

"Sure. Shouldn't take long with both of us. And you can take plenty home with you. I have more apples than I know what to do with."

After Bonnie left her mare with a ranch hand, the three took the wagon and headed for the orchard. Lydia Anne rode in the back between the baskets.

"I'm sorry about Zack," Casey said. "I know this has to be heart wrenching for you."

Bonnie slowly nodded. "What makes it so difficult is that Zack's behavior is my fault."

"You shouldn't blame yourself."

"Casey, you and I both know that if I'd been a better mother—not so selfish in my own grieving—Zack could have talked to me during this horrible grieving time. At least it's not too late for Michael Paul and Lydia Anne. And I pray Brother Travis is able to help Zack."

"Aren't you being too hard on yourself?"

"Not at all. I'm simply facing the truth." Bonnie took a deep breath and glanced back at Lydia Anne. "I might as well simply say the rest of this so we can enjoy the morning."

"Is something else wrong?"

"No. I hope our lives will now start to mend. I realized some ugly things about myself. Cas, do you remember way back when we first became friends? Mercy, I was eighteen and you were twenty-one. You were running from an outlaw gang and the law. To make matters worse, Morgan was pestering you to marry him. And what did I do? Nothing but spend my time dreaming about Ben and backing away from anything that might upset me. Anyway, I've always been the weak one, and it has to stop."

"That's not entirely true. You were and are my dearest friend. Have you forgotten that I deceived you about my past? Bonnie, I lied to you about being a part of an outlaw gang and even about my name."

"Doesn't matter. You asked me to forgive you years ago. I'm asking you to forgive me now." Bonnie refused to become emotional and alarm Lydia Anne.

"Of course. I love you, Bonnie. You've always been the sister I never had."

"We'd better start talking about something else, or I'm going to cry enough tears to float this wagon."

Casey laughed. "What do you think of Brother Travis?"

"Oh my. He's a good preacher and a kind man, but he's certainly not a dandy."

"I heard Hank offered a free haircut and shave—twice, but he refused."

Bonnie giggled. It had been a long time since she'd felt such freedom. "I'm ashamed of myself, but I have to agree with you. Except he has to be a special man to take Zack into his home in hopes I won't have to place him in a military school. I've already decided the good Lord has a special crown for him."

"You're right. The reverend and Jocelyn think he came straight from heaven."

"I have to agree," Bonnie said. "The first time I saw Brother Travis, I mistook him for a beggar. I was not pleasant."

She and Casey exchanged glances.

"I apologized to him, too."

"Oh, Bonnie, I'm so sorry."

"No need. I'm going to be a better woman through this. And Ben will look down from heaven and know his wife and children are doing fine."

"We have all been praying for you."

"Thanks. Right now I miss Zack. I want to see him, but I'm trusting Brother Travis's judgment as to when's the best time."

"Have you thought about inviting them to dinner?"

Bonnie's heart spun. "What a wonderful idea. I'll send word in the morning with Michael Paul. I hope it's not too soon."

Casey pulled the wagon to a halt by a heavily laden apple tree. "If it is, maybe Brother Travis can give you a better time. At least you'd have something to look forward to."

"Wonderful. I'm ready to pick some apples." Bonnie turned to Lydia Anne with another idea. "We could make an apple pie this evening and send it to Zack and Brother Travis tomorrow."

❦

Travis lifted a fallen branch from beside his front porch. A storm had blown through the night before, and debris lay scattered about the ground. Zack helped all morning, but Travis gave him schoolwork for the afternoon. Travis had some thinking to do, and hard physical work was the answer—that and a lot of prayer.

If he'd known about the church's association with Heaven's Gate, he wouldn't have taken this job. But God knew and had given him clear direction to accept the position. Why? The very horror that had driven him from Tennessee haunted him in Kahlerville. Could he conduct himself as a man of God with the painful memories of the past?

God, why? I tried and failed. I ruined Felicia's life and failed my church. Why am I here?

Maybe he'd been given a second chance to share the gospel with those whom others turned away. He thought of all the fine people of Kahlerville who gave of their time and money. They were different; they did care. He didn't have to walk this path alone.

You've never been alone.

Travis recognized the voice. *So is this part of the healing, Lord? Or part of the lesson?* He dragged the limb behind his house to the pile of other limbs and branches. He picked up the ax. With every crack of the split wood, his muscles burned.

"Sir, I could cut that wood."

Travis lifted his gaze. "Are you thinking a little work might make me a little less angry about Miss Scott's unmentionables flying in the schoolyard tree?"

"Mama always sent me to the wood pile when I was angry."

"Your mama is a smart woman. That's why I'm here, but not because I'm angry with you." Travis hoisted the ax back to his shoulder. "I've already forgotten about yesterday."

"Thank you, sir."

"But you can continue the good manners. I rather enjoy them." He tossed Zack a smile.

"Hello. Brother Travis?" The feminine voice sounded familiar.

"That's Mama," Zack whispered. "Should I go back inside?"

"Not unless you want to."

"Brother Travis?"

"I'm back here, Mrs. Kahler." Travis glanced up at Zack, who slipped back inside the house. Did he dislike her so much that he sought refuge?

Bonnie Kahler made her way around the side of the house. She held up her skirt from the mud with one hand and clutched a towel-covered dish with the other. The woman looked innocent and pure, reminding him of a child.

Travis hurried to her side. "Excuse me, ma'am. I should have thought about the mess back here."

"Oh, I've seen plenty of mud in my lifetime." She smiled and offered him the dish. "Lydia Anne and I picked apples and thought you and Zack might enjoy an apple pie."

"I know I will." He lifted the towel and inhaled the apple and cinnamon scent. "Hmm. This is my favorite pie."

She peered around him. "Zack's, too. Is he here?"

"He's inside." How did he tell her that her son preferred the solitude of the house to visiting with his mother?

Sadness fell across her face. "He's not ready to see me, is he?"

Travis shook his head. "But he's improving." He remembered the prank on Miss Scott and nearly laughed. However, Mrs. Kahler might not find it amusing.

She blinked. "Good. I'll wait until he wants to see me. I wanted to invite both of you to dinner, but it must be too soon."

"I'll ask him. Maybe next week?" Suddenly he felt very self-conscious. "I have something for you. Do you have a moment while I fetch it?"

"Oh, yes. Would you like for me to split a little wood?"

Her teasing eased his nervousness. "I can't pay you."

"Not even a nickel for the huge pile?"

He shrugged. "I'm a poor preacher." They laughed, and he disappeared into the house with the pie. He set it on the kitchen table and noted Zack was in his room with the door closed. Travis grabbed the journal wrapped in brown paper and hurried back outside.

Her blue eyes lifted to his face, and he thought his heart had melted into butter.

"What is it?" she asked.

He handed her the package. "Well, I purchased one of these for you and one for Zack. I thought it might be helpful."

Curiosity etched across her face. She took the package and carefully opened it. "A journal," she whispered. "I used to keep one, but I stopped when Lydia Anne was born."

"I encouraged Zack to write down all the things he remembered about his father. I thought it might help him work through his grief."

"Mama suggested the same thing right after Ben left us, but I couldn't bring myself to pen a single word." She glanced up with watery eyes. "Since a couple of years have passed, I believe I can. Thank you. This gift came at just the right time."

Her smile warmed his heart. The cost of the journals had dug into his meager funds, but her kind words were worth any price. And if it helped her, then he'd be blessed with her healing.

Now, if Zack could only try harder. In moments when Travis wondered if he could ever help the boy, he realized Zack didn't want help—not yet anyway. He'd grown accustomed to his miserable life. The boy needed to find a reason to change, a task that only God could do.

"Guess I'll be going," she said.

The sound of her voice caused a sweet shiver to race up his arms. He remembered when she had touched his arm at the Morning Star. This had to stop. "I'll walk you to your buggy."

The back door opened and Zack stepped onto the porch. His hands dug deep into his overall pockets. "Thanks for bringing the pie, Mama. It smells real good."

Thank You, Lord.

<hr />

Travis had waited long enough to announce the forming of a choir. He'd been excited about the idea, especially with Jenny Andrews playing piano. But now as he listened to the off-key men and women, he wondered what God meant by "making a joyful noise." He thought he'd endured it all until Miss Scott, Zack's former teacher, said she'd like to sing a hymn on Sunday morning.

"Most certainly," he said. "What would you like to sing?"

" 'Amazing Grace.' "

"Wonderful. Mrs. Andrews, would you mind playing that beautiful hymn for us? We'd all like to be blessed with Miss Scott's song."

One note, and Travis thought she might be a bit flustered singing in front of him and the choir. The second note made him wonder if she was getting even for what Zack had done to her clothes. On the third note, he stopped her.

"Let's start again, Miss Scott. Just relax."

"I am, Brother Whitworth. I believe this is my best."

I hope not. He might lose his church if she sang this Sunday. By the time she finished the first verse, his head pounded, and the good folks in the choir were either hiding their laughter or their faces were lined with agony.

When she completed all the verses, he didn't know whether to pray for mercy or thank God the song was over. He'd heard coyotes with better voices.

"So I'll sing this Sunday?" Miss Scott wrung her hands.

"Well. . ."

Jenny Andrews rose from the piano. "Oh, please, not this Sunday. I need time to practice. I would feel terrible if your song sounded badly because of me."

"When do you think you'll be ready?" Miss Scott lifted her chin.

"A few weeks, at least."

In a huff, Miss Scott resumed her position in the choir. One man wiped his face with a handkerchief. Another coughed. Mrs. Rainer mouthed, "I'm sorry."

Suddenly Miss Scott stood. Travis hadn't noticed how plain the poor woman was. Sympathy for her touched him. "Brother Whitworth, I thank you for this opportunity to share my gift of voice. I had doubts about your ability to lead this church with taking in Zack Kahler and all, but your willingness to let me sing proves your true heart. My daddy always said my singing lifted his spirits." She abruptly sat down.

"Thank you, Miss Scott. We'll look forward to your solo once Mrs. Andrews learns her part."

"Why not sing with her?" Mrs. Rainer asked. "I think our church would be blessed with two fine voices."

If Jocelyn Rainer hadn't been the reverend's wife, he'd have considered letting Zack swipe her laundry.

"I'm not sure if that would be fair. Michael Paul Kahler and I plan to sing a duet soon," he said.

"But adults should be first," Miss Scott said. "This way, Michael Paul can hear how to reach the difficult notes. I could work with him after school if you'd like."

Travis nearly choked. "Thank you for your kind offer, but I was looking forward to rehearsing with the boy since his brother is in my charge. Surely you understand."

He was trapped, and the whole choir knew it. All manner of common sense had raced out with the church mice. Why ever had he wanted to form a choir? Then his gaze touched on the three young women from Heaven's Gate. They neither laughed nor looked uncomfortable. They understood humiliation; they'd lived it. Sylvia Hillman draped her arm around Rosie's shoulders. From what he'd heard about the problems in Mrs. Hillman's marriage, she understood humiliation, too. God could heal all of their hurts if they simply let him wrap His love around their aching hearts.

"I look forward to your song, Miss Scott," he said. "If your singing blessed your father, then I'm sure it will bless all of us who are privy to the song. I play piano a little, so if you'd like to rehearse here in the church, I'd be glad to help you."

"We could tonight after regular rehearsal."

He smiled. "That would be fine."

❧❧❧

Travis thought he might not live through Miss Scott's repeated variations of "Amazing Grace." As much as he hated to admit it, her voice sounded like chalk scraping across a blackboard. Other choir members milled about in the back of the church.

"Let's simply listen to the melody before you begin again," he said. "I know you want every note to be perfect."

"And it's not?" Miss Scott asked.

"We all aim for perfection when it comes to the Lord."

Miss Scott stood straight, then closed the hymnal. "I don't need to see the words and notes. I have them memorized."

Travis inwardly cringed. "A little review is always good."

"If you insist." She stepped beside him at the piano bench and smiled—far too sweetly. He'd seen that look before, and it made him want to run like a scared rabbit.

"I appreciate this," she said.

"You're welcome."

He started to play the melody, but she stopped him.

"Would you like to come one night for dinner?" she asked.

Please, I'm not husband material. "How thoughtful of you, but my evenings are spent with Zack."

"He couldn't stay by himself one evening?" She brushed against his shoulders while he remained seated on the piano bench.

"Miss Scott, it would not look appropriate if I came to your home for dinner. Neither of us would want gossip."

"I could invite another couple to join us."

"I'm sorry, but I must decline."

"Zack has told you horrible things about me." She sounded like a hurt little girl.

"No, ma'am. I'm simply not interested in social engagements."

"I shall practice my song on my own. For a man who is not interested in social engagements, you certainly find the time to visit with Bonnie Kahler." Miss Scott whirled around and headed toward the back of the church.

A twinge of guilt rushed over him at the mention of Mrs. Kahler's name. Had anyone else noticed the time he spent with her? Surely not. He was only doing the Lord's work in helping her and Zack. He stared after Miss Scott. He didn't understand women and doubted if he ever would.

CHAPTER 15

Bonnie realized nearly four weeks had gone by since Zack had taken up residence with Brother Travis, and finally tonight the two were coming to dinner. She'd given Juanita the afternoon and evening free so she herself could prepare chicken and dumplings. From what Bonnie had seen, Juanita and Thomas planned a picnic. Wedding bells would be ringing soon; Bonnie was sure of it.

A hot apple pie sat cooling in the pie safe, and fresh cream brimmed a pitcher, ready to be poured over the top of it for dessert. Bonnie wanted everything to be perfect. She'd been told her son had been practicing good manners, and Brother Travis said his schoolwork was exceptional.

But what about Zack's relationship with her and his brother and sister? She'd love to see the three of them laughing and teasing like they used to—before Ben left them. The closer the time came for their arrival, the more nervous she became. Her stomach felt like a band of crickets had taken residence.

Stop it. Dinner will be fine. Surely she'd see progress with Zack this evening. He'd spoken to her at church and thanked her for the pie last week.

"They're here," Michael Paul called. "Looks like they borrowed Grandpa's buggy."

DiAnn Mills

Bonnie took a deep breath and untied her apron. All of the food had been prepared to Zack's liking, and the table was set. If only she'd stop shaking.

Zack spoke little during dinner, but what he said displayed pleasant conversation. She'd always be grateful to Brother Travis.

"Are you coming home soon?" Lydia Anne asked.

Bonnie cringed. She should have instructed the little girl not to question her brother about an uncomfortable situation.

"I don't think so." Zack peered up at his mother. "Brother Travis says I have a lot of bothersome things inside me, and I reckon he's right. I'm mad most of the time."

"At me?" Lydia Anne asked in her sweet little voice. "Michael Paul?"

"Hush," Bonnie said. "Be glad your brother is with us tonight." Heat engulfed her face. She understood his anger was aimed at her. How could she blame him?

A heavy pause separated every person at the table. Bonnie longed to bring her family back together, to see Zack the carefree boy she remembered before Ben died. She gazed into the face of her troubled son. "I'd like to send back a couple of fishing poles with you tonight."

He said nothing.

"Fine idea," Travis said. "We've been talking a lot about fishing, and I could use a couple of poles."

"Living with Brother Whitworth must be fun," Michael Paul said. "Going fishin' and not having to sit in school all day long."

Zack scowled, and Bonnie sensed the rebellion from a few weeks prior about to spring on them all like a cat upon a mouse.

"I don't think the amount of school work I give Zack is enjoyable," Travis said. "The reading and math are harder, plus we've started Latin. His geography lessons are for students two to three years older."

Thank you, Brother Travis.

"I can speak for myself." Zack tossed his napkin on the table. "I don't know what is worse, abidin' by the preacher's rules or being sent off to military school."

"We could find out, but I'd rather not." In the past, Bonnie would have done anything to keep peace and not confront Zack with his rudeness.

"I think you're looking for an excuse to get rid of me for good."

She moistened her lips and placed her trembling hands in her lap. "Whatever made you say such a thing?"

" 'Cause I look like Papa, and you wouldn't be reminded of him."

"That sounds like an excuse to have you stay," she said.

Zack glared into her face, and she battled wits with her gaze. She dared not let him overpower her in an argument. He must learn to respect her and other adults. She smiled at him, then at Brother Travis. Somehow the brief focus on the man's kind face momentarily settled her uneasiness. *Please stop, Zack. Can't you see I love you?*

She placed her napkin beside her plate. "I believe we're ready for warm pie and cream."

"Would you like some help?" Brother Travis asked.

"She doesn't need any. That's what Juanita is for," Zack said.

"Juanita is not here this evening. I cooked dinner. In fact, how about helping me serve pie, Zack?" Her heart thumped against her chest until it hurt. How far had she sunk to be fearful of her own son?

"Grand idea," Brother Travis said.

"I can help you," Michael Paul said.

Bonnie turned to her middle son. "Thank you, but I'd like Zack's help."

He must have wanted the pie more than he wanted to release anger and rebellion toward her, because Zack scooted his chair legs back across the wooden floor. Inside the kitchen, she pulled out plates from the cupboard.

"How about I cut the pie and you ladle on the cream?"

"Why?"

"Cream is excellent with apple pie."

"You know what I mean. Why did you ask me to come in here?"

She proceeded to cut the pie. "We could use clean forks and spoons, please."

He opened the drawer and drew out the silverware. "You didn't answer my question."

"I asked for your help because I miss you—not the angry son who gets into trouble but the son who can be a joy."

"That's Michael Paul—the do-gooder."

She bit back a remark as ugly as she'd heard from him. Instead she handed him a piece of pie ready for cream. "After you top this, kindly take it to Brother Travis. And I do know the difference between you and Michael Paul."

She turned to slice another piece, and he disappeared into the dining room. A moment later, Michael Paul took Zack's place in the kitchen.

Would the situation between her and Zack ever improve? She prayed night and day for it to be so. She refused to give up. Their relationship had to get better.

⌘

Travis had to chew on his words to keep from laying into Zack. He deserved a trip to the woodshed, but that wasn't Travis's position. Neither was he convinced that type of punishment would soften Zack's heart. The troubled boy acted as though he wanted to be left alone, yet Travis sensed a deep need for reconciliation with his mother. In the beginning, he had thought Zack blamed himself for his father's untimely death. Many children did. Tonight he realized Zack's pain and anger came from another source. Something deeper that he hadn't been able to reveal.

"Why are you so angry with your mother?"

"You don't want to know. Everyone thinks Bonnie Kahler is this pretty sweet lady who never does anything wrong. Oh, feel sorry for the Widow Kahler. She's all alone since her husband died." He blew out an exasperated sigh.

"I'd like to hear. Maybe I can help."

Silence. The mare moved toward Kahlerville, pulling against the leather harness, each step rhythmic with the night sounds.

"Zack, I'm your friend, and I'm not going to think any less of you or your mother with what you're upset about."

"It's about my father."

"I figured as much. Go on with it."

In the shadows of the lanterns lit on both sides of the buggy, Zack's shoulders lifted and fell. "I heard Uncle Morgan and Uncle Grant talking before Papa died. Uncle Grant said if Papa moved to Arizona, his lungs would get better. Uncle Morgan asked why he didn't go." Zack picked at the knee of his overalls. "Uncle Grant said Papa refused. Said he wouldn't drag my mama away from her family. That she couldn't handle life alone."

"I see."

"So Papa died because Mama is too selfish to think of anyone but herself."

"Do you mind if I tell her about this?"

"No. I nearly did tonight in the kitchen."

Travis picked up the mare's pace. He hoped this could be explained away. If not, it might take years for Zack to forgive his mother.

~~~⌕~~~

Travis knocked on the door of Grant and Jenny Andrews's home, a stately, well-kept house. He particularly admired the huge oaks shading its bricked walls like soldiers guarding a fortress. Unlike the trees near his Tennessee home, these trees still held on to their leaves. The reverend had told him winters were much milder and the number of frosts could be counted on his fingers.

Glancing at Zack, who had wanted to stay at home, he resisted the urge to clap a hand on the boy's shoulder.

"I know what you're going to talk to Uncle Grant about, and I'd rather not be around," Zack had said earlier.

"I understand, but if you heard wrong, then we need to get this straightened out between you and your mama."

Zack shook his head. "Nothing will change. I know what I heard. Uncle Grant may lie to protect her. I'll never shelter Lydia Anne the way my uncles and my real grandpa did to Mama."

"Are you sure they did?"

"I heard my uncles say so, but Uncle Grant didn't. Just Uncle Morgan and my other grandpa."

"Zack, sometimes when folks love someone, they want to protect them from all that could harm them. Your mama looks frail with her small stature, and she appears to be much younger than other women her age."

Now, as they waited for Grant to open the door, Zack eyed Travis curiously and started to speak, but at that moment the door opened.

The Andrews's housekeeper, Miss Mimi, a round woman with a smile and a warm hug for everyone, greeted them at the door and ushered them inside to the parlor. The elegance of the room in rich emerald green and gold furnishings made Travis want to leave his shoes at the door.

"Good morning, Brother Whitworth and Zack. How can I help you today?"

"We're here to see Grant if he's not too busy," Travis said.

"Is one of you feelin' poorly?" Miss Mimi leaned toward them as if she could offer ready sympathy.

"No, ma'am. God's blessed both of us with good health."

She nodded at Zack. "And how are you?"

"Very well, thank you."

Thank you for your manners. Travis had too much on his mind to discipline the boy. Bonnie Kahler's family and problems had settled on him of late, and he longed for her and the children to be happy.

"Grant is with a patient, but he shouldn't be long. Jenny and the girls are at the parsonage. May I get you something?"

"No, thank you. We'll simply wait for Grant to be free," Travis realized it was best that the other members of the household were absent. He'd been told that Grant hadn't been very happy with Zack's previous behavior in the presence of his daughters.

Miss Mimi disappeared, and the two waited for Grant. Travis studied Zack. He looked tired, and corn rows appeared to be embedded across his forehead. But his facial features were not those of a boy who'd lied. Only weary. Perhaps he carried more than his share of worry—and anger.

"Mornin', Brother Travis, Zack. How can I help you?" Grant sounded pleasant enough at the sight of his wayward nephew and the new preacher.

"Just a brief word with you is all. Do you have a few moments to talk about a matter? Zack shared some concerns with me that I was hoping you could help us sort through."

Grant seated himself in an overstuffed chair. "I'd be glad to help you two in any way I can."

"Do you mind if I talk to Miss Mimi while you two talk?" Zack asked.

Travis hesitated. Zack might not be welcome with the housekeeper, and perhaps the boy should make his claims against his mother face-to-face with Grant. Against his better judgment, he elected to spare Zack another grievous moment.

"It's up to your uncle," Travis said.

"Go ahead, Zack. She made a cake yesterday, and I'm sure there's plenty left. Brother Travis and I will talk in my office."

In the next instant, the two men sat across from each other in a room that smelled of medicine and sparkled with cleanliness. Grant's suit looked like it cost more than everything Travis owned. He wished he'd had some experience with folks who never worried about where the next meal came from or if enough wood had been chopped for winter.

He simply wanted to get by the formalities and discuss Zack's accusations.

"I'm trying to help Zack," Travis began. "At times I think I'm making improvement, and other times I'm afraid he might never change."

"The family appreciates what you're doing. Frankly, we've given up. Neither Morgan nor I want to send him to a military school, but the older he gets, the more dangerous he could become."

Travis nodded. "Last night I asked him why he was so angry with his mother, and he told me. It appears he overheard a conversation between you and your brother before his father died."

Grant glanced out a window to the front of his house then back again. "What did he hear?"

"That Ben Kahler had been advised to move to Arizona for his health but he refused because Mrs. Kahler couldn't bear to be separated from her family."

Again Grant stared out the window briefly before giving Travis his attention. "That's the truth. Are you saying Zack blames Bonnie for Ben's death?"

"Yes. I was hoping he'd heard incorrectly." Travis shook his head. "Mending the relationship with mother and son will be harder than I thought."

"But that was Ben's decision. After Bonnie learned how serious his illness was, she came to me asking what could be done for him. I told her that the dry climate in Arizona could help his lungs. She promptly found a buyer for their ranch, but Ben refused. He forced himself out of bed and paid a visit to the buyer. Canceled the whole thing. Bonnie cried for weeks."

"Zack needs to know this."

"I'll tell him now. I never had any idea that he overhead the conversation. No wonder he's had a difficult time." Grant stood. "Would you like to go with me?"

"I'd rather wait here. I'm still an outsider, and this is family business."

While Travis listened to the clock above the mantle tick by like the years of a man's life, his mind drifted to the family he missed in

Tennessee. Were they glad he'd left for good, or had they grown to regret their hasty words? In time, they might post a letter since he'd written them of his new church.

The silence moved him to pray for his estranged family and for the dear people of Kahlerville. He so wanted Zack and his mother to restore their relationship. A child shouldn't have to live without his mother, especially when they both hurt so badly.

Travis then remembered Lester Hillman and how he wanted Bonnie stopped from volunteering at Heaven's Gate. The man was a powerful influence in the community, used to having people do what he wanted. Lester had proved his self-centeredness when he threatened to pull his money from the church. Let him take his money wherever he wanted. Travis refused to tell Bonnie she was no longer welcome at Heaven's Gate. Lester had accused her of drinking—just as Zack had. As much as Travis refused to admit it, an ounce of truth had to be in their stories for them to make similar claims. A strange situation. Lester wanted Bonnie away from Heaven's Gate. Zack wanted Lester away from his mother. Both had stated she had a problem with drinking.

What was the truth?

Bonnie Kahler stayed constantly on his mind, and she shouldn't. No woman should ever occupy his thoughts like that again. It was like poison for all Travis touched.

Footsteps sounded, and he stood as Grant and Zack made their way into the office. His gaze fixed on the boy, but he couldn't tell if the worrisome lines on his forehead were regret or the same anger.

"Zack and I had a little talk," Grant said. "I told him all I knew about his father's illness and resulting death."

"I think I'd like to see Mama," Zack said.

Travis held back a strong desire to let out a war whoop. "Do you want to talk to her as soon as possible?"

Zack nodded. He turned to his uncle. "Who offered to buy our ranch?"

"Lester Hillman."

Zack set his jaw. "I reckon he had the money to do it. Thanks, Uncle Grant, for taking the time to tell me the truth."

"Glad to help. I hope things between you and your mama work out soon. Brother Travis, would you like to take my buggy?"

"Thanks. I'm saving for a horse, and hopefully I'll have the money saved soon. It's kinda hard and humiliatin' depending on other folks for traveling."

Travis shook Grant's hand, and in short order, he and Zack made their way toward the Morning Star.

"I assume you want to speak to your mama alone," he said.

"I'm not sure. I have a hard time when she cries. Makes me feel bad and usually makes me mad, too."

"Most men are that way. We want to make things right for womenfolk, but when they cry, we don't know what to do."

Zack nodded. Today, he'd been able to face and discuss one of the things weighing heavily on his heart. Praise the Lord.

CHAPTER  16

Bonnie heard the rattle of a wagon and the hum of voices. She glanced up from her mending to see Grant's horse and wagon. Jenny and the girls must be with him. She laid aside Michael Paul's buttonless shirt and hurried to the door just as a knock sounded. Visiting with her family always sounded better than pricking her finger with a needle. She opened the door and was startled to see Brother Travis and Zack.

"Good afternoon, Mrs. Kahler. I hope we aren't interrupting you."

"Not at all. Do come in." She resisted the urge to hug Zack. Their last meeting had been somewhat disastrous, and the thought of having it repeated churned her stomach. Zack wasn't frowning. Dared she hope this could be good? She glanced from her son to Brother Travis. What would the town's preacher do with all that hair come summer? But there was something about the man that affected her in a most peculiar way. Immediately she chastened her thoughts.

"You two look fine today," she said.

"And. . .and you look pretty, Mama," Zack said. "We came because I have to talk to you." He dragged his tongue across his lips. "Can we take a walk?"

Her heart thumped like a dog's tail. "I'd love to. This is an excellent time. Lydia Anne is helping Juanita tend to the chickens."

She turned to Brother Travis. "Are you going with us?"

"I'd like for him to come along if you don't mind." Zack's gaze darted about, but his voice sounded calm—in control.

She shoved aside her trepidations and reached for her shawl on the hallway hook.

Zack twisted the button on his shirt. Suddenly Bonnie began to tremble. What if her son wanted to live with Brother Travis and never return home? *Calm down, Bonnie. Let God handle this.*

"Shall we walk the road toward the pasture?" she asked. "The colts are growing like weeds."

"No matter where," Zack said. "I think I talk better when my feet are moving."

Bonnie glanced at Brother Travis, and he smiled. Surely Zack had crossed a milestone. At least she prayed so. They ventured outside toward the pasture.

"We went to see Uncle Grant this morning because of something I heard him and Uncle Morgan say before Papa died."

She clasped her hands in front of her, determined to let Zack speak his mind without interrupting. A crow called above them, and a rooster replied. Then they repeated.

"Wonder what they're talking about," Brother Travis said. "Maybe they think we look funny."

An image of Brother Travis's wild hair and spectacles crossed her mind, and she covered her mouth to stifle a giggle. He must have realized her incredible nervousness. *Thank you, dear man.*

"Reckon I ought to speak my mind," Zack said. "This isn't easy, but I'll do the best I can. Once when Uncle Morgan and Uncle Grant were at our house before Papa died, I heard Uncle Grant say that Papa needed to move to Arizona. That he might get better where the air was hot and dry. Many folks with lung ailments did. But when we stayed here, I thought you refused to move."

"Oh, no, Zack. I tried—" She stopped herself. Already she'd broken her vow to listen.

"I know the truth, Mama. Uncle Grant explained it all to me."

She had to speak. "Is this why you've been angry with me?"

He shrugged. "Mostly. I'm sorry for blaming you when Papa died."

Bonnie blinked back the tears threatening to gush over her cheeks. "I'd have lived at the bottom of the ocean if it would have kept your father alive."

Zack nodded. "I believe you."

She wanted to say other things, but with Brother Travis listening to every word, she couldn't make the words form on her lips. "We've had lots of bad times between us, Zack. I'd like to try again to be a family."

"Not yet, Mama. I'm not ready. But maybe we can talk without me gettin' mad and bein' spiteful."

"Is there anything I can do or say to help you?"

"Maybe not for me, but for Michael Paul and Lydia Anne."

"Anything, Zack. What would you like?"

Zack appeared to study a six-month-old filly that raced across the field on matchstick legs. He turned toward Brother Travis and then back to her. Deep inside, she sensed what he was about to say. *He knows. Zack knows.*

"Stop drinking the wine that Lester Hillman brings you."

Bonnie struggled for her breath as though he'd thrown dirt into her face. The ugliest of secrets had been exposed to an innocent boy.

❧❧❧

Travis wished he could fade into nothing. The pain on Bonnie's face. The anger in Zack's eyes. How could he direct this conversation, or should he? An inner voice, the One he'd learned to trust, directed him to listen.

Bonnie sniffed, and Travis watched her fight a river of tears. "I tried to hide those days."

"Maybe from Michael Paul and Lydia Anne but not from me—or Juanita."

"I stopped a few days before you left. And I'm so sorry. I—I thought the wine would help me sleep better after your papa left. It took a long time before I realized numbing the pain didn't lessen the grieving."

"What about Mr. Hillman bringing you the bottles?"

She said nothing, but her flaming cheeks revealed the humiliation. Maybe she searched for a way out. "If you're old enough to ask man questions, then I suppose you deserve an answer. Right after your papa died, the Hillmans came to check on us. I told them I was having trouble sleeping. Mr. Hillman said the apostle Paul had instructed Timothy to take a little wine for his health, and I should do the same. The next day, Mr. Hillman came by himself and brought me a bottle of wine." She paused, no doubt to keep her emotions in control. "That was the first of many such gifts. Not long ago, I told Lester if he brought another bottle to this house, I'd tell his wife."

"He's not a good man, Mama."

Zack carried too many burdens for such a young life. Maybe now his life could move forward. Travis prayed so.

"I see that now. At least about this matter. Back then, I was too wrapped up in grief." Bonnie took a deep breath. "Thomas is keeping an eye on the house. Most women would never have told a boy your age this kind of thing, but you're nearly a man, Zack, and you deserve to know the truth. I do ask that you spare Michael Paul."

Zack's face softened. "Thank you for treating me like a man. I'm going to try to act like one. No need to worry about me telling Michael Paul."

"I've made many mistakes. Too many to recall, but I promise you I'm going to live my life so God and your papa can look down from heaven and be proud."

Zack smiled. He stopped walking and turned to his mother. They stood eye to eye.

"I'm glad you look like your father. It's like having him here with me."

He reached over and gave her a hug. Not a firm one, but it was a beginning. Travis watched the sight, and she glanced up through her tears. Her smile eased his soul. What a dear lady. Her husband must have regretted leaving her, for he had a touch of heaven on earth. He reached into his pocket and handed her a handkerchief.

Zack released his mother. "I don't know when or if I can ever come home. There's meanness in my head that makes me want to fight and curse." He combed his fingers through his hair. "I want to love you and Michael Paul and Lydia Anne right, but I don't."

Bonnie bit her lip, and Travis wanted to pull them both into his arms. Powerful hurt stretched across their faces.

"I'll not give up until I have your love and respect back," she finally said.

"Good," Zack said. "I don't want you to give up on me, either. Military school sounds awful to me, but I may need to get away."

"From me, son?"

"No, Mama, from the blackness inside me."

"I'll pray night and day for you."

This time when Zack hugged her, Travis could see the muscles across his shoulders relax. And Bonnie smiled. Once the two recovered, Zack took his mother's hand as they walked back to the house.

"Brother Travis, I'd like to give you and Zack a gift."

That was not at all what he expected to hear from Bonnie's lips. "A gift? You've already given us all kinds of food, blankets, dishes. More things than I could count."

How could one woman possess such loveliness?

"This is different. Zack needs his horse, and so do you."

"I couldn't accept such generosity, but Zack here is different."

"Nonsense. My mind's set, and once a woman has her mind clearly fixed on a matter, nothing can change it."

Travis understood a lot of the truth in those words. More than he cared to think on. "I'd be greatly obliged for the gift of a horse, but it's not necessary."

She smiled. "Oh, yes, it is. Needed and necessary. I'll have one of the hands tie them to the wagon for your trip back to town, and I'll include bridles and saddles."

"Mrs. Kahler—"

"Don't refuse me, Brother Travis. You don't want to deny me a blessing, do you?"

How could he refuse anything she requested?

Years had passed since Bonnie's heart had felt so carefree. A shroud of gloom had kept her encased too long, and now God's blessing of peace had enveloped her. The autumn season, which she had begun in desperation, now turned into a newness of heart as though life had given her a gentle beginning.

Since she and Zack had talked twelve days ago about Ben's death, they'd made good progress. She refused to dwell on the sadness existing between them, but instead focused on the future, a happy one.

Her son preferred living with Brother Travis, and for now she wouldn't press him to come home. The sunshine of hope lived, and she breathed its sweet ardor. She sensed the return of the energy and enthusiasm she had known as a girl. The pages of the journal that Brother Travis had given her overflowed with remembrances of Ben and their years together. What good medicine the writing had become. The first night she received it, she had titled it *The Book of Healing*, and every entry was true to the title.

"Some days I think I could write a book," she said to Mama while helping her prepare the flower beds at the parsonage for cooler weather. She'd told her a little about the conversation with Zack—enough for her mother to relax in the prospect of a brighter tomorrow. "Life's mountains and valleys are forming me into a different woman."

"Perhaps you should consider that very thing. As a child you told me many stories while we did chores or busied ourselves in the kitchen."

"I remember how you encouraged me to write them down, but I was afraid Morgan or Grant would find them and tease me." Bonnie noted the yellow lantanas still had plenty of blossoms along with the mums that normally bloomed until after Thanksgiving. She pulled up a thistle and tossed it into the weed bucket.

"What's stopping you now?" Mama stretched her back.

"Time, I guess. With the children and the ranch, I find myself crawling into my bed shortly after I put the children in theirs." Bonnie laughed. "Has it been so very long ago when I complained of sleepless nights?"

"Our prayers have been answered, Bonnie. We all worried if you'd ever come out of the grief."

"I'm an Andrews. We're survivors. Mama, I feel good. I have a purpose in raising my children and not having to depend on anyone. The ranch has done very well under Thomas's care. In fact, I increased his pay, and we're looking into raising quarter horses. I just posted a letter to a breeder in Kentucky. The Morning Star may become known as one of the top horse breeders in Texas."

Mama's eyes glistened. "Your father would be proud. Oh, how he loved fine horses." She nodded and raised a finger. "But don't discard writing some of those stories swirling around in your head. If you want to take on something new and God wills it, He'll help you find the time."

"I'll ask Him what He thinks, but—"

"Mama, I need you." Lydia Anne's frantic voice snatched up Bonnie's attention. The little girl had wandered several feet away from the women and their gardening. "Mama!" she screamed.

Bonnie held her breath. "What is it?"

"A snake, and it's making a clicking noise."

God, no! "Don't move. I'm coming." She snatched up the hoe and raced across the flower bed, nearly tripping over her skirt and trampling on anything in her path. Her vision blurred with only Lydia Anne in sight.

A rattler, nearly three feet long, arched its ugly head straight at Lydia Anne. Without another thought, Bonnie positioned herself between her daughter and the snake. She lifted the hoe and sank its blade across the rattler's head, severing its venomous intent.

Grabbing Lydia Anne, she stepped back several feet and fell onto the grass. Her breathing came in short, quick gasps, while her heart nearly burst from her chest. Too frightened to speak or cry, she held Lydia Anne to her and rocked.

"Are you two all right?" Mama asked, sounding as breathless as Bonnie felt.

Bonnie nodded. She didn't think that much hate had ever swelled inside her.

"You're holding me too tight." Lydia Anne struggled to free herself. The little girl stared at the snake and covered her mouth. "Mama, you cut the snake's head plumb off. Zack and Michael Paul will never believe this. Can we take it home?"

Take it home? Her precious little princess wanted to take home a headless rattler? "Whatever for?"

Lydia Anne tilted her blond head. "I could put it in my room so I wouldn't forget the day my mama saved me."

Bonnie laughed. *Ben, did you hear your dainty little daughter?* "I think it would look better hanging in the barn."

Her mother plopped herself down on the grass beside them. "Would you look at the size of that? Daughter, I never thought you had it in you to. . .to. . ."

"Save my daughter from a rattler?" Bonnie released her squirming little girl. "As I said a moment ago, I'm an Andrews."

Mama laughed. "You most certainly are. I think you've just written your first story."

"And your granddaughter wants to keep this headless monster in her bedroom!"

Mama startled. "She has more of her uncle Morgan and her uncle Grant in her than I care to think about. Next she'll take off bareback in the middle of the night to see what it feels like to be an Indian."

Ah, maybe it's something I should try with her.

CHAPTER  17

"Brother Travis?"

Travis whirled around to face Frank Kahler's wife, Ellen. She bounced a fussy Frank Jr. on her hip. All of the others who had attended Sunday morning worship had left. Frank stood outside. *Must be waiting on his wife.* "Is there something I can do for you?"

The moment he stared into her eyes, he knew she'd learned the truth about his past in Tennessee. His face grew warm and hers reddened.

"I believe you must have heard from your folks in Tennessee," he finally said.

"Yes, sir. And I'm real sorry about what happened to you. Doesn't seem right for a body to be treated that way."

"It was my own fault. I'll resign this very day. No point in waiting around and deceiving the folks at Piney Woods Church any longer."

Ellen's face blanched. "No, please. I'd never have said a word if I thought you'd consider leaving. Frank and I don't look at the situation as your fault. We decided no one needs to learn about your misfortune. God gave you a second chance, and we want to honor all of your hard work. You're the perfect preacher for Piney Woods."

Relief crept over him, but with it came an air of guilt. "I'll tell the congregation."

"Not on account of us, Brother Travis. What went on in Tennessee is no one's business."

He smiled into the face of a godly woman. "I have to be truthful to those who have befriended me."

She shook her head. "No need. No need at all. But there's something I want to share with you, and then you'll understand why Frank and I feel like we do. If not for the reverend and Mrs. Rainer, I'd be living at Heaven's Gate today or, worse yet, living in another town and not owing my every breath to Jesus." She kissed her son's cheek. "I worked in a brothel until a few years ago when the reverend and Mrs. Rainer offered me a place to live rather than to continue in sin. Frank's parents gave me a job at their general store, and I met Frank. I got my second chance, and you deserve yours."

"I had no idea." Travis wondered if Felicia could have been as fine a woman as Ellen Kahler. He hoped so. He prayed she still remembered her promise to love the Lord for the rest of her life.

"Frank and I thought it best if you knew about us. Everyone else does, but we thought our story might make you feel a little better."

"And what exactly did you learn about me?"

"Enough to know it's no one's business that your last church asked you to leave because you wanted to marry a woman they didn't approve of."

He smiled. Ellen's accounting of what happened didn't sound as bad coming from her. "I'm real glad for your and Frank's friendship." He touched little Frank's bald head. "I believe this one has the finest parents I've ever met."

"Then you'll promise me you won't do anything foolish about what we know?"

He paused to consider what she asked. "For now, I'll keep what happened to myself."

She bid him good day and left the church. Travis glanced about at the empty pews that every Sunday and Wednesday held more and more people. The Holy Spirit was working in this church. Why, one of the young men had surrendered to a call to the ministry, and Travis was spending time discipling him.

The choir had grown—even if Miss Scott's voice hadn't improved. Tonight, he and Michael Paul planned to sing their song. Travis preferred the duet to take place on a Sunday morning, but Michael Paul had balked.

"I've never done anything like this before," the boy had said. "I think I'd do better when it was dark outside."

Travis chuckled. "What makes you think darkness will make your song any better?"

"I heard tell a dog howls when the choir is practicin' on Wednesday nights. I might need me a singin' dog."

Travis laughed until tears rolled down his cheeks. Poor Miss Scott.

The afternoon passed quickly, and as usual, Travis looked forward to the evening service. The folks were in for a real treat. Michael Paul's voice was clear and rarely off key. Already, he envisioned the boy playing piano and singing for many services to come.

Michael Paul arrived early—a little pale.

"Are you ready to sing for God and these folks?" Travis asked.

"I think so, sir, but I'm a little weak-kneed."

"You are going to do just fine. The folks tonight will be blessed."

"We're singing my papa's favorite song. He'll be happy to hear it."

" 'Blessed Assurance' is a fine hymn. And your papa will clearly enjoy your solo on the second verse."

"I hope so. I think Mama will be pleased, too."

"She will. Now take your seat on the front row and ask God to chase away those doubts."

Zack had entered the church and stood quietly while the two talked. "I'll sit with you. I don't want to miss any of it."

Travis grinned. Oh, he remembered the times when his brothers were beside him when he needed them. He also remembered when they weren't. "I'll nod at you when it's our turn. Imagine you're standing before God, and He's asked you to sing 'Blessed Assurance.' Open your heart to the song He's given you, and it will be perfect."

He wanted Bonnie to be very pleased. When did he start referring to her as Bonnie instead of Mrs. Kahler? Shouldn't all of the glory go to God? *I'm sorry, Lord.* He was attracted to her, and it scared him like a trapped rabbit. She'd never feel the same about him, especially with the way he'd changed his looks.

Let her see your heart.

Travis recognized the voice. Confusion rushed over him like a chilling rain. Later he'd think about what God meant. Right now he had a sermon to give and a song to sing with Michael Paul.

The moment Michael Paul reached the first note of his solo, perfection swept through his voice, and the crowd hushed. Travis hated to join back in. Tears filled the womenfolk's eyes, and wide smiles spread across the men's faces. When they finished, Jake Weathers pulled his arthritic knees up and clapped.

"Some say it ain't right to clap in church, but I'm clappin' for the fine voice God has given this boy—by golly, given to both of you."

Others joined in. Travis was proud, as proud as if Michael Paul were his very own son.

Bonnie stepped out of Morgan's law office into a chilling rain. She raised her umbrella and frowned—not at the nasty weather, but at the man approaching her. *Lester Hillman.* The mere sight of him made her want to take a trip to the outhouse. God forgive her, but Zack was right. The man had an evil streak, and it seemed the only people in town who were aware of it were she and Zack.

He tipped his very expensive hat while holding an umbrella. "Good morning, Mrs. Kahler. You look lovely today."

"Thank you."

"I hear Zack is doing well under Brother Whitworth's tutelage."

"Indeed he is. We are all quite encouraged." Why couldn't Lester be this mannerly all of the time?

"I miss our little visits."

"Pardon me?"

"You know exactly what I mean." His voice sounded low and seductive. "We could have had some pleasant times if you hadn't been so prim and proper."

Bonnie reached up to slap his face, but he caught her wrist.

"You are a filthy pig," she said. "How do you run the bank when you're so busy preying on women?"

"What do you mean by that? You're attracted to me, and you know it. Sylvia never need learn about it."

The door of the law office swung open. "Get your hands off my sister."

"Maybe you should teach her some manners." Lester released her wrist, but his face brimmed with arrogance.

"You might think you can tell other folks in this town what to do, but not the Andrews family." Morgan's voice roared above the rain.

Lester chuckled. "Ask your sister about her affair with Brother Whitworth."

This time Bonnie did slap him. "Take your lies and get out of my way. Why Sylvia puts up with the likes of you amazes me."

Morgan grabbed him by the collar. "If I ever hear of you speaking to my sister like this again or threatening her name, I'll personally escort you out of town."

"You and your brother have always been good at taking the law into your own hands."

"The law speaks for me when it comes to the likes of you."

Lester laughed. "Imagine what the good folks of this town will think when they learn the new preacher and the Widow Kahler are having an affair—and Morgan Andrews condones it."

"You disgusting liar," Bonnie said. "Who would ever believe you?"

"All those fine folks who have allowed me to take care of them when they didn't have the money for food or doctoring." Lester whirled around and stepped out across the street.

Bonnie clenched her fists. Lester had a lot of people fooled, but the truth always had a way of surfacing.

"Little sister, if he ever approaches you again, I want to know about it."

"I'd be glad to let you know, if I don't stick his backside with the other end of a pitchfork first."

Shock registered across his face. "When did you get that spunk?"

"When I realized a small stick of dynamite could tear up a lot of ground." She turned toward Lester making his way across the mud-filled street. "Morgan, thanks for what you did. I don't like that man, and God forgive me if that's wrong." She swung her attention back to her brother.

"You're not alone."

His words were a comfort. "He's capable of spreading gossip. With Brother Travis keeping Zack, folks could easily believe his lies."

Morgan's gaze swept beyond her, as though his thoughts were in the past. "You'd think he'd be grateful for the town's forgiving nature after what he did to Sylvia."

"Lester doesn't understand anything but what he can do for himself." Bonnie fretted over telling Morgan about the wine. She chose not to. "Should I speak with Brother Travis about Lester's threat?"

Morgan hesitated. "Maybe so. I can visit with him for you."

"No, thank you. I can do this." She smiled despite the dire circumstances. "Your little sister should have grown up a long time ago. Morgan, you're soaked."

He glanced at his wet jacket and trousers. "I was so mad that I didn't take notice."

She shook her head and twisted the knob on his office door. "Best you get inside, or you'll catch your death of cold."

Morgan grinned. "For a moment there, I thought I was dealing with Mama."

"Thank you." And she meant it. In his dry office, Bonnie set her umbrella on the floor. Water splattered around it.

"Michael Paul did a fine job last Sunday night with his song," Morgan said.

She nodded. "Brother Travis has helped us in more ways than I could list."

He studied her curiously, but she continued.

"That's why I want him to hear about Lester's accusation from me. I'll stay on the porch to keep wagging tongues from having any more kindling."

Travis smelled something horrible—like burning beans. He should have learned by now that he couldn't tend to more than one thing at a time. He jumped up from the table and carried the pot from the cookstove to the back porch.

"There goes dinner again." Zack lifted his head from his reading. "I think God is punishing you."

Frustration inched through Travis. He stepped back inside and glared at Zack. "And why is He punishing me?"

"Shakespeare. No one should be forced to read this."

"Maybe God is punishing you, because now all we have for dinner is eggs and bread with no butter."

Zack laughed. Good. Very good. A boy needed to laugh.

"When are we going fishing?" Zack asked.

"Not today. It's pouring down rain."

"I was thinking about Saturday—maybe asking Michael Paul and Lydia Anne to go along."

A warm sensation traversed through Travis's heart. "A fine idea. Real fine. Hope it's all right with your mama."

"She'll welcome it, and she can fry up some tasty fish."

"Maybe I need to take lessons."

Zack eyed him curiously. "Brother Travis, why do you wear clothes that are too big? And the only time you wear your spectacles is when we go somewhere. Seems like you stumble more with 'em on than without."

How do I get out of this mess without lying? "Oh, a man sometimes has to do things to get by."

The puzzled look on Zack's face told Travis that he hadn't satisfied the boy at all.

"I mean when the time is right, things will be different."

"You make no sense at all," Zack said.

Travis glanced up. "Mercy, your mama's here. We can ask her about going fishing on Saturday."

"See. God wants us to go fishing."

Travis punched Zack lightly on the arm before answering the door. Bonnie wore a deep blue skirt and a lacy white blouse with buttons. The rain dripped off her umbrella, but she looked beautiful. She always did.

"How are you this afternoon?" he asked. "Staying dry?"

She looked pale and offered a shaky smile. "I think I've been better."

Zack made his way onto the front porch and gave his mother a hug. "Do you need to talk to Brother Travis alone?"

"Yes, son, I do."

"I'll just take a walk over to Grandma and Grandpa's."

Travis crossed his arms over his chest. "In the rain? Are you going to get an invite for dinner?"

"My grandma recognizes a starving boy when she sees one."

Travis shook his head. "Get going then, but you aren't finished with Shakespeare."

He grinned. "Mama, can Michael Paul and Lydia Anne go fishing with me and Brother Travis on Saturday?"

"Brother Travis and me," Travis said.

Bonnie smiled. "Of course. I'll pack you a picnic lunch."

Zack planted a kiss on her cheek and bounded off the porch and into the downpour. Bonnie sighed and glanced around. "He's doing so well. Heaven will bless you for all of your hard work."

I was blessed the moment you arrived. "Come inside out of the rain, Bonnie. What do you need to talk about?"

"I best stay out here on the porch. Doesn't look proper for me to be inside your house without Zack."

"You're right. I'm sorry to make the invite."

She sighed. "Lester Hillman is not happy with me. You know the story."

"Yes, ma'am. Is he trying to get you to drink again?"

"Worse than that. When I refused to see him, he said a few things that were not appropriate. Then he threatened me."

Travis felt his face redden. "Then we need to talk to the sheriff or your brothers."

"No need. Morgan was there. I—I hit him. I mean Lester. Slapped him across the face. I suppose that was a sin, but it sure felt good."

He wanted to laugh. The idea of tiny Bonnie walloping big old Lester was better than lit candles on a Christmas tree.

"In front of the town's lawyer? Your brother? In the rain?"

Her eyes widened. "Are you making fun of me?"

"Yes."

"At least you're honest."

"Have to be. I'm a preacher."

Her lips turned up, and she began to laugh. His began as a chuckle, then a roar.

"Did you flatten him in the street?" Travis finally asked.

"No. But I thought he'd look quite dandy in the mud." Suddenly she sobered. "He was really angry. He said that you and I. . . Well, you and I were—"

Travis understood exactly what Lester had insinuated. "Were behaving shamelessly?"

She stared at her folded hands. "That's it exactly. I wanted to warn you because he might tell others."

He rubbed his palms together. No man should be allowed to bully a woman. "Maybe I should have a talk with him."

"Might make it worse."

"Lester's not happy with me, either." *Lord, is it going to happen all over again? But this is different, isn't it? Bonnie is good and kind and respectable.*

"Do I dare ask why?"

"He tried to tell me how to manage the church, and I refused to follow his direction."

"I see. Is there anything my family can do?"

She tilted her head, and he grew even warmer. Travis needed help. This woman had stolen his heart, and he couldn't do a thing about it.

"Nothing except pray. Lester. . .well he's like a drowning man. I want to see him get saved, but he has to reach out for help." He thought about the many people who did not know what Jesus had done for them. "I could give a few sermons about the evils of gossip."

"That might help. Everyone knows Lester gives a lot to the church," she said. "Some folks befriend him because of it."

"But that doesn't mean it's his church. It's not mine, either. The church belongs to God. He'll handle Lester. In the meantime, we need to be ready for whatever he throws our way."

"I'd rather have the devil throw dirt in my face."

Would this woman never cease to amaze him? "You and I have a way of upsetting Lester. I'm not concerned." But he was. The problem could explode like the situation had at his other church.

"This is not exactly an enjoyable thing to have in common." She moistened her lips. "I guess we have two. I forgot about Zack."

"Zack is getting better—and at times he's good company."

She giggled. "I ought to cry over this, and here I am laughing."

"It's the best medicine. I imagine Doc Grant says that."

She nodded, but her eyes misted. He wanted to take her hand and tell her Lester Hillman would never bother her again, but he couldn't guarantee that. If the truth surfaced, Travis wasn't much better of a man than Lester.

CHAPTER  18

"I can't tell if it's going to rain again or not," Travis peered up into the sky. Gray clouds rushed away from them like bubbles in a washtub. Maybe the nasty weather had decided to let them go fishing after all.

"I have a feeling in my bones that the sun will come out," Zack said.

"You sound like Jake Weathers."

Zack limped across the porch in a grand imitation of old Jake and his bad knees. "Good preachin' this mornin'," he said in Jake's booming voice.

Travis laughed. "Hush, before we both get into trouble. All right, let's go. A mess of fried fish sounds good."

They saddled up their horses and rode carrying fishing poles. The Morning Star had the buckets, and Bonnie had promised the other two children would dig for worms.

At the ranch, Michael Paul and Lydia waited outside. Excitement sparkled from their faces as though the circus had come to town.

"Mama has a big lunch for us." Lydia Anne spread her arms wide. "And we're going to have fish for dinner. Lots of it."

Travis swung down from his horse and gave her a hug. For certain, she was the spittin' image of her mama.

"Sure glad it quit raining," Michael Paul said. "Though it made digging for worms easier. We have a whole bucketful."

Travis tousled the boy's hair. *Lord, I hope loving these three as much as I do is all right.* Sometimes his mind wandered to other thoughts—grand ones, except it took only a pinch of reality for him to understand those kinds of dreams weren't for the likes of a preacher who had a shady past.

Zack lifted Lydia Anne into his arms. "You're growing, tadpole."

She giggled. "Mama has taught me how to ride. Next week she's gonna let me ride without a saddle."

Zack laughed. "Whoa, like an Indian princess?"

"Yes, and then we're gonna race everybody in the county." Her blond pigtails bounced with every word. "Mama says we'll win 'cause we're wrong women."

Zack laughed. "You mean strong women?"

She nodded.

Bonnie stepped out onto the back porch with a huge basket. Travis's stomach did a little flip, but he tried to ignore it. When he took the basket from her, he noticed a hint of pink to her cheeks. Ignoring his unsettling emotions, he set their packed lunch on the awaiting wagon.

"Want to join us?" he asked. Hope raised a notch.

She smiled and shook her head. "Not this time. Juanita and I have more than a week's worth of laundry to do after all the rain." She tilted her head and folded her arms across her chest. "Take care of my children, Brother Travis."

"You know I will."

She sighed. "If not for all of this work and my children running out of clothes to wear, I'd be bringing my pole. Maybe next time."

Yes, maybe next time.

A few moments later, the small band took a wagon path that wound through the Morning Star Ranch. Travis started singing "Nobody Knows the Trouble I've Seen." Michael Paul joined in, and soon Zack and Lydia Anne were singing. Travis remembered how that song stayed fixed in his head during the six months he'd stayed alone in a Tennessee cabin while he waited for God to give him direction. The old slave song meant more than a freeing from captivity for him; it meant a total dependency upon Jesus for all of his problems and needs.

"We sound right good," he said. "Maybe we all ought to sing together in church."

"No thanks," Zack said. "I sing worse than Miss Scott at choir rehearsal."

"Now, Zack." Travis fought the urge to laugh.

"I don't think anyone sounds as bad as she does," Michael Paul said.

"You forget she has a wonderful heart for the Lord, and I hear she does a mighty fine job teaching," Travis said. "We all have special gifts to use for others."

"And singin' ain't one of them for Miss Scott or me," Zack said. "I mean *isn't* one of them."

Travis elected to change the subject before the talk about the schoolteacher got out of hand. "Would you look at all this beauty around us? Here it is mid-November, the grass is green, and we barely need a jacket. Where I come from, it's colder, and the mountains can see more than one snowfall."

"But you like it better here, right?" Lydia Anne asked.

"I do. I really do." Oh, how he loved this spot of paradise called Texas and the folks who made him feel welcome.

"Do you have brothers and sisters and a mama?" Lydia Anne asked.

"Sure do. Five brothers, two sisters, and God-loving parents."

"And you miss them?" the little girl asked. "I don't remember my papa, but I miss him anyway."

He swung her a smile. "Early in the morning before the sun comes up, I think about home. Sometimes I can smell coffee brewing and breakfast cooking. I see my father sitting on the front porch in his rocker and smoking his pipe—all the little curls of smoke rising above his white head. If I think on it long enough, I hear Mama humming a hymn. When I was a boy, I used to count the wrinkles in her face. She told me they were from frettin' about her children."

"She must be very old," Michael Paul said.

"I'm the youngest."

"How old is the oldest?" Michael Paul continued.

Travis chuckled. "He's forty-three, and we're ten years apart."

"You're just a few years older than our mama." Zack studied him curiously.

Travis had regretted his response the moment the words left his mouth. His disguise of looking older would no longer fool the twelve-year-old.

"I'd appreciate it if you'd keep my age to yourself," Travis said. "I prefer folks thinking I'm real old."

"Why?" Zack asked.

"Makes him look like a better preacher," Michael Paul said. "Grandpa is real old, and he's good."

Thank you. "Hey, is that the creek up ahead beyond those trees?"

"Sure is," Zack said. "We'll do us some fine fishing today."

The day trailed on, and the fish were in the mood to get caught. Lydia Anne fished until she got tired, and then she played on the riverbank. With her chattering, it was a wonder the fish continued to nibble on their lines. When the sun shone straight overhead, they ate the fried chicken, green beans, biscuits, and raisin cookies packed away in the wagon. Travis wanted the day never to end, and from the laughter greeting him, the children felt the same.

Clouds moved in, and a stillness caused Travis to take note of their surroundings. He studied the sky turning a hideous shade of yellow-green, the same color he often imagined the eyes of demons. The air grew thick, and the weight of it pressed down uncomfortably upon his chest, while the hairs on his neck bristled. A strange sensation in his ears moved him to search all around for signs of danger. Not a hint of a breeze rustled, nor did a bird or an animal utter a sound of life. In the distance, thunder rumbled its warning. He felt Zack's gaze upon him; the boy felt the same foreboding. *Why hadn't he noticed the change in weather?*

"I think we've caught enough fish for one day." Travis pulled his empty pole from the water and noticed a crafty fish had stolen his worm. "This must be a sign for us to head back. The fish are stealing our bait."

"Do we have to leave now?" Michael Paul asked. "Y'all have more fish than me."

"It's fixin' to rain, and from the looks of the sky, it'll storm." Travis grinned. "I don't mind getting wet, but lightning has my respect."

Michael Paul stared up at the strange-looking sky. "I've never seen the sky green before." He pointed toward the east. "Reminds me of the moss under the walking bridge behind our house."

Lydia Anne stood to get a better look, her upturned nose perpendicular to the ground beneath her feet. "I don't like thunder or lightning. Why does everything smell funny?"

"It's the worms," Zack said. "Let me help you with your pole. I'll carry you to the wagon on my back."

"Oh, would you, Zack?" She handed him her pole. "I'm ready. I like you better since you're nice."

He grinned. "You only say I'm nice so I'll give you a ride." He bent down, and she wrapped her little legs around his back and curled her hands around his neck. A crack of thunder caused her to gasp. "One, two, three, four." Lightning flashed. "Oh, I don't like this at all."

Travis sensed Zack's gaze upon him. He hadn't fooled the boy for an instant.

Zack pulled a fish from his pole and threw it back in. "We don't need it," he said to a questioning Michael Paul. "Here, you take the fish bucket, and I'll grab the poles."

Travis snatched up the remains from their picnic and hastily packed them onto the wagon bed. He untied the mare and noted her ears lay back flat against her head. She pawed at the ground, then snorted. The deadly still air sent a silent message. Thunder reverberated around them, sounding like a tree had snapped in two. Immediately, lightning zigzagged across a dark blue sky.

Lydia Anne glanced around her. "What happened to the wind?"

"It's quiet so you can sleep in the back of the wagon," Zack said. "Here, I'll sit in the back with you, and Michael Paul can ride beside Brother Travis."

The little girl seemed satisfied and snuggled up against her brother's chest.

Within moments, the horse and wagon trotted along the road, but the air gave Travis a disconcerting awareness, making him feel slightly dizzy. The pleasant November afternoon had changed into a devil's brew of evil. And they were in the middle of it.

"Brother Travis." Zack pointed to the left.

Travis turned his attention and caught a whirlwind twist against a backdrop of a green sky. It was heading straight toward them.

Oh, God, no. He searched the terrain for safety. At least they were out of the grove of pine and oak trees, but they didn't need to be the tallest objects when the lightning decided to strike. He couldn't drive the wagon straight into the twister; neither did he relish the thought of attempting to outrun it on foot with three children.

"We're right in its path." Travis pulled the horse and wagon to a halt. The children scrambled out. Travis pulled Lydia Anne from Zack's arms, and the boy rushed around to the frightened mare and freed her from the wagon. Rain began to fall in heavy drops that felt like stones pelting their bodies. Lydia Anne cried out, and Travis tried to shelter her with his arm. The driving rain transformed into marble-sized hail and attacked their rain-soaked bodies. This time the little girl screamed, but the boys were silent, perhaps too frightened to speak.

"I see a low spot beneath a hill over there." Travis shouted and pointed to a crevice to the right of them.

Zack tugged at Michael Paul's hand and raced toward their only source of shelter. Travis prayed harder than he could ever remember. Fear mounted in each breath, and each step reminded him of how quickly life could be swept away. The area safest from the tornado set them up as targets for the lightning.

God, I am so scared for these children. They are helpless against the force of this awful wind. I don't care for my life, but for them, I pray Your divine protection.

They headed toward a small indentation at the bottom of a hill. Travis gathered the three together with the boys on each side of Lydia Anne and laid his own body over the top of them. He looked up and shuddered. In the blinding rain, he saw a swirl of wind move on their heels. A sound like a growling beast met his ears, growing louder and louder. Then came an eerie roar that reminded him of a mighty train barrelling down the tracks.

"Pray!" he shouted over the twister's roar. "Pray, children, for our Lord to protect us." He felt Lydia Anne and Michael Paul's bodies shiver, but Zack remained still.

The ground shook, and the sound of nature burst forth like a hundred cannons firing in his ears. He was afraid for himself, too. *If death be for us all, then let it come quickly. But remember these little ones who deserve to live and tell of Your mighty deliverance.*

As quickly as the green sky had spread a net of dread and terror around them, so did the fear dissipate as nature's fury whirled away. The rain softened and slowly stopped. Travis lifted himself from the children, greatly concerned for the well-being of the little girl who lay beneath him. A single tear rolled over his cheek as he viewed each unharmed child entrusted to his care. His gaze focused on the show of nature's destruction all around them. Not five feet from them, a splintered pine had been tossed and thrown much like Zack might have tossed a load of firewood. What trees hadn't been uprooted were bent and leaned precariously to the ground. Travis and the children turned in all directions. Their faces grew pale at the devastation surrounding them. There was no sign of the wagon.

In the middle of the same shattered grove of pines from which they had run to escape falling branches stood a small straight pine, unaffected by the twister.

"That tree is like us," Michael Paul said. "The twister didn't bother it at all."

Travis smiled and wiped his wet eyes. "We need to get on our knees and thank God for delivering us today."

Solemnly, each of them knelt in a circle and held hands while Travis thanked God for His protection. "Is there anything any of you want to say?" he asked. For a moment, only silence met his ears.

"Dear Jesus, I was so scared that I forgot to pray for Mama to be safe," Michael Paul said. "So, if it is not too late, I pray for her, Juanita, Thomas, and the other ranch hands to be all right in the storm cellar and for them not to worry about us."

"Thank You, Jesus, for Brother Travis," Lydia Anne said. "We would have blowed away if he hadn't asked You to save us."

Several more moments of silence followed. When Travis opened his eyes to view Zack, he saw the boy crying silently. "Are you all right?"

The boy nodded. He lifted his head, and the tears continued to flow.

"Would you like to talk, or do you want us to leave you alone?" Travis wanted to take him into his arms and comfort him much like his father would have done, but his attempts in the past had not been well met.

Zack's water-filled gaze bore straight into Travis. "I need to say something," he said. "While I lay on the ground listening to you pray for us, I realized I wanted to be just like you. I wanted Jesus in my life like Grandpa and you talk about. I wanted to live to tell you that I'm sorry for being rude and mean to you, Michael Paul, Lydia Anne, Mama, and all of the other folks around me. I told Jesus I was sorry and asked Him to forgive me. I told Him I deserved to die and let the rest of you live. Y'all are good, and I'm bad. But I want to be good." He swallowed hard. "Jesus must have heard me, for a wonderful feeling came over me. I wasn't afraid anymore. I think Jesus must have come into my heart 'cause He made me feel like nothing would really hurt me or you. . . . Is that what happened, Brother Travis?"

Travis nodded and reached for Zack. Several long moments passed while the boy sobbed and Travis held him.

"I never cried when Papa died," he said.

"Then you go ahead and cry it all out now, Zack."

"I'm sorry for all the mean things I've done."

"I know, and God forgave you."

"You can call me 'son' anytime you want to."

"Thank you."

"And I really do love Mama."

"Perhaps you can tell her that very thing."

"I will, and if she doesn't listen, I'll keep telling her until she does."

"What's the matter with Zack?" Lydia Anne asked.

"Don't you know, Lydia Anne? He got saved," Michael Paul whispered.

When Zack no longer held a single tear, Travis suggested they make their way back home. The rain had soaked them through, and it was a good two miles to warm clothes and their mother's arms. He hoped Mrs. Kahler and the others had found safety from the twister.

Lydia Anne wanted to walk. She said she was a big girl now. For a while, they named the things they were thankful for. Zack talked about his father, remembering the good times they'd shared together.

Travis saw Lydia Anne begin to lag behind, and he wordlessly lifted her into his arms. She wrapped her arms around him and kissed his neck through his heavy beard. At that moment, Travis realized how much he needed these children and their mother. He desperately wanted all of them in his life, permanently. A miracle had to take place for that to happen. A beautiful woman like Bonnie Kahler could have any man she wanted, certainly not a down-and-out mountain man of a preacher who covered the truth with baggy clothes and a mass of hair. It was then that God showed Travis the reasons He had called him to Kahlerville.

Heavenly Father, I thank You again for saving us today. It was another reminder of Your powerful love. Thank You for sending Your Son to die for our sins. Help me to daily take up the cross and follow You no matter where You lead. I don't have to understand the whys of my life; I only have to live in loving obedience to You. Thank You for Zack's decision. He needs strength and courage to turn from his past. Thank You for the many questions You've answered for me today. Show me the way, Lord. Show me how to help those around me. I pray for all those caught in the path of the twister. Lord Jesus, I love You with all of my heart. Teach me to be a man after Your own heart.

"Brother Travis?" Zack asked.

"Yes."

"How many do you suppose got hurt in the twister?"

"I hate to say. I hope none."

"Why does God let some things happen to some people and not to others?" Zack asked.

Travis gathered his thoughts. Zack's question was as old as mankind. "Sometimes God stretches out His hand and protects us from the storms of life, and sometimes He walks with us when the strong winds blow."

"What did He do today?" Zack asked.

Travis paused a moment. "I think He did both."

"Mama's safe, isn't she?" Lydia Anne asked.

Suddenly Zack took off in a run, and Michael Paul trailed close behind.

"Where are they going?" she asked.

Travis couldn't decide whether to call them back or pray Bonnie had taken shelter with all the others at the ranch. "They're hurrying to tell your Mama we're all right."

Lydia Anne nestled against his chest. "Good. Brother Whitworth?"

"Yes."

"I like your hair and beard. Reminds me of a bird's nest."

He chuckled. "I'll take that as a compliment."

"We have to hurry to Mama," she said.

A weight settled on Travis's chest. Bonnie had to be safe. She had to be.

CHAPTER 19

Bonnie, Juanita, Thomas, and three ranch hands crawled out of the dark, damp storm cellar. Bonnie hated it there. Usually snakes slithered about, and today had been no exception. One of the ranch hands had killed a copperhead, but she hadn't been nearly as frightened as in the past. Fear for her children took precedence. When she refused to take shelter just before the twister hit, Thomas had picked her up and carried her inside the storm cellar.

"I've got to search for the children and Brother Travis." She glanced about at the downed trees and surveyed the damage. "And what about our own missing men?"

"I'll find the children and the men." Thomas touched her arm. "You stay here 'cause that's where your family will look for you."

"I have to do something. I'll go insane waiting." She took a deep breath. "I'm sorry I screamed at you. You did the right thing. I thought I was doing wrong by making sure I was safe from the twister while the children and Brother Travis were out there. . .somewhere."

He smiled sadly, then lifted his hat and combed his fingers through silver hair. "Given the same situation, I'd have gone looking for them, too. Pray now. That's the best thing you can do for 'em."

"Brother Travis is a smart man. I'm sure he found shelter. But. . ." Her thoughts left her with memories of past twisters and what happened to those caught in their path.

"I'll hurry." Thomas's gaze swept to Juanita.

"I stay with her," Juanita said. "No worry."

The other two men saddled up and rode in different directions to search for missing men while Thomas disappeared down the path to the river where Brother Travis and the children had headed to go fishing. Bonnie heard the mention of the barn roof suffering damage, and a side of the bunkhouse lay in splintered wood. Later, when everyone was accounted for, she'd assess the damage. Right now, she needed to see her precious children unhurt. Brother Travis had promised to take care of them. He'd have found shelter. She had to believe it.

Juanita wrapped her arms around Bonnie's waist. "We must pray everyone all right."

Bonnie nodded. "Seems like my every breath is a prayer."

"Sí. Mine, too." Juanita blinked and turned her head.

"I wonder about other ranches. And what if the twister struck Kahlerville?"

"One thing at a time," Juanita said. "Our family, our friends first."

Bonnie forced a smile and gazed into Juanita's face. "You and Thomas have something very special. Hold on to it, and never let it go."

"We didn't think anyone knew."

"You may have hid it from the ranch hands, but I saw that special sparkle in yours and Thomas's eyes a long time ago."

Juanita flushed. "How sweet of you to be thinking of us now."

Bonnie sucked in a breath to keep from crying. "I have to. I can't bear to think of anything happening to my children. . .or anyone else, for that matter."

Bonnie couldn't utter another word. She'd prayed for Ben, and he filled a cold grave. Maybe that's why she despised the storm cellar. *No, God, please don't let me bury one of my children, too.*

Bonnie sat in the grass and watched the wagon path to the river.

Many things needed to be done, but she refused to budge until she could reach out and touch her children. She pulled her knees up to her chest and held Juanita's hand beside her.

"You've been with me since Ben built this house," she said.

"We're *amigas*."

"Yes, we are."

"Zack was a baby," Juanita said. "Not even crawling yet."

Bonnie remembered moving into the new home. Ben had carried her inside while she held Zack. They'd laughed and talked about the future.

"I want eight children," she'd told him that day. "And all of them must look like their papa."

He'd kissed her soundly and declared his love.

A tear slipped from her eye. Had she truly told him enough times how very much she loved him?

"Michael Paul was my best baby," Bonnie said to Juanita. "Remember how he slept through the night when he was only four months old?"

"Lydia Anne's good, too."

"Oh, Ben spoiled her rotten, but she's a sweet little girl now." She tilted her head and remembered when each child had learned to walk, their first words, and how she had begged Ben for more children until she learned the truth about his horrible cough.

"Ben was a good man," Juanita said.

"I was thinking the same thing. I wish I'd been stronger and not leaned on him like he was my father instead of my husband." She shrugged and squeezed Juanita's hand.

"Brother Travis is a good man."

"Yes, he is." Bonnie wondered if Juanita meant to comment on anything more than his good works.

"I like him much."

"So do I."

"I know."

Before Bonnie could deliberate Juanita's remark any further, she saw a figure running in the distance. A lump took root in her throat.

"Oh, my." She scrambled to her feet, catching her shoe on the hem of her skirt, and grabbing onto Juanita to keep from falling. Was she seeing things, or was her Zack running toward her? Her heart pounded so that it hurt. Emotion slammed against her chest. *He's running to me!*

Zack waved and called her name.

She lifted her skirts and rushed toward him. Tears fell unchecked, nearly blinding her. Several feet behind him ran Michael Paul.

Zack seemed to fly to her, then stopped abruptly. "I was afraid something might have happened to you."

She shook her head, her hands itching to hold him. "I feared the same for you, all of you."

"We're all fine. The Lord used Brother Travis to save us from the twister." He dragged his tongue over dry lips. "I'm sorry, Mama, for all the trouble I've caused—hurting you, being mean. I want to be a good son. . .and help you with Michael Paul, Lydia Anne, and the ranch. Papa would have wanted that, and I've let everyone down. Mostly God."

"I forgave you when it happened. We've had terrible grief, son."

"But it's no excuse for the things I've done."

"Or the things I've done. But we have the future."

"I believe that, Mama. I got saved when the twister whirled around us. Asked Jesus to live inside me."

All the emotion simmering since the sky turned green burst forth as though a dam filled with love broke inside her. She held out her arms to her precious son, and he fell into her embrace. Each was crying and holding on to the other.

Bonnie had no idea how much time had passed, but when she looked up, Michael Paul stood before her, as well as Brother Travis, who was holding Lydia Anne.

"Thank you." She smiled into his face as she opened her arms for her other children. Staring into the kind face of the man who seemed to have an endless supply of love, she realized her feelings for him had begun to change into something that frightened her.

"We were in a miracle," Lydia Anne said.

Bonnie kissed her while the little girl still rested in Travis's arms. "Don't you mean a twister?"

She shook her head, and her pigtails flew. "No, Mama. Trees fell down around us and everything, but Jesus and Brother Travis kept us safe. Isn't that right, Brother Travis?" Lydia Anne peered up at him.

"It was all Jesus," Brother Travis said. "I was too scared to do anything but pray." He smiled at Zack. "Have you told your mama the good news?"

"Yes, sir," Zack said. "I told her I was living for Jesus now, and I was sorry." He shrugged. "Guess I'm the prodigal son."

Bonnie swallowed to keep from crying again.

"Is everyone else safe?" Brother Travis asked.

Reality shook Bonnie hard. "Two of my men are missing. Thomas and two of the others are looking for them."

"I saw Thomas along the road," Travis said.

"They were out looking for stray cattle. I didn't see how wide the twister's path was to know if they escaped."

"Wide," Brother Travis said. "But if we found shelter, then perhaps your men did, too."

"Looks like the bunkhouse is in bad shape," Zack said. "Brother Travis, you and me—I mean you and *I*—may have a little work to do."

"We could do that." Lines etched Brother Travis's face. Later she'd ask him what happened during the twister, but for now, it was enough to know that her children were safe and unharmed.

Juanita pointed toward the southwest. "Riders come."

Shortly thereafter, Thomas brought in Zack and Travis's missing horses. Behind Thomas, a man was thrown across another horse.

Travis hurried toward them. After entrusting the children to Juanita's care, Bonnie quickly followed.

"Don't come any closer, Miss Bonnie," Thomas said. "It's Roy, and he didn't make it."

She gasped. "Are you sure? We can fetch Grant."

"It's no use," Brother Travis said.

She took another step. They could be wrong. Roy could be unconscious.

"I don't want you to see him," Brother Travis said. "He's not recognizable."

She covered her mouth. *Roy dead!* "I don't think he had any family from around here. His parents were slaves from Mississippi." She peered into Thomas's face. "Do you know of anyone we can contact?"

"Roy never talked of family. I'll wrap him in a blanket and take him into town to the undertaker. Should I take up a collection for the burial?"

"I'll take care of it, and I want to put up a nice gravestone for him at the cemetery," Bonnie said. "If anyone objects, then we'll bury him here on the ranch."

"I should ride along," Brother Travis said.

"No need as long as you can give me a time for the funeral," Thomas replied.

"Tomorrow afternoon at one," Brother Travis said. "I hope he's the only one."

"Haven't found Lance yet," Thomas said.

"The twister moved south, away from town, unless it changed directions," Brother Travis said.

"Once Lance is found, I can send a few of the hands to check on neighboring folks." Thomas turned his attention to Bonnie. "Is that all right?"

"Of course, and if anyone is in need, send them here." Bonnie stared up into Thomas's face. What if he'd been taken? What if her

167

brothers were no longer there to raise their families? What if Mama and the reverend had been caught in the twister's path? What if all that she held dear had been seized and destroyed by the twister's power?

You could go on, Bonnie. I'm with you.

She understood what the voice meant. He'd spoken to her continually since she'd destroyed the bottle of wine. Not only was she an Andrews, but more importantly, she was a child of God. She'd take each day as it came—the good and the ugly, the moments of strength and the times when her very lifeblood seemed to be drained from her soul.

God had plans for her and all those around her. Life would be better because of her son's decision; she could feel it. Zack now knew the source of the courage to face each day and the challenges of growing up without a father. Michael Paul had made that decision shortly after Ben died, and she saw a spiritual awakening in Lydia Anne. Soon all of her children would have their names written in the Book of Life.

Once again, the enormity of the day touched her. Her children had been spared while Roy had died. Lance was missing, and she prayed for him. He and a sweet young lady in Kahlerville planned to marry in the spring. They loved the Lord, and Bonnie wanted a rich life for them.

Lord, I thank You for what you did for me today, and I pray for safety for those who are missing.

"Bonnie?"

She focused on Brother Travis.

"I've been talking to you, but you seemed a million miles away. Are you all right?"

She took a deep breath and nodded. "Yes. We have things to do, gentlemen. Other folks may need us. I'm ready to take on the rest of the day. Thomas, let me know how many more folks will be needing dinner tonight or a place to sleep."

"As strange as it sounds, Lydia Anne and I found a big string of fish," Brother Travis said. "And we found some of the remains of the wagon on the walk back."

His gaze caught hers, and she saw something she'd not seen in a man for a long time. Her earlier realization surfaced. She shivered pleasantly, then she relaxed. One more matter for the good Lord to take care of.

CHAPTER 20

The ranch hands found Lance with a broken arm and black and blue ribs where a tree branch had fallen on him. He rode in the back of the wagon with Roy's body to Kahlerville so Grant could patch him up.

"Are you sure you don't need me to accompany you to town?" Travis asked Thomas.

"Naw. If other folks show up at the ranch, Miss Bonnie will need you here."

"Zack and I will be along later." Travis turned to Zack, who had not been far from his side since the twister.

"Can I speak with you a moment?" Concern rippled through the boy's voice.

"Sure, what's bothering you?"

"If you don't mind, I'm not ready to move back home."

The announcement didn't surprise Travis. "I'm fine with you living with me. You're good company, and I have someone to practice my cooking and sermons on." Truth be known, he'd grown right fond of the boy, and now that Zack had a relationship with the Lord, they'd have more good times than bad ones.

"Thanks. Maybe Mama can show you a few things about the cooking part."

"Well, we can ask her." He clamped a hand on Zack's shoulder.

"I'm proud of you. Today could have made you angrier than before."

"But it didn't. Do I still need to write those papers about the people in my life?"

Travis raised a brow.

Zack grinned. "Didn't think it would hurt to ask."

Travis believed the War Between the States had settled the issues about blacks and whites, but a lot of folks didn't share those beliefs. And that included many white Christians. The man before him had tried his patience until Travis bit his tongue to keep from saying exactly what he thought about basing a man's intelligence or spiritual life on the color of his skin.

Through the night sounds of singing insects, Lester Hillman repeated what he'd already said a dozen times. "Piney Woods Cemetery is full of good white folks. Burying a colored man there defaces those holy grounds. Roy Greely isn't welcome there. And the Dawson family made it clear to me that their mother wasn't going to be laid in the same cemetery as Greely."

"I think you've made it perfectly clear how you feel," Travis said. "Show me in the Bible where God says a man has to have white skin to get into heaven."

Lester chuckled. "Then put the man in a black cemetery, but not where we have family and friends. I understand not everyone thinks like I do, but you're about as far south as you can go. We have our beliefs about how life is. My money—"

"I know what your money does, Lester. But it doesn't buy me. Bonnie Kahler requested Roy Greely be buried in Piney Woods Cemetery. I believe she has a few loved ones there, too."

"You'd comply to anything Bonnie requested."

Travis sensed his temper a mere inch from exploding. "I'll forget your last remark."

Lester leaned forward. "Then bury the man somewhere else, or folks are going to get an earful about a lot of things."

"Such as?"

"You and Bonnie. Her drinking. Whatever it takes. I'm not particular."

And you call yourself a God-fearing man? "Fine, Lester. Not because of me, but because of Mrs. Kahler's reputation. Your lies will catch up with you one day. Mark my word. In the meantime, she offered Roy a final resting place on her ranch." He mentally counted to ten, then started over.

Lester stood and scooted his chair back under Travis's kitchen table. "I think you're learning real fast how I control this town. It's a lesson you need to take note of if you want to survive. I don't mind helping folks and the community, but I expect my say in things."

Travis rethought what he wanted to say and rose to his feet. He eyed Lester straight on. "Any power you might have in this town, God will yank away when the time is right. As for me, I don't need or want your money."

"We understand what kind of man you are," Zack said.

Travis whirled around to see his charge leaning against the side of the outside door, hands stuffed in his overalls.

"You need to teach that kid how to respect his elders," Lester said.

"He has." Zack eyed him evenly. "But he's also taught me that folks have to earn respect. I've seen what you tried to do with my mother. I won't forget it, and if I need to, the whole town will know. The only reason I haven't gone to my uncles is because of Mrs. Hillman. She's a good woman, and I'd hate to see her hurt."

Lester raised his hand as if to strike the boy, but Travis stepped in his path. "Try hitting someone more your size. Then explain it to the good people of Kahlerville."

Lester pushed past Travis and shoved Zack to the floor on his way out the door. Travis started after him, but Zack stopped him.

"No harm done, Brother Travis. I'm all right."

Travis clenched his fists. Lester reminded him of men he'd rather forget. Men from his Tennessee home. He reached down and pulled Zack to his feet.

"I'm sorry you saw how my temper nearly got the best of me." Travis shook his head to dispel his anger.

"You saw mine, too, so we're even. Brother Travis, you ain't—I mean *aren't*—anything like I thought a preacher would be."

"What did you expect?"

"You act like. . .a normal man."

Travis chuckled despite the moment. "I am, Zack. I'm no different from any other man. I do my best to let God guide and direct me in all I do—just like every God-fearin' person. The difference with me is I've accepted the calling of shepherding God's people and telling others the good news of the gospel. Someday I'll have to answer to God about the way I've done my job. I strive to be a good example for others, but I still make mistakes. If Lester had hit me, I'd have turned the other cheek, but hurting you is another matter. I think the mountain man in me might've come through."

"If you had hit Lester, would that be a sin?"

Travis tugged at his beard. "To me—and I could be wrong—if I had let him lay his fists into you, that would have been a sin. Fighting's wrong, but sometimes a man has to choose between two wrongs instead of a right and a wrong."

Confusion burrowed into Zack's brow. "Two wrong things? I thought God showed us what was right and wrong."

"Not always." Travis's mind trailed back to Tennessee and Felicia. Seemed like his mind too often slipped back to those days of bad choices and wrong decisions. Guess he'd never figure out what was right until he met his Maker.

"So tomorrow we have two funerals?" Zack asked.

"Yes, son. Mrs. Dawson at ten, and Roy Greely at one."

"I once saw Roy cut his arm on some barbed wire. His blood was the same color as mine. I didn't think about it much at the time, but now I reckon I'll never forget it."

Zack spoke exactly what was on Travis's mind. Couldn't fault the boy for what he'd said to Lester. Nope, couldn't fault him at all.

Bonnie lifted her pen from her journal. She wrote small so as not to waste any of the paper, but some days, she seemed to swell up with things to say. Zack had walked down to the altar at church this morning to show all that he'd made a choice for Jesus. She'd cried like a baby, but her tears were of joy unbounded. Mama and the reverend shed a few tears, too. Ben must be dancing a jig in heaven. After she carefully recorded every word, she leaned back in her chair and daydreamed a little.

This afternoon she'd had an idea, a simply wonderful way to get the young women out of Heaven's Gate and into the beautiful fall weather. When she drove to town tomorrow for her volunteer day, she'd discuss it with Sylvia.

"What do you think about taking the girls on a pecan-gathering and picnic?" Bonnie asked Sylvia the following morning. "We could even make pies the next day."

Sylvia smiled, a special look that lit up her face and rivaled any sunset. "Perfect, Bonnie. A perfect idea. Let's do it tomorrow. The girls are cooped up here far too often. Rosie and Laura have been quiet, rather distant, and Daisy's been staying in her room. Not sure what might be bothering them, so maybe this will brighten their spirits."

"I stopped at Morgan's office this morning. He has plenty of pecans this year and said for us to pick all we want. Should we ask my mother and the reverend? What about Brother Travis and Zack?"

"Sounds like we're going to have an early Thanksgiving," Sylvia said. "I love the idea. Let's tell the girls right now before Laura leaves for work. While we're quilting, we can plan the picnic." She laughed lightly and touched Bonnie's arm. "Let's all take a stroll to Brother Travis's house and give him and Zack a personal invitation." She stepped closer. "You're spending a lot of time with Brother Whitworth. Be careful about wagging tongues."

"Sylvia, where did you hear such nonsense?"

When the woman didn't respond, Bonnie fought to control her temper. "Was it from your husband?"

The woman glanced away, and Bonnie had her answer. Didn't Sylvia ever question Lester's actions?

The suggestion of something different perked the girls' attitudes. However, Bonnie fretted over the saddened looks still persisting on the girls' faces. Only Rosie used to be this way. What had changed?

"We can leave the moment the bank closes on Wednesday noon. I'll make sure Lester doesn't keep Laura a moment longer as he sometimes does," Sylvia said. "We'll have the food and buckets loaded on the wagon. Oh, I dearly love pecan pie, sugared pecans, and about anything else made with pecans."

Bonnie intended to ask the girls individually what bothered them. All of the young women had pasts that would shock most people, but they'd found the Lord and were living for Him. What had robbed them of their joy?

"We'll have a grand time," Sylvia said. "I'd ask Lester, but he always has so much work to do, and he despises ants. What's a picnic without a few bugs?"

Bonnie laughed with her, but suddenly Sylvia's previous statement sent an icy chill to Bonnie's heart. *I'll make sure Lester doesn't keep Laura a moment longer as he sometimes does.* Surely not. Bonnie pushed the nagging thought from her mind, but it crept back in with more force than before.

Lester had proven his treachery to Sylvia some years before, and he'd threatened Bonnie for reasons she'd never figured out. Surely the man would not approach Laura for. . .favors. He'd known these young women when their profession was not what God desired of them, when he had indulged in the same adulterous type of relationship. Now he claimed to protect and take care of them as if he'd always been a pillar of the community. Bonnie shook her head. Lester had nearly destroyed Sylvia a few years ago with his ways; the poor woman didn't deserve history repeating itself. If. . .if Lester was up to no good, would Laura keep quiet to protect Sylvia? The question rang through Bonnie's mind because she had been in that situation herself.

I deceived her, too. I took the wine when I knew deep down she had no knowledge of it. Bonnie studied Laura's face. Anguish creased her lovely features as though plagued with an incurable disease.

Bonnie vowed to tell Sylvia the truth soon. She'd form the words to make it sound like she'd been to blame and not Lester. Perhaps she'd discuss the matter with Brother Travis first. He'd help her put together the right thing to say.

Promptly at noon on Wednesday, a wagonload of women, a picnic large enough to feed an army, and two preachers ambled toward the Double H. Bonnie wished Zack had chosen to come along, but he wanted to work on a carpentry project. Brother Travis had laid out directions for a chest to hold firewood, and Zack was eager to build it.

Sometimes she wondered if he avoided her. Sometimes she realized he did.

Brother Travis started singing, and the others joined in. Before long, they were at the Double H. Casey joined them, swinging her bucket as she walked alongside the wagon en route to a huge grove of pecans. The other women jumped down and joined her while the reverend and Brother Travis drove the wagon.

"I feel a little out of place." The reverend chuckled. "Sure hope you fine ladies don't plan on talking away the day and making Brother Travis and me gather up the pecans."

"You wouldn't want to spoil our fun," Mama said. "Seems only fair that you pick up the pecans and we make the pies."

The reverend swung a glance at Brother Travis. "We're out-numbered, you know."

"I'd be willing to take them up on the offer," Brother Travis said. "Providin' they take turns in bringing Zack and me dinner. My cooking isn't getting much better."

"I gave you and Zack a few good recipes. Easy ones." Bonnie felt as lighthearted as a girl. Juanita had been right. Brother Travis was a good man, and her heart had unknowingly invited him inside. She sensed his gaze and turned her attention his way. Yes, he had been staring, and she didn't mind at all.

The reverend convinced Travis to climb one of the pecan trees while the women placed old quilts around the trunk. He shook the branches, and the pecans landed quite nicely, making them easy to gather.

The day sped by, and for a while, Bonnie let the worries plaguing her mind about those living at Heaven's Gate and Lester's threats fade into tomorrow. Morgan and Grant were watching him, and if he was up to no good, her brothers would have him apprehended.

❧⊙❧

Travis noted how the younger women from Heaven's Gate stayed close to Sylvia. They loved her. Anyone with any sense could see that, and she openly expressed her love for them. But he needed to talk to Sylvia, so he kept one eye out for snakes among the fallen pecans and the other eye on her in hopes of visiting with her in private.

Finally, Sylvia stood alone, staring out over the rolling acres of the Double H. Travis made his way toward her. She turned and smiled wide.

"A pleasant day, don't you think?" she asked. "Just enough of a chill to make us anticipate Thanksgiving and Christmas ahead."

"I agree. After the twister, all of us needed a little break from our hard days."

Lester's insistence upon not burying Roy in the Piney Woods

Cemetery stayed fresh on his mind. Travis had a difficult time believing Sylvia shared her husband's opinions about many of the things the man complained about.

"The young women from Heaven's Gate sure do love you," he said. "Reminds me of a hen with her chicks."

"Oh, and I love them, too. Lester and I never had any children of our own." She paused. A strange look passed over her face. Then she straightened. "These girls are like my own. So I pretend they are."

"That simple?"

She smiled and nodded.

"Lester has a saint for a wife."

She bit into her lip and glanced away. "I understand my husband has made your job a little difficult."

"I believe he's voiced his views on a few matters."

"I'm sorry."

"No need. It's all a part of being a preacher." Travis studied her face and saw exactly what he suspected—a lonely woman. He realized propriety stopped her from talking to him about Lester. In fact, he imagined she led an empty life apart from her volunteer work.

"How is Zack doing in your care? I was real happy to see him come forward on Sunday."

"He's doing fine. I'm right proud of him. The boy's turned into a good scholar."

"Brother Travis, there's something you should know. I—"

"Miss Sylvia," Laura said. "We've decided to gather more pecans. Do you want to help?"

Sylvia touched Travis's arm. "Never mind. Wasn't important."

CHAPTER  21

"I forgot the prayer requests," Travis said, once he and Zack returned from Tuesday night's prayer meeting. With Thanksgiving on Thursday, they'd changed this week's service. He opened his Bible to double check if he'd stuck the piece of paper inside as he normally did.

"Do you want me to fetch them?"

A crash of thunder shook the house.

"No, I'll hurry back to get it before the storm hits."

"Couldn't the requests wait until morning?" Zack asked.

Travis shook his head and laid his Bible on the kitchen table. "I've got myself into a habit of praying for folks night and morning. Done it for years. I won't be long."

"Dodge the lightning. And don't be long, 'cause then I worry."

Travis laughed. Some days that boy acted like an old man. "I'll be back before you bring in a load of firewood off the back porch."

Stepping into the night, Travis saw the sky light up in a jagged streak of lightning. Since the twister, he'd been a mite nervous with nature's fickle temperament. For certain, he'd not waste time.

He hurried past the various businesses and on toward Heaven's Gate. As he passed the house, he shot a glance toward the side and saw the shadowy figures of a man and a woman. Whether it was the previous profession of the occupants or the fact the young women lived alone,

Travis walked across the road to make sure everything at Heaven's Gate was all right. There was a lot of truth in darkness covering sin.

He heard voices and stopped. *Lester and Rosie.*

"No, I won't, and don't ask me again," she said.

Lester chuckled—the overconfident, cocky, grating sound that Travis detested. *Excuse me, Lord.*

"Now, you don't mean it at all, Rosie. We have something special, and you can't deny it."

"I've had enough. You're a hypocrite. You act like you're a God-fearin' man, even read scripture to us; then you come after us like we belong to you."

"You do. And don't forget it."

"Not anymore, Lester. I care too much for Miss Sylvia."

"Every time we have this talk, you get hurt. How stupid are you?"

Lester had beaten Rosie!

"What kind of a man beats a woman who refuses him—a man who has a wife and other women?"

The sharp crack of a hand striking flesh startled Travis. He headed toward them. Bile rose up from his stomach. Lester had beaten Rosie, not once but twice. "Don't you touch her again."

Lester laughed. "Well, if it isn't the preacher coming to pay a call at Heaven's Gate."

"Where is your decency? To think you cover what you've been doing under the blanket of God's work."

Rosie moved away from Lester. "Leave us, Brother Travis. I can take care of myself."

"Like you did when he beat you the last time?"

"You don't understand," she said.

"You're protecting Sylvia?"

Rosie said nothing, and Travis clearly recognized the power Lester held over her.

"Keep walking," Lester said. "This is none of your concern."

"I'm making it mine. The sheriff will learn about this. There are laws to protect the innocent."

"These girls aren't innocent, and threatening me only means trouble for you."

"I don't see how."

"Who do you think the town will believe? An established pillar of the church and community who generously gives to others or a new preacher who nobody knows anything about?"

"Rosie can speak for what's been done."

"No, she won't say a word, because she's tasted my anger. I'm warning you, Preacher, keep out of my business or you're going to be real sorry."

"Listen to him," Rosie said. "Forget about tonight."

"Won't you go with me to see the sheriff?" Travis asked, incredulous that the young woman refused to seek help from the sheriff.

"No, I can't. And if you do, I'll deny it all."

"Why?"

Lester laughed. " 'Cause she's smarter than you."

Rosie walked to the back of the house and up the steps. The creak of the door told Travis she'd gone inside.

"You need to learn a lesson," Lester said. "I've warned you long enough." He took off down the road toward town as another crack of thunder pierced the air.

Travis watched him. In the blackness, the only part of Lester recognizable was his voice—and his arrogance. *Lord, what am I supposed to do with him? He can't get by with what he does, but he picks on weak folks who are afraid of him.*

Travis stared up at the second floor of Heaven's Gate. A faint light from a kerosene lamp shone dimly through a curtain. He vowed to stop Lester, and he didn't have any problem calling on the Andrews men, the reverend, or the sheriff to do it.

❧❧❧

Bonnie said good-bye to Michael Paul and drove the wagon away from the schoolyard. Odd, Miss Scott had not returned Bonnie's wave this morning. She must have other matters on her mind.

"Are you ready to see Grandma?" she asked Lydia Anne.

"How long are we staying?"

"Not too long. I wanted to invite Grandma and Grandpa to Thanksgiving breakfast as well as dinner."

"Brother Travis, too?"

Bonnie sensed a little flip in her stomach. Ever since the twister, Lydia Anne thought Brother Travis hung the moon. And Bonnie's mind tended to drift his way far too many times. Why, he wasn't the least like Ben, and she really had no idea what he looked like beneath that mountain of hair. He could be one hundred years old, and who would know? Except his beard and hair held very little gray. She'd noticed that—and his light brown eyes with little flecks of gold. Mercy, she was behaving like a schoolgirl.

"Mama, is Brother Travis coming, too?"

"We'll ask him and Zack."

Lydia Anne clapped her hands. "Goody."

At the parsonage, Bonnie helped her daughter down from the wagon and took her hand. Mama and the reverend stood in the backyard, each with a cup of coffee.

"Good morning," she called.

The reverend waved, and the older couple made their way toward them while Lydia Anne raced to lessen the distance between them. The reverend snatched her up and swung her into his arms.

"Reverend, she's getting too big for you to lift."

"I'm old," he said, "not weak."

Bonnie turned her attention to her mother. Added lines to her face told of troublesome matters.

"What's wrong? Are you ill?"

"No, I'm fine."

"You're pale. Bad news?"

Mama peered at the reverend. He cleared his throat. "Best tell her, Jocelyn. She needs to hear it from us, not from someone else."

Irritation threatened to rob Bonnie of her festive mood. "Simply tell me."

The reverend planted a kiss on Lydia Anne's cheek. "How about a biscuit and honey?" In the next instant, the two disappeared into the house.

"Please tell me what is going on?" Bonnie asked.

"It's ugly." Mama's tone startled her.

"Gossip or truth?"

"Gossip for sure."

"Then tell me, Mama."

The older woman's face hardened. "You know I despise folks who try to pass lies off as gospel truth."

Bonnie nodded. "Must be a story from a church member."

"Sylvia came by early this morning with a story about you and Brother Travis."

Bonnie shivered. She could only imagine what Mama'd been told. "What kind of a story?" Lester's threats blared across her mind.

"She said one of the girls from Heaven's Gate saw you two together—in an embrace."

"When? How? Which one of the girls? You know that came from Lester. He put her up to it. I'm sure of it."

"I agree, Bonnie. But Sylvia said Lester is taking this information to the deacons, Jenny—"

"She won't believe a word of it."

"Of course not, but the deacons might. But it doesn't matter whether they do or not; the information will discredit you and Brother Travis in the church and community."

Bonnie covered her face. "There's more to the story, Mama. Much more."

"Do you want to tell me?"

In the morning stillness, with the scent of Thanksgiving in the air, Bonnie confessed her past problem with the wine that Lester supplied, his attempt to bully her when she stopped his gifts, and his visits to the Morning Star without Sylvia. Then she told her mother what happened with Morgan during the pouring rain.

"Why does he persist?" Mama asked.

"I'm not sure, but I have an idea." Bonnie dabbed the perspiration on her forehead, and it wasn't even warm.

"I do, too."

Bonnie's gaze flew to Mama's face.

"You're a beautiful woman, and he has a roving eye."

"I thought he might still be upset because Ben refused to sell the ranch." Bonnie closed her eyes. In an instant, the many times Lester continued to bring the bottles even after she'd asked him to stop flashed across her mind. "Sylvia is the most precious woman I know."

"Is this why you haven't told her of your indiscretion? Don't you think she's an intelligent woman who knows what Lester is doing?"

"I hadn't thought of that, but you're right. Then why wouldn't she confront him about his actions?"

"I think she simply loves him. How did Lester threaten you?"

"He said the information would destroy my entire family's fine reputation."

"Hogwash. We've stood against this town with worse."

"What can I do to stop Lester?"

"Probably nothing until he breaks the law. Some folks are going to believe him, and others will ignore the gossip. Perhaps a talk with Jenny and Grant is in order."

Bonnie nodded. "That makes sense since she built Heaven's Gate. She and Grant had a tough time with gossip long before they were married. They'll understand."

"My point. Remember Lester was more than involved with that gossip, too. If you want to take care of a few things this morning, I'll keep Lydia Anne with me."

"But tomorrow's Thanksgiving."

"I'm sure Juanita has everything under control, and Casey and

Jenny are bringing food."

"All right. I'll go see Jenny and Grant now, then Morgan."

"Make sure your older brother keeps his temper in check. The town may be better off without Lester, but let's not have Morgan handle him."

Bonnie smiled. "I'll reason with him. I hope."

A short time later, Bonnie sat in Grant's office with him and Jenny. She described the recent events, including her problem with Lester supplying her with wine. "Before the day is finished, I'll tell Morgan the truth, too." She waited for one of them to speak.

"He wants you dependent on him," Grant said. "I've seen Lester in action. However, I thought after Martha left town with his boys that he might have changed. I mean, he's built an orphanage, and he's the first to contribute to worthy causes."

"I'm going to talk to the girls at Heaven's Gate," Bonnie said. "What could he have done to convince one of them to lie?"

"I have no idea, but I'll try to find out," Jenny said.

"We'll find out together," Grant said. "Lester may think he's bought this town with Sylvia's money, but some of us can't be bought."

"Grant, what do you mean, 'Sylvia's money'?" Bonnie asked.

"Lester wouldn't have a wooden nickel without her, which could be why he didn't follow Martha. If there's one thing in this world I hate, it's wagging tongues, and I need to shut my mouth before I'm guilty of the same thing." He blew out an exasperated sigh. "Let's go see Morgan and get his opinion about all of this."

He took Jenny's hand. "Depending on how many patients I have, we'll head over to Heaven's Gate when I return. I'll be back shortly. Don't you dare go near there until I return, Mrs. Andrews."

Jenny nodded. "Yes, Doctor. I'll do as you ask."

<hr />

"Lester sure is giving us good reason to run him out of town," Morgan said. "I nearly flattened him a week ago when he accused Bonnie and

Brother Travis of the same thing."

"Shall we go see our favorite banker?" Grant asked.

"Ah, I don't think so. That may be exactly what he wants, and I don't relish the thought of playing into his hand. Which one of the residents of Heaven's Gate made the accusation?"

Bonnie's mind focused on each young woman. She'd established a relationship with all of them—and she thought they were close. "I have no idea. All three appear devoted to God, Sylvia, and living upright lives."

"Jenny and I are headed over there to find out as soon as I have a break from patients. I don't want her going over there alone." Grant stood and paced the floor of his brother's law office. "What does Lester really want?"

Morgan glanced at his brother and then at Bonnie. "It could be as simple as our little sister, the ranch. . .or to destroy all of us."

"But why?" Bonnie asked. "Sometimes I think he has a sickness when it comes to. . ."

"Say it, Bonnie. We're your brothers," Morgan said.

"All right. I think he has a problem with being faithful to Sylvia."

"He proved his unfaithfulness a few years ago with Martha," Grant said. "It doesn't help the situation that I delivered his illegitimate sons and persuaded Martha to talk to Morgan about starting a new life away from Kahlerville."

"And I refused to tell him where she moved," Morgan said. "Which leads me back to the idea that he may want to destroy all of us. Most folks in this town let him have his way because he's the banker. But we don't."

"And neither does Brother Travis," Bonnie added.

Grant continued to pace the floor. "I wonder how he feels about the gossip."

"Maybe he doesn't know," Bonnie said. "He spends most of his mornings with Zack."

Morgan stood from his chair. "Let's go pay him a call."

A short while later, the three sat at Travis's kitchen table. Bonnie sent Zack to the parsonage to fetch Lydia Anne and the wagon.

"Lester threatened to spread that rumor," Travis said. "I caught him red-handed doing something no law-abiding, godly man should do, and he ordered me to stay out of his business. I'm real sorry, Bonnie." If she hadn't been there, he might have stated what he saw happen between Rosie and Lester.

"He threatened me with the same. We've come to the conclusion that Lester is more put out with the three of us than you," she said. "I think you got in his way when you refused to follow his orders."

Travis shrugged. "We've had our share of disagreements about different matters. Last night was the worst. And," he hesitated, "I'm not surprised with this at all."

"What do you want done about it?" Morgan asked.

"Church discipline is the first step." Travis shook his head as though frustration was about to get the best of him. "Of course, since he has a witness to his accusations, he may already have that lined up for me instead."

All too soon, Zack returned with Lydia Anne. Nothing had been resolved. No definite steps to be taken.

"I know tomorrow is Thanksgiving, and all the family will be celebrating at the Morning Star, but whatever you decide, please tell me then." Bonnie said. "I'm not too proud to say that I'm concerned about his next move." She gathered up Lydia Anne, kissed her sweet son, and drove home with a heavy heart.

CHAPTER 22

Travis glanced up at Zack. "I need to send you on an errand so I can talk to your uncles."

"This must be about Lester Hillman." Zack dipped the ladle in the water bucket and drank deeply. "I'd like to listen."

"I understand," Travis said. "But I'd rather talk freely and not involve you. You're real close to being a man, but these are serious matters."

Zack nodded. "Grandma was baking pecan pies for tomorrow. I'll go see if she needs a little company."

Once he disappeared, Travis thought through what he'd experienced with Lester and the questions on his mind.

"I'm amazed at the change in Zack," Morgan said. "You will always have my gratitude."

"Thank the Lord for what He's done, not me," Travis said. "I had no training for dealing with him. However, he is a fine boy."

"Guess we don't need to be looking for a military school," Grant said. "And I told him he's welcome at my house anytime."

"We've been talking about his future, what the Lord wants for his life and his talents. Zack's doing fine, real fine. He likes ranching, but he'd like to go to college first. He even talked about being a doctor or a lawyer; then he said he wanted to be his own man."

The brothers laughed. They all understood the strange workings of a young man's heart and mind.

Travis took a breath and forged ahead. "I'd like to have a conversation with you that can't go any further than right here."

Morgan smiled. "I have many of those conversations."

Grant chuckled. "So do I."

"I want to know all about Lester and Sylvia Hillman. I've heard bits and pieces already, but since I'm being accused of behaving improperly with your sister, I want to know what I'm fighting."

Morgan rubbed his palms together. "Do you have information of your own to tell us?"

"Yes, but I need to state what's on my mind first. Lester's a proud man who is fond of being the largest contributor to the church. Most folks think he's a saint because he gives to so many good causes, but I question the reasons why he puts up such an outstanding front. Zack doesn't like Lester, and he has good reasons not to. I need the truth about him before I tell you what I've seen and heard."

"Go ahead, little brother," Morgan said. "You know more about the whole situation than the rest of us."

Grant appeared to deliberate the request. He stood from the chair and paced across the room, opened the curtain, and stared out into the street. Finally he turned around. "I'm not one to gossip. Despise it. Y'all know that. So what I'm about to tell you is the truth, just like you asked."

"I feel the same way. I don't hold any stock in hearsay." Travis hoped and prayed what he'd experienced last night with Lester could somehow be explained away.

"Before Heaven's Gate was built, a brothel stood there. Lester and the woman who owned it were involved for several years. I had firsthand knowledge about their relationship because they had two sons together. I delivered them but kept my mouth shut until a few things happened here in town, and I confided in Ben Kahler, who was sheriff at the time. Through a series of unfortunate incidents, Sylvia found out about Lester and his relationship with the brothel's owner, but she didn't leave him. Shortly afterward, the brothel burned to the ground." He held up his hand. "I know what you're thinking. Sylvia didn't set it on fire; a scoundrel managed that all by himself. The mother of Lester's sons left town, and Sylvia and Lester supposedly worked out their problems. He got back into church and has been a model citizen ever since—despite his past. Our town is a forgiving community. Many fine folks. You already know that Sylvia works tirelessly at Heaven's Gate, a good, good woman. Lester does quite a bit of work there, too, but mostly he tries to find work for the girls who live there and contributes money to keep it running. In the beginning, there were six young women. The other three moved away from town."

"You've confirmed one thing I believe—Sylvia must love Lester more than I could imagine," Travis said. "Or she loves God more and would not consider breaking her marriage vows."

"Probably both." Grant eyed him curiously. "Has Zack given a reason as to why he dislikes Lester?"

"He's made a few comments. One of which puzzles me. He said everybody thought Lester was a fine church man, but there were things about him that folks were afraid to say. Later he said he didn't like the way Lester looked at his mother." Travis stopped. "Zack knew about Lester supplying his mother with wine."

"He's got good reason to dislike him. But stating a man is evil implies Zack has witnessed something else," Morgan said. "He's a twelve-year-old and too young to remember what happened a few years ago. Grant, have you left anything out?"

Grant shook his head. "I never cared for the man and his showy ways, but that's my personal opinion. And the more I learn about what he's doing, the more I'd like to lay a fist alongside his jaw. Pardon me, Brother Travis."

Travis had long since felt the same sentiments, but he dared not reveal it. God was already dealing with him about not loving Lester like he should.

Grant raked his fingers through his hair. "Disgracing Bonnie makes my blood boil, and I can't seem to make sense of him taking offense to her refusing his wine. Unless. . .bringing her the wine guaranteed him a visit there without Sylvia. If he really wanted Bonnie's affections, those visits increased his chances to convince her to his way of thinking."

"So everyone thought he changed after the woman left town and took his boys," Travis said, his thoughts taking voice. "He and Sylvia are real active in the church, but I don't believe for one minute that his heart is committed to God. There's too much about him stating otherwise." He wondered if he'd said enough. Some folks would consider his observations akin to gossip, and he should stick to preachin'.

"You seem to know something you're not saying," Morgan said.

"Must be a lawyer in the midst of us." Travis attempted to add a little humor to the bleak situation. "I hate to keep making accusations against the man without knowing the whole truth, which is why I wanted to have a little more information."

"Since we told you what you asked, what have you experienced?" Morgan asked.

Travis dampened his lips. "Weeks ago when the reverend and I went to see Rosie, she made a statement that stayed fixed in my mind. I've mulled it over, and after last night, I think I understand."

"Don't leave us dangling like two possums," Grant said.

Travis offered a thin-lipped smile. "Lester had just left the room after reading scripture to the three young women housed there. The reverend and I visited briefly with them, mostly Rosie, since she'd just been beaten the night before. As we were leaving, Rosie said the reverend was like Jesus to her. . .then she added Mrs. Hillman, Jenny, Bonnie, and Casey. But she didn't mention Lester, and he'd just left the room."

Morgan set his jaw. "Want me to look into it a little deeper?"

"I sure do. I know I'm a preacher, not a lawman, but we're talking about folks who are a part of my flock."

Grant blew out a heavy sigh and turned to his brother. "Morgan, can you get someone to tail him?"

"That may not be necessary," Travis said. "I caught him at Heaven's Gate last night. I'd forgotten the list of prayer requests and was on my way back to the church when I stepped into a hornet's nest. Lester was talking to Rosie, more like trying to persuade her to do something. Of course it was pitch dark and fixin' to storm, but I recognized both of their voices. She refused his request, and he hit her. I shouted at him to stop. Let me just say, he didn't appreciate my interfering in his business."

"Rosie needs to report what happened to the sheriff," Morgan said.

"I tried to make her see that, but she wanted me to stay out of it. You gentlemen may have already figured this part out, but Lester is the one who beat her."

"No surprise to me," Grant said. "He has to be stopped."

"Well, Rosie isn't the one who'll help us," Travis said. "I'm convinced she's more concerned about Sylvia learning about Lester than her own safety. She told me if I went to the sheriff, she'd deny it. Anyway, Lester told me the church would believe him before they'd believe me. He also said I needed to learn a lesson. The gossip must be what he was referring to."

"Trust me, gentlemen, Lester Hillman has met his match when he takes on this family." Morgan's ice-cold stare gave no doubt to his position. "I will find out his motives for all of this, and I'll put an end to the preying on the womenfolk of Kahlerville. His affair with Martha is not old enough for folks to have completely forgotten what he did to his wife. Let him initiate more gossip, even church discipline for Brother Travis. But he doesn't have the hand of God on his side."

"Amen," Travis said. "Tomorrow is a day of thanks, but I think for us it needs to be a day of prayer for what lies ahead and which road we should take. Bonnie has things she knows. You two have had different encounters with him just as I have. I'd like for us to write down all we've experienced so we can compare the findings."

"Sounds like you should have been a lawyer." Morgan laughed.

Travis joined him. The laughter eased the seriousness of their conversation. "Well, if Lester is successful in his plans, I might need a job."

Grant walked back to the table. "I'll write down all I know, including what I learn at Heaven's Gate today. I'm not so sure I want Jenny there anymore without me. If Lester is threatening Bonnie, Rosie, Brother Travis, and whoever else might get in his way, then my wife might be next." He paused. "Poor Sylvia. I wonder if she really knows her husband."

"I imagine she does." All Travis could think about was Bonnie. *Oh, Lord, haven't we been down this road before? I'm not good at defending women. The last time I lost.* But as much as he vowed he'd never again become involved in separating gossip from truth—and then taking a stand—here he stood knee-deep in it again. His heart ached for Bonnie's happiness and peace of mind. She'd come far, just like Zack, in climbing out of a well of despair and trying desperately to live for the Lord.

Surely Lester had more sense than to hurt her. Morgan and Grant were God-fearing men, but they'd not put up with any more of Lester's tricks. He'd hurt Rosie more than once, and Travis believed she most likely started Lester's gossip—out of fear. Travis had heard the threats. Would the man do the same to Bonnie? What was his motive in all of this?

Sweet Bonnie. She was no match for the man. . .so tiny and frail. . .

Thanksgiving had not been the celebration Bonnie had envisioned, but the entire family was together, and she felt whole for the first time in years. As the children played outside, the women chatted in the parlor and the men walked to the horse barns. Bonnie found it hard to concentrate on women-talk. Recipes, new babies, weddings, and quilt patterns interested her today about as much as a man enjoyed embroidery.

"So are we going to discuss the snake pit here in the middle of us, or pretend the creatures will slither away?" Casey asked.

"Oh, you mean Lester Hillman," Jocelyn said in such a matter-of-fact tone that it was almost amusing. "If I wasn't sixty-six years old, I'd fill his backside with buckshot."

"You're sixty-eight, Mama," Bonnie said. "And is that any kind of talk for a preacher's wife?"

"I was a mama and a wife and handling the recoil of a rifle and shotgun long before the reverend asked me to marry him."

Jenny giggled. "If some of my old friends from back in Ohio could hear our conversation, they'd be mortified." She shrugged. "Until I met Grant and got introduced to real women, I'd have been the same way."

"What are your thoughts about the whole thing?" Bonnie asked Jenny. "Other than packing our guns and running Lester out of town?"

Jenny paused a moment. "I'm remembering why I originally came to Kahlerville. My sister had run away from home, become a woman of questionable employ, and given birth to a baby girl before she passed on. My heart goes out to all the women who have ever found themselves a slave to prostitution. That's why Grant and I built Heaven's Gate." She looked around quickly. "Goodness, all the children are outside, aren't they? I can't believe I was so blunt."

Casey waved her hand. "Yes, we're alone."

"My point is that Heaven's Gate was established to protect those women from the ugliness of that life and to help them get started with changed lives. Lester has taken advantage of his position in the community and church—along with Sylvia's kindness—to frighten

Rosie into a life far too similar to what she led before. He makes me want to do things a good Christian woman shouldn't ever consider. Sometimes I wonder about Sylvia. Does she ever let him know that he's not following God's path?"

"Probably not," Mama said. "Why she loves that man is far beyond me."

"You might have noticed that he hasn't been bothering me," Casey said. "For once, I'm glad my past reputation as an outlaw has scared him off."

The women laughed, and Bonnie thanked God for her precious family.

"Honestly," Jocelyn said. "I feel badly about Brother Travis. He's in the heart of a mess that he didn't bargain for in accepting the call to pastor Piney Woods Church."

"I cannot let the day go by without giving him my personal condolences regarding all the trouble I have brought his way," Bonnie said. "I owe him my gratitude for what he's done for Zack. Instead, he's a victim of gossip."

"Are you sure those are your only feelings?" Jocelyn asked. "Daughter, you have changed considerably since Brother Travis arrived."

Bonnie sensed a deep flush rising up her neck. "Mama, I had determined to live for the Lord and not myself before he came."

"He's a good man," Casey said. "And I think there is more to him than—"

"Hair and beard?" Bonnie asked in an attempt to make light of the conversation. Odd, Juanita had stated the same thing about him the day of the twister. Suddenly she felt ashamed of herself. "I'm sorry. He is a jewel." She stood. "I'm going to talk to him now before you three embarrass me any further."

"If you are embarrassed, then it must be the truth." Jocelyn covered her mouth, but a laugh still escaped. "Marrying Brother Travis means your brothers wouldn't worry about you any longer."

"Hush, Mama, before someone hears." Bonnie hurried from the

room before she had to explain the heat flooding her face. Besides, a good walk would help the uneasiness in her stomach—not from eating more than she should but from all the turmoil in her family.

The men all leaned against the corral like young cowboys bragging about all the horses they'd broken and the young girls they'd impressed.

"Are you admiring my horse stock?" she asked.

"Possibly," Morgan said. "Somebody's done a fine job."

She laughed. "I'll give Thomas the credit. He's attempting to teach me ranching, and I'm trying to learn." She glanced about. "I'm sure he could tell you our plans for raising thoroughbred quarter horses."

"We saw him earlier, walking with Juanita," Grant said.

"Ah, best leave them be," she said. "I suspect a wedding in the future."

"Thomas and Juanita?" Morgan asked. "There's a bit of an age difference there."

"To quote our mother," Bonnie began, "love isn't measured in years." She then remembered her mother's words from a few minutes before. Mama didn't have all the answers. Did she?

"What brings you out here, pretty lady?" the reverend asked.

Oh, my. "I wanted to tear Brother Travis away from you for a little while. I'd like to learn a little more about my son and his schooling. That is, if he doesn't mind." Why did her heart beat faster than a hummingbird's wings? This was ridiculous.

"I'd welcome a walk after all the wonderful food," Travis said. "Let's head toward the river." He grinned. "Do you suppose we can escape a twister?"

"With everything that's happened lately, I doubt it," she said.

As the two turned and walked toward the path leading to the river, she heard her brothers laughing. Now, what could be so funny?

CHAPTER  23

"Thanks again for inviting me for Thanksgivin'. Don't know when I've had such a fine meal and good company."

Was it Bonnie's imagination, or did Travis appear nervous?

"We enjoyed having you here. It's been a long time since I've seen Zack this happy. With all you've done, I believe you've established yourself as part of this family."

"That's right kind of you, Bonnie." She appreciated the deep sound of his voice and the way he said her name.

"You wanted to talk to me?" Travis asked as they ventured farther from the house.

"I said back there that I wanted to talk about Zack, but actually I wanted to say how very sorry I am that you've been dragged into this horrible predicament with Lester. I've apologized to you in the past, but after yesterday, I wonder how many times you must have regretted your decision to come to Kahlerville."

"Never. I was called to this community, and God has a reason for all the misfortune."

"Have you figured out the reason?" Her heart raced at his nearness. How could such a strange-looking man affect her so?

"No, have you?"

"Are you sure you didn't make God mad about something?" Oh,

teasing Brother Travis was a whole lot easier than the uncomfortable moments of acknowledging how the poor man had become entangled in a series of problems.

"Probably." He laughed, then sobered. "I'm afraid for you, Bonnie."

"I'm fine. Lester would have to be an idiot to come out here with my brothers looking for an excuse to fight him. Then there's Thomas watching the house like a hawk."

"You forgot Zack and me."

She swallowed hard. "Yes, my son is very protective, and I respect your concern."

Silence. Not a single topic of conversation entered her head.

"Since you apologized to me, then I need to do the same. The gossip is my fault."

"My brothers said you'd make that claim."

"It's true. Folks are going to spread more rumors each time they see us together."

"Over the years, my family's been the root of more than one nasty rumor. Some of them have been true."

"You'd think Lester would have picked a more handsome man to accuse you with." Travis laughed.

Bless you, Brother Travis, for lightening up the tone. "For shame, Brother Travis. The good Lord gave you fine looks." *If you'd let Hank give you a shave and haircut, we might all benefit from what's there.* "I'm wondering if we should avoid each other until the gossip fades."

"We could, but the moment we start talking again, the tongues will wag."

"I suppose you're right, and we have a boy in common." What was she thinking? Her comment sounded. . .sounded very improper. "Pardon me, I meant Zack living with you."

"I understood exactly." He paused.

"Thank you." But she wondered what thoughts rolled around in his head about her.

"Miss Scott is also hurting from the gossip."

"Why?"

"I'm not sure if this is something I should repeat, but I trust you will keep it to yourself and pray for Miss Scott."

"Certainly."

"She mistook the help I gave her for her solo as genuine interest. When I corrected the situation, she became quite upset. Still makes me feel bad."

"I'm sorry. She is a good woman."

He shrugged. "Not sure why I felt compelled to tell you."

They made their way to the riverbank where trees had been uprooted from the twister. Brush and grasses had been swept away as if a huge bird had plucked them for its nest. The landscape would grow come spring, but the memory of the tragedy was embedded in the hearts of those who'd endured it.

The problems with Lester were like the twister, but worse. He was relentless in his accusations and evil. Today had been like the eye of the storm. Where did he intend to strike next? Whose life would he blow through and threaten to destroy?

Bonnie felt a twinge of fright, but no one would find out. Some of the afternoons while Lydia Anne slept, she saddled up her mare and rode to a secluded spot to practice with her rifle, a Colt Lightning with a caliber that allowed her to shoot larger animals and protect herself. The beauty of the lightweight rifle was that it didn't send her scrambling in the dirt and bruising her shoulder. She'd had enough of that attempting to use one of Ben's rifles.

Amid the serenity of songbirds and the timeless seasons, she wove a mixture of prayer and target practice. Some folks might think her habit an unholy alliance, but with every cartridge that kissed its target, she prayed she never had to rely on her marksmanship to protect her family.

Travis climbed up onto his horse, and Bonnie handed him a basket of food. She'd done the same for Zack. Travis hated to leave the ranch, and he hated his feelings for Bonnie at the same time.

"We'll be able to eat for a week," Zack said. "I hope the good Lord gives Brother Travis the gift of cooking real soon."

"I'm not bad compared to you," Travis said. After a moment's contemplation over some of his disastrous attempts, he reconsidered. "I suppose we could put my cooking on the prayer list. Yours, too."

"You're welcome here every night," Bonnie said.

From the flush on her cheeks, she must have been thinking about the town's gossip.

"Thank you." His mouth suddenly felt dry. How could one woman consume him like Bonnie Kahler?

Felicia.

His heart hadn't yearned for her in months. He again prayed she remembered her promise to Jesus. But the idea of being married to Felicia had left him when he'd lived out his sabbatical in the mountains. If he'd truly loved her, then she'd still be in his mind and heart, and he'd be assaulted with guilt for dwelling on Bonnie.

So maybe he'd never loved Felicia at all. Another revelation of his character. Made him wonder if a man ever truly knew himself.

"Brother Travis, I'd like to ask you a question," Zack said.

"I'm not carrying your basket, if that's what you want."

Zack chuckled. "I have the rolls and the desserts, and I'm not giving them up." Lately his voice had started to deepen with cracks and sputters that reminded Travis of a stream rushing out to sea. He'd reach manhood soon enough with all of its challenges.

Travis looked forward to seeing the patchwork of Zack's life unfold. More so, he longed to be a part of it—and his mother's life, too. "Then ask me what you will."

"Would you help me make something nice for Mama's Christmas present?"

"I believe we could take on a project. What did you have in mind?"

"Something simple. . .like a small hinged box to put Papa's watch, their picture, and his Bible inside. Right now she has them in a drawer. I could sand it smooth and stain it."

"I think she'd treasure a gift like you're wanting to give her. We'll get started on it one day this week."

"I'm worried about her."

"I'd not be truthful if I said there's no reason to be."

"Remember the night I hung Miss Scott's clothes on the school-house tree?"

"Yes." Suspicion plodded across his mind at the recollection of what he'd seen and heard only two days before.

"When I walked past Heaven's Gate, Lester and Miss Laura were talking. They didn't see me. I stopped to listen."

"What did you hear, son?"

"Cursing like I never heard from anyone before. I mean the ranch hands sometimes say a curse word, but nothing like this. Lester was real mad at Miss Laura because she'd gone home from the bank that day without staying late. I didn't understand why he was even at Heaven's Gate, it being so late and all."

"Did anything else happen?"

Zack's silence told Travis there was more, and the boy couldn't quite bring it to words.

"Zack, I'm a preacher, but I'm still a man. I've experienced a lot in my days, and I doubt if I'd be shocked. You may have been privy to information that could help us end all the trouble with Lester."

"He said if she told anyone about Rosie's baby, he'd kill her."

Bile rose in Travis's throat. Had Lester beaten her because she was with child? Possibly his child? Why else would he want to keep the news quiet?

"I'm real sorry you heard all that."

"It's been really bothering me. I thought about telling you and my uncles yesterday when they came to talk, but Mama was there. Then I realized I wasn't supposed to be out so late anyway. Lester could deny it all, and Miss Laura. . .well, I know how she used to live.

So I reckoned our word against Lester's was worthless."

Unfortunately, Zack's conclusions were right, unless Rosie and Laura could be convinced to talk to the sheriff.

"Why does he bully women who can't defend themselves?" Zack asked.

"Because he can," Travis said. "Which makes all of this difficult. He has his good points, and that's important for you to know. Just like I preach that none of us are perfect, inside every evil man is a dose of good. Tomorrow, I'll tell your uncles about this. They're smart men and will know what to do with your information."

"I'll tell whoever I need to. I'm not afraid of Lester, but I am afraid for my mama and those ladies at Heaven's Gate."

Oh, Lord, help us figure out a way to stop Lester. Protect those in danger. . .and use me to Your glory.

Bonnie wiggled in the chair while Morgan copied every word from her, Grant, and Brother Travis. All her sense of propriety in a lady displaying patience had faded years ago. Between the four of them, she hoped enough evidence had been gathered to stop Lester.

"All right, I think we have it all down on paper." Morgan set the pen back in the inkwell. He grasped the paper in his right hand and eyed his sister, brother, and preacher.

"Read what we have," Grant said. "Ought to be something there to put him behind bars."

Morgan raised a brow. "Don't be too sure of it. Lester may have broken laws, but if no one will testify against him, we have nothing." He took a deep breath. "From Bonnie: Lester wanted to buy the Morning Star, but Ben refused to sell. After Ben's passing, Lester began supplying her with wine. He also made visits without Sylvia, offered to find a military school for Zack, and when Bonnie let him know he was no longer welcome, he indicated others could learn about her drinking and ruin her reputation.

"With Grant: no problems with Lester since his relationship with Martha was exposed three years ago. However, if Lester has an ailment, he travels twenty-five miles to the next town for a doctor.

"With me. Well. . .I helped Martha leave town with his sons, and I refused to tell him where she went. We've never gotten along, but why should we? The day he cornered Bonnie outside my office, I nearly hit him, but my wild sister beat me to it." He grinned, and she poked him.

"Then there's Brother Travis: For being here such a short time, you've certainly had plenty of run-ins with Lester. He tried to remove Bonnie from volunteering at Heaven's Gate, but you refused to oblige him. He then threatened to pull his money from the church, and you let him know Piney Woods didn't need his financial support. Now that you witnessed him in action with Rosie, he's out to get rid of you.

"Zack is the one I wanted to keep out of this, but he witnessed the reality of Lester's bad habits and temper."

Bonnie blinked back the emotion. She'd wanted her son's innocence protected for as long as possible. The cost of his foolish prank against Miss Scott was more than he'd ever bargained for.

Morgan placed the paper on his desk, sat back, and folded his arms over his chest. The ticking of the clock on his desk rhythmically broke the silence.

"There's nothing we can do," Travis finally said. "It's his word against ours; the witnesses are too frightened to speak up."

"That's right, Brother Travis," Morgan said. "But we know he's preying on defenseless women. The problem is we don't know why."

Grant cleared his throat. "When Martha was carrying the boys, Lester doted on her. And after they were born, he spent a lot of time with his sons. When he discovered she had plans to leave town, he told her he never wanted to see her or her bastard sons again. Excuse my choice of words."

"Could his anger and apathy have been to cover up what he really felt?" Bonnie asked.

"As in vengeance against women for Martha leaving him?" Travis asked.

"Possibly," Morgan said. "I haven't formed a strong conclusion, but I do believe that he will continue until we find a way to stop him."

"If Rosie is with child, how long before she sees me or it becomes apparent?" Grant asked.

"I want to try talking to her," Bonnie said. "Maybe if she knew that Lester has made my life miserable, too, then she'd be willing to tell the sheriff."

"It's worth a try," Morgan said. "Brother Travis, what do you think?"

"Perhaps Bonnie and I could see Rosie and Laura together. We could offer to go with them to talk to the sheriff."

"Lester would come after you two with both barrels," Morgan said.

"Grant can patch us up," Bonnie said in hopes of tearing down the wall of tension between them.

Brother Travis appeared to study her. "Are you ready to talk to Rosie and Laura right now? I'm not sure when Laura works at the bank, but we could try."

She nodded, although remembrances of Lester's domineering influence still haunted her. Deep inside, she found the courage to fight the fear. She had Brother Travis beside her, and they both had God.

But Lester was a powerful man who manipulated others to follow his orders.

CHAPTER  24

Travis knocked on the heavy door of Heaven's Gate. He glanced at Bonnie, who offered a trembling smile. She should have stayed clear of this wolf's den until the truth met the light of day. The fear in her blue eyes tore at his heart.

"I wish you'd have let me handle this," he said.

"We're in this together—my son. . .the gossip."

"I'd like to spare you from every unpleasantness of this world. It—" He closed his mouth abruptly. Already he'd said too much.

About the time he decided to walk her to the parsonage and handle this alone, the door slowly opened. Rosie blanched at the sight of them.

"We'd like to come in and talk to you and Laura," he said.

"I—I don't know." She stole a look behind her.

"Are you ladies alone?" He smiled.

She glanced at her feet, then back to him. "Laura and Daisy are working right now. But—"

"Are you not supposed to talk to us?" he asked.

Rosie nodded.

"Just a few minutes," Bonnie said. "I think you, Laura, and I have more things in common than you may realize."

Rosie tilted her head. The turmoil on her face spoke of years of suffering. He'd seen the indecision and confusion in Felicia when confronted by the haunting of her past.

"I'm afraid, too," Bonnie said. "We have to stop him, or others will be hurt."

A tear slipped from Rosie's eye. "We could talk for a little while before I go to Mrs. Hillman's."

Inside the house, Rosie led them to the parlor. Travis seated himself in a chair while Bonnie and Rosie sat on the sofa. Polite conversation filled the air, but Travis longed to be finished with it. Heaven's Gate still made him uneasy. He hoped that would change someday.

"I know why you're here, and I'm sorry." Rosie turned to Brother Travis. "You're a fine man, and Bonnie is good and proper. I realize those rumors are lies."

"Do you know who started the gossip?" Travis asked. "I simply want to understand why anyone would want to hurt Mrs. Kahler and discredit me."

Rosie stared down at her folded hands. Perhaps she reflected on Travis halting Lester's brutality.

"Did Lester insist you, Miss Laura, or Miss Daisy spread the rumor?" he asked softly.

"I 'spect you thought it was me after—"

"I've told Mrs. Kahler what happened the other night with Lester. So did he force you to make the claim about us?"

"I refused him," Rosie said. "I couldn't spread lies about you two no matter what Lester threatened or did."

"I'm proud of you for standing up for what is right," Bonnie said. "Especially when I've learned he's beaten you."

Travis stole a look at Bonnie. His silent message told of his caring and how he fretted over her safety. She needn't display bravado on his account.

"He's threatened me, too," Bonnie said. "But I ignored him and clung to God to help me. You did what pleased God by not letting him force you."

"I'm not a good person." Emotion clung to her words like cobwebs in barn rafters. "And I must find a place to go, far away where he can't find me. Like Martha did with her sons."

Bonnie placed an arm around the young woman's shoulder. "How long has Lester been beating you?"

Rosie leaned her head against Bonnie's shoulder and sobbed. "Since Martha left. What he wanted from me is wrong. He claims I'm a wicked woman and will never be able to give up my past ways."

"You've been forgiven," Travis said. "He has no right to tell you such lies."

"I keep thinking about how Ellen Kahler left the brothel and is so happy with Frank and her little son. I love Jesus, but I'm afraid of Lester."

"Will you go with us to talk to the sheriff?" Bonnie asked. "He'll protect you, and I'll help you find a place to hide."

"I can't. Do you have any idea how this would hurt Mrs. Hillman? And I don't have any money. Lester is supposed to pay me for cleaning and cooking at their house, but he hasn't. He tells her he doesn't know what I do with the money, when the truth is that he keeps it all."

"Sheriff Arthur will not let Lester hurt you, and someday Mrs. Hillman will learn about her husband's actions. Better it be now when he can be stopped than later after he's tried to destroy other people's lives," Bonnie said. "Brother Travis, don't you think we could talk to Morgan about finding a place for her and Laura to stay?"

Rosie gasped. "How did you know about Laura?"

Travis saw the wisdom in not revealing what Zack had heard and seen. "We have the word of someone else—about Lester's temper. Did she start the gossip?"

"No," Rosie said. "Not Laura."

"Miss Daisy?" Travis asked.

Rosie said nothing, and he understood all three of the residents of Heaven's Gate had been living an earthly hell. He concluded Lester had used all three of them to meet his physical needs. The words to delicately state the truth jumbled in his mind.

"Does he force all of you to conduct your lives as you once did?" he asked.

"Yes, sir."

"Are there other men involved?"

Rosie's sobs kept her from speaking. Travis and Bonnie exchanged glances. Bonnie's eyes moistened, and she blinked back the wetness. Rosie lifted her tear-stained face.

"Yes. He makes the arrangements while we are in Bible study. Except for me."

Travis's stomach churned. He dug his fingers into his palms. The image of what Lester was doing made him want to stomp through the bank doors and haul him out into the middle of the street.

God might not appreciate Travis passing judgment and punishment, but the thought sure gave him a bucketful of satisfaction.

"Brother Travis and I would be happy to accompany the three of you to the sheriff's office," Bonnie said. "And from there, we'd go see Morgan to secure a safe place for you to stay until Lester is behind bars."

She nodded as though another place to live was the answer. "You must understand that I can't leave without Laura and Daisy. He'd be very hard on them."

"Of course," Travis said. "I'd like to talk to all three of you. When do you think that would be possible?"

She sighed. "Perhaps after church tomorrow night. We could talk there without Lester getting suspicious. But the sheriff might not appreciate us bothering him on a Sunday night—"

"Let me handle the sheriff, and I'll alert Morgan to what is happening so he can make arrangements."

"I don't think any of us would feel comfortable staying at Heaven's Gate because the. . .the men come here late at night."

"We'll take care of you." Travis would help her deal with a probable baby once they were away from Lester. "And we'll be praying. In fact, let's pray right now for God to shelter you ladies with His protection and peace." His attention rested on Bonnie. God help him, but he'd fallen in love with her. He prayed aloud as his mind and heart ushered him to the front door of the troubles that had caused him to leave Tennessee.

For Travis, Sundays normally sped by with a worship service in the morning, a noon meal spent in the company of a church family, and then the evening service. Today, however, the time dragged at a snail's pace. The day before, Rosie had stated she was ready to stop Lester's tyranny at Heaven's Gate. Oh, how he prayed she had convinced Laura and Daisy to join her.

One thought tormented him: How did Lester keep his actions from Sylvia? She was highly educated with a remarkable memory for names and places. Could she love him so much that she ignored his sinful ways? Travis shook his head. Sylvia was a plain woman, and Lester struck a fine image. Could it be she chose to abandon her conscience for the sake of keeping the role of Mrs. Lester Hillman?

As soon as the evening service concluded and the congregation slowly ambled from the church, Travis searched for Rosie, Laura, and Daisy. They sat in a pew near the middle of the church. Bonnie and Zack replaced hymnals while Morgan and Grant talked and laughed with their families. Unfortunately, Lester and Sylvia lingered beside him.

"I have a problem with my girls at Heaven's Gate," Sylvia said. "Oh dear, I don't mean to be complaining. I simply need advice."

"What is it?" Travis's mind whirled with the three young women discussing the change in their future—their destiny.

Sylvia offered a thin smile. "All three of them work either for us or at the bank. Lester pays them handsomely for what they do, but none of them ever have any money. When Jenny Andrews asked me to oversee the home, our goal was for it to become self-sufficient." She shrugged. "If I didn't supply them with food, they'd have nothing to eat."

"I advised her to let them go hungry," Lester said. "A few days without eating would instill good stewardship in them."

Travis barely contained his anger. He'd witnessed how Lester treated Rosie, and Zack had reported the same treatment of Laura. How could the man look in the mirror when he bought and sold these women like slaves, then refused to give them money?

"I don't mind talking to them about the problem." Travis nodded in their direction. "I'll do so before they leave here tonight."

"Bless you, Brother Travis," Sylvia said. "Lester said we could count on you. I'm very upset about giving all my free time to those who don't try to help themselves."

Lester chuckled. "He knows how important it is to have us in agreement with what goes on at Heaven's Gate, especially with the rumors of late concerning him and Bonnie Kahler."

Sylvia gasped. "Lester, we're in church."

"Can't think of a better place to talk about the reputations of God-fearing people," Lester said.

"I understand you were the first to hear it," Travis said. "Where did the rumors begin? I want to talk to that person so the lies will stop."

Lester pointed to the three young women. "Right there. Said they'd witnessed the indiscretion. Can you imagine? Here you and Mrs. Kahler volunteer your time to see to their physical and spiritual needs, and they spread gossip." He patted his wife's arm and leaned in closer to Travis. "Sylvia and I have tried to direct them toward the ways of our Lord, and look how they repay us."

"That will be another matter for me to talk about," Travis said. What was Lester attempting to do? At times, he doubted the man's sanity.

"Tell Brother Travis the rest of what we've decided," Lester said to Sylvia.

She took a deep breath, and Lester supported her waist. "Unless the situation changes in the next month, I will have to cease my work there. I plan to tell Jenny in the morning."

"Her resignation also means a withdrawal of financial support," Lester added. "We believed in what we were doing at Heaven's Gate, but it has become a thankless and weary job."

"I understand," Travis said. "And I'll share your decision with the young women in question."

Lester toyed with the brim of his felt hat. "Come along, Sylvia. Brother Whitworth has plenty to do this evening." He took his wife's arm and nodded at Travis with a smile that more resembled a sneer.

The man puzzled Travis. He couldn't figure out why Lester involved himself with such treachery. Was it the money? He already had more than anyone else in town. Travis took in a deep breath. *I should be trying harder to reach him for the kingdom of God.* His past efforts had been met with contempt, but Travis refused to give up on him.

While the Andrews and Kahler children enjoyed cobbler at their grandparents', their parents visited in the back of the church. Travis approached Rosie, Laura, and Daisy. He had noted Daisy appeared to be the shyest of the three, and she rarely made comments in Travis's presence. Her timid personality kept others at a distance, or had she given up on life?

"Have you reached a decision?" Travis asked the three.

"What did Lester want?" Laura's pallor told of her fright.

"He and Sylvia are concerned about none of you having any money to pay for the expenses at Heaven's Gate."

Rosie nearly stiffened. "How dare he when he refuses to pay us for all our work?"

"I'm trying to figure out the same thing." He glanced into the face of each young woman in turn. "Sylvia plans to resign from her work there if the money situation doesn't change."

"Lester can then do anything he wants without her finding out," Rosie said.

"Another reason why he must be stopped. If you're ready, we can see the sheriff now. Morgan and Grant Andrews have homes large enough for all of you."

"I want to stop him," Rosie said. "He'll only continue beating me."

Laura slid her a sideways glance. "I've tasted his fists once too often myself. I'll go to the sheriff as long as Brother Travis can keep us safe."

"What if he starts beating Mrs. Hillman instead of us?" Daisy's large dark eyes held the haunting story of agony and defeat.

Rosie shook her head. "I hadn't thought of that. I couldn't bear to have her hurt."

"We deserve what happens to us," Laura said, "but not Mrs. Hillman."

"You're wrong," Travis said. "What's stopping him from beating her now? Has. . .has he beaten all of you?"

Each young woman nodded.

"Then put a halt to this now," he said.

Rosie and Laura exchanged glances, but Daisy looked away.

"Daisy, I believe your friends are willing. What about you?"

"I can't." Daisy's gaze focused on the stained-glass window, the one depicting Jesus as the Good Shepherd.

"Why not?" Travis asked. "Are you afraid?"

"Not for me. Mrs. Hillman has been like a mother to me. Better than mine ever was. I can't expose Lester or humiliate her or have him angry enough to hit her. I can't. I refuse. Besides, Mrs. Hillman loves her no-good husband." She stood and, without looking at Rosie or Laura, whisked past them and on to the door.

"Daisy, please," Travis said. "Let's talk a little more."

The young woman paused for a moment, then continued out of the church.

"We can't go to the sheriff without her." A sob escaped Rosie's throat. "I'm sorry. Maybe she'll change her mind. God help me, but I understand how Daisy feels." She stood, and her body trembled. Laura joined her.

"You have no idea what Mrs. Hillman means to us, Brother

Travis," Laura said. "We are condemned if we stay, and we condemn Mrs. Hillman if we leave. I'd like to do what you ask, but all of us fret over Mrs. Hillman."

Travis stared long after the young women left. Desperation and a fear for the residents of Heaven's Gate, who loved Sylvia more than their own lives, yanked at his heart and mind. He had a miserable feeling about the outcome of this situation because it looked like no one was willing to testify about Lester's evil nature.

A hand clamped on his shoulder. "From the look on your face, it appears they are too frightened of Lester to stop him," Grant said.

"They are," Travis said. "Rosie and Laura would go to the sheriff tonight, but Daisy loves and respects Sylvia too much to risk her getting hurt or humiliated. In fact, Sylvia is the reason why the other two are hesitant."

"There will be a special crown in heaven for Sylvia Hillman." Grant turned and motioned to Jenny. She stepped to his side and hooked her arm into his. "I've told Jenny all that we've discussed. We're trying to figure out if there is anything we can do since the house belongs to us. As of yet, nothing has come to mind. We had no luck in speaking to the girls, either."

"Prayer is all we can do," Travis said. "And hope the girls change their minds. I do understand how they feel about Sylvia, but it doesn't make the situation right. Although they have such low opinions of themselves, they are risking their lives for the sake of a beloved woman. How many others in this church would be willing to sacrifice their lives for another?"

Morgan and Casey walked toward them. "I can guess tonight's outcome," he said. "Am I assured in believing none of us have given up?"

"We can't," Travis said. "Lester is pretty confident right now that no one will expose him. He's done a good job of preying on those who cannot hurt him, but I believe if we bide our time, he'll make a mistake. Right now, would you join me in a prayer for guidance and wisdom? I'm real concerned about those young ladies."

CHAPTER 25

The following Tuesday, Bonnie drove Michael Paul to school on her way to her day of volunteering at Heaven's Gate. She wore her coat, knowing by midafternoon she'd shed it for her shawl. Usually Lydia Anne came with her, but today Juanita kept the little girl. The two planned to bake bread, which suited Bonnie fine. Lydia Anne didn't need to see or hear any nasty lies that might arise as a result of Lester's bidding.

Miss Scott ignored her again when Bonnie bid Michael Paul good-bye. The gossip about her and Brother Travis weighed heavily in the air, and Miss Scott fancied Travis in a big way. Bonnie had seen the way Miss Scott stared at him. The memory made Bonnie feel really sorry for the woman.

Not that Bonnie blamed Miss Scott. Last night she'd lain awake wondering if Ben was disappointed in her. She loved him then and she loved him now, but Bonnie's thoughts lingered more and more on the preacher, whose real appearance under that beard had proved a mystery to everyone. She'd fallen for his heart.

Before fulfilling her responsibilities at Heaven's Gate, she wanted to see Zack and Brother Travis. The food from Thanksgiving had probably disappeared, and she had a ham and canned vegetables in the back of the wagon.

The thought of more gossip entered her mind, but she pushed it away. Those who insisted on spreading rumors would continue, and those who knew her as a moral and upright woman would understand she had a need to see the preacher who cared for her son. However, she hoped Zack or Brother Travis would see her coming so she could avoid entering the house.

Zack met her outside before she had time to jump down from the buckboard. Good. A prayer answered.

"On your way to Heaven's Gate?" Zack asked.

"Yes, but I brought you a ham and some vegetables first."

He grinned. "The food you sent from Thanksgiving is gone."

"I figured as much."

Zack snatched up the ham and two jars of vegetables. "I'll be right back for the rest."

The front door slammed, and she looked up to see Brother Travis. Zack held up the ham.

"I'm saved again from your cooking," her son said. "There's more in the wagon."

Brother Travis wasted no time in gathering up the rest of the canned vegetables and a loaf of bread. His gaze met hers, and she sensed her cheeks flush warm.

"Thanks, Bonnie. You know just when we run out. I can cook, and I'm not that bad. It's simply not the fine meals you and Juanita prepare."

Zack hurried back and took the remaining items from Brother Travis. "Grandpa is expecting us this morning. He's going to help me with Latin."

"I have plenty of time, if you'd like for me to drive you gentlemen to the parsonage," she said.

Zack shook his head. "Mama, I'll drive the wagon if it's all right with Brother Travis. A man doesn't allow a woman to do all the work."

"I'd be honored."

Travis chuckled. "Let me grab my hat and Bible."

Luckily, it was early enough that few folks were out and about. Bonnie's idea of avoiding gossip meant not to be showy. One minute she cared what folks thought and said, and in the next she wanted to shake her fist at them. Lester walked by and tipped his hat. Instantly she swallowed her relief. The whole town would hear their fill of lies.

At the parsonage, Brother Travis tied the horses to the hitching post. "Zack, why don't you visit with your grandpa? I'll be inside shortly." He tossed a smile Bonnie's way. "Do you have a moment to help an overworked preacher look through the hymnals for Christmas music?"

She couldn't think of anything better. They ambled toward the church.

"Christmas will be here before we have time to appreciate the cool weather, and I want to have lots of music on Christmas Eve."

"With solos?" She stifled a laugh.

"Yes." He didn't muffle his laugh. "But I'm not doing the selecting."

"Who is?"

"Each person who wants to sing a solo will do so in front of the choir. They will choose, not me. I also want the children to give us a glimpse of the first Christmas in a little play. Having Michael Paul sing is at the top of my list."

Just when she was ready to offer her help with the children, he stopped cold. She trailed his gaze and saw that one of the stained-glass windows was broken, shattered.

"Oh my," she said. "How did this happen?"

"I don't know, but I aim to find out." He took long strides to the church and up the steps two at a time. Swinging open the door, she saw him startle. He swiped his hand over his face as though he couldn't believe his eyes.

"What is it?" She hurried his way.

"Trouble."

She followed him inside. His gaze swept around the sanctuary. Frustration seeped from the pores of his face, then pain as though he fought the urge to cry. The stained-glass window on the opposite side had been broken, too, its shards of glass sprinkled across the wooden floor. Torn hymnals lay strewn about—in the aisle and on the benches—and the pulpit teetered precariously on its side.

Travis walked to the front of the church and set the pulpit upright. He avoided Bonnie's intense scrutiny and appeared to fight his own private war. His eyes narrowed.

"I'm so sorry," she said. "Who would do such a thing?"

He shook his head. "And why? Destroying property belonging to the house of God? May He have mercy on whoever has deliberately done this."

She picked up an open hymnal to reveal its torn pages and placed it on a pew. "I'll go get the reverend. Maybe he saw someone."

"No need. I'm here," the reverend said from the back of the church. "I saw your wagon and then the broken glass. I haven't seen anyone whom I could suspect."

"I've shaken hands with defeat and despair before," Travis began, "and this is near the top of the list." He stiffened as though keeping his feelings in check. "I could simply be tired from dealing with all the problems of late." He picked up two more hymnals.

"I'll go fetch the sheriff," the reverend said.

"Reverend, I'm sorry," Travis said. "This is the church you started for the community. I have no business feeling sorry for myself. After all, this is God's church. Imagine how He feels."

"We're both upset," the reverend said. "I—I can't believe someone could be low enough to damage the house of God." He sighed wearily. "I'll be back in a little while."

Bonnie wished she could disappear. The sight of Travis and the reverend visibly grieving ripped at her heart. They should be alone to deal with their sorrow. The reverend's boots on the church steps sounded like the slow thud of a funeral dirge.

"Would you like to be alone?" she asked.

Travis turned and offered her a slight smile. "Next to God, you are the person I really need right now." He shook his head. "I didn't mean to offend you."

"Not at all. I'm humbled." Her fledgling feelings and his must be the same. How strange. How very peculiar.

"I haven't been this angry in a long time."

"You have every right to be. I'm furious—and saddened." She made her way up the aisle toward him, walking around hymnals, torn pages, and pieces of glass.

"The windows won't be replaced until Christmas or after, and stained glass is costly, but it will still be the celebration of our Lord's birth. Tomorrow night's prayer meeting will be well spent."

She released a sigh. "After all the turmoil we've endured, this happens. I wonder when God will call a halt to the ugliness plaguing our little community."

"God has a lesson for us. I'm sure we'll understand in His timing."

He returned to the pulpit. "The Bible is missing." He searched the floor. "Surely it's not destroyed."

"Who could be so evil?" she asked.

"Only someone who hates the people of God."

In the moments following, Bonnie and Travis picked up the remaining hymnals and the pages. They sat side by side and pieced the songbooks back together until they heard men entering through the back of the church. The reverend and the sheriff talked in low tones. Travis stood to meet them.

"Sheriff Arthur, thank you for coming. Mrs. Kahler and I are attempting to put the church in order, beginning with the torn hymnals. And the Bible from the pulpit is missing."

"We have a witness to the vandalism," the sheriff said. "He saw the culprit who broke the windows."

"Who did it?" Travis's voice echoed deep.

"Zack Kahler."

Travis reached Bonnie before she collapsed. Once he righted her on a pew and the reverend tended to her, his gaze flew to the sheriff.

"Zack did not do this. Whoever accused him was mistaken." He nearly said he'd stake his salvation on it but thought better of it.

"My. . .my son loves the Lord. He'd never damage the church," Bonnie said.

Her blanched face mirrored Travis's heart. His devotion to Zack was that of his own son. "He knows the Lord. It's impossible."

"The witness is a model citizen in our community."

"Who?" Fear snaked up Travis's spine.

"Lester Hillman. He came by my house before sunrise this morning. Said he usually rides to a secluded spot while it's still dark to pray and think about the day. That's when he saw Zack throw rocks at the window."

Bonnie abruptly rose from the pew and stomped toward the sheriff. "How could he tell it was Zack if it was dark?"

"Calm down, Bonnie," the sheriff said. "I asked him the same thing. Lester said he called out to the boy and recognized his voice. I hate to do this to you, but I'm gonna have to put Zack in jail until this is resolved."

"You will not." Bonnie whirled around to Travis and then to the reverend. "Stop him. We know Zack didn't do this. Lester is lying. He's. . .he's. . .trying to destroy us." Her sobs burst like cannonballs piercing the air.

Travis fought the urge to draw her into his arms, but the reverend comforted her instead. *Lester. He'd found yet one more way to plague them.*

"Where is Zack?" the sheriff asked. "No point in hiding him. It'll only make matters worse."

No one chose to reply, so the sheriff repeated his request. "I can swear in a few men to find him."

"No. I'll get him," Travis said. "I hope you remember that he's a boy, not a grown man. Certainly not a criminal."

"But he's committed a crime against the town, the church, and God. You, of all people, should see the seriousness of his actions."

"I do," Travis said. "But I believe in his innocence. In fact, I have a good idea who is responsible."

"Who, then?" Sheriff Arthur asked. "I'll go question him now and get this settled."

The reverend waved his hand. "Don't, Travis. Let's talk to Morgan and Grant before we act rashly."

Travis understood the wisdom of the reverend's words, and reality yanked him back to the roots of common sense.

"The reverend's right," Bonnie whispered.

Listen to them. Trust Me.

Trust You? When an innocent boy will suffer for a crime he didn't commit?

"All right," Travis said. "I'll get Zack, and then we'll see about justice. God will right this. I'm sure of it." He bore his gaze into the sheriff's face. "I know you're doing your job, but I promise you that Zack is innocent."

"Yes, sir. I hope you're right. Looks like he'd made some good changes after that Sunday in church." Deep lines fanned from the sheriff's eyes. No doubt, arresting Zack ate at him, too.

Bonnie blinked back the tears and glanced at the reverend. "It'll be all right," she said. "I'm sure of it."

"God knows our Zack's heart," the reverend said.

Travis made his way to the back of the church with Bonnie at his side. His earlier words of having her beside him now needled him. He assisted her down the church steps and on across to the parsonage.

"Go ahead and cry." He pulled out a handkerchief—the only way he could help.

"Not now. I want Zack to see me strong in my faith and in his innocence."

That's my sweet lady. "Which one of us should tell him?"

"You are the one who's helped him through his troubles. I think he'll take it best from you."

Travis nodded and knocked on the door. Jocelyn opened it and offered a sad greeting.

"I'm sorry about the church," she said.

"We're all suffering because of the damage," Travis said. "Can we see Zack?"

Confusion settled on her face, but she merely turned. "Zack, Brother Travis and your mother want to see you."

"We'll talk to him out here," Travis said.

"What's wrong?" Jocelyn asked.

"Hell has come to Kahlerville," Bonnie said.

Before anyone said another word, Zack appeared in the doorway. "Does Sheriff Arthur have any idea who broke the windows?"

"Oh, the person did more than that," Travis said.

Zack shook his head. "The man needs to be shot. What else has been done?"

Staring into the boy's eyes, Travis realized right then that his original sentiments about the matter were true. "The hymnals are torn, the Bible from the pulpit is gone, and the pulpit overturned. When I righted it, I saw a chunk broken off the end."

"What can I do to help?" Zack asked. "Is the church fit for prayer meetin' tomorrow night?"

"We'll make do."

Zack peered at Bonnie. "Mama, you aren't saying much."

When tears moistened her eyes, Travis wrapped his arm around Zack's shoulder. "Lester has been up to no good."

Zack's eyes widened. "He did this?"

"No, not exactly. Well. . .possibly." How did Travis tell a good boy that he'd been accused of something he didn't do? Would this undo Zack's progress, or was Travis showing a lack of faith?

"What are you not telling me?" Zack's gaze darted between Bonnie and Travis.

Travis squeezed his shoulder. "He accused you of it. Before sunrise this morning, he went to see the sheriff. Said he saw you break one of the windows."

Zack stiffened. "Me? I was in bed." He sucked in a breath. "He's getting back at us, isn't he?"

"I'm afraid so."

"Am I going to jail?"

Travis hated to respond.

Zack's expression changed to anger. "I could kill him with my own hands."

"Zack—"

"I don't care if it's wrong, Brother Travis. He keeps hurtin' folks, and it's never gonna end."

Travis tightened the grip on Zack's shoulders. "I promise you that Lester will be stopped. Don't you know I'd gladly go in your place if I could?"

Zack blinked back the emotion. "What will happen to me?"

"For now, go with Sheriff Arthur. Your mama and I are heading to see your uncles. We'll figure out a way to get you out of there."

"How long will it take?" Zack asked.

"I hope a matter of a few hours. Pray, Zack. God is with you."

"I think God is mad at me for the bad things I've done."

"No, son. What is happening to you is not from God. But He will use it for you to grow closer to Him." Perhaps Travis should listen to his own advice.

Zack finally looked at his mother. "I'm real sorry about this, Mama. Folks are going to be talking about you even more."

Bonnie shook her head and hugged him. "I don't care what anyone says. My love for you and my belief in your innocence are far more important."

LIGHTNING
LACE

Zack shook his head. "Let's go, Brother Travis. I'm real mad right now at Lester. I don't think things can get any worse."

Travis glanced at Bonnie. He read the terror in her eyes. Things could get worse. Much worse. This proved Lester was capable of anything. He reached out and touched her fingertips, when he longed to draw her to him.

"We'll get through this," he said. "I'll do all I can."

CHAPTER 26

"Lester *what*?" Morgan stood from the chair, his eyes blazing like hot coals.

Bonnie wanted to soothe him, but compassion for Zack ran even stronger. She swung her attention to Travis and then to Grant.

"You heard right," Travis said. "How do we get Zack out of jail?"

"Lester's gone too far this time," Grant said. "He can ride the twenty-five miles to another doctor to patch him up once I'm finished with him."

Morgan's red face displayed the thoughts hammering against his brain. "Let me have the honor, little brother."

Bonnie tapped her fingers on Morgan's desk. "You two can tear Lester apart after you figure out a way to get my son out of jail."

"I imagine the sheriff would release him to me as long as I accept responsibility for his actions," Morgan said. "That's probably a good idea since I could keep him at the ranch and away from Lester."

"What about with his mother?" Bonnie asked. Sometimes she thought her brothers didn't understand her position in all of this. Zack was *her* son.

"Considering the problem at the livery when he ran away from you, I doubt if the sheriff would agree to releasing him to you. Good ole law-abiding Lester would make sure the whole town knew that Zack was released to his mother, who couldn't handle him."

"I'd gladly take him," Grant said, "but he'd be confined to the house like a criminal."

Bonnie gasped. She didn't mean to, but the implication of the word *criminal* scraped at her heart. "When will all this end? Has anyone thought about going to Lester and asking him what he wants?"

"I have," Grant said. "Remember I hid the knowledge about his sons from the whole town until he stepped over the line with the law. Maybe it has something to do with that."

"Don't think so," Morgan said. "Lester would just as soon do away with all of us because we stand up to him, but I think Bonnie is what he wants. We've discussed this all before." His gaze penetrated through her. "Be careful, little sister. He knows he can get to you through Zack."

The thought made her want to throw up, but the idea wasn't new. "I'm going to talk to Rosie again. I think she's on the verge of telling all she knows." She crossed her arms over her chest. "I'm ready to tell Sylvia about the wine, and I understand she may take Lester's word for it all. But at least I can plant a seed of suspicion in her mind."

"Do you want me to escort you to the Hillmans' home?" Travis asked. "What if Lester is there?"

"This discussion will be woman to woman. I refuse to believe she's blind to his actions." She studied Travis before speaking. "Has anyone told you that Lester bought those stained-glass windows?"

Travis grimaced. "So our friend looks even more the saint."

"Lester's smart, and whatever he's schemed has been carefully planned," Morgan said. "Right now, I'll see what I can do about getting Zack out of jail."

"And I'm heading back to the church to clean up glass," Travis said.

"And I have patients to see." Grant swung a grin at Bonnie. "Despite the mess we're in, I can't help but tease. If you blow a hole through Lester, make sure no one's around."

Morgan chuckled. "And I'll give you legal advice—free."

"Although you two are incorrigible, you're still the best brothers a girl could ask for."

A short while later, Bonnie knocked on the door of Lester and Sylvia's stylish home. Lester was always adding and changing something to the two-story structure. Of late, a hexagon porch had replaced the previous one, and the brick home had been given green wood trim that twisted and curved in every area imaginable. Various shapes of stained-glass windows had been added when Lester purchased the ones for the church. She'd heard Sylvia speak of replacing much of their furniture and rugs. The Hillman home stood as the regal envy of Kahlerville. Bonnie took a deep breath and noted the chill.

She didn't dare do this in a place where anyone could overhear their conversation, and she regretted the need to tell Sylvia about Lester's behavior. Seemed like the poor woman had suffered enough from Lester's actions. Before Bonnie had a moment to contemplate the dire straits of Sylvia Hillman any further, Daisy, who worked as a maid for the Hillmans, answered the door.

"Hello, Daisy. May I speak with Sylvia?"

The young woman invited her inside just as Sylvia walked into the hallway. Surprise registered in the older woman's eyes.

"My dear Bonnie, Lester told me about Zack. How your heart must be breaking. Please come in." She turned to the young woman. "Daisy, you can continue in the kitchen."

"Yes, ma'am." Daisy neither smiled nor offered another greeting.

Bonnie stepped inside and noted the elegant furnishings. But fine things did not make a person happy. "I apologize for calling unannounced. The devastation at the church has distressed all of us. My brothers and I, along with Brother Travis, feel Lester mistook Zack for the culprit."

"But Lester's sure." Sylvia touched Bonnie's arm. "My sympathies to all of you in this grave matter. And we shared so much hope for Zack."

"Thank you." Bonnie took a deep breath and vowed not to take her anger out on this sweet lady. "We will not give up until we find out who committed the crime."

"Let's visit in the parlor. I see you're very upset, and I want to help. We can pray that the resolution to this will be the end to Zack's rebellion."

Bonnie bit back a retort and followed Sylvia into the gold and deep purple parlor. "Everything has been changed since I've been here. It's lovely." The heavy drapes kept out the sunlight, but a cheery fire warmed the room. A three-tiered crystal chandelier hung from the ceiling, and an elegant rug dressed the floor.

She wanted to cry, not tell this woman about her and Lester's indiscretion.

"Would you like coffee or tea?" Sylvia asked.

"No. Sylvia, I have a confession to make."

The woman tilted her head. Even in the shadows of the elegant parlor, the woman's face paled.

"All I ask is that you let me finish before we discuss the matter."

"Certainly."

Suddenly Bonnie wished she hadn't gone this far, but it was too late. Best the truth come from her. "After Ben died, you and Lester were some of the first people of Kahlerville to check on me. I appreciated your caring at a time when my loss was almost more than I could bear." She swallowed hard. Her throat scratched raw. "I remember stating that I had difficulty sleeping. In the course of the conversation, Lester suggested I try a little wine before retiring. He stated the apostle Paul suggested Timothy use a little wine for his health. It seemed like a good idea, so when Lester brought me a bottle, I accepted."

Sylvia's face stiffened. She shook her head. "I don't recall all of that conversation, only the part where you spoke of being unable to sleep."

"Perhaps you were with the children at the time." Which was true—some of the time.

"I see."

"About two months ago, God shook me soundly, and I realized the habit had to stop. I spoke with Lester and told him I no longer needed wine."

"And what did he say?"

Bonnie's stomach rolled like storm clouds. "He thought I—I might still need assistance in going to sleep."

Sylvia wrung her hands in her lap. "Did you collect the wine at the bank?"

"No, Sylvia."

"Then he delivered it to your home?"

"Yes."

"Without me?"

"Most times." Bonnie dampened her lips. "Juanita was always present."

Sylvia appeared to study her hands, then raised her gaze. "Bonnie, I know my husband better than you may think. He is very attracted to beautiful women."

"Oh, Sylvia, believe me, nothing ever happened except the exchange of wine."

"I believe you. You are too fine a woman to allow the charms of a married man to lure you. If it were otherwise, you would not be here today."

"Thank you," Bonnie whispered and noted her irritated throat felt worse. "I care for you very much, and although this confession may damage our relationship, I could not go on another day without being perfectly honest with you."

"I appreciate your honesty, but this is very difficult." Sylvia blinked and glanced into the red-yellow glow of the fire.

"I think I'd better leave."

Sylvia continued staring into the fire. "I need to be alone."

"I ask you to forgive me. I've received forgiveness from God for using wine to mask my grieving and for neglecting my children. I also asked Him to forgive me for accepting the bottles from a married man. Now I ask you."

Bonnie arose from the chair. Her skirts rustled stiffly, like the tension between her and this dear woman. The moment she climbed back into her buggy and lifted the reins, she remembered someone else who might be able to help.

                        ✺

Travis always looked forward to Wednesday night's prayer meetings. This special time offered countless blessings to those who attended. He believed offering prayers for each other was a vital part of every Christian's spiritual life.

Tonight Zack was the one in need, and the thought of his charge being blamed for the damage to the church nearly brought Travis to tears. Definitely to his knees. He stood and faced the congregation with broken windows on both sides of them and prayed for God to give him the right words.

"Folks, this is a grim occasion. Here we are looking forward to the Christmas celebration, and our building is vandalized. The Bible that has rested on the pulpit of our church is missing." He held up his own worn Bible. "This is still the Word of God, and the gospel will be preached regardless of the building's condition. What's worse is that one of our own has been accused of the crime. Zack is in the custody of his uncle Morgan until those of us who love him are able to find the person who has done this horrible crime. I'm asking—no, I'm begging—for prayer tonight. I believe Zack Kahler is innocent of any wrongdoing. I am convinced that someone else broke the windows, tore our hymnals, and took the Bible. I've prayed that whoever has the Bible is reading it and that the Holy Spirit will bring another soul into the throngs of heaven."

Travis surveyed the crowd. Sylvia and Lester were there, and the pews were filled except for Bonnie and her children.

"Not so long ago, Zack came forward to publicly acknowledge his decision to live the rest of his life for Jesus. Many of you remember the angry young man who came to live with me. He grieved the loss of his father and had a bushel of sadness and regret weighing on his heart. I realized only God could change him, and He did. During the recent twister, Zack, his brother, sister, and I were caught outside with no shelter. God spared our lives while trees fell around us. That was when Zack reached out to Jesus. He was saved from the twister and from the wrath of God. Now I'm asking God to save him again from injustice. Would you join me in this prayer?"

Some of the folks scowled. Couples exchanged glances. One man nodded, but Travis couldn't tell if his look was for or against Zack. Lester stood, and Travis feared what he planned to say.

"You all know I saw young Zack throw the rocks. Because of me, the boy was put in jail. What I want to say is that I don't know why he chose to destroy the house of God, but I will pay for all the repairs."

How was Travis to respond to that? He nodded at Lester. "Thank you for your generous offer."

Jake Weathers slowly pulled himself up on shaky limbs. "I've seen a change in young Zack. I haven't much money, but I'd rather see what little I have be used to replace hymnals and fix broken windows than send a boy back to the misery he knew before finding Jesus."

Bless you, Jake.

"He needs to be punished for this tomfoolery. After all, Lester Hillman saw him break one of the windows," Eli Palmer said. "My boys never did half the things Zack Kahler has done. And to think his father was the best sheriff this town ever knew. The poor man must be twisting in his grave."

"I believe Lester made a mistake, and whoever did this could have been passing through town. It was before sunup," Travis said. "To show my sincerity in the matter, take the repairs out of my pay instead of allowing Lester to carry the burden of the repairs."

Zack's family said nothing—neither the Kahlers nor the Andrews—and that was good. If the people of Piney Woods Church were to open their hearts to the boy, it must be without persuasion from family members. His grandma Kahler dabbed at moisture beneath her eyes.

"Whoever did this hurt God more than us," Miss Scott said. "I remember how difficult Zack was in school, and I haven't decided if he's really living for the Lord or not. But the truth is clear. Zack or someone hurt God's house."

"What are you suggesting?" Travis asked.

"I'd much rather answer to one of you than anger God. If Zack's guilty, God will deal with him. And if he's guilty, he'll resume the same type of behavior, and the next time none of us will have any doubts. Like Brother Travis, I'd like to give him another chance." She smiled, causing Travis to question whether her position was because she believed in giving second chances or because she wanted him to think better of her.

"We're the ones who need to decide," Jake said. "I'd like for us to drop the charges. About half of the hymnals are all right. Folks like me can't read 'em anyway, with the print being so small. And we got along just fine before Lester bought those fancy windows, although I do feel sorry for him."

Eli stood. "Yer wrong, Jake. That boy's guilty as sin. I think we ought to take a vote."

Travis silently prayed for God to direct his flock to the truth. "That's fair, Eli. First let's have a few moments of silent prayer. Then we'll have a show of hands to decide whether we drop the charges against Zack. If the vote goes for him, then he returns to my home. If the vote goes against him, then he stays at Morgan's ranch until the judge decides what should happen. Would a paper vote suit you better?"

"I'm not ashamed of how I feel," Eli said.

"Me, either," Jake said.

"But none of Zack's family can vote in this. You, either, Brother Travis. We already know how you folks feel. This is church business." Eli raised his fist as though he had the confidence of the Almighty.

The prospect of having two old men fighting in the middle of church crossed Travis's mind. Both men had long since determined never to agree on anything, and this matter was no different.

The reverend and Pete Kahler, Zack's other grandfather, stood at the same time. "We agree."

The prayer time seemed to last for hours instead of minutes. Finally, Travis asked for those who believed Zack was innocent to raise their right hand. He purposely didn't ask for those who believed he deserved a second chance. He wanted Zack free of any accusations.

The show of hands was three over half. Travis's shoulders lifted. *Praise God.*

"He'll be murderin' us in our sleep." Eli shook his fist. "Mark my words."

CHAPTER  27

Travis closed his Bible and grasped his sermon notes for the following morning. He'd wrestled all week with what to preach about. Forgiveness? No, that meant Zack was guilty. Love thy neighbor? That sounded too obvious—like beating his congregation over the head with a Bible. However, Travis worked hourly on trying to love Lester, but he'd rather wash pigs. *Excuse me, Lord. That wasn't necessary, just honest.*

Travis reached for his coffee and downed the lukewarm brew. Topics from tithing to taking care of widows and orphans had plodded through his mind, but every reflection reminded him of Bonnie or Zack. He'd finally settled on a sermon about God's miracles and the birth of John to Zechariah and Elizabeth. Certainly fitting for the season. He reread his notes and the Bible passage.

He pulled his pocket watch from his trousers. *Ten forty-five.* The weekly *Kahlerville Times* would be ready by now. He stood and made his way out onto the back porch where Zack was gathering and stacking wood.

"Zack, want to walk with me after the newspaper?"

"Yes, sir. I want to see what it says about the church." He laid an armload of wood in a dry corner of the porch and swiped his hands together. The two walked around to the front of the house and then toward town and the newspaper office.

Morgan had brought Zack back on Thursday morning. Travis had missed him more than he imagined, and the thought of his one day returning to his mother's ranch left a dent in Travis's chest. Fortunately, Zack and his cousin Chad had renewed their friendship, and the Christmas holiday promised to be full of fun—and probably with a little mischief between the two boys. Travis shook his head in rebuttal of his own thoughts. Zack and Chad were no longer boys. They were young men.

"How do you want to spend your afternoon?" Travis asked.

"I reckon I'll work on Mama's Christmas present. Did you have something for us to do?"

"I want to plan the Christmas Eve service and pray about the music. Auditions for solos are this Wednesday."

Zack grinned. "I feel sorry for you. Some of those folks sing like hound dogs."

"And I've already been accused of having favorites. That's one of the reasons why the choir will do the choosing."

"Are you going to sing?"

"Only if I'm asked."

"Brother Travis, you and my little brother have the best voices in the church. I'm sure you'll be asked."

Travis smiled. His charge had come so far from the hostile boy of a few months ago. After the sad business of Zack being accused of destroying church property, Travis had held his breath for fear Zack would return to his old ways. But that showed a lack of faith in God.

"Do you mind fetching the paper while I check at the general store for any mail?" Travis asked. He'd ordered a book for Bonnie for Christmas, but he wanted it kept secret in case it didn't arrive in time.

After Mrs. Rainer had confided in him that she had encouraged Bonnie to write stories, he decided he wanted to do his part, too. The *Houston Post* advertised a book by Eleanor Kirk called *Information for Authors*. He'd promptly mailed his request to the author, indicating he wanted it to give someone for Christmas. Lots of time remained before the celebration, but Travis wanted to read the book before he gave it to her. Some writers said things about God that he didn't approve of.

In front of the newspaper office, Travis gave Zack three cents, and they parted company. "I'll meet you at the general store. Your grandpa may be working today."

The sound of the bell over the door of Kahler's General Store welcomed Travis inside to the crowded shelves brimming over with goods. He smelled a mixture of cinnamon and leather. "Morning, Pete. How are you doing?"

Pete Kahler passed him a grim look. "I've been better, Brother Travis."

"What's wrong?"

"Have you read this morning's paper?" Pete leaned on the counter.

"No. Zack's getting it now."

"You won't like it. Won't like it a-tall." Pete pounded his massive fist on the countertop. "There's gonna be a special set of coals for Lester Hillman, and I plan to be there to light the kindling."

"Whoa. What's it say?" Travis sensed a slowly rising panic. What had Lester done now? "Do you have a copy?"

"I threw it in the stove as soon as I read it. I should have taken it to the outhouse." Pete glanced out the window. From the size of him, a man might think twice before riling him. And Pete Kahler was definitely riled.

"What does it say?"

Pete nodded toward the window. "Here comes Zack now. Looks like he's reading it. Wish I could spare my grandson what's written there."

Curiosity had nearly gotten the best of Travis, but he waited until Zack entered the store and handed him the paper. His pale face told Travis more than he wanted to know.

"And I didn't think it could get worse." Zack walked to the pot-belly stove and warmed his hands.

Without a word, Travis read the headlines: "PINEY WOODS CHURCH VANDALIZED." The beginning of the article ran straight as to what happened until a section regarding Lester Hillman caught his attention: "I take an early morning ride to pray and think about what the good Lord wants me to do that day."

That alone made Travis want to rip the paper into pieces. "I saw Zack Kahler throw a rock at the church, and I heard the window shatter. I shouted at him, but he told me to mind my own business. He cursed me, too. I then reported the incident to the sheriff. As much as it grieves me to see one of our town's youth destroy church property, I am prepared to replace the Bible, the windows, and the hymnals. Brother Whitworth has been trying to guide young Zack, but obviously his work has been in vain. Due to my respect for the deceased Ben Kahler and his widow, I elected to confer with Morgan and Grant Andrews, the boy's uncles, to find a suitable military school for him. I feel prompt attention to the matter will increase the chances of this wayward youth mending his ways."

Travis lifted his gaze from the newspaper, too angry to speak, too dumbfounded to think clearly. "Does the man have a conscience?" he finally asked. "He lies as though every word from his mouth is gospel truth."

"You and my uncles aren't planning to get rid of me, are you?" Zack narrowed his eyes, first at Travis then at his grandpa. "I'll run away. I swear I will."

"No. Listen to me, Zack. It's another one of Lester's ways of making himself look good," Travis said.

"If Ben were—" Pete started then stopped himself. "Zack, neither of us can live in the past. What Lester had printed is wrong. All of us who love you know it."

"But I don't understand. Why is God punishing me? I'm trying real hard to do all that the Bible says, and horrible things keep happening. I give up. I give up." Zack turned and dashed out the door into the street.

"Best go after him." Pete leaned on the counter. "I've got a notion to pay Lester a visit. He's given this family trouble since before Frank and Ellen were married. That man can spread more gossip than a dozen old biddies."

Travis remembered Ellen's story and her deliverance from Kahlerville's brothel. Lester had manipulated the citizens of this town for quite a while.

"Wouldn't help a bit, Pete," Travis said. "He'd have more stories to spread." He watched Zack disappear toward their home. "I need to see to Zack."

"You suppose he'll run off?"

"I hope not." *But I ran when the going got tough.* He made his way to the door.

"Thanks for all you've done for us, Brother Travis. I hope someday we can repay you."

Travis despised statements like that. His past wasn't worth the newspaper print for Lester to tell the story. "This is my life. I only want to help."

As he suspected, Zack was throwing clothes together in a small bag; his Bible lay on the bed. All had not been lost.

"Where are you going?"

"Somewhere away from this town and Lester Hillman."

"The world's full of men like him. They just have different names, different reasons to hurt folks."

Zack glanced up from his furious packing. His reddened eyes revealed the scar across his heart. Travis would have done anything to take away the agony etched in his young face, but Jesus had already done that.

"You don't know what it's like, trying to live a good life when Lester seems to want me dead."

"Not just you, Zack—your uncles, your mother, and me."

"Why? What have we done to him? Is he still mad 'cause Papa refused to sell him the Morning Star?"

"I believe there's more to it."

"No matter. I've made up my mind. I'm leaving. Tell my mama 'bye for me, will you? Don't want her worrying."

"She will. All of us love you, Zack. Stay. Fight this thing with Lester. We will win."

"I can't. I'm tired, and God keeps punishing me for all my sins."

Zack's words echoed from the past when Travis was convinced that God had him tied to a whipping post. He couldn't let the young man live with the doubt of God's love and power in his life.

"You're on your way to being a fine man. Don't let Lester spoil what's ahead for you. I was in your shoes not so very long ago. I understand your doubts and how misfortune seems to stalk you like a wildcat looking for prey. I'm going to tell you a story that I've never told anyone. I'm not proud of it at all. Sometimes I toss and turn in bed at night and wonder what I could have done differently."

In the quiet of that first Saturday in December, Travis revealed to Zack what had driven him away from his Tennessee home. How he'd befriended a woman from a brothel, asked her to marry him, and lost his church when others disapproved.

"And now you're here," Zack said. "Is what happened in Tennessee the reason why you look and dress a little strange?"

"I 'spect so."

"Are you still hiding from yourself?"

The question penetrated Travis's soul. He hadn't reasoned the situation like that before. "Maybe I am. I think I need you here as much as you need me. Will you stay?"

Zack stood from the bed. "I reckon I don't have any choice. If I run off, Lester might go back to bothering my mama again."

Not if I can help it.

The young man forced a smile. "Someday I might find out what you look like under all that hair."

Travis chuckled. "You might at that. Right now we need to go see your mama before she reads the newspaper."

Bonnie blew out the lamp and snuggled under the warm quilt of her bed. The unexpected visit from Travis and Zack had unnerved her for a little while, but she'd come to expect the worst from Lester.

Her poor son. She prayed his life soon returned to that of a normal boy. As she studied him tonight, she saw her soon-to-be thirteen-year-old son was no longer a boy. Travis referred to him as a young man, and she had to agree.

Sylvia Hillman. Had she approached Lester about her knowledge that he had given Bonnie the wine? Or had she tucked it into the secluded part of her heart where Lester's infidelity with Martha lay? Lester had pushed all of them to the limit. If the man turned up dead, a dozen or more folks would be questioned. And she'd be one of them.

Unable to find a comfortable spot in the bed, she opened her eyes and touched the opposite side of the bed. How long had it been since she'd done this? The habit ended weeks ago, and she hadn't been aware of no longer leaning on the past. Odd that tonight she sought the comfort of one who now lived with Jesus. Perhaps the turmoil around her brought on a need for love and reassurance or maybe the twinge of guilt at recognizing the incessant tugs at her heart for Travis.

"Am I being unfaithful to you?" she whispered in the darkness. How many times had the question echoed in her mind?

Nothing but night sounds responded, yet the angst in her soul dissipated. The Bible gave her freedom to remarry, and although Travis appeared as the most unlikely man for her to give her affections to, somehow that very thing had happened. She laughed lightly in the darkness. She, who had always believed a man must be as handsome as the day was long, had fallen for a man she could not see. Blind to her eyes except for the part of him that God loved the best. Mercy, what was she doing robbing her body of sleep by dwelling on a man like a lovesick girl?

Bonnie promptly closed her eyes, determined to sleep and cease this foolishness. He might detest her. She held her breath and remembered Thanksgiving. She'd seen the look in his eyes—the only visible area of his face. *Go to sleep, crazy woman!*

Squeezing her eyes shut, she deliberated everything from Lydia Anne's riding lessons to Michael Paul's piano and schoolwork to the grotesque situation with Lester, who had now dragged Zack through the manure.

Maybe she didn't feel love for Travis at all. Maybe her weary mind simply needed a diversion until Lester stopped his torment of her beloved family. *That's it. I'll not spend another moment deliberating on Travis until my precious son, family, and friends are safe from Lester Hillman.*

Tomorrow after church, she'd talk to Frank and Ellen Kahler. Days ago she'd considered the possibility of Ellen helping her in this war with Lester, but digging up the past was often painful.

CHAPTER  28

Bonnie turned to Michael Paul as soon as the last "amen" rumbled through the church. "Please keep an eye on Lydia Anne for a few minutes. I want to talk to Uncle Frank and Aunt Ellen."

"Yes, ma'am. Can we visit with Grandma and Grandpa while we wait?"

"If I'm not back by the time they're finished bidding everyone good-bye, go ahead."

She wound through the crowd and avoided the disapproving glances and frowns of some of the congregation. Those folks must have left their Christianity at home and decided to believe ugly rumors. Standing on the tips of her toes, she searched the crowd for Frank or Ellen. When the couple was nowhere to be found, she continued looking outside. Just as she decided they must have chosen not to mingle with the others this morning, she caught sight of Frank Kahler—a man hard to miss since he'd inherited his father's huge frame.

Bonnie held back her impulsive nature and slowly made her way to Frank and Ellen. "Morning," she said to Ellen and nodded at Frank. "How are you doing?"

"We're fine. Just fine." The strawberry blond shifted Frank Jr. to her opposite hip. "Oh, Bonnie, I'm so sorry about all the gossip. Is there anything I can do?"

Bonnie took a deep breath. "As a matter of fact, there is. Do you and Frank have a moment to talk to me?"

"Of course. I meant to ride out to the Morning Star yesterday, but Frank Jr. is cutting teeth and running a little fever."

Bonnie touched the baby's head. It felt warm. "Did he run a fever when cutting his other teeth?"

"Oh yes. I should have come by to see you. I'm sorry."

"Ellen, that wouldn't have been necessary. I know you too well, and listening to gossip is not a part of you."

Ellen tugged on Frank's arm, and they moved away from the small crowd.

A few minutes later beneath a live oak on the far corner of the church grounds, Frank and Ellen waited for Bonnie to speak.

"I need help," she said. "Lester Hillman is up to no good, and he's getting bolder."

"My brother would have skinned him alive for some of the things he's done and said," Frank said. "Whatever you need, count us in. Our family has had our fill, too. Lester crossed over into fightin' territory when he accused Zack of vandalizin' the church."

"What I'm going to say might make you uncomfortable."

Ellen nodded. "I have a feeling what this is about, and I'll help in anyway I can."

"Thanks." Bonnie took a deep breath with a quick prayer. "Do you recollect what Lester was like back when he and Martha were. . . spending time together?"

"I sure do," Ellen said. "He was bossy—tried to tell Martha how to run her business. That ended in a lot of arguments, but it was the only thing they fussed about."

Bonnie's next question seemed out of place in the churchyard, but it had to be asked. "Was he involved with any of the other women there besides Martha?"

Ellen frowned. "Oh yes. Shortly before I left, he approached me."

"By any chance do you know if any of those young women were those at Heaven's Gate?"

Ellen focused her attention on Frank, then to their baby.

"Honey, answer her question. If we can do anything to help, then we must."

Ellen hesitated. "When Martha was out running errands, he'd find the time to be with all of them."

Bonnie closed her eyes and nodded. That was the information she needed. Lester no doubt still used the residents of Heaven's Gate as he'd done for years.

"Tell her the rest of it," Frank said, then reached for the baby. "Tell her why you don't volunteer at Heaven's Gate."

From the tone of Frank's voice, Bonnie guessed the reason.

"Once Sylvia took over directing the home, Lester made it clear that I was not welcome there."

"But you ministered to those girls before the brothel burned. You helped some of them go back to their families. You and Jenny are best friends."

"Lester gave his terms." She peered up at her husband. "Frank started after him, but then we got word about Ben not being expected to live beyond the day. So I told Jenny being around Lester reminded me too much of my own past sins."

"I'm so sorry," Bonnie whispered.

"It's all right. Now I help with the older folks."

Bonnie smiled. Ellen was always taking a meal to someone or making sure Grant knew about one of the elderly who felt poorly. "Did Lester ever threaten you?"

"Frank would never have stood for it." She laughed lightly. "I think he's afraid of my Frank."

Bonnie glanced at the huge man devoted to his wife and son. "Thanks, Ellen. Do you mind if I pass this information along to Morgan and Grant?"

"Not at all. From the gossip I've been hearing, best Brother Travis hear it, too. I want Lester stopped. So many people think he's a good Christian man, but he's proving he's not." Ellen's voice quaked.

"Bless you. We're trying hard to put an end to all of this."

"I pray it's soon. He has a temper."

"Did he ever hit any of the girls at Martha's?" Bonnie asked.

"A few times. One of the girls threatened to tell Martha, but she left before Martha found out."

Or did Lester make sure she left?

By Thursday of the following week, Travis had endured as many nasty comments about Zack as he could handle. The newspaper article blaming him for the church's damage had turned more folks against the young man. Travis even heard a rumor about the church voting again on dropping the charges.

Travis knew he must pay Lester a call as soon as he settled Zack into his lessons. He wasn't sure what he'd say; God would have to put the words in his mouth. Forgiveness perched at the top of his list along with finding love for Lester. Christ called Travis to love all men—no matter what they'd done or would do in the future.

Being a man of God sure could test a fellow's patience.

"I'm going to see Lester," Travis said.

"Leave your rifle here," Zack said, not lifting his eyes from a page of arithmetic.

"Very funny. I'm going on God's business."

"Lester won't listen to anything you or God has to say."

"Maybe this time he will."

Zack picked up his Latin book. "I think you're wasting your time."

"God's time."

Zack shook his head and seemingly turned his attention to his lesson. He started to say something, then closed his mouth abruptly and focused on the Latin.

Travis left him to his studies and made his way to the Kahlerville

Bank in the business part of town. He had no problem determining Lester Hillman owned it. The floors were polished so bright that if Travis took a mind to, he could see himself reflected where his boots rested. Deep wine and gold wall coverings framed a huge chandelier, and the wooden partition leading to the tellers' area was in dark mahogany. He clasped his arms behind him and studied the walls. Ornately framed pictures of the different aspects of Kahlerville's history hung for all to see—and Lester stood in every one of them. Travis nearly laughed. He moved his attention to Laura standing behind the teller window and scribbling on a pad of paper. They were alone.

"Good morning, Miss Laura. Is Lester around?"

She lifted her sad eyes and smiled. "He's in the back. Would you like for me to fetch him?"

"If you don't mind. And if he's busy, I can wait." Now that Travis was at the bank, he was eager to make his peace with the man.

She disappeared and returned a few minutes later. "I can show you back to his office."

Travis took long strides down a hallway to a fine office, an even more flamboyant representation of Lester Hillman. Right behind his desk hung another stained-glass window. The man probably had his own glass factory.

Lester hunched over a ledger but straightened when Travis stepped inside his office. "I have considerable work to do, so make this quick."

"I appreciate your allowing me a small bit of your time."

Lester nodded at Laura. "Please close the door behind you."

It shut with a certain finality that caused Travis to wonder if he'd ventured into a lion's den. Sure glad he'd read the whole story and knew who won.

"You can sit down if you like."

"Thank you, I will." However, Travis questioned if he was dressed appropriately.

"So does the church need money?"

"No. We're fine."

"I said I'd replace the Bible, stained-glass windows, and the hymnals. Are you wanting something else, too?"

"This has nothing to do with the church."

Lester sat back in his leather chair, which resembled the color of dried blood. His suit fitted perfectly to his frame, every hair in place, his mustache perfectly waxed. "I don't have all day."

"I've come to tell you that I forgive you for all you've done to me, to those I care about, and especially to Zack."

Not a muscle moved on Lester's face.

"People I care about have been hurt. I can't help them or you as a preacher with bitterness in my heart. That's the reason for my visit, to ask for your forgiveness."

Lester leaned forward and folded his hands on his desk. "If this is a ploy for me to retract my statement about Zack breaking the church windows, you can leave my office now. I've done nothing in my dealings to be ashamed of."

"What about the young women at Heaven's Gate?"

"What about them? I assist my wife in Bible studies there and make certain they are gainfully employed."

"You know exactly what I'm talking about." Travis recalled word for word what Ellen Kahler had said to Bonnie. And he hadn't forgotten about the night Lester struck Rosie.

"Keep this up, Brother Travis, and you'll be looking for another church."

"Lester, let's talk sensibly."

"Grand idea. I've been trying to get you to see my way of doing business since you arrived. You do your preaching and visiting sick folks, and I'll run Kahlerville. If I need you, I'll come calling."

"No thanks. I'm not interested."

"I've lost patience with you, preacher man. Leave my bank before I throw you out." He made his way to the door and opened it wide. "Good day."

"God loves you, Lester. Let Him heal and lead you."

"Mind your own church affairs, and you'll not get hurt." He walked to the bank's entrance and opened that door.

The walk home gave Travis time to pray for Lester—the first time he'd honestly sought God to touch the man's heart. Until today Travis had believed Lester could be reached, but his heart was rock hard. He had the most money in town. He had a wife who adored him. He owned much of the land in and around Kahlerville. He had the power to persuade others for Christ if he'd let the good Lord work through him. Instead, Lester chose to satisfy his lusts.

Back at home, Travis called for Zack. No answer. He made his way to the backyard and called again. No answer. Back in the kitchen, the Latin book lay facedown on the table. No vocabulary words copied. No note.

He spent the next several minutes doing chores. Everything Zack owned was in its place. When Zack had still not returned, Travis sat on the front steps and watched the road while he clutched his pocket watch in his left hand and his Bible in his right.

"A wedding in February?" Bonnie asked. "Juanita, are you telling me that you and Thomas are getting married in February?"

The Mexican woman's eyes shone like the stars had been plucked from the sky and mounted in her dark pools. "Sí, Miss Bonnie. He asked me this morning when I brought him coffee."

"Just like that? He was romantic, wasn't he? I mean, did he get down on one knee and tell you of his undying love and beg you to marry him?"

Juanita covered her mouth. She laughed until tears rolled down her cheeks. "You do not know Thomas very well."

Bonnie laughed, too. Just thinking of Thomas on one knee was hilarious. "Are you going to tell me how he proposed?"

Juanita lifted her lovely face, the color of coffee with lots of rich cream. "I gave him a biscuit with honey, and he said they'd be busy today."

Bonnie waited on the edge of the kitchen chair. "And?"

"Then he asked me if I liked living in the big house with you. I said very much. Then he asked me if I could be happy living with him in his cabin. I asked why, and he said he'd like to get married." Juanita shook her head. "He didn't get on one leg. His knees hurt."

Bonnie giggled. "Didn't he tell you he loved you?"

Her eyes widened. "Sí. I forgot that part."

"That's the most important part."

"I think 'Sí' is the most important. But he told me he loved me after he said he like to get married."

"Good. I can see you love him, too. Why wait until February? Why not a Christmas wedding?"

"Thomas want to fix up the house for me."

Bonnie hugged Juanita and planted a kiss on her cheek. "You will be the prettiest bride this territory has ever seen."

"I'll be the happiest. I've loved Thomas for long time. Now God has blessed me with his love."

Bonnie chatted on about having a grand wedding and making sure Juanita and Thomas had a few days to themselves after the ceremony. She allowed herself to dwell on Travis for a slight moment, then shooed the thought away. Silly woman. With all of her problems, why ever would Piney Woods's preacher be interested in her?

CHAPTER  29

The shortened winter day ushered in the shadows of night, but Zack still did not return home. Travis stared at the empty road, as he had for the last four hours. He considered cooking dinner, but the fear mounting in his spirit for the boy kept him on the porch. Waiting. How he hated not knowing where Zack had gone. The more darkness gathered around him, the more thoughts swirled about his head.

Had Zack grown afraid of Lester's lies and run off? The threat of a military school in newspaper print would scare off the most stalwart heart. And Zack could have suddenly become distrustful of adults again. Travis longed to go looking for him, but where?

One more hour, and I'll go see the reverend and Mrs. Rainer. Zack may have had need to talk to his grandpa and forgot to leave me a note.

The time crept by as though he viewed each particle of sand from an hourglass slowly trickle downward. Travis's prayers grew more earnest. Unthinkable and cruel images of what could happen to Zack stomped across his mind. He shook his head. Faith, he needed faith. Closing his eyes, he lowered his head and nearly wept.

"Brother Travis?"

His gaze flew to the shadowed face of the young man, and he grabbed his shoulders. "Where have you been, son? I–I've been worried sick."

"I'm sorry. I had something important to do, and the time went by faster than I thought. Never meant for you to fret over me."

"Where were you?"

"Heaven's Gate. I needed to talk to Miss Rosie and Miss Laura."

Travis released him. "Come on inside and tell me what is going on while I fix us some dinner."

Zack peered around. "I wondered why the house was dark. Have you. . .have you been sitting here all this time?"

Travis nodded. "When you care about someone, simple things like time don't matter."

"I am real sorry."

Together they mounted the steps.

"I believe Miss Rosie and Miss Laura will go to Sheriff Arthur," Zack said.

A dozen questions slammed against Travis's mind. "You've been there the better part of the day? What did you say?"

"I told them how Lester kept bothering Mama, and how she had to stand up to him. And if they went to the sheriff, he'd stop bothering them, too."

"Zack, you convinced them when the rest of us have gotten nowhere. How did you do that?"

"I brought a copy of the newspaper and read it to them. Told them Lester didn't care about the lies he told to hurt folks. And I didn't think he cared about anyone but himself."

Travis lit the lamp and blew out the match. He pictured Zack sitting in the parlor of Heaven's Gate reading the newspaper to Rosie and Laura. "I don't understand how your reading something they already knew changed their minds."

"I prayed first, and I cried in front of them. Didn't mean to." His voice cracked. "I pointed out every lie and reminded Miss Rosie and Miss Laura what he'd done to them."

"God was with you, Zack."

"I know. I could feel Him. It was like when you put your hand on my shoulder. I wasn't alone."

"When are they going to the sheriff?"

"Not till day after tomorrow. They need to talk to Miss Daisy first. I tried to get them to go tonight or tomorrow, but Miss Daisy wasn't there, and they had a lot to talk to her about."

Travis suspected her whereabouts, but Zack had already seen and heard things far beyond his age.

"Hope you don't mind, but I told them we'd be at the sheriff's office at two o'clock that day in case they wanted you to pray with them."

Travis had thought he loved Zack as if he were his own son, but now he knew the profundity of those affections. "I'm very proud of you, and I'm sure God is, too. What you have done will ensure the safety of the women at Heaven's Gate and other folks who have been in Lester's way." Travis smiled broadly. "Today you've shown God how much you love Him and His people."

"I've been thinking about being a preacher." Zack shrugged. "I like ranchin', too."

"God will let you know what you're supposed to do with your life."

"After you left today, I thought about Lester and what you were doing in forgiving him. I didn't agree with you, but I wanted to do my part. Every time I tried to study Latin, I kept wondering what I'd do if Miss Rosie, Laura, or Daisy were my sisters. They're afraid, and a man shouldn't scare a woman. One day Lydia Anne will be grown, and I want her to be safe. So I tried to do something to help."

"You got a whole lot further than I did today. Lester didn't appreciate my visit. In fact, he escorted me out of the bank."

Zack's eyes narrowed. "He won't be so high and mighty when the sheriff hears what he's been doing."

"I hope so. Before we go to bed, we'll ask God to watch over all of them."

"Brother Travis, I'm powerful hungry."

"Me, too. What do you say we have breakfast for dinner? We've got sausage, eggs, and taters."

"Good. I'll even peel 'em—nice like you like without taking half the tater with the peeling."

Travis grinned. "How do you feel about going hunting first thing in the morning?"

"I know a good spot. One that Papa showed me. I have his rifle, but I still land on my backside once in a while."

"You're growing like a weed. It may go easier on you tomorrow. We could set out at daybreak."

"I'll be ready. Brother Travis. . ." Zack paused. "When the time is right, you're going to be a good father."

⌒⌒⌒

"Are you sure this is the best huntin' spot?" Travis asked. "I don't mind a hearty walk, but on the way back, I plan to be totin' a deer."

Zack laughed. "These woods are full of them. Papa always brought down a good-sized deer. I'll carry it back, unless we both bring one down."

They'd tramped for a mile in dense woods and not seen a thing but an occasional scolding bird or squirrel. The path looked beaten down as though someone else had recently been hunting, so Zack must have been right about the area. Travis had no intentions of complaining, but the longer they walked, the heavier the rifle grew. Now he understood what Grant Andrews meant when he said that the only thing that kept him in good shape was regular trips to Morgan's or Bonnie's ranch. They walked farther into a low-lying area where black mud oozed up midway to their boots, but they could see deer prints.

"I do have a hankerin' for fresh venison," Travis said.

"I can almost smell it cooking. Juanita and Mama can make the best venison sausage. My mouth waters just thinking about it with a big mess of fried taters and jalapeño peppers."

"I've never in my life seen anyone eat food as spicy hot as you."

"Mama says that's the Grandpa Andrews in me."

"Still, it would set my stomach on fire." Travis peered into the thick woods. "Two deer, you say?"

"We could smoke 'em and be set for a long time."

"I was thinking about the hide, too."

"Yeah, we'd have a fine time. Brother Travis, can I ask you a personal question?"

Travis let the request roll around in his head for a moment. "I reckon so. You already know more about me than anyone in this town." Then he remembered Frank and Ellen Kahler. "Ellen Kahler grew up where I'm from, and she has a little of the story."

"This is nothing about that."

"All right. Ask me."

"Do you like my mama?"

Travis thought he'd been doused with cold water. "She's a godly woman, and I admire her determination to run the Morning Star and raise her children according to the Bible."

"I mean, do you like her enough to marry up with her?"

He forced a laugh. "Whatever made you ask that?"

"Because she's pretty, hasn't a husband, and you're not married."

"Zack, two people are supposed to love each other to consider marriage. And look at me. I'm no prize. Besides, your mama is a beautiful woman."

"Remember our Bible reading the other morning about God looking at the heart?"

Travis was snared and skinned. "Yes, I remember."

"Your not wanting a haircut or shave has nothing to do with it. I've seen how you two look at each other. I'm not a man, and I don't understand all of the things that go with love, but I'm not blind."

Out of the mouths of babes, Lord. "I sure hope you haven't had this conversation with your mother."

"She'd deny it, too." Zack stopped in the middle of the path and pointed. "We need to be quiet from here. Don't want to scare them off. You can think on my question and answer me later."

Amused, Travis nodded. They veered off the path and made their way through the woods. What a fine young man Zack was turning out to be, even if he was entirely too observant. Since the tornado, he'd been real company. Still, he hadn't said a word about returning home. Maybe he thought the old Zack might take root again.

Travis reached out and placed his hand on the boy's shoulder. They'd both seen a buck not thirty feet from them sporting a magnificent pair of antlers. "You take it," he whispered. "I'll get the next one."

Grinning, Zack lifted the Springfield to his shoulder and braced himself for the recoil. He took aim, squeezed the trigger, and almost lost his balance. The buck startled then fell. With a whoop, Zack regained his balance, handed Travis his rifle, and rushed toward the downed deer. Suddenly he stopped in his tracks. Not a muscle moved.

"Brother Travis." His voice trembled, and not with the sound of a young man's voice journeying into manhood.

"What's wrong?"

"I see something awful over here. A body. It's a woman, and I think she's. . .dead."

Travis's heart pounded hard against his chest. He thrashed through the underbrush to Zack's side. The boy pointed.

"Stay here while I take a look." Travis recognized the color of her hair, and a moment later he recognized the face. *Rosie.* Her chest was stained red with blood. She'd been stabbed. He bent to her side. No one would hurt her again; she now lay in the arms of Jesus.

"Who is it?"

"It's Miss Rosie."

"Is she—"

"Yes, Zack. She's dead." Travis swallowed hard. "Son, I need you to head back to town for the sheriff. Tell him what happened. He'll know what to do. You might want to fetch your grandpa and do whatever he asks of you."

"Did Lester do this?"

"We can't judge a man without proof."

"Yes, sir. I'm real sorry. She treated me nice, and I liked to hear her singing in the choir. Yesterday she was ready to go to the sheriff."

"We'll talk later, Zack. Right now, we need to get a few things taken care of. I don't know what good I can do here, but I feel like I should stay."

Zack disappeared through the trees, and Travis sat beside the body and hoped he was wrong about who had killed this sweet young woman. Like Zack, he suspected Lester or one of the men he sent Rosie's way, but Travis had no proof, and blaming an innocent man was a terrible sin. From all apparent signs, all Rosie ever wanted was a chance to live for Jesus. Vengeance stirred inside him, hot and mean. God would handle the matter—he understood that, but it didn't stop the fury of injustice.

Fear seized him and caused him to tremble. If Lester had killed Rosie, no doubt she'd refused to give in to his demands about something. Laura. Daisy. Bonnie. They weren't safe, either. And what of Zack? Travis rubbed his face and began to pray more fervently than when he thought Zack was missing.

He glanced at the deer not far from Rosie's face and the rifle leaning across its body. Death held God's creatures in an inescapable snare. He stared into the young woman's face. His attention moved to her red-stained chest. From the size of the hole, the knife had been fairly large, and there were no telltale signs of burnt fabric like a bullet hole would cause. He stood and studied the ground. Two sets of footprints caught his attention: Rosie's and a set of man's boots. She had walked to her death.

Dear Lord, will this ever end? He shook his head and wept. *Yea, though I walk through the valley of the shadow of death, I will fear no evil: for thou art with me; thy rod and thy staff they comfort me.*

Bonnie and Lydia Anne walked through the horse barn after a good ride earlier in the morning. Today Bonnie stood her daughter on a stool and showed her how to brush down a horse after a ride. How she cherished this time with Lydia Anne. After school, she and Michael Paul often spent special time together, too. Although he enjoyed riding and learning about the ranch, he preferred music and books. His interests pleased Bonnie. She wanted her children to grow up with a wide range of possibilities for their lives. With Zack, she had no idea where his future might take him. He loved the outdoors like his father, but he'd been concentrating on his studies, too.

"Mama, Brother Travis and Zack are here," Lydia Anne said. "And so are Uncle Morgan and Uncle Grant."

Bonnie waved to the group, but the solemn looks on their faces worried her. Surely Mama and the reverend were all right. They were in good health and hadn't been complaining about anything. The men dismounted, and after a few greetings, Bonnie sent Lydia Anne to tell Juanita about the guests.

"Tell me what's wrong," Bonnie said as soon as her daughter disappeared.

"Go ahead, Brother Travis," Morgan said.

Her attention flew to the man. He stepped closer, his eyes filled with sadness. "While Zack and I were hunting this morning, we found Rosie's body."

Bonnie covered her mouth. "She's dead?"

"Yes, ma'am. I'm real sorry."

Her gaze whirled to Zack. Horror gripped her. "You were there?"

Zack stepped forward and embraced her. "I saw Miss Rosie first; then Brother Travis stayed with her while I went to fetch the sheriff."

She studied his face, her brothers, and Travis. "What happened?"

"Mama, she was stabbed."

"Do you know who did this?"

Morgan cleared his throat. "We have no idea."

"What about Laura and Daisy?" Bonnie's stomach churned.

"They're very upset. Sylvia came right away to be with them." Morgan swung his glance to Grant. "Jenny and Grant thought the other two women should stay with them for a few days."

"I have a deputy at my house while I'm gone. Frankly, I don't think my wife is safe, either," Grant said. "And we think someone needs to stay with you. Is there a way Thomas could move into the main house until this is settled?"

Shaken, Bonnie struggled to keep her wits about her. "I suppose so. Why?" Then it hit her hard. They suspected Lester.

Zack wrapped his arm around her waist. "Mama, I have to tell you what happened yesterday—before this happened to Miss Rosie."

She tried her best to concentrate on what he had to say while he told her of convincing Rosie and Laura to go to the sheriff about Lester's activities.

"Do all of you think Lester killed Rosie?" Her head pounded— not with pain but with a numbness as though her spirit refused to accept the truth.

"There's no proof," Morgan said. "Sylvia was real quick to say that Lester and she were together last evening."

Bonnie had her own opinion about Sylvia possibly covering up for her husband. "I assume Laura and Daisy now refuse to go to the sheriff."

"Mama, I asked them, but they're scared," Zack said.

"Are you all telling me that whoever did this will get away with it?" She blinked back the tears until later—later when she could grieve in private.

"It's too soon to reach a hasty conclusion," Morgan said. "What's important to us is that our womenfolk are protected."

She nodded, doing her best to digest every word without succumbing to tears. "Of course, and I'll speak with Thomas right away."

"Do you want me to come home to protect you?" Zack asked.

As much as Bonnie had longed to hear those words, she also understood her son faced danger, and he didn't need the responsibility of defending his family in the event of danger. "I want you in Kahlerville with Brother Travis. Thomas can look out for us here."

"All right, but if you change your mind, I'll come home. I can use a rifle."

For a moment she nearly relinquished, but if Lester came calling. . .

No, she refused to think about what the man might do.

Long after they left and she'd spoken to Thomas about staying in Zack's room for a while, Bonnie sat in the kitchen and remembered all the special things about Rosie. Her life had been hard. When her parents died, she took to prostitution rather than starve—a hard lot for many to understand. She'd been at Martha's brothel before it burned, along with Laura and Daisy. The reverend and Mama had taken them in, and the three lived at the parsonage until Jenny and Grant built Heaven's Gate and Sylvia offered to work with the young women. They were young—none of them twenty years old—but years of pain were etched into their eyes. They'd begun this life at fourteen and fifteen while most girls their age sat under the guidance of their mothers.

Repeatedly, each of the young women stated how much they loved Jesus, but they felt unworthy of His blessings or the gift of life. All claimed to want to leave Kahlerville. Now Rosie's wish had come true. No painful memories or physical abuse to plague her ever again.

Tears slipped from Bonnie's eyes, and she swiped them away. In the confines of her bedroom, she'd weep but not where Michael Paul or Lydia Anne might see. They'd watched her shed too many tears. A hand lightly touched her shoulder.

"Miss Bonnie, the children are outside. You can cry."

Bonnie reached up to grasp Juanita's hand. "Thank you. Rosie

LIGHTNING
LACE

was so young and beautiful. She had years of life ahead of her, and now she's gone."

"It's always sad when young people die."

"She gave her life to a ruthless man who had no respect for the living." Bonnie's words spouted venom, and she did nothing to conceal it.

"Sheriff Arthur will find him."

"I pray you're right." She glanced up into Juanita's face. "Thomas will be staying in Zack's room until this is over."

Juanita nodded. "He told me. I feel better that he's close by." Her eyes clouded.

"I'm afraid I suspect someone."

"We think the same, Miss Bonnie."

CHAPTER 30

"Sylvia says Lester was with her on Friday night, which means he couldn't have killed Rosie." Morgan massaged neck muscles, then peered up at Travis. They'd been talking in the lawyer's office for better than an hour. "But that doesn't mean he was ignorant about it, and it doesn't mean Sylvia wouldn't lie to cover for him."

Travis waited a moment to compose himself. Frustration had his head in a whirl. "How do we find out the truth?"

"The same way we tried before—Laura and Daisy."

"That's like milking a bull." Travis thought twice about his words being fittin' for a preacher, but too late. He released a heavy sigh. "Rosie's murder had me awake all night—frettin' over the others at Heaven's Gate, Bonnie, Jenny, and anyone else who's gotten in Lester's way."

Morgan leaned in closer. "I talked to Frank and Ellen to see if they'd convince Laura and Daisy to speak up, but Frank doesn't want Ellen involved. A couple of years ago, Ellen nearly died when a madman attacked her. It was right after the two were married, and Frank's been real protective ever since. But he did promise that he'd talk to them apart from Ellen."

"Can't blame him." A picture of Bonnie entered his mind.

"I imagine you feel the same way about my sister."

Travis's eyes widened. "Not sure I understand."

"No point denying what the rest of us already see, Brother Travis."

Beads of sweat broke out across his forehead. "I wouldn't want her to know, and I promise to do better in hiding. . .my feelings."

"Why? Bonnie has a sparkle in her eyes that's been gone for a long time. We're glad. Real glad. You've done a miracle with Zack and my sister. Michael Paul and Lydia Anne are happy. I'm obliged."

Travis grappled with each word. Morgan had no idea about his past, and if the man did, he'd run him out of town with his rear full of buckshot.

"You're pale, at least what I can see of you." Amusement spread over Morgan's face. Travis recalled his own brothers teasing him when he was younger. Morgan wagged a finger at him. "Maybe you need to have a come-to-Jesus meetin' about Bonnie."

"I'd never be good enough for your sister." Travis leaned back in his chair. Talking about her made him hot and cold all over—even weepy like a lovesick schoolboy. "She's the most beautiful woman I've ever seen, and her heart is pure gold."

Morgan chuckled. "You have it real bad. I won't go into all of her faults. You'll find them out soon enough once you're married."

A preacher seldom groped for words, and Travis always thought he could think as fast as a cat could land on its feet. But not when it came to Bonnie Kahler. His mind had just frozen like a creek in winter, and he couldn't find any thin ice.

"No need to ask me or Grant if we approve. We've already decided you and Bonnie should get married as soon as possible."

Had the whole family been talking about them?

"Now that I've embarrassed you and had a good laugh, let's get back to the business of proving Lester is behind Rosie's murder." Morgan's countenance changed to one of concern as he spoke.

"Seems to me that if we could figure out why he says and does things, then we could understand how he thinks."

"As I've said before, you'd make a good lawyer. I've been thinking." Morgan paused. "I know a man who owes me a favor. Having him follow Lester around makes sense. One of these days, he's going to get so sure of himself that he slips. And I want to be there to make sure he's behind bars for a long time."

"I'm glad Sheriff Arthur appointed a deputy to protect Laura and Daisy. I'm hoping Lester doesn't know about it."

"Talked to the sheriff last night about that very thing, and he agreed. Although, like so many folks in this town, he believes Lester can do no wrong because he gives money to the church."

Bonnie sorted through the leather trunk of Christmas ornaments and decorations. The nativity set that Ben had given her for their first Christmas—the one carved by his great-grandfather from Germany—lay on the top. As she carefully examined each piece wrapped in scraps of old fabric, memories of Ben and the lovely Christmases spent with family flowed gently over her cheeks. Unlike last Christmas, when she despaired until crawling into bed for two days, the tears today became a healing balm. At last she was able to put the past in proper perspective. She'd proven her mettle and made more progress as each day passed. Ben had given her the gift of love and three precious children. Forever she'd love him, yet to continue living in grief was wrong—and selfish. She dreamed about the future and whoever God put in her life. The fear of giving her heart again sometimes gripped her, but God understood her turmoil, and He promised to walk with her until she met Him face to face.

Less than a week remained until Christmas, and the preparations were well under way. She and Juanita worked daily on planning the holiday dinner and baking. Bonnie completed gifts for family and friends and items for the ranch hands, helped Juanita with housecleaning, and assisted the women of the church in taking care of those less fortunate. Thankfully, the many rehearsals for the

Christmas Eve service had produced a fine program. The children would act out the first Christmas while the choir supplied the music. Michael Paul and Travis planned to sing "O Come All Ye Faithful," and Michael Paul would play the part of Joseph. He'd also sing "Silent Night." Lydia Anne had a white costume for her role as an angel; however, she wanted to be a shepherd. Her little daughter's tomboyish ways were a source of amusement in the family.

Rarely did a single member of the family have Thanksgiving and Christmas at their home in the same year, but Bonnie had won out this season. Her family understood her desire to make up for previous holidays. Her only regret was that the Kahlers' celebration on Christmas Day conflicted with hers, but she and the children would visit the other grandparents on Christmas Eve before church.

Christmas Eve services. The reverend and Travis had boarded up the broken windows at church to keep out the weather, and although Lester had boasted of paying for the repairs, nothing had happened. The services would still be meaningful; nothing stopped good people from celebrating Christ's birth.

She smiled happily. Then a gray cloud took residence above her. Sheriff Arthur had not found out who had killed Rosie. Like her brothers and a few other close friends and family, Bonnie suspected Lester. After all, if Rosie carried Lester's child, Sylvia might not be so forgiving this time, and she provided the funds for Lester's many investments.

Bonnie shuddered. Had anyone given thought to Lester putting an end to Sylvia's life, too? He'd be in fine shape with no money problems and able to seek out all the women he wanted. Surely the idea had crossed the minds of her brothers and Travis. Reason told her that Lester might get away with Rosie's passing, but Sylvia held a high position in the community. Folks would not rest until someone was arrested. The thought sickened her until she turned to prayer to rid her mind of another tragedy.

Decorating the house to celebrate the birth of the Savior and contemplating the probability of another woman's death did not mix well. Bonnie set aside the box of Christmas items until Michael Paul returned from school. The children could help her with the decorations before supper.

⌘

"Merry Christmas!" Morgan called the moment he entered the house on Christmas Day, his arms laden with packages. "And I'm hungry enough to eat a horse."

Bonnie had not felt this excitement in a long time. All those she held dear to her heart were gathered near to her.

Casey and the children filed in behind him, carrying food and wearing smiles. Grant and Jenny with their little girls, Mama and the reverend, Juanita and Thomas, Zack, and Travis crowded in the parlor around the nine-foot Christmas tree.

"It's beautiful," Mama said.

"Michael Paul and Lydia Anne helped Juanita and me," Bonnie said. "Of course, we ate more popcorn than we strung on the branches."

"When do we eat?" Grant asked. "I don't want to feast on a horse, but a couple of pies will do. Of course, the only thing that keeps me in shape is working here or on Morgan's ranch."

"You two are teaching your children wonderful manners," Casey said, and Jenny promptly agreed. Her two sisters-in-law were so different: Casey with her height and vibrant auburn hair and petite Jenny with a mass of thick, dark curls.

"If we'd eat, that would solve the argument," the reverend said. "I'll read the Christmas story, and then we can feed this hungry family."

And the Christmas celebration began.

When everyone had eaten their fill of dinner, they found a place to sit in the parlor around the tree. Bonnie set her gifts aside and watched the others open their packages. She especially adored the looks on the children's faces as they tore into the wrappings and dipped into their stockings.

"Your turn, Mama," Zack finally said.

She smiled and opened each package as though it were the most precious gift of all. Zack's box to hold Ben's personal belongings brought tears to her eyes. Michael Paul had made a beautiful card and a Christmas tree ornament in school, and Lydia Anne had helped Grandma Kahler crochet a shawl. Bonnie came to the last gift, and she knew without asking that it was from Travis.

The brown paper package felt like a book. Ah, another journal for the one she was fast completing.

"It's not a journal," he said.

She glanced up as she gently tugged at the wrapping. "Are you reading my mind?" *Don't flirt. Morgan and Grant will start teasing and never quit.*

The clothbound book turned easily in her hand: *Information for Authors,* by Eleanor Kirk. She opened it. *December 25, 1898. To Bonnie, May this book assist you with your writings. Fondly, Travis.*

She peered into his face, which appeared anxious with little lines across what she could see of his forehead. "Thank you."

"You're welcome."

She turned another page, conscious of her entire family's eyes studying her every move. But she didn't care. This little book would help her to write properly. All the stories floating around in her head could be written and possibly sent to a publisher in New York City. The thought thrilled her. The first page displayed the author's name and address. It also listed the author's fees for reading and giving an opinion of the manuscript. How wonderful. In the preface, the author stated the book's contents and how it would especially aid the beginning writer. The chapters brought another surge of excitement: the appearance of a manuscript; methods of literary work with paragraphs on inspiration and how to arrange a schedule to write, literary qualities, the varieties of literary work, different types of manuscripts, information about editors, the making of books, and publishers.

"What a perfect gift," she said.

"I thought you might help me with some of my sermons. I mean after you read it and have the time."

"I'd be honored to."

Morgan chuckled. Grant coughed. The reverend covered his mouth, and Zack had a grin that spread from ear to ear. She closed the book and lifted her chin. Too late—the teasing had begun.

CHAPTER  31

After Christmas, Travis settled in to creating sermons and having Bonnie read them so she could give her opinion. It gave her an opportunity to apply the techniques about writing from his gift and for her to see if she enjoyed what she learned.

The time together also took its toll on his heart to the point where he wished he hadn't asked her to help him. Every moment made him feel like he was on the losing end of a tug-of-war.

"I think this sermon needs more scripture," Bonnie said. The two sat on Travis's front porch. Although it was a bit chilly, she refused to set foot inside his house even if her son was there. "I corrected a few misspelled words."

He chuckled. "Two weeks ago, you didn't say a word about my spelling."

"That's because I assumed you knew how to spell those Old Testament names and cities."

"Don't tell Zack. He thinks I never make any mistakes in my writing."

She laughed, and oh how he treasured the musical sound. "What should I ask for in order for me to keep quiet?"

A kiss would ease this heart.

Bonnie must have read his thoughts, for her face reddened. He'd not trade a minute of the time spent with her. "Bonnie, I'd give you about anything you wanted."

She nibbled on her lip and focused her attention on the paper with his sermons. "I like the part where you suggest folks memorizing more scripture to keep God's Word buried in our hearts."

He should apologize. He'd most likely offended her, and she didn't have the heart to scold him. But what stayed foremost in his mind was the murderer who walked the streets of Kahlerville. Either Lester had killed Rosie, or he knew who had. Laura and Daisy avoided Travis, and Bonnie reported that the young women were sullen and said little. Travis prayed for answers and kept his eyes and ears open.

"I wish the sheriff could have found out who killed Miss Rosie," Zack said the following morning as the two took their early walk. The weather had dropped to freezing the night before, and the brisk pace helped warm them.

"You and a whole lot of other folks," Travis said.

"When my uncles, you and I, Mama, and my papa's family think Lester had something to do with it, why doesn't the sheriff arrest him?"

"No proof, son. Unless someone comes forth with information that ties him to Rosie the night she was killed, we have nothing but suspicions."

"I wake up in the morning and go to sleep at night worrying about Mama. She's made Lester plenty mad."

"Thomas is there with her."

"I know, and that makes me feel better. Sure wish she was more like my aunt Casey. You can be sure Lester would never cross her. Have you talked to Mrs. Hillman?" Zack sank his hands into his pockets.

"Once, right before Thanksgiving when several of us gathered pecans at Morgan and Casey's ranch."

Zack's question twisted in Travis's thoughts. He'd been thinking about talking to Lester's wife again. Their conversation that day in

November had gotten interrupted. Maybe now, she might feel like talking. Especially when she'd told them how she loved the residents at Heaven's Gate.

"Brother Travis, are you listening to a thing I say?"

Travis snapped back to Zack. "Sorry. I was thinking about Sylvia."

"Maybe God wants you to pay her a visit."

He chuckled. "Has anyone ever said you can be quite persuasive?"

"A few." Zack grinned. "I might be a preacher yet."

"All right, you win, Brother Zack. After breakfast, you work on your studies, and I'll spend time praying and then go see Sylvia."

Shortly after nine thirty, Travis walked to Heaven's Gate where Sylvia volunteered a few hours most mornings. He often wondered what she did there every day since Laura worked at the bank and Daisy helped take care of Sylvia and Lester's huge home in the afternoon. Most likely, being at Heaven's Gate gave her purpose. However, Lester had just given notice that she'd not be volunteering past the end of February.

The overcast day brought a cold wind out of the northwest, and a sprinkling of rain chilled Travis to the bone. He hoped the dreary weather did not contribute to Sylvia's mood during their conversation.

Hesitantly, he knocked on the door. An empty hollow sound met his ears, like the spirits of those who lived inside. They were afraid, and no one should live in fear. The verse from 2 Timothy 1:7 came to him: "For God hath not given us the spirit of fear; but of power, and of love, and of a sound mind."

Ofttimes, Zack reminded him of young Timothy from the Bible, and Travis did sense God calling the young man into the ministry. Or maybe it was wishful thinking on his part. Whatever lay ahead for Zack, he'd be a success.

The door opened, and Sylvia greeted him. Her flushed face disturbed him, and the quivering smile she offered did little to settle his concern.

"This is not a good day for a visit," she said.

"Is there something I can do to help?"

In the background, he thought he heard weeping. He sharpened his hearing while determined to engage Sylvia in more conversation.

"No. Nothing. But thank you for your kindness."

"Are you or one of the young women ill?"

"Daisy is feeling poorly, and I'm tending to her."

He listened again. "She must be in a bad way, because I hear her crying. Perhaps Doc Grant should take a look at her."

"No," Sylvia said much too quickly. "She'll be fine."

Uneasiness crept all over him much like the sensation he'd felt just before the twister struck. "I'd like to talk to her."

"I can't let you do that, Brother Travis."

"I could pray for her. Or possibly read scripture."

Sylvia stiffened. "She's not up to visitors."

"Has she been beaten?"

She pressed her lips together for a moment. "Why ever did you ask such a thing?"

"Sylvia, too many women are hiding things in this town. Afraid of someone or something. My guess is Daisy is in a bad way. I wish you'd let me come in. I really want to be of help. Have you forgotten who found Rosie's body? How many times was she beaten before someone killed her?"

"I can take care of Daisy just fine."

"Sylvia, I don't mean to be rude or a nuisance, but I'm not in the mood to bury another one of the young women from Heaven's Gate."

"Surely you don't think I had anything to do with Rosie or—"

He shook his head. "No, but I think Daisy knows more than what she told the sheriff about Rosie's demise. Maybe you do, too."

"I don't need to listen to this. My Lester—"

Travis realized he'd gone too far. Seemed like all the pent-up anger about what was going on at Heaven's Gate and Lester's evil nature had caused Travis to sprout horns. "I'm sorry. I'm really sorry.

I believe your only role in what has been going on here is protecting those you love. I am terribly sorry for my harsh words."

He whirled around and retraced his steps, but instead of heading home, he walked on toward the church. He needed to get right with God for his outburst. He wasn't a sheriff, or a lawyer, or a doctor. He was a preacher, and his calling meant tending to the spiritual needs of his flock, not condemning other folk who didn't live up to his expectations. For certain, Lester would have him thrown out of Piney Woods Church after hearing he lashed out at Sylvia.

Travis hesitated outside of the church. He didn't deserve to step within its holy walls. The agony of disappointing God, again, thundered against his senses. The screams of a hundred demons pronounced him unfit. *You do not love God. You do not love His people.*

A wave of sickness swept over him. Memories of the days in Tennessee slammed against his thoughts.

For thy name's sake, O LORD, pardon mine iniquity; for it is great.

Trembling like a leaf in the wind, he grasped the door handle and entered the Lord's house. The silence pounded in his ears. Bile rose in his throat. He despised himself. Courage and strength pulled his gaze to the cross, the symbol of what Travis's sins had cost his heavenly Father.

Somehow he managed one foot in front of the other to the altar and there lay prostrate on the floor. He begged forgiveness for what he'd said to Sylvia. His words to her had not been righteous indignation in upholding the gospel but revenge against Lester. How he'd hurt God.

Travis prayed for Sylvia and Lester. He begged for a heart to love Lester and to see him through the eyes of God. His entreaty moved to all the folks involved in the evil he'd seen of late. He called each person by name and asked God to protect them and draw them closer to Him. Then he wept. He prayed again for Lester and the men who abused Laura and Daisy. Travis pleaded for guidance in the hours and days ahead—the unknown. Not since his church in Tennessee had shut him out had he shed so many bitter tears for his own actions. Today, like so many times in the past, he questioned why God had called such a sinful man into the ministry. Folks looked up at him to be a representation of Jesus, and look how he treated them.

He needed to produce fruit, not the sour grapes sickening his spirit. That's what pleased God. *"But the fruit of the Spirit is love, joy, peace, longsuffering, gentleness, goodness, faith, meekness, temperance. . . ."* Travis couldn't offer good fruit if he did not love others as himself.

His prayers ended, but he couldn't bring himself to move. Scripture came to mind. Words from hymns comforted him. With his eyes tightly closed and his heart heavy with his own worthlessness, Travis sensed he was not alone. Without opening his eyes, he realized he was feeling the presence of the almighty God. Peace whisked him up and held him as though he were wrapped in a cocoon. Forgiveness had been granted, and once more Travis recommitted his life to the will of God.

"Brother Travis? Are you all right?"

The voice of Jocelyn Rainer brought the communion to an end. Part of him wanted the time with God to continue, and the other part understood he must get on with His work.

"I needed forgiveness," he said.

She stayed in the back of the church, and he appreciated her discretion regarding his misery.

"Would you like to be left alone?"

"No. I'm finished." He pulled himself to his feet and faced her at the opposite end of the aisle. "Sometimes I wonder how God puts up with the likes of me."

"We all question that." She laughed lightly, and he smiled in response. "The reverend often asks the same thing. Don't be too hard on yourself. You're a man, not God."

"I just hurt a wonderful lady, and I don't think my apologies eased her damaged spirit."

"I'm sure she's forgiven you."

"I've never seen an ounce of selfishness in Sylvia Hillman. Makes me downright ashamed of myself, but the damage is done."

"Let God heal the problem."

"Sounds like you were privy to my prayers." He walked toward her.

"It's a universal one." She smiled again. "How about a cup of coffee before you take on the world? Got a few biscuits left from breakfast, too."

Wisdom. Jocelyn Rainer held more in her little finger than he'd earn in a lifetime of preaching.

"You'll be fine," she said "Many of us are praying for you."

"I appreciate your soothing words. Just what I needed to hear. Some days I think I have more in common with the apostle Peter than Jesus."

"But look what Jesus did through Peter. He learned to love himself because Jesus used him in a mighty way."

Travis chuckled. "I see your point."

"I don't need to know what went on with you and Sylvia, but I do think she needs to open her eyes to what is happening in this town."

❧❦❧

Bonnie had a few minutes to spare before picking up Michael Paul from school, so she decided to stop at the parsonage. The reverend was upstairs taking a nap when she and her mother sat down to chat.

"I understand you've been helping Brother Travis with his sermons." Mama's eyes held a special gleam in them. "He told me about it this morning while we enjoyed a cup of coffee and a couple of the reverend's biscuits."

"I'm only practicing what I learn from the book he gave me at Christmas."

"Hmm. Seems like an excuse for him to spend time with my daughter."

Bonnie wrinkled her nose and laughed. No point in hiding the obvious, even if Travis had never said a word about the two of them. "Hush, someone will hear you, and then the good folks of our town will have more to talk about."

"How are the plans going for Juanita and Thomas's wedding?"

"Oh, very good. I've made a list of guests, although Juanita and Thomas want only a few people there. We're nearly done with her dress, a very pretty blue."

A knock at the front door stopped any further discussion about the upcoming wedding.

"Goodness, what a busy place this is today," Mama said. "I hope whoever's here doesn't want the reverend. He gets cranky without his full nap."

"Do you want me to chase them away?" Bonnie asked.

Her mother shook her finger. "Never mind. I'll handle it."

Bonnie stayed in the kitchen, knowing that the reverend received most callers when serious illnesses and death occurred. The hum of voices grew louder until she chose to find out what was going on.

"Lester, this time you've gone too far. Does Sylvia know what you're doing?"

Bonnie held her breath. *What was Lester up to now?*

"I haven't shared this with her yet."

"Why do you persist in spreading rumors and causing trouble?"

"I expected you to stand up for Brother Travis since he's carrying on with your daughter."

Bonnie had heard enough and hurried to the door. "What is going on?"

"Lester is letting us know that he plans to approach the deacons about church discipline for Brother Travis. He feels he is not a fit preacher for Piney Woods. The rumors about you two are disturbing too many of the church members." Mama's face flushed red.

"What about church discipline for you?" Bonnie stepped between Mama and Lester. Disgust oozed from the pores of her skin.

"Are you going to hit me again, like the last time I pointed out a truth?" Lester shoved his hands into his trouser pockets and leaned against the side of the door. "Watch out, Mrs. Kahler, you might be the next one to face the good people of Piney Woods Church. After all, you are the one involved with Brother Travis."

Bonnie dug her fingers into her palms to keep from wiping the smirk off Lester's face.

"I think you'd better leave," the reverend said.

Bonnie whirled around to see her stepfather standing on the stairway.

"I'm only informing you of what I'm doing. Seems rather obvious to me that the church is vandalized and a young woman is killed soon after Brother Travis comes to town. I heard from one member that Brother Travis might be covering up Rosie's murder, and some folks think Zack's a part of it, too. If I were him, I'd resign before facing church discipline."

"You're not Brother Travis," the reverend said. "Take your lies elsewhere."

"I want the address of his former church. The deacons will want to know everything about him."

"I have the correspondence if they want to read it. But all you're getting from me is a request to leave my home. And if I ever hear of you accusing my grandson of murder again, I'll write the next newspaper article."

Lester nodded and left. Silence clung to the hallway like cobwebs longing to be swept away. Bonnie was too angry to speak.

"He'll never get folks to remove Brother Travis," the reverend said. "He's the man God brought to us and the man God will protect. I'll go tell him now."

CHAPTER 32

Travis sat on the back porch and watched the cloak of night embrace the trees before him. The bare branches reminded him of the long arms of God reaching out to the world. Judgment had come to Travis Whitworth—the preacher. Soon everyone would learn how he'd failed his flock before coming to Kahlerville. Only time stood between Tennessee and Texas. He'd been a fool to think his sins rested in the past like a grave full of live bodies.

God's forgiven me. That's the only thing that matters. But the consequences were still to be reckoned with.

What hurt the most was Lester's accusation that he or Zack might have had something to do with Rosie's murder. Eli Palmer's words about Zack echoed in his mind. *He'll be murderin' us in our sleep. Mark my words.*

How many others had Eli made that claim to? Could he and Lester be working together?

Prayer was supposed to change things. God heard every plea, and if a man prayed in faith and confidence, then He answered. Travis clung to the promises of God; he preached them at every opportunity. But the situation in Kahlerville had gotten worse. The more he prayed, the more folks were hurt—or killed. The problem must lie with Travis.

Why had he believed God had forgiven him and wanted him to continue in the ministry? Had he mistaken the Lord's voice for his own desires? Travis wished he knew. In times like these, he wanted to think the good he'd done in Kahlerville made up for the wrong in Tennessee. Yet he understood that God didn't look at deeds to cover up wrongdoing; He looked at a man's heart. Travis had been broken over his sin in Tennessee, and his relationship with God had been restored by true repentance. But now he doubted every move, every prayer, every piece of scripture that he felt God had given to him.

"Brother Travis, don't feel so bad about what Lester is doing. You told me the story about your old church, and you're too hard on yourself. You tried to help a woman like those living at Heaven's Gate."

"Thank you, Zack. I have to tell the deacons what happened a week from Sunday. They've called a meeting with me after the evenin' worship. It will be up to them to decide whether I continue as their preacher." He hadn't the gumption to tell Zack about Lester accusing them of Rosie's murder.

"But Uncle Morgan and Uncle Grant are deacons."

"So are Eli and a few others who aren't happy with me right now."

"That's because they believe lies and not the truth."

Travis smiled. "Sit with me here a spell. There are a few things I'd like to say to you before I meet with the deacons, and tomorrow I might change my mind."

Zack seated himself beside Travis. All the while, night settled in.

"The time's come for you to return to your mama. She needs you, and I'm being selfish by wanting you here with me. I couldn't be any more proud of you—or love you more if you were my own son. If the good Lord ever blesses me with a family, I hope I have a son as fine as you." He paused a moment to stop a tear from rolling down his face and to collect his emotions. "Michael Paul and Lydia Anne need you, too. They are beautiful children, but without a father, they need someone to look up to. It's a lot of responsibility for a young man nearly thirteen years old, yet I have no doubt of your abilities. Tell them you love them. Tell them when you make mistakes. Guide them, but let them learn about life on their own. It's a balance. Encourage them to seek God's face in good times and bad. Memorizing scripture should be a part of their life, like breathing. Can you do that for me?"

"Yes, sir. I'll do my best. I don't believe the deacons will make you leave Piney Woods. I believe God has other plans."

"You're sounding more like a preacher every day."

"I think God might be calling me there."

Travis placed an arm around Zack's shoulders. "Keep listening. When the call on your life consumes you first thing in the mornin' and the last thing at night, then you'll know it is God's will."

"What about Mama?"

"What do you mean?"

"I see you care for her, and I'm not jokin' about it. She cares for you, too. Seems like God would want you to do something about it."

Travis swallowed hard. "If the good Lord wants your mother and me to be together, He'll have to work out the problems to make it happen."

"All right. When. . .when do you want me to move back home? I understand what you're saying, but I will miss you."

Zack nearly swallowed his words, and for a moment, Travis thought both of them would weep. Then they did.

Travis finally squeezed Zack's shoulders. "We can still see each other. I'll miss lots of things between us, too. I talked to Miss Scott, and she says you're welcome back in school."

"I don't think anyone could ever teach Latin or the Bible like you."

"I reckon those classes could continue." Travis took a deep breath. "I'm thinking this Sunday afternoon would be a good time for you to move home. We'd have three more days together."

That night, Travis lay awake. He'd done the right thing with Zack, even though it had been hard. If the deacons kept him at Piney Woods, he could visit Bonnie and the children. Of course, the deacons could very well insist he stay away from them. The only thing he knew for certain was that God rode the waves of uncertainty with him.

His mind trailed back to the many happenings in Kahlerville since he'd first arrived. God had placed some wonderful people in his path, and their friendship had tempered the misfortune.

His thoughts rested on Rosie's death. Who had killed the young woman who carried a child? The murder had snatched away two lives. How tragic. How futile.

Could Lester have been so ruthless as to destroy her? She hadn't been beaten. There was only the single thrust of a knife to her heart. Whoever had committed the killing either planned her demise or had done so in a moment of anger. What puzzled him was that Lester had used his fists in the past to persuade Rosie. Not a mark had been found on her.

Did this mean he was innocent of her murder? But who? The father of her child? One of the men Lester brought to Rosie's door? Travis pieced together what he remembered about the morning he and Zack had found her body.

The path had been trodden by Rosie and another man. He had led her to the clearing and stabbed her with a large knife. The sheriff said the blade was larger than one typically used for hunting. What else had the sheriff found? Travis concentrated on the findings. Nothing came to mind.

Suddenly Travis sat upright in bed. The knife. Could it have been a kitchen knife? A thought sickened him. Where could that hideous thought have come from? Still it persisted until he could not let it go.

Sleep had evaded Bonnie ever since she learned that Lester had succeeded in having the deacons call a meeting about church discipline of Brother Travis. If the rumors were found true, then

Brother Travis was unfit as a preacher and possibly linked to Rosie's murder—along with her son. At the very least, Travis could be asked to leave Piney Woods—or worse yet, face the sheriff for questioning about Rosie. And what of Zack? Lester was getting his way again.

Dear God, protect Travis and Zack. Bring the truth to light. You know Travis's heart, and you know he and I are innocent of the gossip. And you know my Zack would never hurt anyone. Please, I beg of You, help us all through this trial. And guide me in my feelings toward Travis.

The days ahead would pass slowly until the deacons met. She could only imagine the heaviness weighing on Travis and dear Zack. He'd come so far in his faith. She prayed again for her son to remain strong and not to allow the sins of man to dissuade his faith.

Bitterness rose in Bonnie until she flung back the quilt covering her and walked to the window. For a moment she thought she'd be physically ill. *Lester.* How could one man cause so much trouble for so many people? God instructed His children to love their enemies. He'd help rid her heart of hate, or she'd be no better than Lester.

Right now she needed all the help she could get.

A sky full of stars grasped Bonnie's attention. Her father used to sit her on his knee and tell her that, just as God had taken time to mount the stars in the heavens, he'd surely listen to her every prayer.

Travis realized he needed to do something about his suspicions. The thoughts refused to let him go no matter how hard he tried. At first he blamed Satan for trying to persuade him to think evil about an innocent person, but after much prayer, he believed God was urging him to find the answers. Travis intended to follow his hunch, but he needed someone to go with him. Morgan Andrews was that man.

As Travis lifted his fist to knock on Morgan's office door, he didn't know whether to pray he was right or wrong. Neither alternative settled well. The situation reminded him of the time when he spoke to Zack about choosing between two wrongs. Taking a deep breath, he rapped on the office door of Kahlerville's lawyer and waited for him to respond.

"Door's open."

Travis knocked the dirt from his feet and prayed once again for truth. In the moments that followed, he revealed some of his speculations.

"You want me to help you prove what?"

"Not prove, simply look into the matter," Travis said. "It's far-fetched, I know."

Morgan studied him curiously. "You're thinking a kitchen knife was used to kill Rosie, possibly one from Heaven's Gate?"

"The sheriff never found the murder weapon, and he said it was larger than a hunting knife."

"All right. Let's stop at the boardinghouse and pick up a loaf of bread first. I hope you're wrong, Brother Travis."

"So do I."

With the loaf of bread under Travis's arm, he and Morgan set their sights on Heaven's Gate. Neither man spoke. No doubt Morgan's mind whirled as fast as Travis's.

"Sylvia may be the only one there," Travis said.

Morgan didn't respond. With what Travis had suggested, what could he say? Once on the porch of Heaven's Gate, the two men went into action. Sylvia opened the door and greeted them.

"Are Miss Laura and Miss Daisy in?" Morgan asked.

She cast a wary glance at Travis. His last conversation with her had not been forgotten. "No. Can I help you with something?"

Travis handed her the brown wrapped package. "We were at the boardinghouse, and the bread smelled so good that Morgan snatched up a loaf. We wanted to see the young ladies but didn't want to come empty-handed."

"That's very considerate of you. I'll make sure they thank you properly."

"Do you mind if we come in?" Morgan asked. "We'd like to talk to you for a moment."

"Lester would not approve."

"That's my fault, and once again I apologize," Travis said.

"We only want to talk about the young ladies and ask a few questions," Morgan said. "I think we may have a possible suspect in Rosie's death."

"Oh, my. In that case, come on in. I surely want the horrible situation resolved." She ushered them to the parlor.

Someone walked across the upstairs floor. Travis assumed Daisy was recovering, but he chose not to mention whomever was on the second floor.

"May I offer you gentlemen some coffee?"

Morgan glanced at Travis. "I don't ever refuse a cup of Sylvia's coffee."

"I hear she makes the best."

"Yes, thank you, ma'am. Know what? I'd like a slice of that bread. Made my stomach growl when I smelled it, and the feeling hasn't left me." Morgan chuckled.

"Certainly." She smiled and disappeared. The sound of clinking cups and saucers came from the kitchen, and soon she returned carrying a tray with the coffee, cream, and sugar. "I'm so sorry, but I can't find a knife to slice the bread."

Travis inwardly cringed.

"One of the girls must have misplaced it," she continued.

"My goodness, just when a man has a hankering for warm bread."

"And I have freshly churned butter, too."

Morgan pulled a pocketknife from his trouser pocket. "Would this help? I cleaned fish with it the other night."

"I don't think so. The knife we always use has a wide blade and slices through bread quite nicely without chewing it up."

"Must be a fine knife. Did you purchase it for the kitchen here?" Morgan asked.

Travis's heart hammered too hard to think of any fancy, lawyerlike questions.

"As a matter of fact, I did. A fine one, too."

"Maybe next time then." Morgan picked up his coffee.

"I remember you Andrewses drink your coffee black," she said, "and you, too, Brother Travis."

"Yes, I always thought the stuff folks put in coffee ruined the taste," Travis said. "You have a good memory."

"Thank you. Now what did you want to ask me about Laura and Daisy?"

Travis glanced at Morgan for him to begin.

"Do you know where they were the day Rosie disappeared?"

Sylvia tilted her head. "I told this to the sheriff, but I will repeat myself. Laura and Daisy were at the bank. Lester had extra work and needed the help."

"What about later on in the evening? Were all three girls here?"

"Rosie wasn't when they returned from work. They assumed she was with me."

"Obviously that wasn't the case." Morgan took another sip of coffee.

So did Travis. If this made him this nervous, how would he handle the deacons' questioning?

"Did the girls all get along?" Morgan asked.

"For the most part. Three women in the same household can sometimes be a bit stressful." Sylvia gasped. "Surely you aren't thinking one of them had anything to do with dear Rosie's misfortune?"

Morgan twisted his head. "Well, Sylvia, someone did this terrible thing, and all three of them have lived pasts that saw violence."

"Mercy. Mercy." Sylvia fanned herself.

"And the knife is gone." Morgan shook his head. "Brother Travis, do you think we should go see the sheriff with this new evidence?"

"Seems like a good idea to me."

Morgan swung his attention back to Sylvia. "I know how you

feel about Laura and Daisy—like they are your own daughters—"

"I can't believe either of them would do such a thing. Brother Travis, you've visited with them, just as Lester and I have done. But I know they lived a hard life before Heaven's Gate. Does such a tragedy seem possible to you?"

"Any thought of wickedness is troublesome to me. Lester and I have had our differences, but I know he conducted Bible study with them, gave them jobs, helped support them. This is all downright ugly."

Sylvia folded her hands in her lap. "Maybe it is a good idea for you to take this information to Sheriff Arthur and let him figure out what's best."

"Can I count on you to make sure Laura and Daisy don't leave town?" Morgan asked. "I mean, if you hear of any plans, you'll go to the sheriff about it?"

"Naturally. To think I am with those two nearly every day. Makes me fearful for my own life."

"Do you mind if we look about the kitchen to see if the knife could simply have been put in another spot?" Morgan asked. "I sure wouldn't want to be thinking one of them is guilty only to find the knife is really here. I hope you understand my interest in this case has grown since rumors are that Brother Travis and Zack might be involved."

"You go right ahead. We all want the truth."

Morgan whistled as he and Sylvia moved things here and there in the kitchen. Sylvia removed all of the dishes from the cupboards while Travis made his way to the back porch.

"I don't see how that knife could be out there," Sylvia said. "But you go ahead and look, nevertheless."

Travis took in the neatly arranged jars of fruits and vegetables, a small stack of newspapers, and jackets for cooler weather. "Nice backyard," he said. "Looks like y'all had a good garden this past year."

"We did. Had more tomatoes and green beans than we knew what to do with."

Travis finished with the back porch and made his way to the garden. He saw nothing suspicious, but why would the killer put a knife there anyway? In the corner of the yard, a large oak tree shaded a small area that faded into thick brush. A perfect spot to pray about what he and Morgan were doing.

As Travis pondered the realization of the missing knife and the likelihood of someone at Heaven's Gate killing Rosie, he kicked at the brush and stared into the thick undergrowth.

Boots. He moved closer to study them. Strange, a pair of men's boots covered in mud had been carefully placed near a small sapling, as though waiting for feet to fill them up. They were expensive ones, too. He picked them up and carried them to the porch steps. He opened the door, detesting what he'd found.

"Sylvia, I found a pair of men's boots in the brush."

She clopped across the kitchen to meet him. "Oh, those are Lester's."

CHAPTER 33

"Do you honestly think we're going to find that knife in these woods?" Grant asked.

"If God wills it." Travis picked up a fallen log. "Yesterday Sylvia helped us search for it. She was real anxious. I imagine she'd have come with us today if we'd asked."

"I think you're both crazy to think it's here."

Morgan bent to examine the ground not far from where Travis and Grant worked. "Little brother, are you complaining?"

"Not at all. Just questioning the good sense of what we're doing. So what if the knife we find came from Heaven's Gate? You're still looking at a handful of suspects."

"Don't forget the boots," Morgan said.

"That doesn't mean Lester killed Rosie." Travis regretted his words the moment they hit air. His hunch hadn't played out yet, and he surely didn't want to look like a fool.

"What do you mean?" Grant asked. "Aren't those boots and the missing knife why we're here?"

"Think about it." Travis gave the log a toss. "Do you honestly think Lester would tramp through anyplace where his boots might get dirty, then not make sure they were cleaned?"

When neither man responded, Travis braved forward. "And if he wanted to hide them, why in the brush behind Heaven's Gate?"

"Go on," Morgan said. "I want to know what you're thinking."

"I'm saying Lester is a rotten apple, but I don't think he killed Rosie."

"Then who did?" Grant asked. "One of the girls?"

Travis shrugged. "I'm thinking it was a woman."

Morgan studied him. "And you don't think it was Laura or Daisy, do you?"

"Maybe not."

"As I said before, you think like a lawyer." Morgan stood and looked around. "I want to find that knife."

For the next hour, the three men combed the area. Travis planned on turning over every stick and pile of leaves until the knife surfaced. There was no need to rush home. Zack had his schoolwork, and later he planned to visit his mother and tell her about his plans to move home. She'd be elated; Travis already felt miserable, selfish for wanting the young man to stay.

"Hey, I found it." Grant picked up the blood- and dirt-coated knife. "Looks like the killer gave it a toss. So do we take this to the sheriff?"

"Not sure yet. Anything unusual about it?" Morgan asked.

Grant turned it over in his hands. "Yeah. It has the initial "H" carved in the handle. That eliminates Laura or Daisy being a part of the killing."

Morgan turned to Travis. "Are you still thinking the same thing?"

Travis nodded. "Even more so. I've never been a man to accuse another for a crime without proof, but I'm afraid Sylvia killed Rosie."

Grant handed the knife to his brother. "As gruesome as it sounds, the evidence does point to Sylvia. However, someone could have stolen the knife."

Travis took a deep breath and told him what he thought really happened to Rosie. "With the poor girl carrying a child, probably Lester's, and with his having had an affair before that produced children, Sylvia had reason to kill."

"Doctoring is a whole lot easier than what we're trying to do," Grant said. "What happens now?"

"We have to ask a few more questions." Morgan said. "Want to come along?"

"By all means. Lester may not be real happy with your showing up at Heaven's Gate wielding one of his knives and asking Sylvia more questions about the night of Rosie's death. Somebody might need to get stitched up."

"He'll be at the bank, and we'll make sure Sheriff Arthur is due to pay a call." Morgan turned his attention to Travis. "Brother Travis, I think you need to do the talking."

"This doesn't come under the work of a preacher," Travis said.

"But Sylvia is going to need you," Morgan said. "You're the best man for the job."

Travis wished Morgan or Grant would handle the disagreeable situation, but he understood why he must be the one to talk to Sylvia. This was going to be hard. Real hard.

～✺～

Bonnie wished her brothers or Travis might have had the consideration to tell her what they were up to. But they hadn't. Sometimes men behaved like little boys. Jenny said Grant had left their home in the company of Morgan and Travis just after sunrise.

"I'll be back later," Grant had said. "Got something important to do. Hope there isn't an emergency while I'm gone."

How very responsible.

"How long are you going to wait?" the reverend asked.

She shook her head. "Not a minute longer. I have work waiting for me at home. Guess if this is anything crucial, I'll hear about it later."

"What's on your list for today?" the reverend asked.

"Why? Do you need me?"

He laughed and raked his fingers through white hair. "Just making conversation. You have more energy lately than ten little gals your size."

"I'm making up for lost time. To answer your question, I want to check into how much work it would take to widen the creek bed. Every spring, water sweeps over the bank, but by summer, the cattle have to be herded there to drink."

"Are you planning to help the ranch hands dig it out?"

"Reverend, are you making fun of me?"

"Every chance I get."

He kissed her cheek, and she hugged her mother, who had been quite amused with Bonnie and the reverend's bantering.

"Don't be upset with your brothers and our dear preacher. My guess is they're attempting to find proof of some lies in Lester's accusations."

Bonnie nodded. "If that's the case, they can stay gone until next week."

"Will you be at the house midafternoon?"

"I should be. Are you planning on making a call?"

"Not me, but I know someone who is."

"Who?"

"I'm not saying. It's a surprise."

She made her way to the back door. "If I hurry, I'll be finished by noon or so."

"Afternoon, Sylvia," Travis said. "Can we talk with you a few minutes?"

"My goodness. Three of you. Perhaps I should have Lester with me."

"We can talk outside on the porch if that makes you feel better. I hope you don't mind that we stopped here so close to noon. I understand you're normally at home by this time, but this shouldn't take long." Travis gestured toward the rockers and glider on the porch.

"I need to get my shawl. It's a mite chilly."

She disappeared for what Travis considered longer than necessary. Maybe she was apprehensive. He was—clear to his toes.

The door opened, and Sylvia smiled before taking a seat on the glider.

"Brother Travis, is this about our search yesterday?" She blinked and folded her hands in her lap.

"Yes, ma'am. We found the knife near the site where Zack and I found Rosie. We wanted to see you first before—"

"You found the missing knife?"

"Yes, but it wasn't what we expected. I'd show it to you, but it's not clean."

"Is there something I should know?"

"I'm afraid the knife has the letter 'H' carved in the handle."

She sighed. "That set came all the way from Switzerland. I never dreamed it would someday be stained with Rosie's blood."

Lord, guide me. "Do you want to tell me about the knife?"

She hesitated. "Do you have any idea how much I love Lester?"

"I've often seen it in your eyes."

"When I realized the knife was missing from home, I simply took the one from here."

"But you helped us look for it yesterday." Travis kept his voice calm and his words slow and confident. Praise God for His guidance.

"I know, and I'm sorry. Sometimes it's real hard to accept the truth about someone you love." She smiled first at Morgan and then Grant. "Gentlemen, would you care for some fresh custard pie and coffee?"

"No, thank you," each man said.

"Now, Grant. I've never known you to turn down a piece of pie."

Grant laughed lightly. "Does sound strange, but our topic of conversation has taken my appetite."

"I imagine so when you've dedicated your life to healing—not killing."

Travis stood up from the rocker and seated himself beside Sylvia, patting her hand in sympathy. He prayed silently for the truth about Rosie's' death.

"Can you tell us what happened?"

"Oh, yes. My Lester—" Sylvia's voice broke, but she quickly regained her composure. "He had a miserable childhood, the oldest of twelve children. They were always hungry. In many ways, Lester still is." She paused, and a sob escaped her lips.

"We have all day. And I'm right here."

"Brother Travis, have you prayed for me?"

"I have, and I still am."

She wiped her eyes. "Lester never loved me. He made that clear on the evening he proposed. My father had left me a rich inheritance and his plain looks. Lester was everything a comely woman would want, let alone a homely one like me. I was a fool to think he might grow to love me. It never happened, but my love for him grew daily. He's a wonderful businessman, charming and shrewd. He'd tell me about his dreams, and I'd finance them." She paused and stared into Travis's face. "I really wanted children. Lester wanted them even more than I did. I don't think he was kind to his younger brothers and sisters, and being a father would help him make up for that. He talked about a family constantly until he simply gave up. I think he could have forgiven me for my plainness, but he never got over the fact I couldn't give him children."

Bonnie lifted a dipper of water to her lips. The hard work felt good, but she was ready to get a hot bath and wash her hair while Lydia Anne napped. Her gaze swept across the ranch in a panoramic view. Yes, her ranch. Christmas had been a splendid time, and she lived in the memories of special moments. God willing, there'd be more. She lifted her face to the chilling breeze and smiled. The future looked good despite the problems with Lester and poor Rosie's unsolved death. Tomorrow she'd resume her volunteer work at Heaven's Gate and hopefully persuade Laura and Daisy to speak up.

And dear Travis. Mixed emotions surrounded the mere thought of his name. He'd shown her what it meant to live again, to rely on God for everything. Trust. Faith. Travis had been a rope to grab hold of when she was drowning in her own misery. The tender glances exchanged at Christmas revealed his heart—and hers. How very odd that a mountain man with a soft-spoken voice had become so endearing.

Thomas had taken the wagon into town to pick up a load of lumber at the mill. He was adding on a room to the cabin for Juanita and himself. The addition was the finishing touch to his and Juanita's wedding plans. Six more weeks, and the two would be married. Bonnie shook her head to dispel the envy wrapping around her heart. For shame. She should be elated for the couple, not jealous of their happiness. Thomas had lost a wife to cholera years ago. He deserved a woman as fine as Juanita.

Thomas also planned to collect the mail. They expected a letter from the horse breeder in Kentucky, and she was ready to wire money for a good stallion.

"I'll be back in short order," he'd said. "I've asked Jesse to keep an eye on the house."

"No need. Send him on with the others to help clear the far woods for pasture."

Thomas frowned. "My job is to keep you safe. I gave my word."

"All right. I'll let Jesse keep Juanita and me company."

Thomas's eyes crinkled with his smile. "Thanks. I want no worries while I'm gone."

But as soon as he left with the wagon, she sent Jesse on with the other hands to clear the woods. They needed the extra land for grazing. The idea of being termed a helpless female scraped against her pride. After all, Morgan didn't fret over leaving Casey alone.

The sound of horse hooves drew her attention. The sight of a familiar appaloosa gelding sent a sinking feeling to the pit of her stomach. She thought she'd seen the last of Lester, especially with Morgan's ultimatum that day in the pouring rain. Obviously not. He rode up alongside her. Turning to face him, she crossed her arms over her chest.

"Mornin', Bonnie." He lifted his hat and smiled his jaunty best.

"Lester, I asked you not to come here again. You're not welcome."

His smile may have swept other women off their feet, but not Bonnie Kahler. The thought of him and what had happened to Rosie stayed in the front of her mind. And to think he'd hinted of Travis's and Zack's involvement.

"I'm heading back East tomorrow on business, and I wanted to take Zack with me. I plan to make a stop in Virginia, and my friend at Fishburne assures me there is room for him. The boy wouldn't have to travel alone."

"How many times have I told you that Zack is not going to a military school? He's staying right here with me." Caution settled on her, and she bit back a mouthful of bad-tasting words. "I appreciate your offer, but Zack has everything he needs until he's ready to further his education at a university."

"I normally like kids, all of them, but that son of yours is trouble."

"Then you don't really know him."

"Can we go inside to talk about it?" He leaned against his saddle horn. "I know this is a delicate subject, but have you ever wondered why he found Rosie's body?"

"Get off my land, Lester. This conversation is over."

"A lot of folks claim either Brother Travis or Zack killed her. Think about it. He either stabbed Rosie or is covering up for the preacher."

"Neither of them are killers. You're disgusting."

"The truth always hurts the innocent."

"Get off my land."

He laughed. "You've gotten a bit feisty of late."

"I take after my mama—and my brothers."

He frowned. "I rather liked the old Bonnie."

"You mean the one who needed wine to sleep and cried at the drop of a hat? She doesn't live here anymore."

Lester smirked and then dismounted.

"I asked you to leave. Do you really want to tangle with my brothers?"

"Let me ponder on that a minute. Who in this town would take the word of an Andrews over mine? Morgan married an outlaw, and Grant married a whore's sister."

He stared at her for a minute, and the intensity frightened her more than she cared to admit.

"Thomas isn't here," he said. "I saw him take the wagon into town."

"He'll be right back."

"Liar. I heard him say he had lumber to load."

"That won't take long. I'm warning you."

"Warning me against what? Bonnie, you know I'm in love with you. Have been for a long time. And I think you're in love with me, too."

"Don't make me sick. Need I remind you that you're married? Sylvia is a wonderful woman, and you don't deserve her. I'll never understand why she took you back after your affair with Martha."

"Sylvia's never let me forget that." He rubbed his gloved palms together. "Why did you tell her about our little arrangement?"

"The wine? Because she deserved to know the truth. I played a part in that ruse and needed to ask for her forgiveness."

"You only wanted to cause trouble between Sylvia and me."

Bonnie lifted her chin. "You manage trouble before you get out of bed in the morning." Disgust sprinkled on her like dirt in a dust storm. "I'm asking you one more time to leave, or I'll get help."

He reached inside his jacket and pulled out a revolver. "You and I are going to have a talk inside."

CHAPTER  34

Sylvia wept silently for several minutes before she lifted her dampened face. "I'm sorry, gentlemen. I will do better."

"It's all right." Travis squeezed her hand lightly.

She glanced straight ahead, not at any of the men listening, but beyond Heaven's Gate to a place where agony twisted at her heart. "I expected him to have affairs. He's an attractive man and needed. . .those indiscretions. I ignored them with an understanding that without me, he had no funds to grow his business. He'd never leave me. The hardest one to endure was his relationship with Martha. When I learned her sons were his, I thought he might leave me. He threatened, but she left town before he could stop her. He never forgave me. Thought I'd given her money."

"Did you?" Travis asked. "Not that anyone could blame you."

"No. She didn't need me. Martha was a strong woman. She came to see me the same day she left town. Told me that she had to leave—because of the boys. She'd decided to tell them that their father had died so they'd never be branded with being fatherless. I was very angry with her and Lester."

"Can I get you a glass of water?" Travis asked her.

She tilted her head. "What a dear man you are. No, I don't need any water. If I stop for too long, I'll not have the courage to continue."

"I wish all this wasn't necessary. I see what it's doing to you."

"But we must. You are here because the truth must be spoken." She lifted her hand to Morgan and Grant. "I have a lawyer to hear my story, a doctor to help me when the pain becomes unbearable, and a man of God to walk with me through this living hell."

Travis swallowed hard.

"I believed Lester when he asked me and the church for forgiveness. He said he'd made his peace with God and would never be unfaithful again. And for a long time I trusted him. Jenny and Grant are saints to have built this house where the brothel once stood. When she asked me to direct it, I was thrilled. My days were often long, and it not only gave me something to do, but I also had purpose and something to talk about with Lester. He encouraged me and then asked if he could help. I was pleased. So very pleased."

~~~

Bonnie tried desperately not to show her fright, but fear nearly paralyzed her. Juanita and Lydia Anne were in the house. "Why, Lester? I don't want to have a relationship with you."

"Doesn't matter. I've had every woman I ever fancied."

"Even the ones who abhorred you?"

"None do after they have a taste of my affections."

Bonnie backed up toward the house. "What happens when a woman refuses you? Or is that why you killed Rosie?"

He chuckled. "Can't pin her murder on me. I had nothing to do with it."

"She was carrying a child. Was it yours?"

"If it was my child, why would I have killed her?"

"Sylvia."

"You have no idea what you are talking about. But I didn't kill her."

"You can tell that to all the folks when they learn what really happened. You killed Rosie, and it's only a matter of time before the people of Kahlerville find out."

An odd look passed over Lester. Was it regret? Or remorse? But the look quickly faded to arrogance. He waved his revolver. "Do you really want me to use this in front of your daughter and Juanita?"

"The ranch hands would hear."

He raised a brow. "None of them are around. I looked real good before I rode in. Now we'll step inside so you can pack Zack's things."

"You know he lives with Brother Travis."

"When will Zack arrive? Don't tell me he isn't coming this afternoon, because I heard the good reverend and Brother Travis talking about it yesterday." He laughed. "To think you are such good friends with that revolting-looking man."

"Why do you need Zack? I thought it was me you wanted."

"Oh, it is pretty lady. Having him with me is a deposit on my requests from you. You won't talk to a soul as long as I have your son."

"There is no military school, is there?"

He laughed. "Believe what you want."

"You are an animal."

"I've been called worse. Sylvia has a wonderful vocabulary when it comes to labeling me." He raised the revolver. "Inside."

Bonnie trembled. She remembered years ago when an outlaw had held her, Mama, and Casey at gunpoint. Grant had been shot trying to help them; his blood splattered on the kitchen floor. At the time, she'd nearly fainted with fright. Not this time. Lydia Anne's and Juanita's lives were at stake.

The door behind her opened, and Lydia Anne rushed to her.

"Mama, I can't wait to tell you what happened with my kitty," she said. "Juanita said for me to take a nap, but I wanted you to tuck me in so's I could tell you."

"Of course, sweetheart." Bonnie bent and kissed her cheek.

"You're shaking."

"I'm a little cold." Her throat constricted as though a snake coiled around her. Indeed, he had.

Lydia Anne peered up at Lester. "Hello, Mr. Hillman. Nice to see you."

"I have a cinnamon stick for a sweet little girl." He reached into his pocket and bent down to hand it to her.

He's a demon.

Lydia Anne smiled and took the candy. "Thank you."

"Your mama just offered me a cup of coffee. We're going to have a nice chat while you're sleeping. Can you save the story about your kitty until later? I might still be here, and I want to listen, too."

"I can tell you now."

He touched her cheek, and Bonnie wanted to kick him in the face.

"Oh, sweet girl, you look so very tired."

She yawned as though he'd directed her every move. "All right. I will nap now."

Dear Lord, help me. I don't know what to do. How long would Thomas be gone? Why had she sent Jesse with the others?

Bonnie took Lydia Anne to bed, tucked her in, and gave her a big hug. She wanted to cry and hold her little daughter. Instead, she shut the door and made her way back down the stairs.

"Lester has a soft spot for children, and I thought of the girls living here as my daughters. I thought he did, too. I was not blind to what their lives had been like at the brothel, but God had given them new life, and I wanted to, also. They were my little girls—the babies I never had. I gave them all of me. Just like I did Lester. Then I stumbled onto the truth."

"And what did you learn?" Travis asked.

"That he had his way with Rosie, Laura, and Daisy. I'm not sure about the others who once lived at Heaven's Gate."

"Sylvia, I understand this is so very hard, but we must hear the whole story to help you."

Her lips quivered, but she finally managed a faint smile. "I suspected it all along, but it wasn't until Rosie was beaten the first time that I put the pieces together. You see, my girls love Jesus. They were finished with the sordid life, and Lester wanted them as before. I was so stupid to believe Lester had changed, such a fool to believe he wanted to lead them in Bible study because of concern for their souls. And then he started using them—putting them to work just like Martha had. Except this was worse. My precious girls wanted freedom, and I did nothing. I covered it up in hopes the sin would stop. I prayed. I really prayed."

"What happened to Rosie?

"She had such dark moods, and I worried about her. When I asked her what was wrong, she'd say nothing. The other girls claimed they had no idea. One day, she and I were alone here at the house, and I begged her to tell me what tormented her so. She cried and said she had to leave Heaven's Gate, but that was all. I suggested a long walk, perhaps a picnic. She laughed. Said it was too cold for a picnic, but we went anyway."

"Did you wear Lester's boots?"

Sylvia sucked in a breath. "How did you guess?"

Travis patted her hand. "I assumed it yesterday."

"They're an old pair, and I don't like to get my shoes dirty. It had been raining earlier, and my shoes, well, I didn't want to ruin them."

"So you went on a picnic?"

"Yes, I wrapped a loaf of bread with a bit of ham."

"And the knife?"

"No, I forgot the knife, so we stopped at my house to get one. We walked out to the woods north of town. Well, you know where."

"What happened?"

"We talked for a long time, and then she began to cry. I held her and told her that whatever was wrong, I could help her. When she confessed to me that she was with child, I knew the child had to be Lester's." Sylvia stiffened then shook her head.

"I'm so sorry. What did you do then?"

"I walked away and left her there crying. When I got back to my house, I told Lester. He left and returned several hours later."

"Have you told me all of it?"

"Yes, Brother Travis. The next thing I learn is. . .she's dead." She buried her face in her hands. "Lester must have killed her."

"Are you ready to talk to the sheriff about this?"

"What will happen to him?"

Travis turned to Morgan. "I think you could answer her question much better than I."

Morgan cleared his throat. "With your testimony, the sheriff will arrest Lester. I imagine Laura and Daisy will testify, too. He'll be held in jail until trial."

Sylvia clutched her hands to her heart. "Morgan, could you represent him? I'm sure he didn't mean to hurt her."

"I'll see what I can do. I'm not Lester's favorite lawyer. But if he asks me, I'll represent him." Morgan walked over to her and bent down to his knees. "You have to be prepared for a harsh penalty."

Sylvia paled. "But I'm sure it was an accident."

"A young woman is dead, and she was carrying his child." Morgan stared into her face.

Travis waited. Time seemingly stopped. He hoped Morgan and Grant were praying for the truth. "You know this means that Lester will face trial for Rosie's murder," Morgan said.

"What will happen to him?"

"He'll be executed, or he could get life in prison."

Sylvia gasped. She stood up from the swing and walked across the porch. "Lester has hurt me badly for all the times he was with other women. When I hurt the most was when he gave money to the poor. That was his way of saying he was sorry."

Morgan walked to her side. "Now is the time to talk to the sheriff. I've already asked him to come by here. Lester needs to be arrested."

She nodded. Long moments passed. She shook her head while

tears flooded her eyes and streamed over her cheeks. At last she took a deep breath and looked at Travis. "I thought I could blame him, but I can't."

Travis stood on the other side of Sylvia. "Loving someone when they have done something wrong is hard."

She shook her head. "I can't do this, not even to Lester. I—I lied," she whispered. "I—I stabbed Rosie. I couldn't help myself. I couldn't bear the humiliation of Lester fathering one more illegitimate child. He sold the other two girls to those men, but he kept Rosie for himself."

Travis wanted to believe his suspicions had been wrong, but by her own admittance, Sylvia had killed Rosie.

"I threw the knife as far as I could," she said. "The boots had drops of Rosie's blood on them, so I wiped off the blood and set the boots in the garden. I couldn't look at them."

"Are you covering up for Lester?" Travis asked. "Do you love him so much that you would take the blame for something you didn't do?"

She shook her head while tears flooded her eyes and streamed over her cheeks. "I thought I could blame him, but he's innocent of Rosie's death." She peered into Travis's eyes. "What will happen to me?"

"I'm not sure, Sylvia, but I will be with you all the way. And so will God."

"Can He ever forgive me?"

"All you have to do is ask Him."

"I didn't mean to hurt Rosie. I was slicing the bread, trying to distract her so she'd say what was on her heart. When she told me, I seemed to lose my senses. And then I listened to Lester claim you or Bonnie's precious boy had killed her. I said nothing, too scared to admit I was a murderer."

"I'll help you," Morgan said.

"Do I go to jail now?"

She sounded more like a little girl than a grown woman. Lester had hurt her beyond any human comprehension. She'd been pushed to murder, and now she must suffer the consequences.

"I imagine the sheriff will be along shortly," Morgan said.

She nodded. "I suppose y'all knew I did it. The guilt was torturing me. I kept seeing Rosie with blood all over her chest. I hated myself, but I couldn't take back what I'd done."

They sat with Sylvia on the front porch of Heaven's Gate. She and Travis swung in the glider. Back and forth. Like the mountains and valleys of life. No one said a word. Travis grieved and prayed, and from the looks on Morgan's and Grant's faces, they did the same. She clung to his hand, and Travis wondered when the last time was that Lester had touched her in tenderness.

CHAPTER  35

Lester sat sprawled on Bonnie's sofa, puffing on a cigar. A disgusting man smoking a disgusting cigar in her parlor. She loathed the very sight of him. And to think he sat in church every Sunday making contributions to all the varied needs of the community.

"Sylvia is far too good for you."

"She would never leave me, my dear. What would her church friends say?"

Bonnie considered crashing a lamp across his head. Something. Anything to protect those she loved.

He patted the sofa beside him. "Come, sit down, dear. We have much to discuss."

She lowered herself onto a chair across from him. "What must I do to stop you from taking Zack?"

"Nothing. I plan to take him regardless of what you say or promise. If you want that no-account boy of yours to stay alive, then you'll do whatever I ask, when I ask."

"How do you live with yourself?"

"Quite nicely, thanks to the bank and my investments."

Bonnie chose not to respond. She needed time to plan how to stop him.

Juanita stood in the arch of the parlor. "Good afternoon, Mr.

Hillman. May I get you something?"

"I'm fine, Juanita. Thank you for offering."

She nodded and turned to Bonnie, giving her a questioning look. "Anything for you?"

A gun. Go for help. "Not at the moment."

"Congratulations on your upcoming wedding," Lester said.

"Thank you, sir."

"Sylvia was telling me that she'd like to help with the preparations. I was certain we'd be invited." He shifted on the sofa. "On second thought, I'm a mite hungry. Do you happen to have any eggs?"

Confusion wrapped around Juanita's delicate features.

"I'd love a plate of scrambled eggs and some potatoes to go with them. Do you have time?" he asked.

Juanita glanced at Bonnie, but Bonnie could not give away Lester's threats. He'd hurt all of them.

"I will make them for you," Juanita said.

When Juanita disappeared, he pulled out his pocket watch. "I give you fifteen minutes to pack his things. He shouldn't have much here since he's been living with Whitworth. By then Zack will be here, and you can tell him that you've changed your mind about military school."

Bonnie would like nothing better than to claw his eyes out. "You'll never get away with this. The law will be breathing hot on your every move."

"Not if you want your boy to live. Now run along like a nice mama. Time's a-wasting."

With clenched fists, she rose from the chair. Lester was right. She had no choice but one.

"If I hear any noise or you take too long, I'll be up the stairs."

"I understand."

"Don't look so forlorn. You'll come to enjoy this arrangement. No one else has ever regretted my advances except Rosie. She threatened to go to the sheriff one too many times until a good beating took away her stubbornness. I demand obedience. Perhaps I hadn't made that clear."

"You may have Laura and Daisy bullied into keeping their mouths shut, but not everyone in this town believes you're a model citizen."

He smiled and pointed to the hallway. "I doubt it. Go. You have a job to do. Oh, before you leave, let me give you a clue as to Zack's new home."

Her heart slammed against her chest.

"I have a friend who has a farm in Arkansas. He needs good strong boys to work it. We made a nice arrangement for Zack."

She sank her teeth into her lip to keep from saying anything that she'd regret later. Hurrying up the winding staircase, a plan began to form. She willed her body to cease shaking and her mind to clear. Papa and Mama would have splattered any man's blood across the walls of their house if their children had been threatened. Mama would still do it.

And I'm an Andrews.

Bonnie crept past Lydia Anne's bedroom, stopping briefly to make sure the door was closed. Fear made her dizzy. Later when Lester sat behind bars or was laid out cold in a pine box, she might give in to the terror. But not now. Sudden realization shattered her. She couldn't put an end to Lester's evil, not on her own. She needed God, and she hadn't even prayed.

Lord, have mercy. You are the only one who can help me here. Guide me. Give me strength to see this through.

In the bedroom, she took a quick glimpse out of the window to see if any of the ranch hands had returned. The barns looked deserted. Taking a ragged breath, she turned her attention to the loaded rifle beneath her bed. She dared not make a sound, for she knew Lester had not made an idle threat. She didn't really want to kill a man, but she would. The many times she'd slipped away for target practice now had meaning.

Once her fingers wrapped around the cold metal barrel, she scooted it to the rug beside her bed. Her gaze flew to the doorway and back again. With the ease of a mother who practiced the art of working quietly, she checked to make sure the rifle was loaded. A shotgun would have cut him in two. Not a bad thought.

Rising to her feet, she swung the rifle into her right hand. Her babies were at risk, and no one was going to hurt them. She'd die trying and take Lester with her.

"Mama." Lydia Anne's small voice shook Bonnie's resolve.

"What are you doing up?" she whispered. "You're supposed to be in bed."

Lydia Anne pointed to the rifle. "Why do you have that?"

Bonnie laid the weapon across her bed. In an instant she knelt to her daughter's level and grabbed her shoulders. "You get back to bed this instant, or I will whip you very hard."

The little girl's eyes filled with tears.

"Do you understand me?"

Lydia Anne nodded.

"Do not leave your room until I come to get you. Is that perfectly clear?"

Again, Lydia Anne nodded.

"Now go. If I hear as much as a whimper, I'll not only whip you but take away your kitty."

Never had she spoken so harshly to Lydia Anne. When this was over, she'd apologize. The little girl scampered across the wooden floor and slammed the door. The crash echoed over the house. Bonnie held her breath.

"Bonnie?" Lester called from the stairway. His boots thudded as he mounted each step.

"Lydia Anne got up from her nap. I'll be right down." Her voice sounded more like a frightened child than a confident woman. She snatched up the rifle from the bed and lifted it to her shoulder.

"I'll see for myself."

"No need. I'm on my way down."

She made her way to the hallway. Lester hadn't gone back down the stairs. Maybe he needed a little help.

Lord, my thoughts are so brave, but I'm not. I'm not so sure I can squeeze the trigger, either.

At the top of the stairway, she saw him standing midway on the steps. His eyes widened, then he laughed.

"I didn't know you knew how to hold a rifle."

She took aim. "Lay your revolver at your feet. Now."

His smirk turned to a frown, but he obliged.

"Get out of my house."

"What are you going to do, hit me with the rifle?"

To reinforce her words, she started down after him. "When I was eleven years old, my father taught me how to shoot. No one else knew. The only reason I practiced and listened to Papa was because he said the day would come when I'd wish I knew how to use it. The day's come. Your day of reckoning."

"You expect me to believe that?"

"You'd better, or your blood is going to paint my steps. I've never gotten over your spreading gossip about Brother Travis and me, accusing others of killing Rosie, and vandalizing the church and blaming it on Zack."

He chuckled. "Breaking those windows and destroying a few hymnals hurt my bank account, but it was necessary."

"What about the reverend's Bible?"

"It's in my office."

"Is there anything you won't do?"

"Try me." He planted his foot on the next step.

"Get out, Lester. My finger's itching to pull the trigger."

Lester backed down to the entrance with Bonnie following him. She prayed Juanita would stay in the kitchen. The front door opened wide, and Zack walked in. He glanced up at her with a puzzled stare. Before Bonnie could warn him, Lester whirled around and grabbed

Zack's shoulders. His hand slipped to her son's neck.

"Maybe you'd better drop the rifle." Lester meant business, but so did she.

Bonnie's mind raced back to all the times she'd slipped away in the past few months for target practice. With God's help, she could save her son from this monster.

"What is happening here?" Zack attempted to shake off Lester's hold, but the man appeared to hold him tighter.

"Don't worry, Zack." This time her voice did sound stronger.

"But you don't know how to use a rifle, Mama."

She forced a smile. "Remember the coyote that Thomas found dead outside the chicken house a few months back?"

Zack nodded. "Shot right between the eyes, and none of the ranch hands owned up to it."

"That's because your mama shot it, just like I'm going to finish up the coyote who has his filthy hands on you."

She squeezed the trigger just as Lester threw Zack on the floor and reached for the door. The bullet lodged in the wood just above Lester's head. She raced down the stairs after him, but when she reached the door, Lester had already been stopped. Travis had him pinned to the ground with his knee into his back.

"That woman is mad," Lester said. "She tried to kill me."

"I heard enough of the conversation to know you're lying." Travis glanced up at Bonnie. "Are you all right?"

She nodded. "He still didn't acknowledge killing Rosie."

"That's because he didn't do it."

"Then who did?"

"Sylvia. She confessed earlier today. Laura and Daisy went to the sheriff this afternoon once they learned about the confession and revealed Lester's dealings. He's on his way out here now to arrest Lester for abusing Rosie and the others."

"Sylvia killed Rosie?" Lester winced as Travis tightened the hold on his arms. "She couldn't hurt anyone, not with her gentle spirit."

"Well, Lester, she did."

"But. . .but Sylvia cared for my no-good brothers when they came begging for handouts."

"Love and jealousy often rule a person's judgment." He glanced up at Bonnie. "I'll tell you the whole story later. Right now I need a rope."

"What did you ask me?" *Slow down. You're angry with Lester, not Travis.*

Travis startled. "A rope. I need a rope to tie up Lester."

"I've spent the past hour with a man who was threatening me and my children, and now all you do is ask me for a rope?"

"I'll get one," Zack said. "I want him tied real tight."

All the fear and fury from the ordeal sent shivers up and down her arms while her face flushed hot. "And to think I wanted you to ask me to marry you."

Travis sputtered. "What?"

Realization of what she'd just said hit her like a blast of cold air. Maybe she *was* mad. He hadn't made an unreasonable request. What was wrong with her? She shook all over. "I'm sorry. Oh my, I must go see about Lydia Anne." She whirled around in time to see Juanita staring with her mouth open. Instead of making one more ridiculous statement, Bonnie avoided them all and hurried after her daughter.

~~~

Travis went through the motions of tying Lester's hands while his mind spun with what Bonnie had said.

"Did you see what my mama did? Why, she sent a bullet into the front door right where Lester had been standing," Zack said. "But why did she get so mad about the rope?"

"I have no idea, but I'll find out as soon as the sheriff gets here. He was right behind me. I was afraid of this when your uncles and I found Lester gone from the bank."

The sound of horses' hooves punctuated his words. Within

minutes, Sheriff Arthur had Lester in custody. "I'll take him into town," he said. "Thank God our womenfolk can now live without fear."

"A prayer answered." Travis stood and glanced at Zack, who happened to be grinning.

"What are you smiling about?" Travis asked.

"The look on your face when Mama said she wanted to marry you."

"She must have been real upset," he said.

"You mean upset enough for the truth to come spurtin' out?" Zack laughed. "You best go see what you can do to make her happy. And be careful. She's a good shot."

Travis trembled all over. Without another word, he made his way into the house.

"Bonnie, I need to talk to you."

No answer.

"Bonnie?" He still shook like a scared rabbit. Maybe because he felt like one.

"She's upstairs," Juanita said from the front porch.

Travis made his way up the staircase, all the while rehearsing what he should say, yet realizing the words would refuse to come. One thing he knew for sure: He loved Bonnie Kahler.

"Bonnie?" he called softly. He didn't want her aiming that rifle at him.

"I'm right here."

He glanced up and saw her holding Lydia Anne. Both were crying. How was he supposed to handle that? *Lord, I'm in trouble here, and I need help.*

"Is she all right?" he asked

"I scared her," Bonnie said with a sob. "I said ugly things to her when I was afraid Lester might hurt her."

Lydia Anne snuggled against Bonnie's shoulder. It looked to him like the little girl was doing better than her mama.

"We need to talk," he said.

She shook her head. "I'm sorry. I was upset about Lester and said things I didn't mean."

Standing there in the hallway with the western sun shining through the window, Bonnie looked like an angel, his angel. "I think you meant every word. I—I've been in love with you for a long time, but I never thought you'd have any feelings for a man like me."

She tilted her head, and a fresh glazing of tears sprinkled her cheeks. "That's not true, Travis. You are a fine man, and I love you."

"You do?"

"Yes." She sniffed, and he pulled out a handkerchief for her. "You're always doing this."

"I'd like to do it permanently. Take care of you, I mean."

"Are you sure?"

"I'm more than sure, and I want your children as mine."

"What is Brother Travis saying?" Lydia Anne asked.

"I'm asking your mama to marry me and let me be a papa to you, Zack, and Michael Paul." There, he'd said it, and the words came out just fine.

"Say yes, Mama." Lydia Anne lifted her head from Bonnie's shoulder.

Bonnie sighed, then smiled through her tears. "I don't think I have a choice."

"Do you mind if I come up there and give you a kiss?" he asked.

"Mama or me?"

Travis laughed. "Both of you."

❧⊙❧

Travis walked by the barber shop. How many times had Hank offered him a haircut and a shave? He should get himself fixed up. And he should tell Bonnie the truth about his past. Should have done so the afternoon she agreed to become his wife. In fact, his whole congregation needed to be told what had happened in Tennessee. The days of hiding from the past were over.

If he planned to marry Bonnie and wanted God to bless him and his new family, then the story must be told. Tomorrow morning just before the sermon seemed like the best time. Bonnie always arrived a little early. Then he'd tell his flock. He glanced down at his clothes. Morgan had given him a fine suit, one that would fit. High time he wore it.

Travis retraced his steps on the boardwalk and twisted the knob on the barbershop door.

"Welcome, Brother Travis," Hank said, glancing up from a newspaper. "What can I do for you?"

"That offer still open for a haircut and a shave? I thought the town might want to see what their preacher looks like."

Hank laughed until he held his sides. "Just set yourself right down."

❦

Travis wished Zack still lived with him, but he'd stayed with his mama since the day Sylvia and Lester had been arrested. Travis needed someone's opinion about his appearance this morning. Freshly groomed and wearing Morgan's suit, he looked like his old self. But his heart had changed. God had slowly taken care of his relationship with Him during the past year, from his time alone in the mountains on through his pastoring of Piney Woods Church. This morning he needed God's guidance more than ever. Before lunch today, he'd know whether he still had a church and a future bride and family.

The thought occurred to him of heading over to see the reverend and Mrs. Rainer before church, but did that mean he didn't trust God for the outcome today? No point in taking a chance. He snatched up his Bible and stepped out into the early January air.

His habit was to be at church before anyone else considered getting there. That way he could pray. This morning he needed lots of prayer. He should have left the house before daylight. After all, he'd been awake.

At eight o'clock, the door swung open, and the reverend boomed his familiar, "Morning." Travis swung around from the front pew.

"Is Brother Travis here?" the reverend asked.

"It's me." Travis managed to stand. "I decided it was about time I looked more presentable."

The reverend's eyes widened. "My land. I never thought. . .Why, you're a fine-looking man."

Travis smiled. "We're going to talk about my change in church this morning after I tell Bonnie. I'm going to need a lot of prayer while I confess to everyone what happened in my last church."

The reverend walked toward him. "I knew right from the start what caused you to leave Tennessee. When you answered the call, I wrote one of your brothers, and he told me the whole story. He has regrets about the way he and your other brothers handled the problems there."

"And you still asked me to pastor this church?"

"We have a merciful God, and I wanted to give you an opportunity to start over. I knew someday I'd hear your side of the story."

"Thank you. I'm a mite nervous, but my mind's made up." He glanced about. "No one's seen me but Hank, so we'll see how many other folks won't recognize me."

The reverend chuckled. "My guess is no one, except maybe Bonnie."

Travis stayed seated in the front pew until the church filled up. Why hadn't Bonnie come early? A few folks shook his hand, and Morgan even called, "Good morning," not recognizing his own suit. Travis took the steps to the pulpit, hoping his heart didn't jump from his chest before he got there. Seemed like since he came to Kahlerville, his heart had taken a beatin'. *Help me, Lord. I have to be honest.*

Glancing at the pew where Bonnie and the children always sat, he watched as she and the children made their way down the aisle and took their seats. She stared at him oddly. The color drained from her face. Oh, how he loved this woman. Would she and her children trust him after this morning?

"Good morning," he said to his congregation.

Immediately the room hushed.

"I see that you don't know your own preacher. Hank kept offering me a haircut and shave, so I finally took him up on it."

Everyone laughed.

"I also had a good man give me a suit. So I guess on the outside I'm a new man. What I'm about to tell you is about the man I used to be, the man who was asked to leave his last church. When I'm finished, if you choose to have me step down as your preacher, I'll do so." He stole a look at Bonnie. "I never meant to deceive any of you. I simply wanted to forget about my past and start my life over by serving the Lord with a clean heart and a clean slate."

"Doesn't matter what you say, Brother Travis," Jake Weathers said. "We wouldn't trade you for all the preachers in Texas. Without your help, a lot of wicked things would still be going on."

"I appreciate that, Jake. I hope you still have a high opinion of me once I'm finished."

"Just tell us whatcha got to say," Eli said.

Travis cleared his throat, rubbed his clammy hands together, and prayed for the proper words.

"I led a church back home in Tennessee. It was my parents' church, and my brothers were deacons. I preached there for ten years. Not a single soul found the Lord during that time. I became desperate. Didn't know what I was doing wrong. That's when I started calling on people who wouldn't darken the church's door—not for them to be saved, but for me to look good. I was sure I'd be blessed for all my work." Travis took a deep breath. His mouth tasted like dirt. Women and children were listening. How much dared he say?

"One of the places I visited. . ." He paused. "Well, women of questionable reputations lived there. I started visiting regularly. One of them was interested in knowing more about Jesus. In my enthusiasm to bring a new convert to church, I spent too much time with her. She made a profession of faith, and I thought I'd fallen in love with her. I wanted to marry her, so I told my family. They were very upset, especially my brothers. They said this woman would not be a good preacher's wife. In fact, they told me to choose between this woman and my church. When I refused, my brothers went to see her and informed her that she wasn't fit to be my wife. Not only did I not have any converts in my church, but my only one went back to her previous occupation and refused ever to see me again. She disappeared from the community. My brothers said I wasn't fit to lead their church and asked me to leave."

Travis studied his flock, his congregation. He couldn't bring himself to look at Bonnie. Not now. He couldn't bear to see her disappointment. Zack sat beside her; he alone knew the story. He smiled and nodded, giving Travis a little more courage.

"After I left my church, I spent six months in a mountain cabin. I needed to find out where I went wrong. Why hadn't I been able to bring folks to God? What was wrong with me? God spoke to me there. He said I was full of pride; that He wasn't my first love. I also realized I hadn't loved that woman at all. I'd been in love with the idea of bringing a woman out of her past and makin' myself look good in my church—not understanding it was God's church, not mine. At the end of the six months, I learned about your church needing a preacher. I felt God wanted me to take it, to try again." He swallowed hard.

"I was afraid of allowing anything to get in the way of following God, so I let my hair and beard grow, bought spectacles, and wore those big clothes. I'm sorry to have deceived you, folks. You've been better to me than my own family. You've given me a fine house, sung in the choir, given me the privilege of baptizing some of you. Treated me like family. I'll be forever grateful."

He wanted to look at the reverend, Mrs. Rainer, the Andrews, and Bonnie, but his insides froze, and he couldn't. Travis stepped away from the pulpit and set his sights on the door. A flash of the first day he'd walked into this church swept across his mind. He blinked and took another step.

"Brother Travis, I came here expectin' a sermon this morning," Jake shouted. "What about the rest of you folks?"

"Me, too," another man said.

"Me and Jake never agree, but I do on this one," Eli said.

Travis glanced at Miss Scott. She dabbed her eyes.

"Confession is good for the soul," Pete Kahler said. "Now, let's get on with worshippin' God."

"Weren't you listening?" Travis asked.

"Sounds to me that any problems you might have had got worked out," Morgan Andrews said.

Travis glanced at the reverend. He smiled. His attention moved on to Mrs. Rainer. She nodded as though she knew his turmoil. His gaze ventured to others in the church. No condemnation looked back at him. Zack grinned and nodded again. With his stomach churning, Travis turned his attention to Bonnie.

He met her gaze. She placed her hands on the pew in front of her and slowly stood. "Brother Travis, I believe you have an announcement to make before you give the sermon."

Heat flooded his face. "Are you sure?"

"I'm positive."

"Would you come up here with me?"

Bonnie made her way into the aisle. Her sweet blue eyes never left his face. She held out her hand. Travis hesitated. He didn't feel worthy of this woman, these people, and they were not rejecting him. Just as God had not rejected him. Travis grasped her hand, and she took her place beside him.

"You're completely sure about this?" he whispered. "Don't be saying yes because you feel sorry for me."

"If you don't make the announcement, I'm going to be very disappointed," she whispered. "And you already know what I can do with a rifle."

He chuckled. "Oh, life with you will never be dull." He turned back to the crowd. "Folks, I, or rather, we, have something to tell you. Looks like this morning is full of news. Bonnie Kahler has agreed to be my wife."

A clap rose from somewhere in the church. A whoop and a holler came from the back. Zack and Michael Paul grinned like somebody had given them a whole bag of jelly beans. Lydia Anne clapped her little hands.

"I still came to hear some good preachin'," Jake said when the clapping died down.

"And you will." Bonnie squeezed Travis's hand and walked back to the pew and joined her children—soon to be his children. With eyes filled with tears, she sat down.

Travis couldn't believe his blessings. He had a church, a home, a God who loved him, and a future wife and family who knew his faults and still loved him.

"When's the weddin'?" Jake asked.

Travis dared a look at his future bride.

"Tomorrow?" she asked. "I'm ready."

Award-winning author DiAnn Mills launched her career in 1998 with the publication of her first book. Currently she has nineteen novels, fifteen novellas, a nonfiction book, and several articles and short stories in print.

DiAnn believes her readers should "expect an adventure." Her desire is to show characters solving real problems of today from a Christian perspective through a compelling story.

Five of her anthologies have appeared on the CBA best-seller list. Three of her books have won the distinction of Best Historical of the Year by Heartsong Presents, and she remains a favorite author of Heartsong Presents readers. Two of her books have won Short Historical of the Year by American Christian Romance Writers for 2003 and 2004. She is the recipient of the Inspirational Reader's Choice award for 2005 in the long contemporary and novella category.

DiAnn is a founding board member of American Christian Fiction Writers and a member of Inspirational Writers Alive, Chi Libris, and the Advanced Writers and Speakers Association. She speaks to various groups and teaches writing workshops. She is also a mentor for the Christian Writers Guild.

She lives in sunny Houston, Texas, the home of heat, humidity, and Harleys. In fact, she'd own one, but her legs are too short. DiAnn and her husband have four adult sons and are active members of Metropolitan Baptist Church.

SOME OTHER BOOKS BY DIANN MILLS

Texas Charm

Nebraska Legacy

Footsteps

When the Lion Roars

Leather and Lace (Texas Legacy #1)

Lanterns and Lace (Texas Legacy #2)

AVAILABLE WHEREVER GREAT
CHRISTIAN FICTION IS SOLD

Visit DiAnn's Web site at www.diannmills.com